PAINTED PROMISES

VULCAN UNIVERSITY
BOOK 2

LANIE TECH

CONTENT WARNINGS

This book contains subject matter that might be difficult for some readers, including gaslighting and manipulation in a previous relationship, and sexual intercourse.

To a summer sunset kind of love.

PAINTED PROMISES

CHAPTER 1
RORY

Five simple words should not hold this much power over me.

MAX

You back on campus yet?

I stare at the message from my ex, chewing my lip. I've anticipated this moment for months, but scanning over the text for a third time, my nerves aren't the gushy or fluttery kind.

The heart emoji I never removed from beside Max's name post-breakup reflects the way mine skips in my chest.

Leave it to him to reach out the exact moment I arrive back on campus, like there's a tracker sewn into my sweater.

I should be glad he texted. This is exactly what he promised at the end of freshman year when he shattered my heart, claiming time apart would be good for us because our relationship wouldn't survive long distance over the summer.

A breakup was the last thing I expected. We had just celebrated seven months together a few days prior with dinner and a movie we hardly watched because we were too busy locking lips. Which is why I allowed the conversation to happen at his end-of-the-year party.

I saw through Max's reasoning like freshly polished glass that he subsequently took a hammer to. A slap in the face in the form of a strung together sentence that seemed all too easy for him to admit with a freshly cracked Coors Light in one hand. His words unraveled the cocoon his false love wrapped my heart in.

"I think we should break up for the summer. Take some time to ourselves and reevaluate our relationship once the fall semester starts back up."

Well said for someone who swayed with drunkenness.

Three months later, Max Denton is making good on his promise.

And perhaps I should have blocked his number and said sayonara to the future captain of the Vulcan University football team. The thing is, no matter how much I hate what he did to us . . . I'm still in love with him.

A round of painful memories rushes me despite my hopeless attempts to keep them at bay. I wasted too many hours of the summer replaying the glory days of our relationship: the lingering touches, eager kisses, and passionate sex.

At the time, rekindling our relationship sounded like one of those excuses guys give girls to placate them so they don't cry or yell or cause a scene, all before they disappear from the face of the earth without a trace.

Max did not disappear off the face of the earth. He did not disappear from my head or my heart, did not magically go missing from the hundreds of pictures on my phone, did not pass go. What he *did* do was flaunt himself all over social media, where he made damn sure I bore witness to his vacation in Panama City Beach, partying with plenty of new female friends that seemed more handsy than not.

Getting back together should be as simple as saying yes. We both want a relationship, so why is there a thread of hesitancy pulling at my heartstrings when I reflect on every hurdle we've been through to get to this point?

My stomach knots as my thoughts spiral like a football. On one side of the field, in the end zone with his arms wide open, is Max. He's made his intentions clear, and returning to him will surely help stifle the pain he inflicted. In the opposing goal, the one who helped fill the void Max left, is—

"What an absolute pig!" My roommate's cry of outrage startles me into the present. I fumble with my phone, quickly locking the screen like I've been caught viewing something I shouldn't be—which, technically, is true, since I should have blocked Max's number long before now. I tuck the device between my thigh and the sofa and swing my attention to Quinn, who's pointing an accusing finger at the television stacked on a pile of moving boxes we haven't unpacked yet.

Her fiery glare is latched onto the trashy reality show we've been obsessed with for years. *Love Untouched*, the highest-rated reality dating show since its debut, blasts from the speakers. There's yet another argument in the house of twenty contestants—ten men and ten women—trapped in a luxurious mega-mansion in a tropical country for eight weeks to find love. The catch is, they're supposed to find their happily-ever-after *without* any sort of physical touch. The rule looks just as torturous as it sounds, but the show does make for good entertainment.

A share of $500,000 if the contestants all manage to keep it in their pants doesn't sound too shabby, either.

"Men suck."

"Hear, hear," I praise. My fingers brush the floorboard as I stretch for my cup on the floor, carefully balancing my laptop on my legs as I contort to reach my drink. The glass is slippery with condensation from the handful of ice cubes I stuffed into it before collapsing on the couch for a much-needed break from moving into our new apartment. An icy droplet rolls down my forearm when I raise my glass in agreement, Max's text still at the forefront of my mind.

Cheers to fucking that.

The glow of the TV illuminates the otherwise dark apartment. The sun set half an hour ago, and the disappearance of the natural light signaled the end of what little unpacking Quinn and I managed to do. We arrived back on campus after our long road trip from Seattle to Southern California, more than excited to be in our first off-campus apartment for sophomore year of college.

The deepening blue sky speckled with stars peeks into our fourth-floor apartment through the large living room windows my roommate has been religiously spying out of since ten minutes after unloading the last box from the U-Haul. She barged back into the apartment after a failed attempt to move the truck out of the loading zone. Steam shot from her ears while complaints of a "tattooed fucker" rolled off her tongue as if the words tasted like poison. From what I managed to make out between grumbled curses, said "tattooed fucker" parked his motorcycle between the vehicles flanking our moving truck and refused to move.

As her best friend of more than fifteen years, I've seen Quinn upset, but there is something especially intriguing about how she keeps cursing this man's name. She didn't even notice when I slipped from the room to shower, too busy wearing a path into our already faded wood floors while she plotted her revenge. Three and a half hours later, she's still as salty as she was when the incident transpired.

The vibration of an incoming message tickles my leg. My spine tightens, and I'm not certain if the jumble of knots is excitement or regret. Probably a mixture of both.

I don't dare check the notification. If it is who I assume it is, he needs to learn some patience, and I need to figure out how to respond without sounding desperate. Or apprehensive.

I busy myself with a sip of water. The crisp drink is refreshing, soothing my unease. I take a second swig before returning the glass to its home in the ring of water on the floor beside my ankle. My biceps scream with effort, aching from hauling boxes and furniture up four flights of stairs all day. When I settle back against the cushions, I readjust the laptop across my knees. The webpage for the Royal Academy of Arts in London is open, blaring almost as bright as the TV in our dark apartment. I've been wanting to apply to this summer painting class since my professor mentioned it last year. If I get accepted, it would be a dream come true, but I have no professional portfolio or website to attach to my application. Yet.

I slip a slice of pizza from the box nestled between Quinn and me on our small navy futon that has seen better days. The corners of the cheap fabric are shredded from the few times we've moved—out of the freshman dorms to my parents' basement—exposing a lovely shade of mustard yellow foam beneath. The ugly, uncomfortable piece of furniture barely survived the trek back to Vulcan U this time around.

The couch gives a hearty groan when Quinn climbs off. She weaves around haphazardly stacked boxes, blonde hair swishing behind her as he dips and dodges, all to peer out the window for the umpteenth time tonight.

We could have easily finished unpacking if she hadn't

convinced me to have a sleepover in the living room tonight. It was all too easy to agree while distracted by Max's text, and I hadn't fully comprehended what I got myself into until Quinn started pulling pillows and blankets from labeled boxes and stacked them on the couch. I shoot a longing glance at my mattress through the open door of my room where it leans against the wall, still bundled in plastic casing. There's nothing I want more than to crawl into a cozy bed after all the heavy lifting I accomplished today, both physically and mentally. Instead, navy fabric and yellow foam it is.

My mistake for letting Quinn talk me into a night on the futon that barely fits both of us sitting down, let alone trying to sprawl out lengthwise. I refuse to sleep on the hardwood floor that matches our beat-up couch. I'm pretty sure the bottoms of my socks are black with dust and dirt, but I'm too afraid to lift my foot to check.

"Give it up already," I grunt around a mouthful of cheesy goodness. The summer has been long without the triple-cheese garlic crust from Mad Mozzie's, our favorite late-night pizza spot in town. The pies are decent sober, but they taste like a slice of heaven at two a.m. after a night of partying at Hardwich's best bars.

"I'm still pissed off," Quinn huffs, as if I haven't picked up on her sour attitude from her constant sighs and glares at the window. She plops back down on her side of the couch, appearing mighty similar to an irritated wasp, ready to sting as she picks at the melted cheese crusted to her plate with a sharp glare.

I understand her ire. If it had been me that ran into the boy in the lobby who refused to move his motorcycle, I wouldn't be joyous either. I'm all for supporting my best friend. If she's angry, I'm angry. If she's sad, I'm sad. If she's laughing so hard she cries, there isn't a single chance I'm not wetting myself beside her. And if she's being delusional . . . well, there's only a certain extent of delusion I can excuse, but I'll be right there to set her straight. No woman left behind.

But right now, I'm exhausted. I have little energy to deal with my own boy problems, let alone my roommate's. The jam-packed day we spent lugging our lives to the fourth floor has left me nothing more than a lump on the couch.

At least I'm a lump with a reality show playing and a delicious slice of pizza in hand. Things could be worse.

"I noticed," I respond dryly, blinking hard in a futile attempt to remove the grit from my eyes. I examine my crust. It's buttery, flaky, and my favorite part. I probably look psychotic staring at my pizza like this, but my bestie isn't one to judge.

Okay, that's horribly incorrect. Quinn's been judging the boy downstairs for—I check the time in the corner of my computer screen—almost four hours now.

"Being pissed off isn't going to magically move the motorcycle." I elbow Quinn, slapping on a faux-excited grin when her harsh gaze settles on me. "Oh! Maybe if you *stop* being pissed, it'll magically move. Let's try that!"

Quinn scowls. A retort forms on the tip of her tongue, and I brace myself when suddenly—thankfully—loud music rocks the walls of our apartment. My mouth parts in surprise, my roommate and I sharing confused faces. I'm afraid the building might collapse from the force of the full band next door. A heavy metal band. Twisting in my seat, I pinpoint the location: the roaring composition seeps through the barren off-white wall as if there's nothing separating us from the screeching guitar joining the fray.

To make matters worse, Quinn's room is on that side of the apartment.

This won't be good.

"What the hell is that?" I slide my computer to the cushion beside me and shove from my seat. Quinn sinks further into the couch, head in her hands like the entirety of the day has finally settled on her, not joining as I creep closer to the noise. If I had to share a wall with this, I would be furious, too, but I keep that to myself. I really lucked out today.

"It's like a bunch of metal pans clanging together with a surprisingly nice beat," my roommate answers sarcastically. The wall pulses beneath my palms when I brace my hands against it, buzzing up my arms. In another totally unnecessary move, I press my ear to the paint.

The music is awful. Worse than awful. The man screaming lyrics about death may as well be dying himself. He sounds like he swallowed a cheese grater, and it's difficult to make out the words. My throat burns as I imagine accomplishing such a pitch.

My ears begin to ring. How can anyone possibly listen to this type of music and enjoy it?

Rory and Quinn: 0. Third Street Apartments: 2.

"Should we go ask them to turn it down? That's going to get annoying fast."

"We can always try not getting pissed off." Quinn shrugs from the couch, tossing my words back at me. Her frown twitches, the corners of her mouth tugging with amusement. If it gets her mind off the moving truck incident, I'm more than happy to be on the receiving end of the wisecrack. "Maybe they'll *magically* turn it down!"

"Shut up," I scoff, but can't help the grin stretching my cheeks. Oh no, are we at the point of the night where we're so tired we're finding the worst things funny? Because this is not funny. At all. It's as irritating as a fly buzzing in my ear, and I'm going to do something about it right here and now.

I stalk across the apartment, past boxes that were organized by room at one point in time, to where my shoes await. Somewhere around here is a heavy box labeled "Rory's Shoes, 1/2", and I'd slip into a pair of flip-flops if I knew where the damn thing was. I don't waste time searching with the adrenaline spurring me into action, and shove my feet in the sneakers I spent all day in, bending the heel in the process.

Quinn joins, following my lead. Together, we trudge next-door, where my roommate knocks so hard I'm surprised the door doesn't rattle on its hinges. We wait for a long moment with our arms crossed and the nastiest glares we can muster. Clearly, we weren't heard over the eardrum-shattering screeching, so when the song switches over, I abuse the door with another angry rap. The new track is equally as jarring, like nails on a chalkboard. I shudder.

All I want is to finish our first night in peace, however that may look. Whoever's inside interrupted *Love Untouched*, and by no means is that acceptable, even if we were watching a rerun from last week. Ariana and Johnathan's conversation isn't going to analyze itself. The CEO of gaslighting has somehow managed to make the poor girl believe it was *her* fault he was caught canoodling with Yasmine.

Asshole.

The cinderblock-gray door cracks open. Music spills into the hall, and I'm not only blown away by the sheer volume but also by the boy who stands in the door, eyeing us like we're about to sell him Tupperware.

His jet-black hair is stark against the pallor of his skin. And I thought I was pale. I've got nothing on this guy.

A lock of hair rests perfectly across one of his pinched brows, and I follow the curve to a narrowed gaze so green it borders on jade. His lips are pressed into a thin line as he assesses me. I fight not to shrink under his impassive stare as he sweeps down my pajama-clad frame, then moves to my roommate. The corner of his mouth twitches when their eyes lock.

Every muscle in Quinn's body tenses. Her shudder travels through me where our arms brush, and *oh*—realization hits me like an arrow to the head. This is the "tattooed fucker" from outside. It has to be.

While he and Quinn silently face off, I take my own perusal. His shirt clings to his body like a fine layer of paint, contouring his lean figure. Tattoos peek from the sleeves of the black fabric, and I follow the artwork down strong arms to where his hands are stuffed deeply in the pockets of his dark-wash jeans.

My eyes dip to the waistband of his pants—traitors—and I jerk them back up to his face, pulse hammering in my ears. My face burns, and I don't even need a mirror to know I'm blushing like an idiot. Thankfully, his attention is entirely focused on Quinn, a challenge on his face as if he's tempting her to cross the threshold and do something about the elephant in the room. Or rather, the motorcycle in the room? The metal band in the room?

"Can I help you?" He asks apathetically. His voice is a low rasp, like he doesn't use it much. The roughness could be due to singing along with the music blasting full volume behind him.

"Can you turn the music down? We're trying to sleep." Quinn grits and I don't correct the lie. I'll do anything not to have the daggers she's shooting our new neighbor on me; her scolding stature screams *serious*.

As a longtime fan of love-based reality shows, their inter-action screams enemies to lovers, and I'm hooked.

The boy doesn't so much as blink. They're locked in an

intense glaring contest I can't stop ping-ponging between. Any second now, her claws are going to extend, and he's going to bare his teeth. I wish I had popcorn or candy to chew on as I watch, entrapped. I'd never admit it to Quinn, but this is so much better than *Love Untouched.*

"It's nine-thirty," he says flatly, as if we don't know how to tell time.

Suddenly, I regret ever wanting to meet the boy who made Quinn his enemy on day one. She was right: he *is* a douchebag.

My roommate is about three seconds from jumping him, and not in the sexy way, so I come to her—or perhaps his— rescue. They both startle when I butt in, cutting gazes sharp as razor blades when they swing to me. My instinct is to duck to avoid getting sliced, but I manage to lift my chin. "We know what time it is."

"We would appreciate if you turn it down," Quinn tacks on. Annoyance only ekes into her words a little. I'm proud.

The boy in the door seems less than sorry about our griev- ance. This isn't how I imagined the first night at my big-girl apartment would go. Shit, I didn't expect to be sitting in a circle holding hands and singing songs or anything, but I wasn't prepared for our neighbor's flippant attitude. He doesn't own the building.

Once again, I'd like to restate: if Quinn's pissed, *I'm* pissed.

"We've had a long day," Quinn admits, switching tactics. She coyly twirls a strand of blonde hair around her finger. My spine straightens, the hair at the back of my neck standing on end. I've borne witness to this play before, and Quinn Conroy is definitely out for blood. I may be pissed if she's pissed, but I'm not trying to cut a man down at the knees for something as lame as loud music.

Dread pools in my stomach at the determination in Quinn's eyes. She's going for the kill, and it's not going to be pretty. I don't get the chance to stop her before she fires the shot. "People here park like shit, and we couldn't get our moving truck out of the loading zone, you know?" She cocks her head, taunting him. The muscle in his jaw flexes, and my hand flies to Quinn's forearm, gripping tightly with warning. I'm not afraid to dig my nails in if it means she stops before this goes too far. She ignores me, and all I can do is brace for the bomb drop. "We had to call the towing company to get them to move that silly motorcycle. Isn't that right, Ro?"

Her lie lands like a slap to the face. His eyes narrow to slits, cheeks coloring with anger. Unease creeps up my spine, and I shift awkwardly in an attempt to dispel the simmering hatred beginning to stifle the hall. I should yank Quinn by the arm and run. Hell, I should forget Quinn and make my own escape. Neither of them would notice while they're busy trying to melt each other into the ground.

Their hostility intensifies as the music switches to something faster paced. The drums heighten the aggression wafting off of them in waves. The quick tempo only lends to the stifling tension, and the clashing harmonies reflect their fiery gazes. Any moment now, the walls will burst into flames, and I'm not entirely sure that'd be a bad thing. If anything, it will be an escape from this situation, and for that, I'd be thankful.

When Quinn's lips part, I pray she takes back her bluff, but not so deep down, I know she's reloading.

Before she can apologize—or most likely make the situation worse—the boy slips back into his apartment and slams the door in our faces.

I flinch at the noise. Strands of my brown hair drift from

my face with the force. Stunned, I blink at the gray-painted door.

When his audacity registers, I snap. Any pity on his behalf simmers into a hot flood of irritation. My head swings to Quinn, who offers me a silent "I told you so," propelling me into banging on the door with a tight fist.

The door swings open again, revealing a different boy. One that has the breath *whooshing* from my lungs and the floor falling out from under my feet.

Time stands still when Ace Broden peers down his straight nose at me.

My heart gives a thump of betrayal.

He's just as handsome as the last time I saw him. Dirty blond hair swept back in an unintentionally intentional way, like each lock was carefully selected and methodically mussed into place. His deep blue eyes sparkle like sun glinting across the ocean surface. I sway forward unconsciously, like a warm current drawing me in. My cheeks burn in what I assume is an unimaginable shade of red when he regards me, amused by my surprise.

My blood pounds so loudly in my ears I hardly hear the apology roll off his tongue.

"Sorry, ladies." Ace's attention lingers on me, alight with recognition—and something more. My body reacts as if I grabbed a live wire with both hands, nipples tightening and stomach jumping, rippling with electricity. His poorly contained satisfaction sends the heat from my cheeks shooting between my thighs.

Shit. He's fucking Pavlov-ed me.

"We're getting ready for an event tonight." The corners of his mouth twitch, battling the smug smile threatening to consume his features. My breathing stalls in anticipation of his smile, but it doesn't break through. With a flash of disappointment, I peel my gaze from his mouth, chest tightening when I find his attention on me. We share a brief moment, where he makes sure he knows I'm watching before he drinks me in at his leisure, the same way he did the last time we saw each other. The last time I thought I'd ever see Ace Broden. "But we'll try our best to keep it down."

As if he can't contain it any longer, he sets that self-fucking-satisfied smirk free and shuts the door right in my face.

CHAPTER 2
RORY
CABO

"*I just don't think I can trust myself, and I don't want to hurt you.*"

The words are a broken record in my head, skipping over and over and *over* again since that fateful night.

Fourteen days, six hours, and fifty-three minutes ago, Max Denton reached between my ribs, wrapped his big, dumb, football-throwing hands around my heart, and ripped it right out. Not that I'm keeping track of how much time has passed since I've been able to stomach a full meal, sleep more than a few hours without waking up an anxious mess, or check my camera roll to grieve the relationship I lost.

Despite the hours gained from lack of sleep, I haven't fully processed the finality of the split. How could we have gone from late nights laughing and kissing, to a shell-shocking We're Over™ speech the evening before I left campus for the summer?

The conversation hadn't been long either. Every single second is laser-etched into my brain. Max had been prepared, delivered his spiel like breaking my heart was as easy as throwing a football. And maybe it was, because I'm no six-foot-four, 275lb defensive lineman putting pressure on him. Nope. Instead, it was little old me with my shoes stuck to the tacky floor and the remains of what I hoped was a sneaky hook-up that quickly deteriorated with his words.

I'd been completely fucking wrong about why Max brought me upstairs. Pop music from the end-of-the-year bash raging downstairs crept through the floorboards like a mockery. The yellow-green eyes I'd fallen so deeply in love with hadn't met mine once as he broke the news, as if he couldn't muster the nerve—the *decency*—to say it to my face as he tore my heart to pieces. Maybe that's what hurts the most, because if our roles were reversed and *I* was the one breaking *his* heart, I wouldn't have been such a coward.

It was the following declaration that left me with a seed of hope. *"We can try and pick back up after summer ends,"* he'd said, picking at the label on his beer bottle. I cling to the fraying thread like a lifeline, even though his explanation haunts me to this day. *"I just don't think I can trust myself, and I don't want to hurt you."*

That confession alone should have told me everything I needed to know about Max Denton.

The humid air has either suddenly thickened or my throat has closed up because it's difficult to suck down air in order to keep myself from bursting into tears again. There's a familiar prickling in my sinuses I've been combatting and succumbing to for days, unable to keep my sadness at bay. I'm not nearly close enough to the ocean to blame my tear-streaked vision on the salty breeze. Every time the conversation replays in my head, it's like there's somehow a smidge of my heart left in the pile of rubble to pluck out and stomp on. I'm utterly and completely miserable, and not even the warm Cabo sun splayed across my shoulders does anything to ease the pain.

I promised myself I would take the time away from school to relax. Instead, I'm already acting like a complete and total mess, unable to stop the conversation plaguing my mind.

I've been no good at hiding the rain clouds that have made a permanent residence over my head, either. My heart is stitched on my sleeve, no matter how many hours I spend in front of the mirror practicing the art of swallowing my emotions. My older sisters, Aisling and Peep, have pestered me about my downtrodden mood every opportunity they get, and thus far, I've held strong. Mom's even taking a break from her hard work of influencing me to switch majors, instead using her maternal sway to tempt me into confession.

None of them seem to understand the meaning of the words "I don't want to talk about it."

I'm not even fooling myself. My family isn't dumb. I'm constantly on edge, nervous they'll figure out the cause of my gloominess any second. I haven't been able to mutter the word "breakup" aloud. Not even to Quinn, who found me collapsed against a wall in the hallway of Max's shared home in the aftermath of his admission.

The breakup becomes much more real if I admit it out loud.

Dad has been the only one to refrain from any talk of what's been going on with my attitude lately. I suspect it's because he never really liked Max anyway.

In an attempt to conceal my watery eyes, I dip my chin, blinking rapidly. The brim of my baseball cap serves as a shield, concealing the other mistake I made the moment I arrived home in Seattle following freshman year at Vulcan University.

Bangs fucking suck. *Especially* when you cut them yourself.

The sidewalk beneath my sneakers shifts to smooth, taupe tile as I cross the threshold to the hotel lobby where we are staying for the duration of our family vacation. The wheels of my suitcase snag in the dip where the automatic doors slide shut. With a quick jerk, my lilac luggage tears free. Focusing on the sliver of annoyance accompanying my difficult roller bag, I chance a glimpse of my surroundings. The space is vast and airy, with large floor-to-ceiling windows drawn open, allowing the saltwater breeze to cascade through the luxurious interior.

Past the windows is a pool deck littered with enough loungers and cabanas for each guest to have their own. A horseshoe-shaped pool is a close second to being the star of the outdoors, but could never compare to the ocean beyond. The vast white sands of the beach and the choppy waves call to me like the tide to the moon.

It truly is a beautiful place to wallow in heartbreak.

A low hum in my pocket steals my attention. Swapping my luggage to my free hand, I dig my phone out. The screen is lit with a message from Quinn, expressing how much she already wishes I were home.

Guilt stabs me in the gut. If I had confided in her, I'd be able to beat the "breakup dead horse" as much as I want. The only reason I've avoided mentioning it is because of the bead of hope that Max and I will find our way back to each other. Keeping this from Quinn has proven difficult because I'm used to gabbing about every minor inconvenience in my life. If she found out about Max and me, she'd throw a party in my honor.

The wheels of my luggage whir to a halt beside me while Mom and Dad continue to the front desk. Quinn and I text back and forth, with her updating me on how she's filling her time since I abandoned her this morning. This trip is only two weeks long, but away from my best friend, it's going to feel like ages. It's only been half a day and I'm already having withdrawals.

Knuckles rap across the brim of my hat, spooking me. I lift my chin to meet my father's sensible gaze. We have the same freckles dotting the bridges of our noses. A clump of hair from the mustache he's sporting is stuck together with the sunscreen Mom slathered on his cheeks as soon as we stepped foot off the plane. Despite the shimmer of his skin, he's already pinkening from the sun, cheeks tinted with color. By the end of the trip, the Wilsons will rival a pod of lobsters, clawing our way home.

"Get that pretty head out of your phone, Rory Wilson," he commands. Light bounces off his sunglasses, temporarily blinding me as he leans to readjust the straps of Mom's duffle bag on his shoulder. They dangle from the bright orange cord around his neck, and I'm sure they were cool when he bought them five years ago. "Quinn can wait until later. C'mon, kiddo, you're in Cabo! Time to soak up some sun!"

The sun is not a cure for heartbreak, but I don't tell him that.

Mom slips into the space between us, and I'm met with the obnoxiously large beach hat that shields her bright eyes. With an annoyed huff, she shoves the brim back, icy eyes enhanced with thick, brown liner. She swishes her chocolate hair over her shoulder, offering me a soft smile. The delight I paint over my features is false, and it must show because her perfectly plucked brows thread together.

With a sigh, I heed Dad's direction, stuffing my phone back into the pocket of my denim shorts as I take up position as the fifth wheel of the Wilson family unit. Mom and Dad walk hand-in-hand at the head, and my sisters follow, chattering excitedly about going to the pool to check out the submerged bar or if they should take a dip in the ocean first. I'm the caboose, and my partner in crime is 1,800 miles away.

With no one to occupy my mind, it dips into its favorite pool of misery: Max. If I were majoring in something other than art, I might have an easier time distracting myself. Every portrait I've attempted to paint recently has somehow acquired his features: the curve of his ears, his sandy-brown hair, the peculiar hue of his irises—the perfect combination of yellow and green. Sometimes, my subjects take on his pouty lips or the slight crook of his nose from when he broke it as a boy.

Fuck. I'm doing it again.

Reminiscing does not help pave the path to getting over Max Denton.

Shaking my head to dispel the mental image of Max, I force my focus on the present, lingering behind my family while we wait for the elevator to arrive. Across the lobby, through the open doors and past the deck, a wave crashes against the shore. The mighty ocean, ready for me to take a plunge. The bright white sand is perfectly untouched. The resort must have an entire staff dedicated to combing the beach after anyone so much as leaves a footprint.

I struggle to care about the beach and the perfect weather and the suntan—sun*burn*—that will help mask some of my freckles. I don't care about family dinners or the bonfires on the beach Peep hasn't stopped gushing about. I don't even care about the tropical drinks.

Okay, that's a lie. I care about the tropical drinks *a lot.*

In fact, the sweet juice pumped full of fruity liquor might be the only thing that gets me through this trip. Then, when we return home to Seattle, I can lock myself in my room and wallow alone in my plush bed, which is exactly what I'd like to do right now.

"Aren't you and Mom going to the spa and leaving us to fend for ourselves?" I ask Dad as I step onto the elevator beside him. We just checked in, and they're already abandoning us in favor of the spa. I should be jumping for joy they're giving my sisters and me our own space, but when it's only us girls, as the youngest by three years, I tend to be left out of the conversation more often than not.

"Fend for yourselves?" He scoffs and punches the button for our floor with his knuckle. "As if I didn't raise *three* incredibly self-sufficient women. If you'd like to join your mother and me, I—"

"Honey." Mom tugs Dad's hand, and my shoulders deflate. Strained is too light of a word to describe my relationship with Mom. Since I declared a major in Fine Arts with an emphasis in oil painting, rather than study something more stable like education or psychology—my sisters' respective degrees—we've been on the outs.

We're working on it. Albeit slowly.

Mom's bright blue eyes, mirror to mine, pierce straight through my somber attitude. As soon as our pupils meet, I dodge, focusing on the changing number as the elevator rises. Perhaps my submission is why her tone softens when she addresses me. "I think you can find something to do with your sisters for a while, right? Plus, I saw some cute boys headed toward the pool."

"Yeah," I answer robotically, tucking my lips between my teeth to hide the pucker of irritation. Mom's not a fan of my ex either, and while I should be used to her off-handed comments about my relationship, they still sting. Now that she's officially brought up boys, I could throw myself into the enormous horseshoe-shaped pool with hopes I drown. The last thing I need is another boy to worry about this summer.

Maybe I should jump into the ocean instead.

Nope. Sharks.

I stare at the laces of my shoes. Maybe Dad has a point, I should look on the bright side. I'm in Cabo. All of my problems are in a completely different country. Worrying isn't going to change a thing. With that in mind, I collect the negative emotions swirling in my head, releasing them with a harsh exhale that earns me a questioning glance from Peep. She eyes my sheepish grin suspiciously until she's drawn into conversation with Aisling, murmuring something about a "craft your own shell necklace" event the hotel is hosting.

My shoulders deflate in relief. Now isn't the time to sulk about the boy I envisioned my future with. It's about making the most of my summer. So, I come up with a new mantra for vacation: *you can do this.*

Making the most of my summer doesn't last nearly as long as I hoped.

My sister's enthusiastic chatter rises when they burst through the hotel door, gunning for the beds. The door swings shut with a heavy clash because I'm trailing behind, silently reeling. Mom and Dad's room is across the hall and a few doors down. Part of me is ecstatic we don't have to share connecting rooms with them like we did when we were younger. I won't have to worry about surprise attacks from Mom asking to go shopping or early morning wake-up calls from Dad to get the best spot at the resort's breakfast buffet.

The green light flashes as I disengage the lock with my room key. Abandoning my suitcase by the door, my feet scrape against the drab carpet all the way across the room to the queen bed closest to the window. Three pillows sit perfectly puffed and stacked, and the comforter is crisp and white, just asking to be disheveled. It will be a struggle to wrangle the sheets from where they're pinned tightly beneath the mattress, and I'm actively using all my energy to not burst into a fit of tears, so I rip the hat from my head and faceplant onto the bed in defeat. Not even the pillows' plush caress can lighten my mood.

Why had I been so stupid to check Max's Instagram story in the elevator? *Rookie mistake, Ro*, I scold myself.

While avoiding Mom, I had pulled out my phone to aimlessly scroll through pictures of unattainable beauty standards, *Love Untouched* update accounts, and the occasional kitten video, when the colored ring around Max's profile picture appeared. Like a helpless princess in a trance, my thumb hovered over his name for only a moment. Clicking the story was the equivalent of pricking my finger, consequences be damned. The photo of him and his friends wouldn't have caused my throat to constrict on a normal day, but with the perky girls draped all over them, breathing suddenly became difficult. Their eyes glittered with alcohol, half-lidded and cloudy, showing their beverages off to the camera. According to the location tagged, he's taking advantage of the sunshine and singleness in Florida.

With jealousy gnawing at me like a beast devouring prey, I swiped away as quickly as I could, but the image of their two sizes too small bikinis, bleach blonde hair, and dark tans are burned into the back of my eyelids.

Lovely.

The worst part is, Max didn't seem heartbroken at all.

There was laughter crinkling his features. His body was turned toward a girl with the sky-high ponytail and blinding white teeth. He wore a broad, unbothered grin, like the last seven months meant jack-shit.

I guess being the one who did the breaking up will do that to a person.

"I can feel you brooding all the way over here," Peep huffs from her side of the bed. I hadn't realized she sat down. Memory foam? Total win.

Despite my sister's closer relationship, being the oldest has its perks. Queen Aisling gets a bed all to herself while Peep and I are stuck sharing. Allegedly, my eldest sister kicks in her sleep—or so she claims.

I shouldn't complain, because it's doubtful I'll sleep much on this trip, anyway.

My response is muffled by the pillows I'm trying to smother myself with. "It's not that big of a bed."

"Come *on*, Ro," Aisling groans from across the room. Uh oh, she's using her 'Mom's not here so I'm in charge' voice, which sounds all too much like her teacher voice. "You can't spend all summer sulking."

I don't see why not, but I indulge her anyway. "Why?"

She glares. I feel it prickling the side of my head like a laser. Maybe if I'm lucky, she'll light my bangs on fire. Now that would be a win for both of us.

The air conditioner clicks on, and a force of cool air sweeps across my arms. That's why I shiver.

Before Aisling can go full teacher and lecture me, Peep chimes in. "Let's go down to the pool," she suggests, ever the peacemaker. She emphasizes her words, which means her doe eyes are comically wide as she warns Aisling to chill out. The needles on the side of my head lessen, and I melt further into my pillow. I have no doubt that if Peep gets me alone at any point during this trip, she'll put her psych degree to good use and pick my brain, asking leading questions to trick me into confessing what's wrong. "Have a few piña coladas."

They should leave me to my devices, like usual. Why they suddenly seem to care now when they're usually all about excluding me from their hangouts is beyond me, but if they're extending the olive branch, I might as well grasp it.

Maybe we're all finally growing up.

Drinking my memories away does sound nice. While I mull the invitation over, a beautiful idea sparks to life, lifting my spirits so high I wouldn't be surprised if I'm levitating off the bed. Max is flaunting his vacation all over social media for me to see, so what if I do the same? Then he can see how much this breakup isn't affecting me, and he'll have a taste of his own cruel medicine. If there are cute boys by the pool like Mom mentioned, I might be able to enlist them to post pictures with to further my retaliation.

If Max wants to play, I'll show him how the pros do it.

Holy shit, did I move past the wallowing stage into the revenge stage of the breakup?

With newfound energy, I shove off the pillows to face my sisters. They wear matching devious grins, like I projected my plot for revenge and they're all in. Mom and Dad might care about me drinking while I'm still underage, but it's Mexico, and they're not here. I have *hours* to get drunk before we meet for dinner.

"Fuck it, let's go."

Matching squeals of excitement ring through the room, and we race for our bags. Dodging Aisling slinging her luggage onto her bed, I haul my suitcase to the far corner of the room next to the lone chair, staking a claim on the spot. By the end of this trip, the room is going to appear as if an EF-5 tornado crashed through the place: clothes strewn over every piece of furniture and available space on the floor, shoes kicked off in all directions, and don't get me started on what the state of the bathroom will be. Three daughters, and none of us use the same products.

It's going to be a hellscape.

Rifling through my bag, I pluck out a bikini and examine it with a frown. The flounced top is nowhere near as skimpy as any of the girl's suits in Max's photo. Their tops barely covered their areolas. Insecurity bites at me as I drop it back into my quickly disheveling suitcase. My boobs are a handful at best, and I'm not even close to the tan shade the palest girl in their group is. My hair isn't bleached, and my bangs are atrocious, but I have to try. If I don't, I'll never find out if I'm still on Max's mind the way he is on mine.

Sending a silent prayer to the god of vengeance, I scour for the new one-piece I bought specifically for this trip. Shoving jean shorts and oversized pajama tops to the side, my fingers brush polyester. I fist the fabric and pull. My triumph disintegrates as I hold the garment up, wanting to shove the offending swimsuit so far into the bottom of my bag I won't find it for years. The bright blue, borderline neon, is glaring. It will overpower my pale skin in every way. When Quinn and I were at the mall trying swimsuits on, I had been confident in this purchase. Staring at the asymmetrical top and cutouts, vulnerability plucks a string in my chest. Damn dressing room lighting.

If making Max jealous is my goal, thirst-traps in a one-piece are not going to do it.

Next.

"Ro, hurry up," Aisling complains.

My head snaps in her direction, face contorted in confusion. I gawk at where she's planted in front of the mirror, lathering sunscreen on her face. "You changed already?"

She shoots me a smug smile, which would have more effect if she didn't miss a spot of sunscreen over her lip. "Wore my suit on the plane."

"Ew." Wrinkling my nose, I return to scavenging. Peep calls for sunscreen, and Aisling tosses it her way. The fact my eldest sister isn't calling her out for lollygagging is bullshit, yet expected. They've always been thick as thieves, and I didn't make growing up any easier when I expressed more interest in arts and crafts than playing princesses with them. Unless the princesses had to sit for a still-life to be hung in the royal family hall; my favorite scenario when I did join.

Aisling didn't appreciate sitting still for long, and Peep always rushed out of the room after ten minutes with claims she had to use the chamber pot.

Who said I was the only creative one in the family?

Rushing with desperate determination, I tug out item after item and stack them on the chair to create room. Nothing I unearth is good enough, and I'm beginning to believe my plan to make Max jealous will slip down the drain before I get the chance to post a single picture. I might reverse back into the self-sabotage stage if I can't pull this off. I already have the bangs, and who knows what might come next. A terrible tattoo? An egregious new wardrobe?

Too cute. Wrong color. Who let me buy this in the first place? There must be one more swimsuit. I tug at the collar of my shirt, body warm with worry. In my haste, I don't recognize the next swimsuit, tossing it atop the quickly growing pile of clothes. I backtrack, breath catching as I ogle.

Quinn fucking Conroy, I love you so much.

My best friend must have slipped it into my bag when I wasn't paying attention, that sneaky bitch. I'm forever grateful because it's the skimpiest, sexiest thing I've ever seen. Sleek, black, and *stringy*. It's the swimsuit equivalent of the little black dress: the little black bikini.

It's more than perfect.

Stripping my t-shirt off, I change quickly, mindful of the schedule Aisling has us on. She stands by the door in a brightly patterned coverup, sunglasses propped in her dark hair, towel hooked over her elbow, book in her hand with a look that means business. Any minute now, I expect her to start tapping her foot or counting down from five.

Rushing is the last thing I want to do on vacation, but I'm willing to admit I'm as giddy about hitting the pool as my sisters are. Peep helps tie my top while I slather coconut-scented sunscreen up my arms, SPF 80. I sweep my bangs back and tuck them tightly against my scalp before sliding my hat back on. Seriously, the tension I use to slick them back rivals the tight sheets on the bed.

My gaze trails down the curves of my body in a final once-over in the mirror. With the suit on, I'm more than hot. I'm sexy, confident, and unbothered. The black triangles of the top accentuate what little boob I have, and the strings holding the bottoms together are tied into perfect bows at my hips, revealing much more of my ass than I usually prefer. At least it's perky. Max would have loved this.

I swallow the dejection in my throat and take a deep breath, burying the reaction deep. If this outfit doesn't show him what he's missing, I'm not sure anything will.

The book Peep's been begging me to read is stuffed at the bottom of my backpack. Aisling tuts when I dump the contents on the bed. A watercolor kit and a water bottle clang together on the way out, along with a bag of chips I never got around to eating on the plane. They'll make a delicious drunken snack later. I bite back a grin. My sunglasses and the book topple out next, and I cringe. The corner of the cover is bent. I abandon the bag on the edge of the bed and snatch the book, smoothing out the fold before Peep notices.

Resting my sunglasses on the brim of my hat, I join my impatient sisters by the door. Aisling appraises me with a smug smile, straightening one of my straps. Her cover lifts, showing off a firetruck red one-piece. The hips are cut high, Baywatch style. Her equally dark hair is pulled away from her face in an effortless pony, large, butterfly-style sunglasses perched on top of her head.

Peep hands me a towel and nods proudly, like she dressed me herself, and my confidence rises. She has a lot of faith in her strapless top. It's as vibrant as her personality, electric mauve. Where I would have resembled a highlighter, she pulls it off effortlessly. Her bottoms are skirted, flouncing as she jumps in excitement. Her nearly waist-length chestnut hair recoils with her bouncing, perfect waves shining like a hair commercial. She almost passes for a mermaid with the starfish-shaped gold earrings clinging to her lobes.

My sisters are quick to drop their towels on the first empty loungers they spot. They don't even sit, kicking off their sandals and heading for the intricately shaped pool, the submerged bar calling their names. Wading in shallow water, Peep shouts they'll bring something back for me. I wave them off without a care, because I wouldn't know what to order in the first place. My go-to at school is a basic vodka tonic, and I'd prefer not to taste the harsh burn of alcohol right now. I want it masked with sugar and fruit. I want my tongue blue or green or purple.

The sun is warm on my shoulders as I spread my towel and settle onto my lounge chair, assessing the pool deck. A DJ is hidden safely behind the bar, music pouring from the speakers flanking his turntable. He dons a funky leopard print bucket hat I would trade my boring emerald cap for in a heartbeat. The collar of his gray tank top is damp with sweat, and the thick gold chain around his throat threatens to blind me when the sun glints off the diamonds as he leans forward to playfully shoo away a girl who is soaking wet and leaning too far over his equipment.

Drinks are clearly flowing. I watch, amused, as a guy stands on one of the built-in pool tables and attempts a back-flip. He makes it about halfway before prematurely unraveling from his tuck, flopping into the water with a loud slap. Everyone cheers when he pops up from the pool, hands thrown in the air like he scored gold in the Olympics. I smother my laughter behind my book.

Far away from the shenanigans at the other end of the pool are a few families with children, splashing and laughing. A father tosses his daughter, who wears a bright grin, giggling with glee when she resurfaces. I can't help but smile at the display. A pair of brothers chase down a neon plastic torpedo their mother lobs in the water, reprimanding them when they burst from the water fighting over the toy.

There's a woman caged between tan biceps, possessively dragging her nails down a man's back as they lewdly make out. My lips twist into a grimace at the obvious grind of his hips into hers, drawing a breathy gasp from his girlfriend. Wife? Complete stranger?

With a quick prayer they don't float closer, I adjust my book in my lap. The pages are a comfort as I flip aimlessly, searching for my bookmark.

Within a few pages, I'm sucked into the fantasy world. The couple, the music, the chatter of people all around disappear, making way for the female warrior who runs right into the large, strong body of who I hope is the love interest. The odds of him being endgame are slim because he's blond, but a girl can dream.

A shout startles me. Lifting my gaze, I scan the deck, searching for the noise. The couple has torn apart from each other long enough to climb out of the water. As soon as they find their footing, she falls into him. He swings her up in his arms and stalks toward the hotel. Lucky her. Continuing my hunt, I note my sisters are missing from the bar. Before I wonder where they may have scampered off to, my gaze snaps to a boy and stays pinned. Something stirs in my stomach, and my mouth feels like a desert.

Aisling and Peep better hurry back with my drink soon because *wow,* am I thirsty.

He's the real-life version of the love interest from my book.

Thankfully, he hasn't noticed my slack-jawed leering, focused on slathering what appears to be tanning oil across his abs. I greedily follow the motion of his hand over his toned chest, littered with tattoos. From this far, they're just splotches. Splotches that cause my stomach to flip-flop. The urge to move closer grows tenfold, and I don't even realize I'm leaning forward in my lounger until my book slips from my lap.

He's tall, lean, and embodies the word "summer" with his perfect golden glow and salt-kissed blond hair. Max is broader, but there's a healthy amount of muscle packed onto the boy's arms. A sliver of thigh is exposed thanks to the short seam of his swim trunks, and I'm *incredibly* happy with that trend for men's fashion right now.

Of course, as if my stare has grown fingers and tapped on his shoulder, Beach Babe's chin lifts to meet my gawking.

Or at least I *think* he's looking at me. Ray-Bans shield his eyes, and I curse myself; my aviators are still perched atop the brim of my hat.

Caught red-handed, I squeak, fumbling with my book to

conceal my embarrassment. My hat doesn't offer enough protection from his intense stare. A dizzying current races through me, like I've spent all morning drinking. It's impossible to ignore the sudden rush of heat roasting my body from head to toe, nor the warmth kindling low in my stomach. My skin sticks to the lounger as I shift, suddenly all too aware of how skimpy my bikini truly is.

Ducking my chin, I skim the pages of my book, rereading the same paragraph three times, the words a jumble on the page. With a single glance, Beach Babe has managed to scramble my brain. Impressive.

Time passes by agonizingly slow, and I count the seconds by the beat of my heart, thumping loudly in my chest. It could be seconds or minutes or hours before I'm positive his attention has moved elsewhere. I peek over the spine of my book, telling myself I'm only checking if I've scared him off, only to startle because, horrifyingly enough, Beach Babe's standing at the end of my lounger.

He musses the wet hair plastered to his head and for a brief flash, I'm sad to have missed not only his dive into the pool, but also his lean limbs carrying him through the water. A bead of water falls from his hair, rolling down his smooth chest. I track the droplet like a moth to a pyre, drinking in the hills of muscle. The urge to lean forward and lap up the droplet to wet my parched throat is so strong I have to forcibly remove my gaze from the light dusting of dewy blond hair beneath his navel.

Yeah, he might be the perfect guy to help with my revenge.

"Hi," he greets, and damn, is his smile dazzling. His teeth are straight and white, the color of pearls. "What are you reading?" He slides his sunglasses to the top of his head, revealing blue eyes that rival the color of the ocean. The towel folded at the end of Peep's lounger goes unregarded as he lowers himself onto the chair like I've invited him. I'd be more offended on my sister's behalf if he weren't every woman's wet dream. She'd understand.

My stomach clenches under his intensity. I scan the deck again, searching frantically for my sisters, who are still nowhere to be found. Perfect. They've abandoned me.

Under his leisurely perusal, my body ignites. Even though I was just eyeing him like a rack of ribs, I can't help but readjust. He's watching me like he wants to untie my bikini strings with his teeth, and I might let him.

"Oh." I blink, racking my brain for an answer. It's like wading through sludge. "Um, hi?" I say, because apparently, I've forgotten how to formulate a coherent sentence in the presence of his hunkiness. His abs flex as he settles into the stolen chair, and I wet my lips, directing my attention before he can catch me staring again. Once was mortifying enough, I don't need to give him any more fodder. The warrior on the cover of my book stares back at me, sword raised for battle, and for a moment, I wish I had some of her confidence when facing a potential suitor. Or revenge guy. Whatever.

When I realize I still haven't answered him, I admit, "I don't...I don't really know. I told my sister I'd read it."

I haven't read more than a few chapters. *Because you can't stop thinking about a boy who's in no way thinking about you,* my mind supplies, unhelpfully.

The boy hums thoughtfully and tucks a hand behind his head, causing his bicep to bulge.

This close, we might be similar in age, early twenties. A tattoo of a snake wraps around his wrist, its body made of barbed wire. I dart around his ink, unable to help myself. A heart with a knife pierced through the flesh lies right where his own resides. Another tortured soul?

"Where's your sister?" He interrupts my leering, and my face flames. If I'm lucky, he'll think my cheeks are bright red from sunburn and not because of his perfect body. The quirk in the corner of his mouth tells me I'm not so lucky.

"She's over at the bar." Or, she was. There isn't a single Wilson in sight. In fact, there isn't a soul by the bar, not even the DJ. Music still filters through the air, a pre-made playlist trickling from the speakers. He must be on break, which caused the rest of the tipsy hotel goers to find somewhere else to occupy.

Being solo isn't something to complain about, not when one of the hottest guys I've ever seen is beside me. A picture with him will surely have Max teeming with jealousy, but how can I explain my predicament without sounding like a crazy ex?

"Looks like you might've been abandoned," he chuckles low and smooth, and *wow,* does my body perk right up. His laughter rolls down my spine like I've been doused in the icy ocean, nipples pebbling beneath the fabric of my bikini. "That's okay," he continues, and for a split second, I presume he's referring to my treacherous breasts and their desperate attempt to say hello, but when I turn my attention to my neighbor, his head is fully tilted back, basking in the sun. "I'm with my parents, and they've ditched me, too."

I hum, returning to thumbing through the pages of my book, though the last thing on my mind is the warrior's reaction to her love interest. I'm too busy mulling over ideas on how to ask to borrow his bicep or hand or any body part of his for a picture.

"Would you like to get a drink with me?" He offers when the lull extends too long.

I shrug, half-listening. What bursts out of me is a concoction of nerves and distraction that makes me believe I don't need any alcohol right now. My half-baked ideas swirl like a whirlpool. "I kind of wanted to sit here and wallow in self-pity for a bit." *What the hell, Ro? Think before you speak, you sleep-deprived, heartbroken idiot!* "Maybe catch a tan." I tack on hurriedly, as if the words will somehow erase my unfiltered admission.

"Perfect," he responds with a smirk. The muscles of my thighs jump in response, and hey, there are my nipples again. "I have some experience in that. Need any tips?"

Another tortured soul, indeed.

I'm about to ask, maybe cross a line when I don't even know his name, when my sisters interrupt.

"That's my seat," Aisling bluntly lies. Peep isn't the confrontational type, but the oldest Wilson has no problem fighting for what's hers. It must be part of the teacher thing, not taking bullshit. Her brow lifts in my direction in silent question, asking why I would've invited this stranger to sit in her lounger. The two colorful drinks in her hands with mini umbrellas sticking out of the top really throw off her whole WTF vibe. "Who is this, Ro?"

Her arm is outstretched; offering me a bright blue slush matching Beach Babe's irises. Peep comes to a halt beside her, and they both openly stare at my new friend. The plea I shoot them is ignored. They're in full protective older sister mode.

"Ace," the boy introduces before I have the chance to tell them I have no idea what his name is. "Sorry about your seat. I was keeping your sister company until you made your way back to her." Ace slides from the chair easily, and it's a hardship not to watch the muscles of his back contorting. He gifts Aisling a charming grin, not a smidge put off by her suspicion. "That drink looks great, by the way. Maybe I'll order one myself."

The image of him sipping a fruity drink with a colorful straw brings a smile to my lips.

"Yeah, you do that," Aisling responds, unimpressed. When Ace steps out of her way, she thrusts the cup into my hand. "Here you go, Rory."

"Thanks," I mutter, attention locked on Ace. Disappointment trickles through my veins as I aimlessly stir the drink. I didn't get the chance to propose my idea, though more time to flesh out my plan couldn't hurt. Hopefully, I'll run into Ace again, and soon. "Nice to meet you."

"Nice to meet you too, Rory," Ace says with a smile I'm certain drops panties. I would know, because the strings of my bottoms slowly unravel the longer he grins. He hooks a finger around his sunglasses and slides them down, covering those ocean eyes and breaking my trance. "I'll see you around." My eyes glue to his ass as he saunters away. Totally biteable.

"Well, he's cute," Peep says as she takes a seat on her lounger, completely unbothered by the damp spot Ace's swim trunks left. Aisling unfolds her towel, smoothing it over the chair on the other side of me before stretching out, drink in hand.

"Yeah." I clutch my book to my chest, watching Ace disappear into the lobby. "He is."

CHAPTER 3
ACE

I am *so* fucking screwed.

Not only is the girl I spent two weeks of summer vacation hooking up with my new neighbor, I also slammed the door right in her pretty, shocked face.

God, she looked good, too. Her pink lips parted in surprise stirred up every X-rated memory of what we shared. Not that they were buried deep down or anything. No, Rory has been my go-to fantasy since we began fooling around in Cabo.

The last few months have been good to her. I didn't think it possible for her to be any prettier, yet here we are. The sleepless circles beneath her ice-blue eyes are gone, instead ignited with annoyance, much livelier than when we first met.

The bangs she hated so much have grown out, too. The brunette strands don't stick straight out from her forehead anymore but caress the curve of her cheek.

Opening the door to her had nearly struck me dumb. I figured I must have been dreaming, but the heavy metal song my roommate refused to change would never be the sound-track in any of the fantasies I conjured. How can the girl I haven't been able to banish from my mind be *here* of all places? Right next door, like some sort of sick joke. Like the cosmos aligned and set this forth as a giant "fuck you, Ace," when I haven't done anything wrong . . . other than not upholding my half of the promises we made to each other over vacation.

Cruel, cruel world.

Seeing Rory roused the same spike in my heart rate as it did the first time I set my sight on her. The warmth tingling through my body as she assessed me was visceral. It took more effort than I would ever admit to remind myself of the deal we struck and to shut the door on her instead of threading my hand through her hair and pulling her into me.

The way she softened as soon as she recognized me is burned into my head. Her shoulders falling from where they were pinned tightly to her ears in aggravation. The shock on her face that kept me locked in the door's threshold. Her mouth parted in that perfect fucking "O," ready to swallow me whole. Time seemed to slow, and yet it was only a fleeting moment before the situation fully hit her: our roommates hadn't left the best first impression on each other, and they were fuming. She reinforced her walls quickly, stacking sandbags and reloading, her spine straightening and chin lifting, once again protected like I'm not privy to what happened between her and her ex.

One of the conditions I agreed to—and there were *a lot*—was not to ask any personal questions about each other. The rule hadn't stopped Rory from spilling tidbits of her life every time her ex posted something new to social media.

Selfishly, I did nothing to stop her.

After my roommates and I all but publicly declared Rory and her friend enemy number one, my night had taken a trip down memory lane, projecting every moment we spent together in my head. The party we were hosting was long forgotten, the urge to hole up in my room like Knox or stalk next door to confirm she hadn't been a figment of my imagination was way more appealing than the girls who offered me their batting eyelashes and salacious dancing. All I could think about was *her*.

When the last drunkard stumbled from our apartment and I managed to crawl into bed, my mind wandered so far and wide I couldn't sleep. What is she doing at Vulcan University? Why haven't I seen her around campus before? Does she miss me at all? And most importantly, is she back with her ex?

Burying myself in one of my sci-fi novels—a guilty pleasure as much as it is the inspiration behind my paintings—didn't help, either. Instead, I spent the midnight hours staring at the words, desperately trying to ignore the ache between my legs begging me to find Rory, strip her bare, and lay myself over her. To taste her. To touch her.

Somewhere between star-wielders, spaceships, and intergalactic war, I must have drifted off.

The soft, sage-green sheets are kicked to the foot of my bed, proof of my restlessness. One of my pillows has found a home on the floor. Sunlight peeks through the blinds, casting stripes of light across the beige walls of my room, and my first notion of the day is Rory Wilson.

With a forlorn sigh, I snag my phone from the charger on my bedside table. I click into the text thread Rory and I share, or *shared,* rather, since she followed through on her side of our little deal. Messages I've sent gone unread and unanswered sit with no sign of delivery. The blue bubbles of my desperation mock me.

I may as well tattoo a picture of a clown across my forehead.

Of course, she wouldn't answer. I was stupid to believe Rory—stickler for the rules Rory—would ever unblock me; that we could be friends.

Friends, because I can't offer more. I don't do relationships, I don't date, and I certainly don't involve feelings. Not since she-who-shall-not-be-named, the girl I'd given myself to completely at the ripe age of sixteen. The catalyst for that rule. The one who cheated on me with my closest friend, right under my nose.

Or should I say right under my fucking sheets.

So, hookups it is. Never staying the night, never emotions, never secrets.

And Rory had fit that bill to a T.

Now, I'm cursing the damn deal we made on the beach. We agreed fooling around was a "vacation only" situation, and we'd block each other's numbers as soon as one of us left Cabo. I couldn't. Something inside me couldn't let her go. Something I fought day in and day out until I finally accepted she would never be a number I erased from my phone. Someone must have cashed in their karma against me, because this deal has clearly come back around to kick my ass.

Maybe Rory was shocked when I answered the door because she wanted what we had to be just that—a wild summer vacation with a stranger she'd never see again. Maybe I was always meant to be a story she told her daughter going through her own relationship problems someday. Maybe she's already gotten what she set out to do. Maybe she and her ex are no longer exes at all.

Maybe our fooling around actually worked.

Acid churns in the pit of my stomach. I sit up, groaning, not quite ready to roll out of bed but not willing to lie in sorrow any longer. My room in our three-bedroom apartment is fine for what it is. Four cream-colored walls with no visible dents, a door that shuts *and* locks—thanks to Knox's insistence to keep Slate from barging into our rooms—and a window overlooking the street. The view isn't anything spectacular—the parking lot to Third Street Apartments and a single tree—but the natural light is great for painting.

A cherrywood easel—a gift from my parents—sits near the window. Landscapes are my subject of choice, and I've painted this exact street many times, at each season change, at different times of the day. It's my favorite warm-up before I'm consumed by my talent.

My parents would lecture me until my ears bled if they saw how my canvases lean haphazardly against each other in the corner of my room. Dad would say every painting should be cherished and treated with respect. Mom would offer to hang them as a collection in one of their galleries.

There is no order or flow in my workspace. A rolling cart holds my supplies: jars stuffed with brushes and so many tubes of paint I wouldn't be surprised if I had enough inventory to open an art supply store of my own.

A palette sits on the highest shelf, paint piled in dried mounds on top. I haven't touched it in days. Each time I sit to finish the details of the two planets hurtling toward each other at light speed, my mind shifts from galactic encounters to the girl who seems to have me under some sort of cosmic spell.

My body pops with protest as I rise from bed and exit into the quiet apartment. The morning sun glows across the living room, bathing our black leather couch and water-ring laden coffee table in warmth.

The floorboards creak under my weight as I pad to the bathroom beside my room. On the opposite side of the apartment, Knox and Slate's rooms butt right against the home of our new enemies. Neither of them will hear me puttering around as I get ready for my shift at the local art supply store: Art Haven.

I began working at the small shop in the middle of Hardwich's quaint downtown last semester. My parents are humble, and they've raised me as so. To prove how responsible I can be, I had to find a job. Not that I ever wasn't responsible, I was a good teenager . . . for the most part. And the graffiti stint with my roommates last year didn't last *that* long. It wasn't my fault we got caught. I swear.

Mom and Dad agreed if could keep my grades up and find a source of income to bankroll alcohol for my parties, they'd allow me to bring my car to campus for senior year.

That's the day I yearn for. No more ripped cloth seats in Slate's Bronco. No holes in the framework or flaking rust. No more thick black smoke rolling in through the open windows because the air conditioner doesn't work. Truly, my parents don't understand how much I've been suffering since Slate purchased the car the first week we moved into Third Street Apartments, and I'll be damned if anyone ever catches me riding princess on Knox's motorcycle. I'd rather walk.

I'll be living in the lap of luxury when my beloved Bimmer, Birdie, is waiting outside for a joyride, all shiny, silver, and fast.

One more year. For now, Art Haven it is.

Lavender permeates the air from my shampoo. I inhale deeply, shoulders falling as I release a heavy breath. My eyelids slide shut, mind drifting. Hot water runs rivulets down my skin and pelts the shower floor, reminding me of Rory at the hotel pool; Rory swimming in the ocean; Rory as I pressed her up against the shower wall and fucked into her—

Arousal spindles throughout my body. Shit. This is going to be a problem, isn't it?

Get it together, Ace. My body is only reacting like this because I haven't been laid since. I'm pent-up. Instead of focusing on soaping my body, my cock twitches as Rory's "O" face appears in my head.

I'm careful not to run a hand down my excited cock. Groaning, I twist the knob to cold, letting the icy spray snuff out the flames of lust. By the time I successfully manage to calm down, my fingertips are white and my jaw aches from clenching it shut.

Shutting off the water, I snag my towel from the hook behind the door, drying myself before folding it around my waist. I go through the motions of moisturizing, slathering a copious amount of lotion on each tattoo littering my skin. I drag a brush through my hair and muss it right after, shaping it into the perfect unkempt style I prefer.

Brewing coffee greets me when I exit the bathroom, the aroma thawing the chill in my veins. I beeline for a cup, passing Knox, who nurses his own mug at the island.

He acknowledges me with a dip of his chin. His morning glory mirrors mine. His green eyes are half-hidden behind sleepy lids, and his movements are tired as he raises the cup to his lips. He takes a long drag of the drink, savoring every ounce. Black hair sticks up in every direction, like he spent the night battling his pillow and the pillow won.

"Morning," I greet, scouring my options for mugs amongst our mismatched collection. A red one with an innuendo and a chip in the lip, a national park mug, a simple terracotta one that's shaped so oddly I wonder why no one's thrown it out yet. Pushing those aside, I snag a white one decorated with a worn Vulcan University logo. I received it as a gift from my parents after accepting my offer of admission. It's served me well these past two years, and is still holding strong.

Steam wafts from the pot as I pour myself a generous mug of caffeine-filled goodness. It isn't perfect without a little milk, and by a little, I mean almost half the glass. If I can taste the bite, there isn't enough milk. I have no idea how Knox drinks it black. The bitterness must have burned off all his tastebuds by now.

He responds with a grunt that's not unusual for my roommate. He's quiet, thoughtful, and prefers to keep to himself. The complete opposite of Slate, who shares every detail of his life, down to the dirtiest bits.

I know more about his sexcapades than I'd ever want to.

Propping my hip against the counter, I lift my cup for a hearty sip. The whisper of the coffee's nutty, toasted flavor warms my soul, rejuvenating my mood.

Slate's door is tightly shut. Faint snores travel through the wood. He won't be up for hours, and after the sleepless night I endured, I'm more than jealous.

"Sleep well?" Knox asks. There's a hint of amusement in his tone, which suggests he knows *exactly* how well my night went.

His gaze stays fixated on his cup, but the corner of his mouth quirks at my incoherent response. He traces the side of his mug with a fingernail, like he's deep in thought about his next drawing. "What are you doing today?"

He huffs as if whatever is on his schedule is affronting to what little peace he had this morning.

"Slate's forcing me to go to some Cars and Coffee event." A heavy sigh accompanies Knox's complaint, like he's going to have to give himself a mental pep talk to attend. "And he's not letting me bring my bike. He said, and I quote, 'It's *Cars* and Coffee, not *Bikes* and Coffee. Requirement is the vehicle must have four wheels.'"

Envy bleeds into my response. *I'd give my right arm to*

go. Maybe even a leg, too, if Birdie were here. "Dude, seriously? I can't wait until I have my car so I can show her off. Cars and Coffee is legendary, you should consider yourself lucky."

He pins me with eyes so desperate I almost choke on my coffee. *"Please* call in sick so you can take my place." With his monotonous tenor, the gripe sounds sarcastic.

A chime pings from my room. I tamp down my FOMO and abandon the kitchen, shooting Knox a sorry glance. Hopefully, the notification is from Rory, finally answering my silent pleas to unblock me. Maybe our interaction churned up the same desperation it did for me and she's jonesing for what's been cloying my mind for agonizing hours. Sex.

I whip my towel off, abandoning it on the end of my bed as I reach for my phone. My shoulders deflate with disappointment when the message isn't from Rory, but my coworker, Paula. According to her text, she's come down with a sudden cold and can't make it to Art Haven this morning for her shift. Scowling deeply at the screen, I choose to ignore her message completely.

This isn't the first time she's pulled this stunt. Does she think I want to work the day before classes start, too? I *swear* she was at our party last night, slamming back shots during a game of tipsy cup that ended with a second round of Shirts vs. Skins. I was on team Skins, rocking my summer tan at least three girls couldn't stop ogling.

Unfortunately for them, my mind was too occupied by Rory to do something about their fuck-me faces.

My eyes flit to the time in the corner of the screen, and I sigh. It's much too early on a Sunday to open the store alone, but Paula's left me no choice. Asking any of my other coworkers to cover for her is futile; everyone will have some excuse in their arsenal as to why they can't come in. The only thing I can do now is strike petty and disinvite her from all future parties, though I'm sure Slate will re-invite her as soon as he finds out.

I yank a pair of boxers from my dresser, stepping into them quickly. A boring green tee is the first thing I pluck from the drawer beneath, and on it goes, along with my favorite light-wash jeans.

"By the time you get there," I comment to Knox, pausing by the door to slip on sneakers, "it's going to be over."

"That's the hope." Knox offers a rare grin. "Hey, bring me an eraser when you get off?"

"Sure thing," I call back, shouldering my way out the door.

If the blonde girl who hastily stalks down the street, paper art supply bag clutched tightly to her body, feels the sharpness of my glare as she flees, she doesn't show it. Her steps are rapid, like she can't get away fast enough. The sentiment is mutual; as soon as I glanced up from my magazine to catch a familiar glower I've seen too much of in the past twenty-four hours, I wanted her gone.

The less than lovely run-in with Rory's roommate has only soured my morning further.

Our interaction had been like pulling teeth. My first mistake had been referring to her with a term of endearment that sounded about as endearing as stepping in shit. There was a condescending edge in my tone. After Knox's story of their encounter, I was petty enough to rile her up on my roommate's behalf, which only dug the hole we're in deeper.

Then, selfishly, I tried to pry for any information on Rory, pretending not to know exactly who stood outside my door last night. Pretending I don't know what her lips taste like, don't know how soft her skin is, how she liked it when I circled my tongue around her nipple tantalizingly slow before taking the hardened nub between my teeth. Like I don't know every curve, noise, taste, and touch of Rory Wilson.

Quinn had given me nothing but scraps in return.

Remorse stirs in my gut as she slips out of sight, head down. I figured the chances of running into Rory at Art Haven were high; however, I didn't consider her roommate might be majoring in the arts as well. If Quinn is working toward a degree in The Art of Making Enemies, she is off to an amazing start.

She'd probably say the same about me.

It became clear rather quickly that Quinn has no idea who I am or what I shared with her roommate. Why wouldn't Rory have mentioned to her best friend the two weeks she spent in bliss? Disappointment tightens my ribs, and I busy myself with cleaning the front desk, moving the penny holder just to put it back, adjusting the expensive pens in the glass case I've never seen anyone take a second glance at.

Rory and my relationship was strictly physical, and I use the term "relationship" lightly. What we had was more of an agreement than anything. With fondling. Lots of fondling.

I miss the fondling.

The stack of boxes I pulled from the stockroom isn't going to unpack itself. They would if Paula was here. Begrudgingly, I snag a box cutter and begin opening the stack while my mind continues to reel. Does Rory miss what we shared? Did she think about me at all, or has she found herself in the exact situation she'd been hoping for when she returned to campus?

A piece of tape clings to the back of my hand as an idea buds to life. I shake my arm to rid myself of the sticky offender. Now that Rory lives next door—praying she's still single—we can continue our bargain for however long it takes for her ex to get his head out of his ass and realize what he's missing.

The lingering irritation from the stuck tape intensifies at the idea of Rory in an exclusive relationship with him. From what she's told me, which granted, isn't much, he doesn't deserve her in the slightest. Despite the blaring red flag of splitting up for the summer, Rory was ready to crawl right back into his arms the minute they returned to campus. If he's what she truly wants, I won't step into that mess, but I miss her. Hell, I'd even settle for a friendship with Rory at this point. Platonic, non-physical *friends* who talk about their days and shit.

Who the fuck am I kidding? If I had the chance to sleep with Rory again, I'd jump at it.

I unpack stacks of drawing pads, placing them on the counter before mindlessly reaching for another box. They must be together by now. Only an idiot wouldn't want her. She's stunning, for one. And witty. An incredible artist, from what I've seen. Sexy, too.

I can't imagine how stupid a man would have to be to give her up in the first place.

My limbs seize as anger flares, cardboard crumpling beneath my fingers. I'm irrational, but I don't care. If dipshit had never broken up with her, I wouldn't have gotten a taste of Rory Wilson. I should be thanking him.

Psh. Yeah, fucking right.

I'm no better than him. I can't give her what she wants, what she deserves. I'm just not sure he can either.

Scowling, I abandon my progress and tug my phone from

my pocket, pulling up her contact. The nickname I saved her under only serves as a painful reminder of the girl I spent a few fleeting weeks of euphoria with.

> Officially met your roommate. She's nowhere near as peachy as you were when I first met you, Rory-O.

My thumb hovers. If I press send, the message won't go anywhere. It will forever live in the purgatory of undelivered texts along with the rest of my attempts.

Rory was a breath of fresh air. The first time I saw her, something clicked, like I had met her in another lifetime. I couldn't stay away; a magnetic force all but dragged me across the pool to her.

She had an all too familiar heartbreak in her pretty blue eyes. I recognized it because it was the same one I wore when she-who-shall-not-be-named and I ended things. A heartbreak so great it alters your life forever. Moments you can never erase from your mind no matter how much time passes or how much you try to forget. Of a pain so deep, it seems impossible to open up to someone new.

Suddenly and selfishly, I wanted to be the reason she smiled again.

A breeze jingles the wind chimes hanging outside the pastel-painted door, drawing me to the present. With a sigh, I delete the message, and I'm about to lock the screen so I can get back to work when my phone chirps. My heartbeat jumps to my throat, only to deflate just as quickly at the text.

> MOM
>
> Hi sweetie! How are things going?

Unwarranted irritation flares. Like she has a weekly alarm set, Mom asks how I am. Sweet? Yes, if there wasn't a hidden meaning within her question. What she's really asking is if I've decided I want to become one of her clients when I graduate.

She's nothing if not persistent. I still have two years of schooling to get through, and I'm fairly certain she's been gunning to be my manager since I picked up my first crayon. Somewhere in our crawlspace is a box the size of an elephant stuffed with every piece of artwork I've ever made. She could fill all the galleries she and my dad own with them, and she's tried a time or two. If Dad hadn't been around to stop her, some poor soul would've admired a sad picture of a red tulip with an equally red stem. I lost my green paint one afternoon and stubbornly refused to leave my flower without a colored-in stalk.

My parents are like the super-couple of the art world. Mom is a manager and consultant for several artists, which is why she was elated I made the decision to turn my hobby of painting landscapes into declaring a major in Fine Arts.

Dad owns galleries all across the states, including their newest venture: an over-the-top remodeling of a historic storefront in Malibu. He'd invested in the spot when I committed to Vulcan University, only a mere two hours away. Dad said the entire ordeal was coincidental, but Mom gave up their jig when she gushed over the possibility of exhibiting my work for the grand opening in the early spring.

I'd talked her out of that all too quickly.

It's not that I'm not thankful for the connections my parents have to the art community, because I am. I would never have gotten to travel as much as I have, visited the most iconic and historic galleries to view the most iconic and historic pieces of artwork the world has to offer. I would never have received private lessons from some of the country's best artists. When I expressed interest in a new medium, they didn't hesitate to find the best teachers and classes. When I went through a phase indulging the history of art from Ancient Greece, they took me on a trip to see exactly what I learned about. When I spent a summer inspired by Claude Monet's landscapes, they booked a vacation to Giverny, France, where we toured his home and gardens.

The art world has always been my playground, and my parents' support has left me more than spoiled. I might seem haughty to some, but I never flaunt my experiences, and I do understand how lucky I am to be in this position.

What smidgen of peace I have left is held onto tightly as I reply to Mom.

Between missing Cars and Coffee, Paula calling in sick, and the Quinn run-in, there isn't much left to dredge up.

> Good, mom. Working right now, so can't talk much.

MOM

Okay, honey, just checking in. I love you.
Have a fantastic day!

Bitter resentment sours my tongue. I haven't agreed to become her client, and she's acting like it's a done deal. While I respect Mom's job, I'm worried about working with her. My parents have provided for me in every capacity, but with their heavy coddling, I'm terrified my work isn't actually good enough to make a name for myself. I'd like to be represented by someone who doesn't want to work with me because of my last name, but because of my talent.

This is the last thing I want to stress over right now. I'd much rather focus on school. Or Rory. Most definitely Rory.

> Love you too. TTYL.

I don't expect a reply to my short response. Returning to the partially opened box to finish the job, I flip the tabs back to find kneaded erasers inside. How my life can go from the worst of luck with Rory's roommate here to finding exactly what Knox asked me to bring him so quickly is beyond me.

I have some dumb luck indeed.

CHAPTER 4
RORY

For the third time in the past hour, I want to slam my laptop shut, shove it off the edge of the counter, drop my head into my hands, and scream.

"Try dragging it over here," Quinn directs, tapping the opposite side of the screen from where my mouse hovers. The pressure I use to hold onto the element rivals the Hulk's strength. Like releasing the trackpad might alter time and space itself. My roommate is braced against the island with a hand, leaning so far over my shoulder the back of her blonde head nearly blocks my vision from the screen I've been glaring at for the past sixty minutes.

The first week back has been slow; professors going over syllabi and material lists for art classes. With the downtime before assignments, studying, and parties start to stack up, there is no time like the present to begin building my portfolio.

I didn't account for how difficult it would be to move a damn picture box.

All the ads and reviews claimed Webspace's build-your-own-website tool was simple, but it's most definitely not. I'm still in the process of crafting the homepage, and it truly was a miracle I was able to edit the headline text, even if I accidentally spelled my name wrong.

I haven't managed to fix it yet, and at this point, I may have to start adding an extra "y" to my paintings when I sign them. Surely that will be easier than fixing this mess.

The tip of my finger is white with the amount of pressure I use on the trackpad, doing everything in my willpower to keep the selection box in my cursor's grasp.

"I am! The damn thing won't let me," I grit, sliding the component to where Quinn's polished fingernail points. With bated breath, I send a silent prayer up above before releasing the cursor. Apparently, no one is granting wishes today because the box flies right back to where it first appeared when I clicked "add image."

Perhaps it's called a cursor because it's cursing me with the inability to work Webspace's website builder.

Quinn hums thoughtfully, scrutinizing the screen, as if any second a neon-colored pop-up will blare step-by-step instructions. With pictures. A girl can dream. "Are you sure you're in editing mode?"

Frustration throbs behind my eyes. Squeezing them shut, I slump back in my stool with a defeated groan. If I continue to sit any longer trying to fuck with the impossible, I may combust.

"What do you know about building websites, anyway?" My grumble is rude, and I shoot my best friend a silent apology. Quinn waves me off, unoffended. I don't mean to snap, but at this pace, my portfolio won't be completed until cars fly. My to-do list to complete the application before finals begin in December is long, including photographing my paintings.

My stress meter is steadily rising, and the immovable image box only threatens to push my radar from moderate irritation to severe exasperation. Combined with my confliction over Max and the feud with our next-door neighbors, I haven't fully relaxed since move-in day.

My mind wanders. Ace hasn't tried to reach out yet, or if he has, I wouldn't have seen, since his number is in phone purgatory. Per our agreement, I only hope he blocked my number like I did his, otherwise, he'd be getting an earful right now about how he slammed the door in my face, and the way he treated Quinn when she ran into him at the art supply store on Sunday.

He's so unlike the Ace I met over the summer. Summer Ace was carefree, funny, and sexy. Magnetic. He was someone I felt good being around, and not only because of the mind-altering orgasms we shared. There was a lightness in my chest. I didn't have to worry about when I'd see him next or what to wear for parties. There was no overthinking or misunderstandings; I was simply carefree. College Ace is snarky, rude, and . . . Well, he's still sexy, but his new attitude makes avoiding him much easier.

My phone buzzes on the counter, diverting my attention, and my heart skips at the name on the screen. Max.

The vibration barely fades before my hand darts out, flipping the phone over as Quinn's gaze sweeps toward me. Thankfully, she doesn't seem to notice the sudden tension pulling my body tight, pushing away from the counter.

Quinn is not my ex's number one fan. While Max and I were dating, I hadn't been the best of friends. She'd been happy for me at first, as excited as I was, but as our relationship grew, and I opted to spend more time with my boyfriend than with my best friend, an unspoken strain stretched between us. Quinn stopped attending football games with me, stopped accepting invitations to our hangouts with Max and his friends, and I didn't care to ask why. As bad as it sounds, I hardly missed her presence, too wrapped up under the guise of new love.

In the end, it had been my best friend who had been there. Who consoled me as I bawled beneath my blankets, unable to make sense of what happened. She didn't pry for details I incoherently choked out between hitched breaths and a water-fall of tears, despite the protectiveness burning a fire in her eyes. She'd been there when I took the scissors to my hair, even tried to talk me out of it, but I'd been adamant about change.

Guilt spins my stomach. Quinn has always been my biggest cheerleader, and her not being privy to my life hasn't been easy. My secrets are nearing their boiling point, and it's only a matter of time before I burst.

"Honestly, I know as much about websites as you do," Quinn answers distractedly, scouring the fridge. There isn't much to choose from, shelves mostly barren. We need to go grocery shopping, and soon. We won't last on takeout, no matter how appealing a juicy cheeseburger or chicken wings sound right now. "But this is just sad, Ro. No offense. You've been working on this for days, and you've barely gotten your name up there. It would go much faster if you got help from someone who actually knows what they're doing."

A subsequent vibration nearly makes me groan. With the half-dozen messages begging to meet gone mostly unan-swered, I'm surprised Max's name isn't permanently burned onto my screen.

Nerves aren't the only thing keeping me from throwing caution to the wind and jumping in the deep end with Max. A slew of emotions accompanies his name on screen or his face in my head; anger, heartbreak, jealousy, longing . . .

And the niggling in the back of my mind that appears in the form of blond hair, blue eyes, and a sinful smirk.

It's obvious Ace is open to revisiting what we shared months ago. I'd be lying if I said the heat swirling in his gaze every time we catch eyes didn't make my core tighten with need. Ace was better than good in bed, and my betraying body hasn't seemed to pick up that our agreement has ended. From here on out, it's nada from Ace. Zip. Zilch. None. Just like we agreed.

Is un-Pavloving myself possible?

I consider opening a new tab to search for the answer. Swiping over the trackpad to awaken the screen, my curiosity for reversing the effects of conditioning morphs into irritation when my portfolio appears, the still selected image box daring me to give it a nudge.

I never pictured myself inept at the internet—I'm as speedy as can be when the voting for *Love Untouched* opens every week. As soon as the code appears on screen, time is a flurry of fingers across my keyboard, pulling up the polls and slamming the option to keep my favorite couple in the house. Perhaps technology has taken two-leaps forward since last season, especially since I spent most of the summer buried in beaches, daiquiris, and *Ace.*

"From who?" I question absently, giving in and clicking on Max's thread.

MAX

C'mon babe, you said we'd talk this week,
and I have plans later.

Coffee?

Caffeine *would* ease the grating pulse behind my eyes. Dropping my phone into my lap with a small sigh, I turn my attention to Quinn, carrying a bowl of cherries. The glass container clinks as it hits the counter. She pops the lid off the Tupperware, plucking one out with a shrug. "I don't know. We're in college. Go stand outside the computer science building and wait for someone to offer their services."

My hand thumps against my chest, and I pair it with a dramatic gasp. "Are you insinuating I proposition someone in exchange for help with my website?"

She grins, red teeth and all.

"Well, you do need to get laid," she teases, tucking the pit into her cheek to make room for another piece of fruit. It reminds me of a chipmunk, and as adorable as Quinn can be, right now she's much the opposite. "Maybe sex would make you less snappy."

My cheeks flare. What she doesn't know is I've had plenty of sex since Max and I broke up . . . only, our hot neighbor was the one satiating my arousal.

"Like you're one to talk," I gripe. Ace's sun-kissed, inked skin flashes through my mind, and with it, a wave of guilt for drooling over a boy who wants nothing to do with relationships while I have one in my messages who does want to date me. Keeping my phone in my lap, I discreetly respond to Max's demand, accepting. He won't stop bombarding me until we talk, and right now, burrowing myself in his strong arms for a dose of comfort sounds a lot more appealing than this website.

Meet me there at 3.

Now, I have to figure out how to slip out of the apartment without Quinn questioning where I'm headed.

"Yeah," Quinn sighs, long and loud. She blinks longingly into the bowl. "I need to get laid, too."

I bite a fruit from its stem. "And be less snappy," I remind her with a smile as sweet as the taste of cherries on my tongue.

A glare hardens her features, sliding to the wall that separates our apartment from next door. "I'll stop being snappy when *they* decide to apologize," she snips, turning her nose up. She clicks the Tupperware lid back onto the bowl and returns it to the fridge, spitting the pits in the trash before she heading toward her room. Over her shoulder, she calls, "Don't be too loud with your website. I'm going to nap while the other side of the wall is actually quiet."

Well, that was easy.

Max is infuriatingly late.

It's not five minutes past when we agreed to meet. It's not ten minutes past. It's not even *twenty* minutes past.

It's *thirty-five fucking treacherous minutes* I've been sitting here like an idiot.

I've forgone coffee in favor of twiddling my thumbs where they're folded atop the table. I figured I'd wait for Max to arrive and *maybe,* just maybe, he'd be gentlemanly enough to buy me a cup.

Apparently, he's not even gentlemanly enough to arrive on time.

And from the annoyed puckering of the barista's lips while the shop is clearly suffering through their rush hour, she's about as happy as I am regarding Max's tardiness.

At least she isn't the complete fool waiting this long to talk to her ex.

I'm pretty sure I've memorized every nook and cranny in

Sip & Sonder: the planks of wood making up booths, the cobweb in the corner of the window, the number of coffee beans in the decorative jar on the shelf behind one of the two vacant seats at my table.

I'm on the cusp of letting mortification win and slink back to my apartment with my tail between my legs when the bell above the entrance rings, pulling my gaze.

My heart swells painfully at the sight of Max. Social media has never done him justice, and he doesn't post often outside of a quick 24-hour story. He appears older than the last time I saw him, more mature. The shadow of hair dusting his cheeks makes me ache to brush my fingers across his jawline to feel the rough stubble against my skin. He's bulkier, too, like he's spent the entire summer training for the upcoming football season, shoulders straight and standing tall.

His sandy brown hair is freshly cut and styled to perfection. His bushy brows almost blend in with the tone of his skin, warm and tanned from the sun. I admire the way he fills out his VU tee—a staple in his wardrobe, which consists mostly of college paraphernalia given to him for being on the football team.

There's a gleam in his yellow-green eyes as he roams the coffee shop. They halt, then rove back over someone for a fleeting moment. My spine straightens in an attempt to peer over the heads of studying students and other patrons here for an afternoon pick-me-up, but I'm unable to catch a glimpse of who may have caught his attention before his gaze finally comes to rest on me.

Max's features brighten, and my heartbeat stumbles at the genuine smile curving his lips. His shoulders slacken, as if he wasn't sure I'd show up despite his persistence, when in fact, it's the other way around.

"I'm late, I know." Max rushes to his defense as soon as he's within spitting distance. He yanks out the seat across the table, focus entirely mine. The girl sitting behind him throws a nasty glare over her shoulder when his chair runs into hers, and I'm glad I'm not on the receiving end, although her venomous stare goes unnoticed by the man it's intended for.

I stay silent. Other than reprimanding him, I'm not sure how to respond, and that isn't how I want to begin our second chance. My throat is painfully tight, like there's a lump of clay preventing me from swallowing. Every single word I've recited in my head for each minute he was late vanishes in his presence.

Max clears his throat as if to dispel the awkwardness between us. That's the only acknowledgement of his lateness he's going to offer? After I've been waiting over half an hour for his attendance? He's not the apologetic type; he's not wired that way, but I thought he'd be able to muster up some sort of excuse or regret for his tardiness.

Maybe the time apart hasn't changed Max all that much.

"I got you something." He tugs the hair at the nape of his neck. It's difficult not to lean forward and remove his hand to intertwine our fingers at the sight of this habit. One he normally reveals right before a big game. Before falling into the compulsion, I latch onto the bracelet wrapped snugly around his wrist. Its pink and gray threads are woven into a chevron pattern, the knot fraying from wear.

Last time we were together, the only accessory he wore was the flashy wristwatch from his father. Someone must have gifted him the bracelet, and I'm not inclined to believe one of his football buddies made it.

A question burns on the tip of my tongue as a white-hot spark of jealousy temporarily blinds me. To keep myself in check, I gnaw the inside of my cheek. Unlike him, the summer has changed me. There will be no diverting my attention with flowers, gifts, or the promises of something later. No shifting my focus with questions about me, how school is going, or how much he's missed this.

If this was last year, I wouldn't have blinked at his lateness. I was a girl head-over-heels for the school's football star. Too doe-eyed and gooey in the brain to notice, I would have forgiven him instantly. I would have reassured him everything was fine, insisted I wasn't upset, and consoled him with a comforting touch or my lips.

Not today.

I don't bother asking why he's late or what he got me. I sit in my chair and wait.

To my horror, Max slowly slides the bracelet off his wrist, offering it across the table. Examining it, uneasiness stirs in the pit of my stomach. I used to make friendship bracelets exactly like this with Quinn in middle school. Mine were more intricate, thread woven carefully into perfect hearts. The pink and gray making up this unimpressive bracelet are glaring, two colors I detest. The pink is so hot it almost hurts to look at, and the gray so dull concrete is a party in comparison.

"It reminded me of you." Max murmurs earnestly. His soft features thaw some of the iciness in my heart, despite the fleeting notion that maybe we shouldn't start our relationship over again. He requested the break, admitting he wasn't sure he could be faithful whilst we were so far from each other. I was the desperate one to believe the sentiment was honest and caring, not wanting to accidentally cheat or hurt me, though the admission felt like he was cheating on me, nonetheless.

I can't pull my gaze from the bracelet quickly enough. Rejection wafts from him, probably because I haven't jumped from my chair in excitement and started gushing over the used gift. My hand discards the ugly bracelet, reaching across the table unconsciously.

Memories of our relationship play as I scrutinize him. Our first date at the fanciest restaurant in town. How he appeared so unlike the stereotypical quarterback engrained in my head, cheeks red like apples, how he latched onto my every word like I was the most interesting person in the room. I remember the night he asked me to wear his jersey to his games, and how I dragged Quinn along with me, screaming my head off despite not knowing the first thing about football. How he called me his good luck charm and asked me to be his girlfriend right before the homecoming game where they won 35–22.

My arm jerks to a stop, and Max's eyes dim when I retract it, only to fold my hands carefully on my lap. Emotion thickens my throat, making it difficult to swallow the shame rearing its head at my hatred for the gift. I should appreciate him thinking of me when he saw this—and missed me enough to give it to me.

"Thank you," I break, accepting the gift. My stomach churns as I slip the ugly thing on, hanging loose around my wrist, worn from the life it's lived with Max. His beaming grin is the perfect distraction.

"Anything for you, Ro."

Anything except staying with me.

The sharp thought sours my mood. My chair creaks as I shift, mind wandering. When I envisioned seeing Max again, I didn't think it was going to be all flowers and rainbows. I've been hyperanalyzing our relationship, making lists and notes in my head of talking points, but now my brain is completely empty.

The bell above the door rings, the perfect excuse to turn

my attention to the boy who walks into the coffee shop. My pulse skitters at the sight of blond hair. The muscles of my thighs tighten beneath the table to stifle the spark of excitement flaring to life, only for the heat to rush to my cheeks when he lifts his head and I realize it's not Ace who wandered inside.

Ace. I can't think about him without my nerve endings lighting with desire. Almost every memory I have of him is of the sexual kind, because I didn't allow us to get to know each other. Cabo was supposed to be my one and done. Come the fall semester, I wanted a relationship with Max more than I wanted air to breathe. I never thought in a million years I would see the hottest—and only—fling of my life again.

Max clears his throat purposefully, startling me out of my mortification. If he notices the way my face resembles a tomato, he doesn't mention it. I blink, fighting the impulse to slide down my chair until I'm hiding beneath the table. His lips are set in a thin line; eyes narrowed in a way that makes me itch. One of his brows is raised, and I realize he's waiting for an answer to a question I never heard, too distracted by another boy.

I force my limbs to relax, scratching a nail across the wood grain of the table. "Sorry," I apologize on instinct. "You were saying?"

A muscle in his jaw ticks. It's how I conclude I've missed something important. Situating myself straighter in an attempt to prove how much this conversation means to me while simultaneously ignoring the lingering buzz between my legs.

"I was in the middle of begging you to give me another chance," Max answers with an edge.

I gape. Begging? Max has never begged for anything in his life.

Something in my chest keeps me from reveling in the spoils of his admission. I've fantasized about this moment, but I never imagined our romance would begin again with an ugly bracelet and a spark of annoyance rather than love.

"Look," Max sighs, scrubbing a hand down his face. "I know I fucked up, Ro. Taking a break during the summer was the worst decision we've ever made."

A scoff crawls its way up my throat, and I manage to bite it back by the skin of my teeth. *We?* There was no *we* in that decision.

Annoyance sears my veins. Max's mouth opens, but I can't hear what he says over the blood boiling in my ears. My fingers curl into fists in my lap.

It takes work to unclench my jaw. Voicing that our breakup was in no way my decision won't get me the answers I seek. Instead, I ask, "Why didn't you say something earlier?"

Max winces at the stiffness of my tone, irritated demeanor deflating. "It seemed like you were having fun." He shrugs sadly, and my heart cracks at his dejection. "I didn't want to bother you."

My plan worked. Instead of a surge of triumph at his acknowledgement of my petty revenge, acid rises in my throat. He didn't reach out because of *my* posts? Everything I did was an exact reaction to what *he* started.

Regret strikes my nerves. Maybe I shouldn't have flaunted myself with a stranger all over the internet because all it seems to have done was hurt both of us more.

I swallow hard. "What about those girls I saw you with over summer?"

Max runs his hands down his jeans. "Some of them were random people we met, hopping into pictures. You know, college kids bonding over a few drinks." He refuses to meet my gaze, and it's difficult to gauge whether he's hiding because he doesn't want me to see the wound my actions inflicted or for an entirely different reason. "Some of them were Philly and Cutter's girlfriends' friends," he explains, mentioning a few of his taken teammates he vacationed with. My ribs constrict at the mention of them. They *wanted* to spend their summers with their girlfriends, while Max was more than willing to be the only single one in the group.

After a tense beat of silence where we're both trapped in our heads, his pleading eyes meet mine, begging me to believe him. "I didn't do anything with them, Ro."

"You should have told me." Remorse clouds my voice. My sinuses prickle with regret, and I tear myself away from the heartbreak on Max's face, blinking rapidly in a futile attempt to keep the tears at bay. I focus on the couple near the window. The man pulls his chair around the table to sit as close to her as he can, their knees bumping. He gently tucks a strand of hair behind her ear and leans in to whisper to her. She blushes in response, a small smile gracing her lips.

They're so in love it makes me ache.

I had those moments once. With the boy across from me.

Max's dry laugh startles me back to my table. Gone is the sadness weighing his shoulders. His stare is sharp, smile bitter. "When? While you were having the time of your life, gallivanting around with that tattooed fuck?"

He has a point, but the blame isn't solely mine. None of this would be happening if it weren't for what he started. We can sit here and talk in circles about the wrongs we've both made, but the barista is still glaring daggers at me, and I'd rather not make more of a scene than we already have. The pair of girls at the table behind Max are making a poor attempt at pretending they're not listening because they haven't spoken or moved since they craned their ears toward us at his accusation, making faces in silent conversation.

This was a terrible place to talk.

Exhaustion slams into me. The lingering headache from my website crisis is slowly building as my thoughts race quicker than I can follow. Home seems like a dream.

"So, what do you want, Max?"

The fight ekes from his body. The chair groans as he leans forward, elbows braced on the table, extending a hand. I chew my lip. My heart screams that this is everything I wanted, but my brain protests, howling to go about this rationally. Taking his hand would only mitigate our conversation.

Reluctantly, I place my hand in Max's. He doesn't attempt to intertwine our fingers, to grasp onto me like I'm the lifeline he's been missing these past three months. He lets me lead, and I settle on stroking my thumb across his, allowing the familiarity of his calloused skin to soothe me.

Max releases a breath, admitting, "I want to be with you again, Ro. I want Rory and Max, together forever."

An incredulous noise jerks up my throat so fast it almost slips. *Rory and Max, together forever* was the message written in the Valentine's Day card he gave me in February, three months before he broke things off.

My limbs stiffen. These are the exact words I'd been hoping to hear since the moment Max mentioned the possibility of rebuilding our relationship, and yet a sense of wrongness swirls in my gut. "You're going to have to work for it."

Max squeezes my hand, features brightening with a spark of hope. "I'll do anything, Ro. I promise."

I study my ex for a long moment; unsure I believe his sweet words. I drink in every inch of him while my mind replays moments from our unfortunate ending. How easy it was to walk away from the *Rory and Max, together forever* he claims to want more than anything now.

"Okay," I eventually decide. Max's relieved grin does little to ease the foreboding cloud accumulating above my head.

CHAPTER 5
RORY
CABO

My breath stills when Peep shifts in her sleep, rolling over to face me.

Her cheek is smashed into the fluffy pillow, lips parted with her soft snores. My face scrunches and I flip over for the umpteenth time tonight, turning my back on her. Her ability to sleep peacefully is enviable. I wish I were blissfully dreaming about rainbows or kittens or, in Peep's case, Sam Conroy, my best friend's older brother.

They've shared lingering glances followed by rosy cheeks since Quinn and I were eight and obsessed with the idea of true love. We'd duck behind the couch when our giggles drew their attention, scrambling from the room when their complaints began.

For as long as I can remember, I've craved my other half. Someone who understands me so wholly, so completely—there's no force on Earth that can break us apart.

A sliver of light leaks through a slit in the curtains, and I'm drawn back to the view I've been admiring all night. The sky has gone from a quiet midnight to a serene blue hour, and the sun will break the horizon at any moment. The waves lapping the shore in a soothing symphony weren't enough to distract me from the thoughts jackhammering in my head.

Max wasn't the only man running rampant during my mind's moonlight rendezvous. Ace managed to burrow his way into my brain with his stupidly charming smile and captivating cerulean eyes. His presence washed away my sadness like a crashing wave, dragging the image of Max with his arrogant smile and arm around another girl's shoulders into its depths.

It was with Max's post in mind that I began formulating my plan for payback.

The soft cotton sheets tickle my thighs as I slip from the bed with a quiet sigh, careful not to disturb my sister. Rubbing the grit from my eyes, I carefully dance around scattered shoes, towels damp from the pool, and a string bikini that threatens to take me down when it catches on my toes. I'm exhausted down to my bones, but sleep will only continue to evade me until I can think about something other than Max.

On my way into the bathroom, I snag my new sweatshirt from the back of the armchair. Yesterday, I stopped in the gift shop to peruse while on the phone with my best friend. We were engrossed in conversation about *Love Untouched*, how Maddox Rhind and Harriet Gibson finally called it quits for what we hope is the final time, when the design caught my eye. CABO splays across the white cotton breast in large, emerald letters. Palm trees flank the words on each side, and as soon as I saw it, it had to be mine.

The lock *snicks* softly. My fingers drift blindly across the wall in search of the light switch. When they flicker to life, the burst of brightness burns my retinas. I squint for a solid two minutes while brushing my teeth, waiting for my vision to adjust. Cool, crisp water shocks the grogginess from my body as I splash my face, then take a towel to it. I avoid my puffy bangs in the mirror, stuffing the sweatshirt over my head before dragging a brush through my tangled hair. My eyes betray me, impulsively glancing at my reflection, proving the hood does little to hide the strands sticking straight out from my scalp. They don't submit to my glare, and frustration throbs in my temples.

The air conditioning unit kicks on when I double back for my baseball cap, startling me. My heart jumps, breath stuck in my chest while I wait for one of my sisters to stir. Neither of them so much as moves a muscle, completely out cold, and I take the chance for my escape. I break for the door, only to pause when I remember the watercolor kit in my bag. If I'm up this early, I may as well practice painting.

A tube of sunscreen takes my feet out from under me, throwing me off balance and skittering under Aisling's bed. With a squeak, I catch myself against the edge of the mattress, cringing when my sister murmurs something unintelligible and tugs the sheets higher, her breathing evening out. Phew.

The escape isn't my best effort. No, that would've been when I was fifteen and grounded for taking Peep's phone and messaging a guy she was into, asking him to hang out. He said yes, but I was still reprimanded when my sister tattled on me. I would've accepted my punishment if Quinn and I hadn't been invited to our first ever high school party, which I wouldn't have missed for the world. So, I snuck out and had my first kiss the same night, and my parents were none the wiser.

The hotel door latches heavily behind me, and I release a breath of relief, unsticking my shoulders from my ears. A coffee sounds great, but a peek at my phone reveals it's just after five o'clock, which means there's still a few hours until breakfast at the resort's restaurant begins. My sisters won't be up for hours, but Dad is an early riser. Maybe I'll meet him for breakfast.

The lobby is calm when I step off the elevator. The employee at the front desk looks up from where she's typing away on her computer. She wishes me a good morning, and I smile sheepishly in return, headed for the patio.

The large sliding doors are shut for the night. The glass is cold against my palm as I push outside, the morning breeze kissing my cheeks. My bangs tickle my forehead as I move, and my flip-flops clap against the patio, shattering the serenity of the early hours.

When I reach the edge of the deck, I kick off my shoes and step onto the beach. The sand seeps between my toes with each step, cool to the touch. Rippling waves caress my ankles as I stroll along the shore, admiring the scene while I search for the perfect spot to watch the sunrise. There are a few early risers milling about, but it seems we're all in an unspoken agreement not to disturb the quiet the morning has to offer.

When I find the perfect vantage point for my painting, I untuck the small porcelain pot from the kit and bend to collect water. I meander to the top of a sandbar and settle crisscross, digging the bowl into the sand so it doesn't spill, then arrange my tools. A shiver crawls up my spine as the chilly sand penetrates my sweatpants, goosebumps pimpling my legs.

Waves spider up the beach, and I study them for a moment, plucking the brush from its holder. They're quick to retreat, as if skittish of the shore. The sky shifts, yielding pink and orange hues as the sun rises.

With one last task before I settle in to paint, I pull my phone from the pocket of my sweatshirt. A stab of sadness slides between my ribs from the lack of messages. Ignoring the sting, I snap a picture of the sunrise to use as reference because of the animated waves and rising sun.

It doesn't take long before I begin to lose myself in the familiar strokes of the paintbrush as I bring the canvas to life with the perfect mix of color. Swirling my brush clean in the pot of water, I slide it through the blue and take it to my paper. The salt absorbs the pigments of the watercolors to create a starburst of color, enhancing the waves.

The sun casts a spray of color across the ocean so beautifully, I'm struck still for a moment. The various tones of the water stir with the swell of the waves. The bubbling foam as it crashes against the shore, reaching out for me. The cotton candy clouds, perfectly parting to make room for the sun's golden glow.

Everything around me falls away as I work, my hands drawing their own movements. The screech of a seagull, the rushing ocean, the sweep of my brush against the textured paper. My knotted stomach wanes with each stroke, the lingering worries of a sleepless night unraveling.

It's only me, the sunrise, and my—

"Wallowing again?" A familiar voice startles me—the pad slips from my grip, landing in my lap. Thankfully, the paint is quick to absorb into the paper, thus saving my off-white sweatshirt from its own early-morning masterpiece.

I crane my head in time to watch Ace plop down beside me, amusement dancing in his features. He's perky like he's had the best sleep of his life, all wide-eyed and energized, and I'm envious. His blond hair is salt-kissed, and I wonder if he's already taken a dip in the ocean this morning or if his hair is always so effortlessly tousled.

"Huh?"

Pearly white teeth gleam with his widening grin. I blame

my artist's eye for my staring, attracted to beautiful things, and Ace is no excuse. Warmth leeches into my cheeks when his dimple appears, and I stick my paintbrush in the pot of water to avoid his gaze. "I asked if you were wallowing again, and I have to say, this view trumps the pool." He sounds pleased with my location change, appears so when he digs his toes in the sand like he plans on sitting beside me as long as I'm around. That works for me, because it might take me an hour to work up the courage to ask if he'd like to join my plan for revenge on Max.

I ignore the wallowing comment, not because he's right—that's *exactly* what I set out to do—but for my own personal reasons. I need Ace's smile to disappear. It's a weapon of mass panty-melting, and he knows it.

"Good morning, Ace." I refuse to begin my day reminiscing over my embarrassing slip-up, mostly because I spent too much time last night overanalyzing it between spells of all things Max. "You're up early."

"The same could be said for you, Rory-O," he replies, and my nose scrunches in disdain. We aren't quite on nickname level yet, but if I intend on inviting him to pretend to be my summer fling, he can call me whatever childish nickname he chooses.

Doesn't mean I won't question it. "Rory-O?"

Ace shrugs innocently. "Yeah. Like Oreo, but with your name."

I pair my brow raise with a dry look. Whooshing waves fill the space between us, and the squall of seagulls in the distance really adds to my sarcasm.

"Yeah. I gathered that." Ace scoffs at that, but I continue. "No one calls me that." Except for Jared King in the third grade. He stopped pretty quickly when he found a lizard in his backpack after recess.

Ace's head swings my way, mouth gaping like a fish. "Oh, *come on*," he says in disbelief, blue eyes wide and piercing. My fingers clasp the paint pad as warmth coils low in my belly. "It's like the most obvious nickname ever."

A smile threatens to reveal itself at his dramatics, and I bite the inside of my lip to stifle it. His face is a mask of pure horror, and my laughter cannot be contained. "I didn't say the joke has never been made. I said no one calls me that."

"Well, you better get used to it, Rory-O, because you're stuck with it now." I refrain from mentioning that when my vacation ends, no one will ever call me that again.

A thought strikes me: is asking Ace to be part of my plan the equivalent of him giving me a nickname when we only met yesterday?

It's not, I decide before I can talk myself out of it. "Whatever, Acey-boy."

He grimaces. "Point taken."

I grin, tossing his words right back. "Better get used to it, Acey-boy, because you're stuck with it now!"

Ace shakes his head and playfully kicks sand at my legs, my toes already burrowed in safety. The motion knocks over my pot of water, which he finally takes notice of as he straightens the container. His gaze slides to the paint pad in my grip, and his features brighten in a distracting way.

"You paint?"

"I do," I reply proudly, showing off this morning's painting. Despite my lack of experience with watercolors, I'm happy with how my piece turned out. The waves have a speckled-texture due to the saltwater, and the rays of sunshine blend seamlessly across the ocean's surface. "Though I prefer oil paints."

"Really?" Ace lights up more than he did when he thought he was the first person to call me Rory-O. "Me too."

I eye him suspiciously. What are the odds I find another creative who shares the same medium on vacation? For all I know, Ace could be blowing smoke up my ass.

"You're just saying that to get me to talk to you."

"Am not," he huffs, jutting his lip out. My eyes linger on his pout.

Grains of sand slip between my fingers, granules clinging to my skin as I pluck the paint pad from my lap. I snag the paintbrush and offer both to Ace. "Prove it, then."

A dimple pops in his cheek with his answering grin. I suck in a breath, heart flipping at its appearance.

He takes the supplies, flipping to a fresh page. Within a few strokes, it's apparent he is, in fact, an artist. A *good* one, too. I don't realize I'm leaning closer until the heat of his body penetrates my sweatshirt, and the warmth only makes me want to move closer, to bask in it. Catching myself, I force distance between us, allowing my inspection to wander to the tattoo of a scorpion on the back of the hand holding the brush steady.

Curiosity urges me to question the meaning behind the ink, but when I open my mouth, my attention is diverted to the cinch between his brows, tight with concentration. Passion wafts from him in ropes. His skill is honed, and I'm enthralled as the sun rises without either of us realizing.

Sitting on the beach with him, bonding over art, provides a comfort I've been missing. Max and I didn't have much in common, but our differences weren't important. He's on the football team and enjoys more active dates like hiking or going to the gym together, whereas I prefer creative and chill dates such as painting at Tipsy Canvas or the movies.

Despite our differences in date preferences, we were both on the same page when it came to our explosive sex lives.

My stomach curdles at the reminder. Tilting my head

back, I squeeze my eyes shut, allowing the sun to wash over me. I pray the heated bands of light will burn my ex away. Here I am, sitting beside a handsome boy who knows his way around a canvas, and my mind is on Max.

"Wow," I breathe in awe when Ace shows off his finished product. He's used the same subject, but our paintings are vastly different. His colors are much more vibrant; his strokes blend seamlessly, with no hard-edged marks or streaky washes. "Color me impressed!"

"That's not the only impressive thing about me," he winks. I'd roll my eyes at the crass joke, but his flirty banter is the perfect segue into the imposing question I've been contemplating.

It's now or never, Rory, so woman up and do it. I mentally psych myself up, uncurling my fingers from the sand. My breath whooshes from my lungs in a nervous exhale I didn't realize I was holding.

"What's wrong?" Ace nudges my shoulder with his. I remind myself to learn to hide my emotions, because if Ace, a stranger, can read them this easily, my family must have known about my breakup the moment I stepped across the threshold to our home in Seattle. "Am I witnessing the famous Rory-O wallowing again? Need a piña colada to sulk into? What's up with that, by the way?"

"Piña coladas?"

It's Ace's turn to shoot me an unimpressed stare, but all I notice are his pink, pursed lips. "The sulking," he deadpans. "I hear frozen, fruity drinks are supposed to mend moods, not make them worse."

It's difficult not to gape. *Shit,* I really *am* that transparent.

My anxiety builds as I scramble for a response. The urge to bury myself in the sand is strong, but I doubt my family will be pleased with my disappearance.

What I come up with is to *deflect, deflect, deflect.*

"And what do you know about bad moods?" I bait.

Ace stiffens. He breaks contact in favor of scanning the ocean, a faraway sheen glossing over his pupils. Whatever his experience with heartbreak, it mustn't have been pretty. I sink further into myself as guilt nips at me.

"Let's just say I don't do love anymore," Ace answers roughly, confirming my thoughts.

"I'm sorry," I murmur. Something terrible must have happened if he doesn't believe in love at all, and it's clear he's not in the mood to divulge.

He shrugs, and the silence extends between us as we both lose ourselves in thought. Why would he never want to be in love again? Just because his relationship didn't work out once doesn't mean there won't be others. Love is . . . *everything.* Like plunging into ice-cold water, all my senses awakening in a rush. It's the highest highs, and I revel in it. Being loved is the best feeling in the world.

Ace wouldn't appreciate my sentiments, so I force my tongue to form different words. "So, alcohol heals a broken heart. Is that it, or do you have any more sage advice, Acey-boy?"

The corners of his lips tip up in a smile, arrogance twinkling on his face. "Getting under someone else. Or, in your case . . ." His gaze sweeps down my body in a long, slow stroke that sends sparks shooting down my spine. I straighten my legs and press my thighs together tightly, swallowing hard, startled by the fuzziness I didn't expect so soon after being dumped. "I'd suggest getting on top of someone else."

Little does he know, he's given me the perfect in.

I lift a brow. "Are you propositioning me?"

Ace's grin turns wicked. "Couldn't pass up the opportunity to hit on a pretty girl like you."

I bark out a laugh. "Your game could use some work, Acey-boy."

"Oh, we haven't even started playing yet, Rory-O. This is the warm-up."

The challenge in his tone causes heat to creep up my throat. I resist the urge to tug up the hood of my sweatshirt and pull the drawstrings tight.

"So, you want what? To sleep with me?" I sound breathless, and my heart beats loudly in my chest. The salt-spun breeze trickling by does nothing to dispel the burning in my blood at the image of Ace's body draped over mine.

Sleeping with him wouldn't be a hardship by any means, and from the dampness between my legs, there are no protests from my side. Ace is one of the most attractive men I've ever seen, with his toned figure and perfect blue eyes. His summer tan is a golden glow all the way down to his swim trunks, and I wouldn't be surprised if the color continues beneath the waistband. His tattoos are something worth exploring—in more ways than one—*and* he's made it perfectly clear he doesn't do love anymore, so there's no danger of either of us catching feelings.

This would be strictly pleasure.

My plan might work.

"Amongst other things," Ace flirts, bemused. If he's picked up on how flustered I am or the sliver of excitement that's taken root in my veins, he doesn't say. I curse myself again for showing my emotions so openly. After I seal this deal, my next task is to find a mirror and practice the art of stoicism, ASAP.

Pretending to mull over my options, I nod to myself. My mind is more than made up, and by the cunning grin on Ace's face, he knows it, too.

"There's one thing I want in return."

This piques his interest. He turns fully toward me, and I ignore the jolt zipping up my leg when our feet brush beneath the sand. "I'm listening."

There's no good way to propose my idea, but I'm sure he's already read the nerves on my face. He resembles the cat that got the cream, so I blurt, "I want to make my ex jealous."

The smile slips from his lips. He studies me for so long I begin second-guessing if this is a terrible idea.

A retraction forms on the tip of my tongue when he finally answers. "And what does that entail?"

Tension I hadn't known crept into my shoulder's eases slightly. It's not a flat-out rejection, and I'll take it. "I have a few things in mind. Mostly posing for pictures." I explain, and at the way his brows thread, I continue quickly. "Your face won't be in them, I promise. I'm posting on social media in hopes he sees them and feels as shitty as I do." I immediately cringe at the overshare.

Ace nods with finality, offering me those dimples again. They distract me so easily, I almost miss his acceptance. "I have nothing better going on. Let's do this thing, Rory-O."

CHAPTER 6
RORY

"So . . ." Peep trails off, sifting through the mostly soggy stack of fries on her plate. She resembles an archaeologist on the most important dig of her life, lashes narrowed with focus, lips pursed in concentration. Her brunette hair falls in waves over her shoulder as she leans closer for a better vantage point.

I await the end of her sentence patiently, although, from her apprehensive tone, I don't want to know what topic she's trying to breach. Uneasiness settles like a stone in my stomach. A tendril of hair slips over her shoulder, precariously close to the salad bowl beside her fries. Stretching across the table, I catch the clump before it hits its mark, saving her from smelling like Caesar dressing for the rest of the day.

She offers me a grateful smile, and her face brightens further when she spots the fry she's been searching for. She pops it in her mouth with a satisfied hum, and the following crunch makes me long for my own crispy fry.

As if sensing my jealousy, Peep pushes the plate to the middle of the table, giving me free rein of her picked-over dish. I have little hope there's another jackpot of crunchy goodness anywhere to be found. The remaining fries resemble a pile of limp noodles.

Leaning back in her seat, Peep threads her fingers through her long hair as if the way I flipped it over her shoulder wasn't to her standard. Her gaze flits around the restaurant—a new French-inspired bistro a few blocks from campus—and I follow suit.

The relaxed atmosphere does little to ease the anxiety itching my arms. The exposed brick walls with vines clinging to the mortar remind me of an alleyway. A monstera sits behind my sister, so large the leaves droop heavily over her head. We decided to try Bleu Moon Bistro for lunch, but with the rigid iron chair beneath my butt and sodden fries on my plate, I'm not inclined to dine here again anytime soon.

There aren't many patrons inside. Maybe word of mouth has spread already and missed the Wilsons. Two waitresses behind the bar converse quietly, completely unaware of the shift in mood at our table.

Peep's salad was crisp and fresh, and my sandwich was alright. It could have used another slather of garlic aioli to moisten the ciabatta. Peep's limp fries—arguably the most important item of the meal—give Bleu Moon Bistro a low score on the RRR: Rory's Restaurant Ratings.

She straightens her tank top beneath a pink corduroy button-down while I busy myself with a bite of food. Despite the sweltering end of summer, the bistro's air conditioning is on full blast, and I envy her second layer as the chill penetrates my bones.

My sister's movements are meticulous—braiding her hair only to wring it out and start anew, her nervous tell. Dread rots the food in my mouth. I swallow the sludge with effort and set the rest of my sandwich on the floral-decorated plate.

The longer she takes to speak, the tighter my muscles grow. I'm a rubber band of tension waiting to snap.

"What is it?" I pry, unable to hold this conversation at bay for another moment. She could be preparing to ask me several questions, and I sift through my brain for any gossip that could have made its way to her in the one month we've been at school. Is she going to ask if I'm back with my ex? Because it hasn't happened yet. Is she going to ask if I fucked my new neighbor? There's no way she would. Ace and I kept our deal under wraps while in Cabo. *No one* knows about our little agreement.

Her cursory skim of the café does nothing to sate my unease. I roll the edge of my napkin between my fingers nervously. Whatever news my sister is about to break, I'm not going to like it.

Peep and I have been texting about a lunch date all week. Now that it's no longer the first week of the new semester, our schedules have been packed. Despite attending the same college, my sister and I rarely see each other around campus. When I'm not traipsing around the art buildings, I've been busy with portfolio fails, reconstructing my relationship with Max, and a riveting war with my neighbors. Peep is usually holed up in her psychology classes or studying, working toward her master's degree.

When I made the decision to attend Vulcan University, I was worried my parents might force Peep and me to keep tabs on each other, but she and I respect each other's space. By the time I showed up at VU, Peep had an entire life built already, and I wasn't going to wedge my way into it. I wanted my own experiences, my own friends and activities, so we didn't see much of each other. We stayed out of each other's way, but always had each other's backs.

"The homecoming game is coming up," she says tentatively. Her fork scrapes against her bowl as she sifts through her salad, much more interesting than watching the way my face almost fractures at the mention of football.

I blink harshly. Meeting with Max a few weeks ago only accomplished dredging up the emotions I've been trying to banish since summer began. Our conversation did nothing to appease me about reconnecting. If anything, his tardiness proved how unimportant our relationship is, and yet, I still ache when he's near.

His plea echoes in my head. *I want to be with you again, Ro. I want Rory and Max, together forever.*

My heart clenched at his sincerity. I yearn to get back to what we had, but without my permission, every time I consider getting back together, memories of what he's done rear their ugly heads. How he went about ending things in the first place, the pictures of him with a retinue of girls and spending his summer without a care in the world, like I didn't take up an ounce of space in his mind.

I might be a sad, desperate fool, but Max Denton is mine. I asked for change, and so far, he's keeping up his end of the bargain. Every morning, I'm greeted with a sweet text that begrudgingly brings a smile to my face. Every night, I drift off with a fond memory of our relationship via voice note.

"I know you're probably going to be at the game supporting Max, but Jessy, Dani, and I are throwing a party. I'd really like if you could come, even if it's just for the after-party. And you can bring whoever—"

"Yeah, I'd love to come," I cut into her rambling, decision made.

Peep blinks. "Really?"

"Yeah." I shrug, tracing the pattern on the table. "Sounds like fun."

Instead of excitement, her brows slant in suspicion. "Max won't be upset?"

Considering we're not officially together, I don't think he'll care.

Now would be the perfect opportunity to tell Peep. She never really made her true opinion of him known. If I was happy, she was happy.

The rocks in my stomach forbid me from finishing my sandwich, but the fries are fair game. Hopefully, keeping busy during the game will help take my mind off Max, and if not, the loads of alcohol and Peep's roommates' famous Jello-O shots will be there to bury myself in.

Stabbing a fry with my fork, I shove it in my mouth for something to do. It's cold and squishy and bland. I grimace and pluck another fry to scrape the sides of the accompanying ketchup container. While I jam the food into every crevice to swipe up the remnants of sauce, my phone vibrates. I stuff the bite into my mouth and regret it immediately. The ketchup helped, but the texture of the soggy fry has me grimacing in disgust. Quickly exchanging the utensil for my phone, my shoulders drop at the sight of my best friend's name.

QUINN

Where are you?

Lunch with Peep.

Before I can lock my screen, Quinn responds.

QUINN

Again?

I wince. I used the same excuse when I went to meet Max. As soon as I arrived back at our apartment, worn and weary, my best friend interrogated me about my whereabouts.

Caught off guard that she was up from her nap, I realized I'd completely blocked out the sound of music thumping through the wall. The coffee I brought wasn't enough of a distraction to deter her onslaught, so I fibbed. Lunch with Peep was the first excuse to pop into my head.

Lying to Quinn fills me with grief, but if I had told her the truth, I would've never heard the end of it. Max was at the top of Quinn's shit-list after the breakup, and even though I'm pretty sure Knox has taken over that spot, I don't plan on bringing up Max until I'm completely sure of our relationship. As long as our neighbors continue acting like dicks, perhaps it'll be easier for Quinn to accept Max back into the fold.

Peep sighs softly. She has heart-eyes directed at her phone and is biting back a smile I'd be able to pinpoint a mile away. A lovey-dovey one. Elation bursts through my festering angst. I have an inkling of who she's texting, but I'm nice enough not to mention the unacknowledged attraction she has to Quinn's older brother, Sam. Peep will deny my questions as quickly as her tongue can form the words, so I take the moment of distraction to respond to Quinn.

> Yeah, what's wrong with that?

QUINN

> Because you went to school together all last year, and you hung out with her, what, twice in the span of ten months?

Shit, she's right.

> We grew closer in Cabo, I guess. I think she's texting Sam as we speak. You want me to bring you back anything from Bleu Moon?

My diversion works.

QUINN

Omg so you've noticed them, too? I thought
I was going crazy!

When you get home you need to tell me
EVERYTHING!!

Nah, I'm good. Thanks!

I almost groan. Great. Now I have to dig for info about my sister's love life while mine is in shambles.

A slurp draws my attention. Peep's draining her lemonade, cheeks tinted pink. Quinn's message goes unanswered as I abandon my phone on the table and plant my elbows, leaning closer to my sister with interest.

"Who's that?" I nod to her cell gripped tightly in her hand. I'm going to attempt to make good on this conversation for Quinn.

"No one," Peep answers quickly. Annoyance bites at my ankles like a puppy. It's like I'm twelve again, not allowed to join the whispered conversations about boys or giggle over TV shows with my older sisters.

Her phone jolts and Peep startles in her chair, the metal feet scratching against the stone tiles.

Her eyes go round as saucers, caught. I raise a brow. "No one?" I prod. "It couldn't possibly be a certain Conroy, could it?"

The pursing of her lips confirms my claim.

I grin triumphantly.

"No, it's not Quinn, and it's *definitely* not Samuel Conroy." She scrunches her face as if speaking his name might make him appear out of thin air.

Peep can pretend there's nothing going on between them

all she wants, but I have my doubts. She's about as good at masking her emotions as I am. Must be a Wilson trait.

"You sure?" If my love life—or lack thereof—is a topic of conversation, hers should be fair game, too.

Desperately, she glances toward the bar, where our waitress has joined the two bartenders. She doesn't pick up on Peep's plea for the bill, too busy giggling at something the girl with a bouncy bob says. She clears her throat, returning her attention to her bowl, mindlessly moving pieces of lettuce around. "Have you and Quinn watched the latest episode of *Love Untouched* yet?"

My shoulders deflate at the distraction. For once, I'd like to be the sister she confides in. I might be three years younger than her and five years younger than Aisling, but I'm not a kid anymore. I'm almost twenty, for fuck's sake. If we can't talk to each other about things, *especially* boys, what kind of relationship do we have?

Tamping down the loneliness like I have so many times before, I stare at my half-eaten lunch. The corners of the bread are too dark for my liking; the contents between slices gone. Yeah, this totally doesn't pass the RRR.

I force out, "I can't believe Brea re-coupled with Miles right after she made up with Simon."

Peep fully abandons her salad to launch into a long-winded theory about how they made this plan before going into the house. She's in full-on fangirl mode now, completely overlooking my struggle to not stew in my seat.

No matter how much I adore *Love Untouched*, this isn't what I want to talk about. I'd rather hear about what's going on in Peep's life, the *real* things, but if she's not ready to talk about whatever may or may not be happening between her and Sam, I have to give her that grace.

Heaven knows I'm keeping secrets from her, too.

CHAPTER 7
RORY

The charcoal feels out of place in my hands.

I yearn for the comfort of a brush instead, thick paint poured from plump tubes, and a canvas larger than my torso: the bliss of my favorite hobby.

Instead, I suffer through Drawing 201. Charcoal darkens the tips of my fingers, and my nose has chosen this particular moment to itch. Perfect. The portrait I'm working on is medi-ocre, too. The model's features aren't proportional, and I blame it on the subtle shift he made halfway through the session. One eye is bigger than the other, and his ears are uneven. On top of everything, my ass is numb from the wooden drawing horse I've been sitting on for the past two and a half hours.

I check the clock above the door. Only two minutes have passed since the last time I glanced over. In eighteen minutes, I'll be free.

Biting my lip, I force myself back to the present. All morning, I've been lost in my head, so distracted that the shape of the model's lips I'd been trying to perfect began to morph into a certain someone's: sharp and tight, with one corner stretched so high a dimple formed in his cheek.

My face warms at the mistake. I fumble for my eraser, attacking the paper like the smirk is going to start moving at any moment, spilling cocky remarks that would send tingles shooting between my currently spread thighs—

"Rory!" A pinch of pain in my glutes accompanies my lurch at the voice cutting through my daydream. I blink at a worried Quinn, who waves her hand in front of my face. Reid —a new friend we made the first day of class—sits beside her, packing up his pencils. From the concern written on his face, my roommate must have been trying to get my attention for some time.

Dazed, I frown. My arm burns from the vigorous erasing, and the paper flakes from how hard I tried to remove any trace of the smug smile.

"Sorry." I offer each of them a sheepish shrug as my surroundings creep back into the present. Drawing class. Chattering students. My sketch pad with a tear. Damn. "You were saying?"

My hips and ass protest as I swing my leg over the horse to stand. My bones will be creaking like rusty door hinges in no time. Twisting my torso side-to-side, my spine pops, releasing the tension trapped between my joints. I exhale in satisfaction.

"We were talking about getting some coffee," Quinn replies as she slips into the same routine as Reid, cleaning up her workspace. I follow suit, shoving pieces of chalk into my pencil case, thankful class has ended.

I groan. A latte would be divine. "That sounds amazing."

Reid offers to store our sketchpads in our cubbies, and I graciously accept. They're as big as posters, and it's too much to lug them to and from class twice a week. "Hey," Quinn nudges me when we're alone, face pinched with worry. "You okay? You were spacing out pretty hard there."

What she doesn't know is I was only a few strokes away from fully turning my portrait into Ace, so I offer what I hope is a reassuring smile, trying to brush off the bitter taste in my mouth as the lie rolls off my tongue. "I'm fine. Was just thinking about Peep's party."

The homecoming party. The party that is basically in honor of my ex.

"Have a good weekend, everyone," Professor Beatrice calls, cutting off Quinn's response. I meticulously scrub my fingers on a cloth to rid the charcoal from my skin before stuffing it into my pencil bag, zipping it shut. "And don't do anything I wouldn't do!"

Laughter flurries throughout the classroom, bouncing off the boring white walls and paint-splattered concrete floor.

Shouldering my backpack, I head to the sinks to scrub away the lingering traces of class. By the time I come back, Reid has rejoined us by our drawing horses, which we drag to the stack in the corner of the room. I pile mine on top before trailing the students flooding through the halls.

My mood brightens significantly when I step into the sun, basking in the beautiful day. Students huddle together as they walk down the sidewalks, conversing. A pair of squirrels chase each other through the grass, and a girl nearly jumps out of her skin when they skitter too close. We amble toward Sip & Sonder, our conversation light. It's the best coffee shop in town, perfect for studying, hanging out with friends, or the occasional meet-up with your ex.

I assumed getting back together with Max was going to be a walk in the park, but there's a kernel of doubt in my mind that's just waiting to pop.

I'm scared, I realize, kicking a rock. It cracks against the sidewalk before skipping under a bush. I'm afraid of giving my heart back to the boy who broke it in the first place. Terrified of the possibility he'd do it again. Or worse. And I don't know if I'll be able to scrape myself together a second time.

Do I miss him terribly, or do I miss the connection? The excitement of seeing him at the end of the day: the touches, the kisses, the long talks. What Max and I had was good, great even, but the time away has taught me a lot about myself, what I want in a relationship, and what I deserve.

A war of confusion edges closer to my protected territory. I need to give him an answer to *Max and Rory, together forever*, and soon. Ironically, he won't wait for me forever.

"What are you planning on drawing for the assignment?" Reid asks, and I'm thankful for the distraction.

Quinn's unfocused stare is pinned to the winding sidewalk. She offers a lame shrug in response, and I frown. Something is up with her. Her straight blonde hair is shoved beneath a hat. The brim does little to hide the faint circles under her lashes. She seems overwhelmed, and guilt swirls for not noticing sooner. She's been in a mood since we moved back to school, all thanks to the boys next door. More specifically, Knox. His nightly death metal is no lullaby, and he hasn't shut the music off no matter how many times we threaten to call the landlord. I've even contemplated unblocking Ace's number just to give him an earful but was too scared he might easily distract me.

Slate has been of little help either.

"I'm not entirely sure yet," Quinn replies distantly.

Our assignment is to copy the work of a well-known artist to better understand the process and techniques the masters used while creating their artwork.

Reid's brunet curls bounce as he turns to me with the same question. "How about you, Ro?"

Excitement bubbles over, smothering my concern. When Professor Beatrice announced the assignment, my favorite artist popped into mind, and I knew exactly what artwork to focus my project on.

As we turn the corner into downtown Hardwich, the coffee shop comes into view. The emerald storefront stands starkly against the neighboring businesses. A group exits the building—jibing a boy whose cheeks are redder than the shirt he wears—bringing the inviting scent of coffee with them. I inhale deeply, eager for a drink of my own. Reid takes the door from the last person in their group, holding it open as Quinn and I duck inside with thankful smiles, bookending the short line.

Sip & Sonder is one of my favorite coffee shops, and that's saying something hailing from the city of coffee culture. The atmosphere is homey, and the warm scent wrapping around me is like a hug. The terracotta floors reflect the sun beaming through the large front windows. The glossy green tiles of the counter modernize the shop, and the wooden tables and booths littered throughout the space in perfectly lined rows complete the tranquil vibe.

"I plan on copying something by Élisabeth Vigée Le Brun. Her work is breathtaking." I gush, only wishing to create something half as good as hers someday. "But I'm not sure if I'm using one of her landscapes or portraits. How about you? Did you pick anyone yet?"

Reid gleams with excitement, just as eager for this project, too. "I'm drawing something by Santiago Calatrava for sure," he says with a sure nod. From the corner of my vision, Quinn stares hard at the menu hanging above the counter as if she doesn't contribute to the conversation, we'll forget to ask. The urge to question her about what's wrong prickles the back of my mind, but out of respect, I won't in front of Reid. I'll be digging into what's going on with her later. "He's brilliant in the way he combines architecture and art. It will definitely help me better my skills."

The line slowly creeps forward, and I converse softly with Reid, keeping an eye out for Quinn every other step. It's clear she isn't in the mood to join in on our enthusiasm about drawing class, so with a shrug at Reid, we change topics to something safer, like how many espresso shots it would take to taste colors. I said seventeen, while Reid placed his bet on twenty-nine. Quinn turns to venture her guess, her hazel eyes latching on something over my shoulder, and quick as a flash of lightning, her demeanor switches from subdued to defensive, her jaw clamping shut.

Anxiety shoots through my veins like said espresso shot, straightening my spine and raising the hairs on the back of my neck. My fingers tighten around the straps of my backpack. That look can only mean one of two things; either Max has entered the coffee shop, or one of our neighbors did.

Swallowing roughly, I chance a peek, shoulders easing at the lesser of two evils.

Ace stands in the doorway in all his college glory, dressed like it's the middle of fall when summer hasn't quite let us out of her clutches yet. The navy sweater stretched across his shoulders matches the color of his eyes. My eyes dip eagerly, drinking in the sleeves shoved to his elbows, flaunting his impressive ink.

His light wash jeans are worn, sitting low enough on his hips that the band on his boxers greets me when he lifts his arms. Fuck, I've missed the cutting lines of his hips, the dusting of hair above his navel—

I tear my eyes away, praying he didn't witness my ogling. I'm practically screaming to be caught, face as red as a stop sign and staring straight at him. To further my humiliation, my gaze lifts, body taut with anticipation at the thought of seeing the smirk he might be wearing, only, I skip right over his features to where he's rearranging the backward navy hat atop his blond hair.

I didn't think it was possible for my face to burn any hotter, yet here I am. He's wearing my hat.

My lips part, and the smirk I was hoping would grace his features distracts me from my surprise. I thought I'd lost that hat to the ocean, not realizing Ace must have plucked it out of the water and stuffed in the pocket of his swim trunks. I didn't think much of the loss at the time with three other hats sitting in my suitcase, but seeing him wearing it brings a flutter of arousal between my thighs.

Devastatingly red-handed, sliding my attention to the floor does nothing to ease my desire. My heart matches his stride as he makes his way over. I've successfully managed to avoid him both on campus and in our apartment building recently, and though I knew we'd inevitably run into each other again, I'm not fully prepared.

To avoid meeting his cheeky grin, I check on Quinn. Her attention is zeroed in on the entrance, where the door swings open, Slate appearing. He's beaming as always, like nothing in the world could ever sodden his mood. His wavy chocolate hair is barely long enough for the knot it's pulled into at the nape of his neck, fallen chunks caressing the firm cut of his jaw. Clinging to his wide torso is a white shirt that makes his tan skin appear even darker today, and the smile he gifts us with when he recognizes us is as dazzling as the sun.

Slate joins the line, and I can't help it; I join Quinn in watching the entrance with bated breath. All they're missing is Knox, who I pray isn't about to walk through the door for my roommate's sake.

Ace sidles up to me, and the heat of his body caresses my

shoulder as our arms brush. Like I'm under a spell, my focus slips swiftly from the entry to the boy who leaves tingles climbing up my spine.

Quinn all but falls into the hug Slate offers, and Ace's grin only grows.

"Do I get a hug?" He asks innocently. His face is anything but, and I almost choke on the laughter bubbling up my throat.

"What?" I splutter. His lips purse playfully. "What have you done that warrants a hug upon greeting?"

"What has *he* done?" Ace defends, hooking a thumb over his shoulder at Slate. Teasing him is more fun than the hug that would surely plunge me into memories of all the times I spent in his arms.

To drive him crazier, I easily accept Slate's embrace. Ace's eyes narrow to slits.

"Well, for one, he apologized," I note.

"Yeah, Ace," Slate tacks on. His grin is contagious, and mine grows. "Feel free to take a page from my book anytime." He winks.

Ace arches a brow. A muscle in his jaw pops as he clenches his teeth.

His glare bounces off Slate's shoulders, who is too distracted by the pastries behind the window to notice.

Ace's features soften as he returns his attention to me. "You know I'm sorry," he murmurs, and I gape.

What is with the men in my life lately not owning their wrongs?

"Do I?" I place a hand over my chest with a dramatic gasp. "I didn't know you were a mind reader."

If he wants to play the arrogant part, I'm more than happy to continue my role in the "I can't stand you" department. It makes avoiding him much easier.

"I *am,*" Ace insists. "I'm sorry for slamming the door on you."

His mesmerizing eyes are soft, sincere in a way that begs for forgiveness. I chew my lip. Accepting his apology could end in disaster. I never expected to see him again, and his sudden reappearance in my life brings a slew of bodily reactions I tried not to give thought to after Cabo. A few strides down the hall and we'd be right back where we were over the summer, and the temptation alone stirs flutters in my stomach.

Against my better judgment, I nod in acceptance. His shoulders droop in relief.

"What are you ladies doing this weekend?" Slate asks, shuffling forward as the line moves. The question is a thankful distraction from Ace's lingering stare.

I answer without thinking. Anything to dispel the residual tension between Ace and me. "My sister's throwing a party for the homecoming game, if you want to join." Fuck. I regret the words as soon as they cross my lips, shrinking back as Quinn's hot glare lands on me.

"Sounds like fun," Ace answers quickly. I wince, hoping Slate would've responded first, if only to ease my roommate's simmering rage.

Thankfully, Quinn is called forward by the cashier. Without the sour look of betrayal on me, what I've done fully settles in.

I invited the summer fling I swore I'd never talk to again, to a party to celebrate my ex.

What the hell did I just get myself into?

As if the mere thought of running into Ace solidifies my fate, when I exit the creaky elevator the next afternoon with my head buried in my phone, I run straight into him.

"Shit, sorry, oh—" The words die in my throat as I realize exactly whose chest is well acquainted with my face. I don't need to lift my chin to know it's *him*.

Hands find my hips to steady me as I teeter. They're firm, strong, and the last time he held me like this, he was guiding my hips while I rode his cock. I would've never guessed they'd be gentle enough to hold a paintbrush.

From my periphery, the ink on his forearms teases me. I remember tracing those lines with my fingers, lips, and tongue. The tenor of Ace's groan when I did so rings in my ears, shooting up my spine. I shudder as the memory of the way his hips bucked into mine appears like a screenshot, flooding my body with arousal.

The speed with which my mind recalls the instances is astounding, and the full-body blush sears my skin like sunstroke.

Ace's fingers flex against my hips, drawing a sharp breath from my lungs. His scent invades me. Lavender with a lingering hint of sun cream, as if it still hasn't washed away from summer.

My muscles are coiled tight. He towers over me, waiting for me to tilt my head back and meet his gaze.

The soft fabric of his shirt nearly brushes my nose. Instead of giving in to the urge to bury my face into him, I take one large step back. Or maybe it's two. I can't seem to focus on anything other than his fingertips falling from my waist, leaving a hot brand in their wake.

When I chance a glance, Ace's face is a steel trap, void of all emotion. His stare is carefully blank, as if the two inches between us aren't a tangible cloud of attraction. I wish I could tell if he is as affected by the storm as I am, but he offers nothing besides a lifted brow, stuffing his hands in his pockets. "*Oh*? That's the only greeting I get, Rory-O?"

No. My stomach clenches in excitement, but my mind surges with panic. I fight the urge to drop my gaze to the ground at the sound of my nickname. He can't start calling me that again. It brings up *way* too many memories of the time we spent together; of the things I promised to forget.

Caught up in my inner turmoil, I almost fail to notice Ace inching closer. *Almost.* There is no room for me to step away with the elevator at my back. The chill of the metal does nothing to ease the fire in my veins as I splay my palms against the surface. Not when Ace looks like he wants to devour me whole.

I swallow hard, hoping I'm not shying away from him on the outside like I am on the inside. On the contrary, on the inside I'm clawing against my last restraint keeping me from throwing myself into his arms, to press my mouth against his.

I need to keep him far away from me because Ace in close proximity always equals trouble.

"You can't call me that." My words are breathless, and with the heated glimmer in his eyes, this is *exactly* how he likes me to sound. I'm not anything like the cool, calm, and collected Rory I wish I was, but then again, I've never been any of those things around Ace. He brings out a side of me I've never seen before, one I'm not sure how to navigate. Like all my walls come crumbling down in front of him. I'm open, beaming, and undeniably giddy in his magnetic presence. Around him, everything else seems to melt away.

"*Oh*?" he teases. His preferred language is banter and innuendos, and with Ace, they go hand-in-hand. My fingers curl against the metal when his smirk appears, threatening to buckle my knees. *Fuck*, he knows what that smile does to me, but damn it, I can be strong for once. I have to be. "And why is that?"

"Rule number two." He presses in closer, hips threatening to slot against mine. My hand plants on his chest. The tempo of his heartbeat beneath my palm matches mine, racing wildly. His smile falters in surprise, and for a moment, I have the high ground. "No pet names."

Ace cocks his head in mock-confusion.

My teeth grind, annoyance zipping through my body. With his wide eyes and perfectly disheveled hair, he appears perfectly innocent, but from where I'm standing, his face is that of a shark, and I'm chum in the water.

"I seem to remember rule number two differently," he counters, extending his arm to rest his hand flat against the door beside my head, trapping me. Warmth blooms between my legs as Ace shifts, bringing him even closer. His bicep bulges beneath the sleeve of his white t-shirt when he leans his weight into it, the jump of his muscles accentuating the shark inked there.

Fitting.

I roll my eyes so hard it hurts. "*Nicknames* and *pet names* are the same thing."

"Darling and sweetheart are *pet names*. Rory-O is a *nick-name*, and therefore, fair game," Ace replies with a smug smile. I want to wipe it off his dumb, handsome face.

With my lips.

A scowl works its way onto my mouth. I shove away from the elevator, dipping beneath Ace's arm to free myself. I'm not upset about the nickname. On the contrary, it causes a burst of tingles across my skin every time it rolls off his tongue. No one calls me Rory-O, but it's never stopped Ace, even with my vehement complaining. It's like he's in on my little secret that I find the nickname endearing.

I slink past him, but he's moving with me, and his presence tightens the knot in my stomach. The heat of him at my back isn't something I can disregard easily. If I halt in my tracks, his body will be up against mine again, and I'm sure Ace wouldn't mind. I'm not sure I would either.

My phone pings, and my core grows taut with shame, like I've been caught red-handed in my less than pure thoughts of Ace.

I fear I know exactly whose name awaits me on my cell. The boy who's *supposed* to be on my mind. My steps quicken, and I pass an ugly abstract portrait that clashes with the dreary cream walls. The door to my apartment is just ahead. A few more feet and I'll be safe from temptation.

Ace calls after me. "Where is sweet Rory from the coffee shop yesterday?"

I squeeze my eyes shut and swallow harshly, unable to dislodge the rock in my throat.

At my silence, Ace continues, defeated. "What, so now we can't even be friends? You've been avoiding me for days."

"What happened to rule number one?" I argue futilely, staring at the carpet as my steps crawl to a stop. If Ace had kept his side of the deal, we wouldn't be in this position. I wouldn't be wondering *what if*.

Rule number one: whatever happens this summer, stays here. No reaching out to each other after vacation. Certainly, no thinking about each other.

I'm as guilty for breaking the last part of the rule as he is. There were days when I was unable to keep him from popping into my mind, easily overtaking my thoughts. Days when all I could think about were his smiles, his hand in mine or his fingers tracing lazy patterns across my skin. He wasn't so easy to forget.

His shoes enter my line of vision as he stops beside me. Scuffed sneakers with the laces shoved under the tongue like he didn't have enough time to tie them. The hem of his light-washed jeans are distressed from dragging on the ground, looser at his ankles, and I'm careful to keep my breathing steady because I know they're tight around his waist.

My eyes have lifted of their own will, slipping up his thighs, and I'm going to have a much overdue boundary talk with myself later. *We do not ogle asses in the hallways. Especially those that belong to the boy you're not supposed to be thinking about.*

I continue lifting my gaze—there's no point in pretending I wasn't about to greedily drink in an eyeful of his taut waist. I ignore my body perking in response to knowing exactly what he looks like beneath his t-shirt, only for the arousal to shrivel up and die when I reach Ace's face. He's staring at me the same way I did when he slammed the door on me: like he doesn't know me at all.

"That was before I knew you lived next door." He speaks carefully, calmly, but there's a hint of something more I can't pinpoint. He sounds . . . pained by the revelation, almost.

"Like that should change anything?" I protest weakly, swallowing the hysterical emotion threatening to claw its way up my throat. I fist the straps of my backpack in an attempt to dispel the urge to fall into him for comfort.

"Well, it's a hell of a lot closer than Colorado is to Washington," Ace scoffs. I wish he would leave me alone, turn around and go about his day. He knows *exactly* why we shouldn't be friends. "I can walk next door whenever you come calling instead of hopping on a goddamn plane."

My heart fractures. Whenever I come calling? Like I'm some lonely, desperate girl who can be placated with a quick fuck?

Pressure stings my sinuses, and a lone tear sears a path down my cheek before I can stop it. He'd rather sleep together than have a friendship. That's all there is to us. Yet another reason we should stay away from each other.

My phone vibrates in my pocket, reminding me of the conversation I left unanswered when I ran into Ace. The one I'm having with the boy who *does* want more than sex. Max invited me to the homecoming game as his good luck charm, claiming he's never lost when I'm there, though his theory isn't holding up well since we're five weeks into the semester and the Pinto's haven't lost a game yet, but the sentiment is flattering.

"You don't have to worry, Ace," I start, and damn, I'm proud when my voice doesn't waver. "I won't come calling."

More than ready to retreat, I continue the trek to my apartment in an attempt to put space between us. I should know by now Ace doesn't give up easily. He follows, eating the distance in a single stride, and his breath is hot across the back of my neck with his reply.

"Oh, I'll make you come calling, Rory Wilson." He's smirking, I fucking know it. The image of the smile alone has my legs trembling with arousal, and the certainty in his tone sends shivers skittering down my spine. Warmth floods my cheeks, and I'm thankful he's behind me, even if I almost rock back into him with his sensual words. "And it'll be my name you're calling when you do."

My body's reaction is visceral. Everything tightens in response to his words; my throat, my nipples, my pussy. *Yes, my mind screams. Yes—*

I whirl before the hypnosis fully kicks in, and I drag him into my apartment with me. Thankfully, my jellified legs keep me upright, even if I do stumble. My mind is still whirring, but somehow, I manage to poke a finger into his chest. I would shove it into his taunting dimple, but fear that would make me cave keeps me from doing so. "Let's get one thing straight, Ace. There isn't going to be any calling or coming." His smile stretches, sending fire shooting through my veins. "If you think you can handle just being friends, you can still join us at my sister's party. If not, I'm sure you and your hand can find something else to do."

Hunger streaks across his vibrant eyes, and my throat dries. He liked that?

His weight shifts subtly to his other foot. He *liked* that.

"You also have to apologize to Quinn." I continue, frantically grasping for anything that will wipe the satisfaction from his face.

My ultimatum hits its mark. Ace's jaw snaps shut with a crack, and I almost preen under his hardening features. Mission accomplished. "If she agrees to give you a chance at friendship, then I'm all yours." The words are out of my mouth before I can stop them, and dammit, I almost had the upper hand. "Not like *that*," I snap before Ace can retort with a witty remark. "*Just* friends."

His eyes simmer at my challenge. He stares at me for so long, I wonder if he's about to say "fuck it" and swoop down to kiss the daylights out of me.

Nope, don't go there, Ro. He's definitely wondering if he can strictly be friends with you or figuring out if he's capable of apologizing to Quinn at all.

I don't wait for a response, because the longer I stand here, the weaker my resolve gets.

I turn and head for my door.

CHAPTER 8
RORY
CABO

"Let's go over some ground rules," I say, stumbling over a particularly strong wave that threatens to take my feet out from under me. Ace's hand shoots out, but before he can catch my arm, I've regained my footing and shoo him away.

My phone is safe on shore, tucked between the folds of my towel after posting the first photo of Ace and me, our toes in the sand, the blue water inching closer. The following five minutes were spent obsessively checking the views with my heart in my throat, waiting for Max's name to appear. With each refresh, the lack of his username caused my stomach to coil tighter and tighter until Ace distracted me, insisting we take a dip. As much as I didn't want to part with my cell, since he's doing me a huge solid, it's the least I can do.

We're alone at the beach. My sisters are hotel hopping with a few people from the bar they've befriended, and my parents are trying their hand at snorkeling. Mom and Dad think I'm bonding with my siblings, and Peep and Aisling assume I'm searching for turtles. It's the perfect gimmick, as long as no one asks about my day at dinner.

The cold water swells around my waistline. I shiver as my mind wanders. Part of me can't believe the only reason Ace agreed to help with my revenge is because he's bored. Most guys would probably call me crazy and run the other way. Not Ace. He's been more than willing to play into my delusion, but it was impossible to miss the flash in his eyes when our thighs brushed as we situated ourselves for the perfect photo, which is why now is the perfect time to lay down the rules that have been running rampant since his smoldering face and the heat of his body wouldn't disappear from my mind.

I don't know what excuse he used to get away from his parents, but he's here, rolling his eyes and splashing in the ocean like a child. Droplets splatter my arms and chin, and he ignores the glare I shoot him.

We wade deeper until the rippling ocean covers my breasts. Ace's glorious pectorals are on full display due to our height difference, and I unabashedly trail the water cascading down his broad shoulders and chest. He resembles a siren with his alluring smile and wet hair, drawing me in.

"How about no rules, since this is a vacation?" He counters, kicking his feet up to float on his back.

"This is an agreement, not a vacation," I reply, hastily tucking a fallen lock of hair under my hat to busy myself from ogling his muscular form. The short strands are annoying as fuck, and I wish they'd grow faster. My face hasn't been getting nearly as much sun as I'd like due to hiding the hideous haircut beneath hats. "So, rule number one should be: whatever happens this summer stays here. We don't reach out to each other after our vacations end, and we certainly don't think about each other."

I tug my lip between my teeth, mulling over my proposed rule. It's open-ended, like there's room for a little more than the few innocent pictures and videos I have planned. Like next time he rests his hand on my leg, it might trail higher than my knee.

Whatever happens this summer stays here? Please. Every touch of his has already burned itself into my psyche. This vacation will go down in Rory Wilson history.

"Are all your rules going to be so obvious, Rory-O?" Ace asks, muscles flexing as he treads water. Dark sunglasses hide his eyes, his chin tilted toward the rays, allowing me the full view of his lean body. My eyes linger on the realistic heart inked on his pectoral.

"Rule number two." I ignore him, ripping my gaze away to search the ocean for anything else to focus on instead. *Please, let a dolphin jump out of the water,* I silently urge. If Ace continues lounging like a model from a perfume ad and calling me *that,* I might start enjoying his company more than I should, and according to rule number one, that can't happen. I flip up a second finger. "No pet names."

"That's a no-go, Rory-O," Ace lifts his head, offering me the smug smirk that makes me want to drown him and smash my lips against his at the same time. I hone in on the former emotion lest the urge overtake me and I try something stupid.

"It better not be, Acey-boy. If anyone overhears how chummy we are, they're going to think we're more than strangers who are exacting revenge together."

Water sloshes as he fully rights himself. He shakes his hair out like a dog, and I cringe away from the sprinkles pelting my skin. My foot brushes something, and my heart rate triples. I'm a millisecond from screeching in fear when I realize it's seaweed and not a crab or shark.

"Isn't that the point?" He questions, brows disappearing behind his sunglasses as they draw downward in confusion.

"No. We're doing this to show Max I've been enjoying

my time with someone else. I don't need the whole resort thinking we're together. Rule number three—"

Ace rips the hat from my head, and I squawk in outrage. My hands fly up to cover the catastrophic haircut, but it's no use, the tendrils are already tangling in the wind in a knotty mess from being stuffed under my hat all morning. I pin Ace with my nastiest glare as mortification warms my body, but he isn't giving up the cap. No, he's too busy adjusting the strap, not paying a lick of attention to my fury.

I weigh my options. If I try to fight him for it, he'll raise the hat over his head where I can't reach. We're in the middle of the ocean, and my towel is on the shore, so there's no fashioning a makeshift hood to cover this mess, which leaves me with one other option. I squeeze my eyes shut and dunk my head into the water, plastering my hair to my scalp.

"Rule number forty-two," Ace declares when I resurface, wiping the salt from my eyes. My teeth clack as I adjust to the temperature, and I lift my head just in time to catch Ace shoving the navy hat on backwards. It makes him go from *ohmyfuckinggod* hot to *pleasebendmeoverrightnow* hot. My nipples tighten and my thighs involuntarily clench, and not from the chilly water. "No hats."

While my mind whirs back online, I breathe carefully. "Then you should take it off, too." I reach for my hat, but he grasps my wrist to prevent me from prying it off his head. His free hand finds my waist and tugs me closer to hold me steady against a large wave.

Ace meets my gaze head-on, his chin dipped, as enraptured with the moment as I am. His blue eyes are a reflection of the vast ocean around us, rippling with interest, keeping me pinned to my spot.

My body zeroes in on his touch, suddenly all too aware of the blatant attraction simmering between us. Each press of his fingers sears against the cold, and I'm surprised the ocean isn't boiling from the tension. If he leans in a few more inches, his lips will be pressed against mine. If I take one step closer, his toned, tanned, beautifully inked body will be pressed fully against me. If he moves the hand on my hip a little further south . . .

I should not be dreaming about Ace's hands trailing to more precarious parts of my body, but here I am, wondering what it would be like to have his fingers brushing along the inside of my thighs, pulling my bikini bottoms to the side to circle my clit. *Shit.* There I go again.

I am single, my mind tries to reason, and it kind of has a point. That's right . . . I'm just a single girl standing in front of an attractive man, trying not to beg for a finger-fuck in the middle of the ocean.

From the heat in his eyes, Ace wants this as much as I do. He hasn't pulled away or splashed me or laughed at me, and there's certainly no chance he could break my heart, because it's not even his to break.

Fuck it, I think, using the same words he said to me when he agreed to my plan. *I deserve this.*

He's already meeting me halfway as I give in to the decision and roll to the tips of my feet, sand squishing between my toes. Our bodies collide a millisecond before our lips do, and lightning sparks down my limbs. Then he's plastered against me, every toned muscle molding against me. A soft moan tears from my lungs at the bulge in his swim trunks. My arms lock around his shoulders, and his hands clutch my waist, pulling me closer until there's no space between us. His mouth is on mine in a kiss that takes my breath away so quickly, it's like something grabbed my ankles and yanked me underwater.

There's no hesitation on Ace's end. His fingers slip

beneath my bikini bottoms as he tilts his head for a better vantage point. Desperation leaves us in hungry moans when our tongues clash. The hat falls from his head as I yield to the urge to bury my fingers in his hair, and I can't find it in myself to be upset with the loss.

Ace tastes like citrus and sea salt, and it's intoxicating. If I could have one of the bartenders recreate the flavor in a delicious icy drink, I would. His mouth on mine has the same effect, too. I'm dizzy, my body buzzing like I've been slugging said drinks back all day. Sunscreen and cardamom and a hint of lavender invade my senses, and my hips roll freely into his. He feels fucking amazing beneath my fingertips, muscles flexing, cock thick and hard where it's trapped between our bodies.

Pleasure crashes over me like a wave when Ace knots his fingers in my hair, guiding my head to the side to deepen the kiss. He splits the seam of my lips and dives his tongue inside hungrily, mapping the shape of my mouth. Tingles erupt in my core, and I cling to him tighter. His confidence is sexy, and I wonder what other areas he's this unfaltering in. He holds me like he's been praying for this since the moment we met, grip firm around my waist. Right now, there are no thoughts of revenge, no exes that don't care. My mind is blaring with my own selfish needs. This moment is solely Ace's, our mouths pressed together, his tongue tracing mine in a way I want recreated between my legs.

A piercing screech tears us apart. Dazed from the kiss, I stagger back. A wave almost finishes knocking me off balance, but Ace is there, saving me yet again, keeping me close. We blink at each other, and I can't help but drink in how wrecked he appears with his blond hair sticking up in every direction, his eyes hot and hooded. Our chests heave, brushing with every inhale, sending electricity zipping through my veins as reality slowly trickles in.

I can't stop staring at his mouth, swollen from my kisses. I'm parched, and unconsciously lick my lips to chase the taste of him, hardly able to contain a shudder of arousal at the way Ace tracks the movement.

I want to jump him all over again.

"I'm sorry," I pant, cutting the silence. I'm not sorry, not really, because I'm pretty sure Ace enjoyed the kiss as much as I did.

The hardness of his cock against my core only confirms it.

"Don't be," Ace echoes, just as breathless. I'm entirely aware he's holding me against him; his hands placed firmly on my ass. When I begin to pull away, his grip only tightens. "I want that to be a rule," he bites out, like it's painful to have me this close and not fall into something more. I mirror the sentiment. "Sixty-four, fifteen, thirty-two, I don't fucking care what number it is. Rule number eighty-seven says I can kiss you whenever I want, because after *that?* There's no way I'm staying away from you."

If only he knew what those words do to me. Seriously, the ocean is turning into a hot tub with how blisteringly my body burns. My lungs are void of air, and my heart beats to a newfound drum, pounding so hard the waves grow stronger.

The spot between my legs pulses in vehement agreement, even when I weakly protest, "Not in front of my family."

Ace rolls his eyes as if to say "obviously." If any of my family members catch wind of what we're doing, they're going to grill me and keep me within their sights for the rest of our trip.

"Yes, boss," he teases, catching me by my wrist when I try to splash him.

He's admiring me as if I'm much more to him than a stranger. The heady look awakens something in me, like a flower blooming after it's been on the verge of death, withered and limp.

"You know, if we're going to kiss," I wave my hand nonchalantly, rifling for the words. My brain is fried and much too interested in kissing him again for coherency. "Rule number three should be no marks where anyone can see them."

Ace's face takes on a dark glint of amusement. His lips curve into a wicked grin as he leans in to latch them against my neck. I squeal as his teeth scrape my throat, my fingers curling into the waistband of his swim trunks.

"No fucking promises, Rory-O."

I'm three seconds away from tossing my phone into the horseshoe-shaped swimming pool ten feet in front of me. I'm not athletic by any means, but I'm pretty sure I can make it to the water from here.

Okay, 98 percent sure. And if the stupid piece of technology doesn't make it into the crystal-clear water, the concrete will surely take care of rendering my phone unusable.

"What are you huffing and puffing about?" Ace asks lazily from beside me. The question is paired with a gentle squeeze to my thigh, where his hand has been resting for the past five minutes while I attempt to snap the perfect picture to post on my private story. The tingle accompanying the motion temporarily distracts me from my annoyance.

Ace doesn't sound interested in my answer. He's too busy basking in the sun, free hand propped behind his head.

"I can't get the picture right." My cheeks heat. I sound like a petulant child, but this snapshot has to be perfect. I won't post anything less. With a sigh, I lock my screen and let my phone fall to my lounger.

I'd throw my head back in defeat if Ace's hand wasn't splayed across my leg like a web, trapping my attention.

Ink dots his skin, and I trail its path. On his pointer finger is a set of Roman numerals, representing a year I'm interested to know what happened that was significant enough to mark himself forever. The date his favorite sports team won the Superbowl or Stanley Cup or whatever trophy they win at the end of the season? His birth year? The date he realized his smile could melt panties? That seems like an accomplishment worthy of showing off.

Following up his forearm, a tube of paint squirts black ink. None of his tattoos have color, and the linework gives me the urge to purchase markers from the gift shop and spend my afternoon coloring. The idea sounds more fun than my failed attempts at photography.

Maybe if Ace dozes off, I'll take the chance.

A barbed wire snake coils around his wrist. It's unique, and I wonder how many of these are his own artwork. Shamelessly, my gaze slides to his wide shoulders, enjoying the view. His body is built for sports, with his defined abdominals and the strong curve of his bicep linking us together.

"Here." He sits up, plucking my abandoned phone, and placing it in my hand. Begrudgingly, I await his next instruction. "Come on, open the camera. I'm going to give you some of my best work."

I'm apprehensive about what his best work contains, but I'm afraid if I ask, all I'll get in return is a cheeky remark. My filthy mind flutters to something much less appropriate for the pool deck, and maybe *I'm* the one with the problem. I tuck my lip between my teeth to stop from entertaining that train of thought and open my camera.

Ace returns his hand to my thigh in the exact same position it was before. When I go to complain about how this isn't going to work, my words die out as he drags his hand closer to the apex of my thighs.

Arousal rears its head, his touch the only thing I'm able to focus on. My instincts scream at me to clasp my legs shut to trap his hand between them. It's sweltering under the sun, but his fingers raise goosebumps on my legs.

If Ace notices my sudden stiffness, he doesn't mention it. Leaning closer, he peers at the phone screen. He's so close his torso brushes my arm, and any coherent thoughts completely fizzle into nothingness. His breath puffs against my neck when he says, "How's this?"

I'm going to need that hand about two inches down and a few more to the right, is how I would reply if I could form words. He's dangerously close to where my aching pussy begs for stimulation. When he begins stroking my thigh mindlessly, I all but melt between the slats of my lounge chair.

"That's . . . good," I whisper. His touch is more than good. It's fucking electric. My chest is so tight it's difficult to remember how to breathe. Ace is right; this makes a much better picture than before.

With a shaky hand, I snap a few photos and hope for the best. I can hardly focus on my phone, entranced by the amount of surface his splayed hand covers. I feel small in Ace's grip, and he must catch on to how his touch affects me because he gives another, more prominent squeeze, and I jolt in my chair like a startled deer.

We haven't kissed since we declared our rules two days ago. Not because I haven't wanted to. I'm ready for *a lot* more of Ace Broden, but with family activities, I haven't had the chance to sneak away until this afternoon. I've imagined Ace's lips on mine as he teases his tongue into my mouth more times than is considered healthy. When I so much as think about making a move, nerves seize my limbs, stopping me from going after what I crave.

I'm not confident in my ability to flirt. When Max and I first met, I was more of a pile of anxiety than human. He was the confident one in our relationship, and I found it sexy how assured he was in every move he made.

A flare of misery explodes to life at his memory, and I hastily shove all things Max away, not wanting to ruin this, even if this moment is a direct result of what he's done. I won't allow him to take this from me.

"Is this okay?" Ace questions. His blond brow appears over the frame of his glasses when he raises it. "I won't stand for 'good.' We're aiming for perfection here." My heartbeat staccatos as his hand inches higher.

My breathing shifts from shallow to a sharp inhale. The rest of the hotel falls away until it's Ace and me, and Ace's knowing smirk.

I hate that smile. I hate that I'm even more turned on by it.

"How about now?" He all but purrs.

It's difficult not to glare. That would mean he's succeeding in riling me up. I swear, if he continues, I might have to excuse myself for half an hour . . . maybe a full one if he's willing to join.

My attention is glued to where our skin meets. "It's pretty close," I reply, and I don't know why I'm adding fuel to the fire. Fuck, of course I do. Because this is thrilling and arousing and *new.* How can a single touch possibly have me burning up this way?

Ace's hand slips from my leg. I trap a noise of protest, only for my jaw to unhinge when he hooks his fingers around the edge of my lounger to tug me closer. So close our arms plaster together when he relaxes back in his seat.

I almost implode.

This is a dangerous game because I haven't been touched like this in weeks. A girl has needs.

"Pretty close?" Ace echoes suggestively. He drags his sunglasses to the top of his head, gifting me with those simmering blue eyes. He tilts his chin to see my screen better, and the movement puts his mouth so close to my cheek I feel the words form on his lips when he speaks. "What can I do differently?"

The image of Ace asking that exact question while his head is between my legs punches the air from my lungs. My thigh twitches in his hold, threatening to close without my permission. I need to smother the fire between them, and fast, preferably with Ace's palm or fingers.

Words have abandoned me. I open my mouth only to shut it, and Ace's grin grows into asshole territory.

"What's going on in that pretty little head of yours, Rory-O?" He heckles, circling a thumb to emphasize he knows *exactly* what's going on in my pretty little head.

"N-Nothing." I curse myself for stuttering and somehow muster the courage to remove his hand from my leg completely. The immediate loss is devastating. "We got the picture."

I ignore his chuckle and the ache of my body. Stretching my legs flat, I carefully cross one over the other, swiping from the camera app to Instagram. I choose a photo at random before I get all worked up again. I tack on a sparkling sunshine sticker and upload the post to the private story I created which consists only of Max, his friends, and Quinn. I came clean to Quinn because the guilt of hiding what I'm doing with Ace was driving me insane.

When I explained the situation to my best friend, I kept the details vague, not mentioning Ace's name or any attributes that would help her pick him out of a lineup. Maybe I'm too paranoid, but since our agreement ends when vacation does, there's no point in divulging the finer details that will only embed the boy beside me into my mind.

While the picture uploads, I notice the ring of color around Max's profile, alerting me to his story. Every ounce of fire in my veins freezes. My stomach churns and my limbs grow numb, pins pricking as I hover over his name.

Ace must notice the sudden change in my mood because his playful tone drops when he asks, "You okay?"

I nod absentmindedly and click Max's name.

My shoulders droop in relief. The picture is of a seafood boil, one that would look mighty delicious if I weren't battling knots in my stomach. The location is tagged, but there's no further text or limbs to decipher, except for the crawfish and veggies piled on the table, so I click away and drop my head onto my chair.

I hate my reaction every time I see his posts, for anticipating a photo of a girl hanging all over him or his hands around their waist. For the urge to reach out and ask how his summer is or if he's thought of me once in the past few weeks.

I should've completely cut ties with him like any smart person post-breakup would have, but I'm still in love with him. I miss him so much it physically hurts. His parting words of how we can pick our relationship back up when school starts again ring in my head with a knell of hope.

My phone buzzes, drawing my attention. Eagerly, I check the notification, silently hoping it's Max. My stomach swirls with disappointment when my sister group chat appears with a new message. Peep is wondering where I've wandered off to. My parents want to take us out for lunch at one of the local spots they came across in town after their scuba diving lesson.

"I have to go," I sigh, slipping from my chair before Ace has the chance to protest. I snag my striped towel and tie it around my waist as dread kicks in. I'm not looking forward to being the fifth wheel with my family, but I don't have much of a choice. They're going to become suspicious if I keep sneaking away, and I don't need an interrogation.

Ace sits up, flicking his sunglasses over the bridge of his nose. "Already?"

I try not to let his note of disappointment burrow its way into my brain. I'm still trying to recover from the unnecessary spiral Max's post has thrown me into.

"I'm sorry, I'll see you soon," I promise, slipping into my flip-flops.

"Yeah," he agrees easily, shrugging me off. I frown as he falls back into the lounger and props his arms behind his head, like he doesn't have a care in the world. He probably doesn't, and the thought has something sad turning over in my chest. "See you later."

CHAPTER 9
ACE

Slate plucks a bright green bottle of alcohol off the shelf and examines the label. I grimace. The liquid looks like straight up acid or a potion from a children's cartoon. *Witches brew.* "What do you think the girls like to drink?"

Daiquiris, Mai Tais, Bahama Mamas, anything frozen and fruity—I recall the sugary concoctions Rory drank over the summer. She forced me to try a sip of each one for every complaint I made, and even though I made a show of disliking them to make her laugh, they were fucking delicious. So much so that I considered purchasing one of those frozen drink machines for the apartment. It's truly a shame the cleanup is more effort than I'm willing to put into having one. I'd kill for a daiquiri right now.

Slate, Knox, and I waltz down the aisles of the best liquor store in town: Bruiser's Booze. The secluded store on the edge of town is the best because they don't ID. We've been shopping here since the second weekend of freshman year when we overheard the rumor. Plus, the owner, Bruce, otherwise famously known in Hardwich as Bruiser, is one of the nicest guys I've met.

Did I mention they don't ID?

Even though my roommates and I are almost all twenty-one—with my birthday in a few months and Knox's in January—we've been loyal to Bruiser's for two years and don't care enough to take our patronage elsewhere, even if we have to drive to the outskirts of town for liquor runs.

"They like anything that doesn't taste like alcohol," Knox mutters like the answer is obvious. I'm not surprised by his knowledge of this, not after the girl he was trying to tattoo at our last party threw her fruity drink in his face. He's still salty about the incident and the fact we've decided to go to the homecoming party Rory invited us to. To Knox, attending is a betrayal of brotherhood, getting chummy with our neighbors when he's clearly drawn the line in the sand and is ready to lead his army into battle any day now.

While he's standing firm on his beef, I'm definitely ready to get a little more than friendly with one of the girls next door.

We're picking out alcohol for the party because we're nothing if not gentlemen beneath our less than stellar attitudes on night one. It would be rude to arrive empty-handed, and I want to make a good first impression on Rory's sister.

"I guess that means lime-apple schnapps is out," Slate says solemnly, replacing the bottle on the shelf. My mouth sours at the name alone, unable to imagine drinking that shit. It looks like it'd slowly eat me from the inside out. Before I can make the comment, Slate perks up, reaching for a bottle on the other side of the aisle. "Tequila, *in*."

Knox and I share a glance. Slate has never said no to tequila in his entire life, not even when he's past his limit. At this point, his blood is probably 98 percent tequila instead of water; *that's* how much Slate loves it.

"Just put it in the cart," I grouse, spotting a mixed margarita blend a few bottles over. Strawberry watermelon, the label reads. Rory would love this.

My pocket vibrates as I place it in the cart beside the case of beer, the only other thing we've picked out so far.

Pulling my phone out, I grin at the contact name and don't hesitate to accept the video call.

"Hey, Mom," I greet, adjusting the camera to show my roommates, who continue to peruse the shelves. Knox wears an annoyed scowl as always, hands shoved into the pockets of his jeans. The tattoos drawn down his arms are on full display. Slate runs his fingers through his jaw-length brunet hair, brushing it from his vision. No matter how much he complains about the longer style, he refuses to cut it, claiming he's been pulling more ladies than ever. He happily grabs bottle after bottle off the shelves, checking the flavor and alcohol content of everything he touches.

Mom squeals at the sight. "Slate, honey, I haven't seen you in *ages*! And look at that hair!" She exclaims proudly. The video shakes as she tries to get my father in frame. I bite my lip to contain my grin, and I'm thankful I'm not five drinks in because the shaking would make me sick to my stomach. "Look, Theo, it's so shiny!"

Slate ambles over at the sound of her voice and hooks his chin over my shoulder. I groan and attempt to shove him off, but the big asshole doesn't budge.

"Hello, Mom? What about me?" I question, feigning betrayal. "The entire reason you called?"

"Yep, there's our son," my dad tacks on. He's reclined in a lounger beside her, basking in the sun. Dad slides his sunglasses down his nose to see the screen, and the same blue eyes I inherited pop against the crimson his face is beginning to turn. "Miss you, bud."

"Miss you too," I respond sincerely. "How's Bermuda?"

Mom's beaming smile says it all. The phone wobbles as she taps the screen forcefully, failing to flip the camera around. When the image finally switches, I'm met with the view of pink sand beaches. The water is crystal clear, and there's not another vacationer in sight. I wonder if they're at a private house instead of an all-inclusive they normally book.

"It's *gorgeous*! We'll have to come back here with you someday, sweetie."

This is what I love about my parents. They always make time for each other, even with their busy schedules. I'd yearn for that if I were capable of giving love a second chance. Traveling the world with the person you love must be an incredible experience.

My mind flutters back to Cabo and Rory, and how spending my time with her had felt similar.

I shove the thought away before I read too deeply as to why she popped into my head in the first place.

"That'd be great, Mom," I agree. Her eyes flit around the screen, scanning my surroundings. I wince, but it's too late to hide where I am, especially when her smile falters and a scold appears on the tip of her tongue.

"Are you boys at the liquor store?" Mom squawks like we're doing something much worse. I'm almost twenty-one, but I'll always be her little boy. "Isn't it Thursday?"

"Isn't that a daiquiri in your hand?" I counter, and grins split both of our faces.

"Like mother, like son," Dad laughs, leaning over to peck Mom's temple. When she turns her head for a proper kiss, I make a noise of revulsion.

My chest tightens at the loving way they stare at each

other when they part. They met in college when they quite literally ran headfirst into each other like some cheesy rom-com and have been inseparable ever since. Mom would say it was love at first sight, Dad says Mom knocked a part of her soul into his noggin that day. They're so smitten it makes me sick.

They've been through everything together. Every downfall, every time they've had to pick back up to climb the mountain again, they did it hand-in-hand, and they've built an incredible life together.

My father owns exclusive art galleries all around the country, and Mom has built a reputation as one of the most sought after art managers, with some of the more popular artisans on her roster of clients.

Her dream is to onboard me onto her list, and as much as I love my mom, I don't want handouts from my parents. I believe in myself to find a manager of my own and weave my way in the art world without their connections. It will break their hearts when I can finally muster the courage to come clean, which is exactly why I haven't dared bring it up yet.

"Hey," Mom scolds playfully, swatting at Dad. The action causes the phone to take a swoop, almost giving me motion sickness, and before I can cut our conversation short, Mom's attention is back on me. She takes a large sip of her drink in defiance. "This isn't a daiquiri, it's a Bushwacker!"

"Bushwacker?" Slate echoes, grin spelling trouble. Something dirty is about to spew from his mouth because that's exactly who Slate is. I quickly mute our side of the phone before he can finish his sentence. "I hardly even know her! *Hey! Not cool, Acey*!"

He reaches over my shoulder to snag the phone from my hand, but I duck away, shooting him a warning glare. The harsh look isn't effective, because it doesn't stop him from coming at me. Mom might believe Slate's charming, but I don't need another lecture about how I better not be repeating those kinds of jokes, too.

Before Bruce spots us wrestling around all these glass bottles, Mom asks, "Where's Knox, honey?"

"He's right here," I answer with a huff, thankful when Slate finally backs off. He sticks his tongue out, and I ignore him, turning the phone to face Knox, who has wisely chosen to stay out of our tussle. At least he enjoyed the entertainment, according to the amused glint in his features.

"Oh! Knox, you get even more handsome every time I see you. Doesn't he, Theo?" Mom gushes. Her face grows as she moves the phone closer to herself, sliding her sunglasses into her blonde hair to squint at my roommate. She's always adored Knox, even more so after learning about his motorcycle accident. They've met on multiple occasions, as Knox normally accompanies me home for school breaks. Mom absolutely cannot get enough of my stoic and brooding roommate. It must be a mom thing.

Knox doesn't always join me on trips to Colorado because he thinks himself a burden, but my family loves him, myself included. I'm pretty sure Mom is ready to officially dub him her second son. And if Knox is her second son, Slate is her third, because he'd absolutely throw a fit for not being included. "You better be around for parent's weekend, honey. I want to see you too!"

"Of course, Mrs. Broden," Knox agrees politely. The shift in his attitude to placate my mom has me biting back a smile. As of late, he's been nothing but his snarky self, especially since declaring World War III on Rory and Quinn. To see him actually smiling—even if it is forced for my mom's sake—is a rare sight.

"What about me, Margot?" Slate butts in, slinging his arms around Knox and my shoulders.

"You too, honey," Mom scoffs like she can't believe Slate asked something so silly. "We'll let you boys get back to shopping. Don't overdo it, and don't blackout!"

We laugh and agree with the most innocent smiles we can muster. None of us makes any promises.

Dad appears in the frame to say his farewells. "Love you, Ace." He fans himself with a menu, and it's either sweltering outside or they're about to order a midday snack. My stomach rumbles at the idea of food. We should get something to eat when we're done here. "See you for parent's weekend."

"Love you, too," I echo as my roommate's trail down the next aisle, abandoning me with the cart currently holding only a case of beer, one bottle of margarita mix, and a handle of tequila. We have some shopping to do before I can get my snack. "See you in a few weeks."

I glare into my cup of punch, the taste of alcohol potent on my tongue while everyone around me enjoys the party.

I'm not having a good time.

From the scathing scowls Knox keeps shooting Quinn where she's laughing with Rory, Rory's sister and her roommates, and Sam—who lovingly has his arm draped around Quinn's shoulders—he isn't having fun, either.

Apparently, Knox doesn't care that Sam is her brother, and that Sam's heart-eyes are glued on Rory's older sister, Peep.

I haven't said anything, mostly because it's too entertaining watching Knox be this oblivious. He might think he's scowling because he doesn't like our blonde-haired neighbor, but everyone else in the room—with the exception of Quinn —knows he's acting out because he's clearly attracted to her. Also, it's sort of nice to have someone to wallow with, even if it isn't a pretty girl who's using me to make her ex jealous.

Of the three of us, Slate seems to be the only one who has an in to the close-knit group, which isn't fair because he can fit in *anywhere*. It's his superpower.

My mood is grim because Rory has done everything in her power to put me in the most miserable position tonight. And not sexually. Even an unfavorable sex position is a better day than most. *This* is all because I made a deal to apologize to Quinn and haven't made good on my promise yet. Her roommate is the most stubborn woman on the face of the Earth, and Quinn's proving it by refusing to give me the time of day—night—to speak my piece.

On the ride over, Rory forced me into the middle seat of the Uber, right between her and Quinn. I brush a hand through my hair over the spot singed to my scalp from her blistering glare she impressively kept up the entire ride.

Slate didn't understand how safe he was in the passenger seat while I was trying my best not to brush any of my limbs against Quinn's, holding my breath and suffering greatly in the back.

The smirks Rory gifts me when everything goes wrong have my heart fluttering to the beat of the song shaking the house. Like I said, she knows exactly what she's doing, but those wicked smiles behind the brim of her cup are worth a bit of torture.

Quinn takes her fury seriously, and she's more than made sure I get the picture she's not forgiving me for the morning at Art Haven.

Isn't it tiring being so stubborn all the time?

She even went as far as to slam the car door in my face when we arrived at Peep's. My first mistake was attempting to exit the vehicle on the same side as her. With a groan of frustration and her sign well received, I shifted back the other way, tailing Rory instead. Her icy blues took note of me, and when she stood from her seat, she mirrored Quinn's actions, shutting the door on me with a grin of pure satisfaction I wanted to taste.

I suppose a door to the face was a well-deserved form of punishment for doing the same to them, and no, it didn't feel good.

I also didn't miss the way they high-fived each other before leaving Slate and me to unpack the alcohol we brought.

Knox arrived late, muttering something about the number of people stuffed in the small house. The kitchen has fewer partygoers than the living room, where all the furniture has been pushed aside for room to dance.

The baby-pink kitchen tiles match the color of the shots one of Peep's roommates, Dani, pours into a circle of plastic cups on the counter. The cerulean walls are the same shade as the Jell-O shots stacked on a shelf in the fridge. It's all very cute that they chose to celebrate the homecoming win with themed drinks. They taste damn good, too.

Surprisingly, Knox accepts a shot glass as we gather around the island. Quinn's brother slinks away to stand beside Peep, his bicep brushing her bare arm as he settles in comfortably beside her. Her cheeks flush and her gaze lingers on him. Rory's staring openly at them, eyes wide and entranced like she's watching her favorite show. She carefully folds her lip between her teeth in an attempt to stifle the smile threatening to split her face in two.

Warmth ignites in my veins, straightening my spine. I want that lip between my teeth.

"Who's toasting?" Jessy, Peep's other roommate, asks, scanning the group impatiently before stalling on the living room like she's more than ready to dance. Her hips are swaying, and her drink is halfway raised, fingers tapping the cup in beat with the music.

Rory's gaze meets mine for a split second, and when she notices my focus is entirely hers, her pretty blues widen and dart away. I grin triumphantly at the blush coloring her throat.

I shift my weight, ignoring my rousing cock as the memory of Rory on her knees with that exact look on her face flashes through my mind.

Fuck, do I want her.

"I'll do it," I blurt. I'll do anything to get her attention back on me.

Surprised at my volunteering, she latches back onto me. Satisfaction floods me, and I'm more than willing to propose a toast. We haven't been able to talk much tonight, and it's not for my lack of trying. She's been avoiding me.

I guess I'll have to try harder.

"Then spit it out," Jessy complains when the song blasting through the house melds perfectly into another party classic. "This is my favorite song!"

"Me too," Slate winks, and I know that look. It's the one that says he might just make her wildest dreams come true. Or at least make her come, if she gives him the chance.

Jessy bats her eyelashes flirtatiously in response, and the deal is as good as done.

"To Picasso," I begin, regarding the circle.

I'm met with varying degrees of confusion. Peep and her roommates exchange baffled glances, unsure of where I'm going with this. Slate doesn't seem to care much about the toast at all anymore, eyeing Jessy as if she's going to slip away at any given moment. Quinn and Sam wear matching frowns. I don't know how Knox doesn't see the similarities; they could almost be twins. Speaking of, Knox's features are flooded with amusement. A smirk tugs at the corner of his mouth, and I'm sure his self-satisfied smile only infuriates Quinn more. Offering a toast she doesn't know and Knox does isn't going to bode well for me when I try to apologize again, but I can't find it in me to care.

Rory's shoulders soften, recognizing my words. She appears almost apologetic for the way the night has gone, for the way she's had me jumping through hoops for her attention. At the very least, I want to be friends with her. Fuck, in total honesty, I want to be so much more than friends with her, but if this is all I'm allowed, I have to be okay with it because having a tiny sliver of Rory in my life is better than having none of her at all.

Besides, I'm good at biding my time, and it's only a matter of when she'll break her rules, just like she did over the summer.

"What?" Dani asks, utterly confused.

Rory explains, "Picasso's last words were 'drink to me.'"

It takes everyone a moment before it clicks.

"*Oh*," Slate grins, clearly enjoying the artistic spin I've added to drinking. "Sick toast, Acey. Drink to me!" He shouts, slamming his shot back.

A resounding round of cheers goes off as everyone echoes my words. I tip my cup back, not breaking eye contact with Rory as I swallow the bite of tequila with a hint of watermelon. Her throat works around her own drink, and I can't help the smug smile gracing my cheeks.

It doesn't take long for her to figure it out. She's quick as a whip, but not quite quick enough. Rory's features sharpen into a scowl when she realizes she just drank in my honor.

The pissed-off frown she wears might be the most beautiful thing I've seen.

I'll make it up to her somehow. I'll drink in her honor if she wants me to. I've been doing that all night anyway, even if she hasn't noticed. She's a fine glass of wine. Her long brown hair is curled in loose waves around her shoulders. The bangs she hated so much over the summer have grown out to frame her pink cheeks. The tight top she wears clings to the curves of her body, and her jeans hug her ass and thighs like they're painted on.

My pants grow tighter the longer I think about stripping them off.

I drag my hungry gaze down her body for the umpteenth time tonight, and she watches. I stare long and hard, taking my time so she understands just how badly I desire her.

When I finally reach her eyes again, those bright blues aren't filled with annoyance and revenge, but with a heat that bleeds oceans dry.

CHAPTER 10
RORY

"So that's one vodka cran, hold the cran," Slate sing-songs with a mischievous wink, passing Quinn a blue Solo cup. She grumbles, and Slate pretends not to hear her over the loud music pouring from the speakers. I bite my lip while our friend shouts across the circle the three of us have made up on the "dance floor," which is really the middle of Peep's living room. Slate thrusts a cup into my hand next. "And one tequila sunrise, hold whatever the fuck else that isn't tequila."

I etch a face of confusion. I'm not sure what's in a tequila sunrise either, but this isn't even close to what I asked for. I take a tentative sip nonetheless, bracing myself. The warmth of the acid-like alcohol blossoms from my stomach to my head and toes, and I smother my choking with a laugh.

Slate takes our empty cups and ambles away, eager to get us as drunk as possible. Quinn and I close in on each other, swaying our hips to the music. The punchy bass filters through my veins alongside the alcohol, loosening my limbs.

The heavy weight of someone's attention licks me up and down, causing the hair at the nape of my neck to stand. The heavy stare has been following me around all night, and there's only one person it can be. Only one person I want it to be.

I take a nonchalant sweep of the room. College students pack the house, grinding and dancing to the upbeat music. Drinks are held high in the air, girls jumping and collectively shouting the lyrics when the chorus hits, and there's a couple making out against the wall so fiercely I'm positive that by the time they break apart, his mustache will have melted onto her face.

I peer over my shoulder to the archway of the kitchen where Slate disappeared. I don't see his frame through the doorway, and the lights have dimmed.

As I'm about to shrug off this feeling and let Ace come to me, I spot him.

He stands against the wall with Knox at his side. He's every bit as effortless as someone can muster in the thick of a party; a beer clasped in his hand, eyes dark and pinned on me while he murmurs to his roommate.

The alcohol has my boldness skyrocketing, and I eye Ace just as greedily. His blond hair is perfectly ruffled, like always. I've been keeping careful watch of him all night, stomach souring with displeasure anytime a girl so much as offers a suggestive flutter of their eyelashes in his direction, and secretly preening into the rim of my cup when he shrugs them off, uninterested.

Ace can fuck whoever he wants, much to my body's protest. I'm on the verge of rekindling my relationship with Max, so if Ace fills the void with someone else, who am I to judge?

He smiles when I glare, like this is some sort of game. He says everything he needs to with the look he offers in return, lighting a fire between my thighs.

Drink to me.

Asshole.

I wish I could say Ace's cockiness was endearing, but I'm nowhere near wasted enough to admit it out loud.

I swirl my hips sensuously, and he greedily latches onto the movement. My heart skips with excitement. To really give him something to ogle, I run my hands across the tops of my thighs, over my hips, continuing to trace my body higher. My head falls back on my shoulders with the music. Quinn dances at my side, so I lean into her, swaying with my best friend, back-to-back.

Ace's gaze darkens, like he's two seconds away from prowling across the living room to tear the clothes from my skin, maybe catch my mouth in a kiss that would knock my world off its axis. I bite back a triumphant grin.

He pushes away from the wall, and my body thrums, the beginning of my fantasy coming to life.

I whirl around and grab Quinn's arm as a thrill of excitement zips up my spine. The chase is half the fun.

"Come to the bathroom with me," I beg. She blinks, dazed. For a moment, I shove aside my arousal, reminding myself to swing by the kitchen on our way back for water because the buzz under my skin is kicking up a notch as well.

Quinn nods and weaves our fingers together tightly, shuffling through the crowd. She's blissfully unaware of the boys hunting us, and I wonder if she knew they were prowling behind us like lions, would her heart be stammering as quickly as mine?

My hand slips from hers when my shoulder snags against someone else's. An unknown liquid splashes across my shirt, momentarily shocking me out of my trance-like state. Halfheartedly, I apologize to the girl who glares whilst I try to shake the alcohol from my arm.

The fabric of my shirt is damp, but not enough to borrow one of Peep's. When I'm finished examining the mess, Quinn has fully disappeared, and I'm stranded in the middle of a forming dance-circle.

Oh, hell to the fuck no.

My sprinkler is rusty from unuse, and I haven't stayed at the YMCA in years. There's no way I'm attempting the worm; the last thing I need is more stains on my shirt or, God forbid, Ace finding me face down on the floor.

Rolling to the tips of my toes, I scan the crowd for Quinn. It's too dark and there are too many people stuffed into the house to make out her blonde hair or pastel top. Maybe she redirected to the kitchen to spy on her brother and my sister. My steps falter, and I almost turn to join because whatever is happening between them is way more interesting than hiding from Ace in the bathroom like a coward.

After a second scan of the room and finding no best friend, I push into the bathroom, both surprised and pleased to find it unoccupied. An empty bathroom this late in the night is almost skeptical, or fate. Whatever it is, I'm taking advantage of this strange gift.

Swinging the door shut, it catches against a body trying to barge inside. Startled, I'm forced backward with a cry of protest. Thankfully, I don't trip over any discarded beer bottles or the suspiciously wet hand towel kicked against the wall.

"What the—*hey*!" I shout, twisting to face the intruder. I should've known. Ace leans casually against the door, and the temperature in the tiny bathroom soars.

"Hey, Rory-O," he greets with his famous panty-dropping smile. "You having a good time?" By the glow in his eyes, he knows exactly how much fun I'm having. I didn't see Peep much last year, but I'm glad she convinced me to attend tonight. I haven't heard a single passing conversation about the football team or how well Max played tonight, and I'm thankful.

Now that I'm alone with Ace, I'm not sure *fun* is the word I'd use to describe my night.

Although I'm sure we could make some fun of our own, like old times.

"Have you apologized to Quinn yet?" I dig up the only excuse I can think of to keep him at arm's length a while longer. My question does nothing to deter him, and I cross my arms to fill the space between us as he steps closer. The bathroom is small. How Peep manages to share it with two other people, I have no idea, because Ace and I are nearly chest-to-chest, and I hate that I like the way his body heat presses deliciously against me, even with the inches of space between us.

His hands find the counter, bolstering me between strong arms. My heart thrums with an uneven beat at the proximity. To keep my emotions askew, Ace leans in, ocean eyes alight with mischief. He's so close I can almost taste him, and it's fucking with me how we're at a party essentially celebrating my ex-boyfriend. An ex-boyfriend who no longer wants to be ex.

Desperate to keep my head, I scoot back, lifting myself onto the cool stone counter. I clench my aching thighs, using my knees as a wall to block Ace from moving any closer.

His scent consumes me as he lowers his chin to speak in my ear. Lavender and cardamom, sweet and spicy, has me inhaling a deep breath. His lips caress the shell of my ear. I white-knuckle the counter to stop from looping my arms around his neck to haul him into me. "Can't I just apologize to you again, Rory-O? I promise I'll make it worth your while." Shit. My self-restraint is wafer thin.

Biting my lip, he tracks the motion. We're so close all I'd have to do is straighten my spine and my mouth would be on his. He'd be kissing me like he did all over Mexico: wet and wild, my legs wrapped around his waist in the ocean, brash and hungry in one of our hotel rooms, soft and sweet like the ones we shared under the stars.

"If you were to," I start, shivering at the idea. Ace's thumb traces the sliver of skin between the hem of my shirt and the waistband of my pants, and I'm thankful I'm sitting because my knees liquefy at the sensation. He's too close. It's making my head spin. "Apologize, I mean. How might that go?" If I wasn't actively trying to swallow back the desire to be touched, I'd already be begging.

The corner of his mouth quirks, and my clit throbs. His hands trail my thighs agonizingly slow. The sensation of his fingers dragging down my jeans sends a blaring signal to my brain: *more.* My choice to sit on the counter seemed like a good idea at the time, but with the way Ace gives in to the magnetism between us, my decision has made it almost impossible to escape.

Ace dips so close his lips brush the shell of my ear with his whispered response. "Would the sight of me on my knees help you forgive me?"

His words send me spiraling. My eyes flutter shut. My heart thunders. My throat dries. My pussy tightens.

Where is Slate with my refill?

His nose brushes mine. His breath caresses my lips, inviting me to close the millimeter of space between us. I keep my eyes fully shut, grasping onto the last thread of self-control like I'm grasping the counter. His hands crawl at a torturous pace back up, sliding over my waist, my skin lighting with desire as his fingers catch on the slits in the sides of the low-cut tank top.

Electricity crackles between us, snapping at my senses. "No," I try to break his intoxicating allure, planting my hands against his chest. His muscles flex, reminding me of how much I've missed his body. "Not good enough."

"What if I used my tongue?" He counters, his words brushing my throat as he continues to tease. His tongue flicks out, tasting me, and my fingers fist in his shirt. "And apologized all night long?"

"I'm not too sure Quinn would enjoy that," I deflect weakly. My words leave me in a breath I'm not sure Ace hears, because I'm not strong enough to raise my voice or all that will escape me is, "fuck me over the counter, please."

His responding growl informs me he heard, but I'm too busy reveling in the vibration of his chest to remember exactly what I said. The words disappear from my mind like a well-timed magic trick.

Ace's teeth scrape my earlobe in warning, and I gasp, craning my neck to give him room. He knocks my legs apart with his knee and forces himself closer, slotting his hips tightly against mine.

His length is hard as he presses into the apex of my thighs, screaming for his touch. This position is all too familiar, dragging up the memories of what usually follows. Fewer clothes, more touches. Lust. Euphoria. Bliss.

This position is dangerous. So very dangerous. There aren't enough layers between his cock and my pussy. Not enough space between our chests to breathe. Not enough fight in me to say no.

"You're so full of yourself, Acey-boy."

"Would you rather be full of me instead?" He taunts, and my threadbare restraint snaps.

"*Ace*," I warn. Or beg. It's hard to tell.

"Tell me, Rory-O." I didn't think we could get any closer,

yet Ace manages to find a sliver of space and presses our bodies so tightly together, until I can't tell if it's his heart or mine hammering against my chest. "What happened to rule number eighty-seven?"

There weren't that many rules, were there? I blink, racking my brain. I *know* there weren't that many rules, which means this is one Ace made up to poke fun at me. Which means I wasn't taking him seriously, so I have no idea what he's talking about.

I'm about to question if there ever really was a rule number eighty-seven when his mouth slants against mine and it rushes me like a tsunami.

"Rule number eighty-seven says I can kiss you whenever I want."

Yes, Ace. Yes, you fucking can.

I return the kiss just as vehemently. I taste the longing on his lips, and it shouldn't be so sweet. Shouldn't make me preen at how much he might have missed this. I've forgotten how much *I've* missed this, the demanding way he splits the seam of my mouth, tongue sweeping inside. My body rushes with excitement. I've never felt so *wanted*.

His fingers curl into the hair at the nape of my neck, and a wild moan tears out of me when he tilts my head. The new angle gives him room to explore my mouth, desperate like our first kiss all over again. Our tongues tangle with a fervor that silences the ringing in my head.

My fingers find the waistband of his jeans, curling into the fabric and grinding his hips forcefully into mine.

The room spins. My head is no longer dizzy from the alcohol; I'm completely drunk off Ace. My nipples tighten, and I keen. Ace greedily drinks the sound from my lips, humming with delight. The vibration runs down my front, all the way to my aching clit.

After a deliciously slow roll of his hips, Ace draws away. A protest forms on the tip of my tongue, but before my complaint shatters this bliss, Ace snakes his hand between my legs, knuckles dragging up the seam of my jeans. My spine arches as I shudder, bucking to meet his touch. *Fuck*, I want him *badly*, consequences be damned. I want to be splayed out under him like when he fucked me into the hotel bed, when he impaled me with his cock in the restaurant bathroom while our families unknowingly ate dinner beside each other. When he licked me until I saw a sky full of stars behind my closed eyes that night on the beach. When my face was pressed into the mattress, fingers curled so tightly in the sheets the fabric gave while Ace had his way with me—

If I'm going to regret anything Ace does to me, it'll be tomorrow's problem.

I fumble with his belt in my haste to get it off. I've never felt an urge so visceral as the one compelling me to pull his cock out and wrap my fingers around his thick length.

Ace is just as eager, easing my shirt up my torso. My head falls back on my shoulders with a sharp cry as he latches onto the soft flesh beneath my collarbone. His teeth pleasurably scrape against my skin, then soothes the ache with his tongue. If he keeps kissing me like this, my panties will be ruined and I'll have the reminder on my flesh to prove this isn't my imagination.

The door shakes on its hinges under the force of an urgent knock, fissuring the lust clouding the room.

We startle apart with heavy gasps, our attention darting to the door. Instinctively, I trace my swollen lips burning with the remnants of Ace, chasing the taste.

"Rory?" Quinn calls through the wood. "You in there?"

Ace and I lock eyes. His pupils are blown, and I'm sure mine aren't much better. He wants this just as much as I do, shaking his head, begging me not to give us away. His gaze is as pleading as it is hopeful that once my best friend gives up her inquisition, we can continue wherever this is headed.

It truly is a shame my head catches up to my body and my stomach sinks with realization over what we were about to do.

Ace must see it in my eyes when it hits me. He's always been good at reading me like a book.

"*Please*," he whispers hoarsely, but my mind is already made.

I'm the one to break our staring contest. We can't do this. Not here. Not *ever*. We made a promise on the beach to forget each other for a reason. A reason billowing in my mind like a warning flag. Ace Broden doesn't do love, and my heart belongs to someone else.

"Yeah, I'm almost done," I croak. Ace stills beneath my hands. It's a Herculean effort to push him away. The two steps he gives me feel like a thousand, a chasm of space between us matching the deepening cavern in my chest. It's impossible to meet his eyes. I can't handle whatever I might find with the devastation surrounding us.

Carefully, I slide off the counter, hyper-aware of every movement. The fabric of my shirt dragging against my pert nipples, the dampness of my panties when I shift my weight, twisting on my heel, careful not to brush against him accidentally, my heart jackhammering, and the sickness swirling in my stomach.

I swear I can feel his breath on the back of my neck. The focus I use to twist the sink on is laughable. All I want to do is spin around and fall into his arms, instead I shove my hands beneath the ice-cold water gushing from the faucet in hopes it will shock me out of this paralysis.

What the hell was I thinking, trying to stick my hands down Ace's pants? We don't do that. Not anymore.

The realization alone tastes like shit in my mouth.

Ace shuffles behind me, the motion startling. I tear my gaze from the water to meet his in the mirror. His face is carefully blank, and he's too quiet. I don't like it one bit.

"She'll go away," he says, and I tell myself it's because he just wants a quick fuck.

"She won't," I disagree, shutting the water off. The hand towel is a lump of dampness on the floor, so I dry my hands on my jeans, my mind racing. I can't believe we were about to have sex in the middle of a party. In my *sister's* bathroom.

Ace and I have slept together before, and it was every bit as wild and crazy as I needed at the time. But things are different now, and we made a promise that the summer would be all we had. That it would be the end of *Rory and Ace's Sextravaganza*.

And to solidify avoiding Ace, I already agreed to a date with Max.

Fuck. I have a date with Max.

My stomach roils as if I've just cheated on him.

"This was a mistake," I whisper, throat as tight as the tiny bathroom. Tears sting my sinuses, and I shake my head to clear them away. "I'm sorry. We can still be friends, but I—I can't do this right now."

Ace calling my name hardly registers as I lunge for the exit. I'm desperate to escape; the walls are closing in. I jerk the door open, only to be met with Quinn on the other side. I forgot she had been knocking only moments before.

Her features contort as she assesses me with a cloudy gaze that clears significantly at the sight of my pinched features. Her brows flatten, lips turning downward in concern.

She opens her mouth, only for her jaw to snap shut when Ace appears behind me. I curl in on myself, hugging my arms as Quinn tracks the movement, eyes widening in realization.

I shake my head to answer the silent question she pins me with. While having Ace this close was something I yearned for earlier, right now, the warmth of his body is haunting, feeding into my guilt. It propels me into action. I thread my arm through Quinn's and lead us into the thick of the party that has been raging on whether I'm making out with someone in the bathroom or stifling tears on my roommate's shoulder.

I don't look back to see if Ace follows.

CHAPTER 11
ACE
CABO

Rory's mauling her ice cream like it's going out of style: her sinful lips wrapped around the cone while her tongue swirls the frozen treat in a display of showmanship she should be rewarded for. For fuck's sake, her cheeks hollow when she sucks the top, and my cock rouses in my swim trunks.

Does she not understand what this is doing to me? That I've been untouched in the week I've been here?

There's nowhere else to look, nothing else to occupy my mind. Every time I pry my gaze away, I find myself watching her again with no memory of turning my attention back on the enthusiastic cone-licking beside me. It's like she has magical abilities, and I'm in a deep trance with no hope of ever escaping the chokehold she has on me. And I'm not even sure I want to. I'm exactly where I want to be. Well, I'd prefer one of our hotel rooms, but I can work with what I have.

Crossing my hands over my lap will only draw attention to the problem quickly arising between my legs. I could take the loss and go back to my room, jerk one out while this tantalizing hypnosis is still fresh in my mind, but there's no way in hell I can stand up right now without a pool-goer noticing my stiffy.

Her tongue pokes between her lips for another taste, unbothered by the tension of my limbs or how I've barely breathed in the past minute. I desire her badly, and I wonder if she's doing this to me on purpose or if this is some sort of sick joke put in motion by the Fates. Rory and I haven't done anything more than make out a few times. There was an accidental boob graze and a brush of the back of her hand across my swim trunks, sending a zap of lightning up my spine. It took all my self-control not to snatch her hand and stick it down my cabana shorts.

If we hadn't been in line for the lunch buffet, I might've done just that.

She is torture personified. There's a distinct craving for her touch I don't quite understand, and all I can chalk it up to is that I haven't touched a girl since stepping foot off the plane. I've felt her body pressed against mine, those perfect handful-sized breasts in my grasp, and her eager hips grinding against mine while we dry-humped each other, and it's safe to say I'm greedy for more.

To top it off, she's not looking for anything serious, which is perfect, because I can't offer anything more. She's truly an enigma.

Hesitantly, I peek from the corner of my sunglasses, and the tormented groan lodged in the back of my throat nearly slips. She's thorough in her work; laving her tongue across the droplet of cream that has somehow managed to escape. She drags the vanilla up the side of the cone in one long stroke—

CRUNCH!

My jaw hangs, appalled as Rory chomps her cone. Eyeing

the missing chunk of dessert, my cock begins to ache for an entirely different reason. The heinous way she chews while the ice cream is still piled high on top distracts me from my impure thoughts.

"No one does that mid-cone," I gape, glued to the divot quickly collecting melting ice cream.

"Does what?" Rory replies distractedly, licking her lips. She doesn't glance my way, and I'm suddenly jealous of the attention she's giving the cone. She's much too focused on devouring her treat than on the hardness in my swim trunks.

"No one takes a bite of their cone while there's still ice cream on it." I shift on my lounger, a discreet attempt to adjust myself. Hopefully, no one decides now is the perfect time to check out the deck. We're entirely too close to the pool where families splash around, and I don't need a trip to the local jail in a foreign country. My parents would be *pissed*. "It's ice cream first, then cone."

Rory pauses her assault for only a moment, enough to grace me with a blank stare I can barely make out with the aviators perched across the bridge of her nose. Her brows knit together, and that's enough to tell me she's looking at me like *I'm* the crazy one.

And then she licks her lips, and I wish I hadn't wanted her attention on me at all.

Okay, that might be the biggest lie I've ever told myself, but I'm struggling here, and she's not helping in the slightest. She could, though, if she would just—

Goddammit, where the hell is my towel?

"But I like the ice cream *with* the cone." Rory emphasizes her words with another bite. This one is more dramatic, removing a chunk like she's a famished shark that's found its meal.

I carefully—*desperately*—try not to notice how wide her jaw unhinges.

"There's ice cream *in* the middle of the cone," I counter, struggling to find something else to focus on. A bead of sweat slides down the back of my neck, and when the hell did it get so hot out? It's still early. Well, early enough for ice cream, that is. "The perfect amount, one might argue."

I can almost hear Rory's eyes roll into the back of her head. "One might mind his own business if he wants any chance at having his cone licked."

I splutter a noise that's something between a laugh and a groan. Excitement rattles down my bones at the idea of her tongue anywhere near my cock. Her joke solidifies the notion that she's been taunting me this entire time. No one would eat ice cream like *that* if she weren't showing me what else her mouth was good for.

"You want to lick my cone?" I muster as much innocence as I can, which, in all honesty, isn't much at all. Any semblance of innocence took a deep dive in the ocean as soon as Rory sat down beside me with her ice cream.

The grin she fails to smother only drives me crazier. Fuck, she's beautiful, and I hate that she's still wearing her hat because it covers too much of her face. Leaning closer so there's no chance the couple in the cabana beside ours can overhear us, I watch her chest hitch as our arms brush. "I want to taste your cream."

Laughter bubbles out of Rory and my heart pounds. Her head falls back, cheeks pulled into perfect circles as she revels in amusement. Her smile is contagious, and I join her.

Rory's still clutching her stomach when she manages to calm herself enough to speak. The cone has been forgotten, a dribble of white cream rolling across her knuckle. "That was not as sexy as you think it was. I really hope this is still the warm-ups to your player ways, Acey-boy, because if not, you might need to be benched."

My jaw drops in offense. Using the cutouts of her electric blue swimsuit to my advantage, I reach over and tickle her exposed skin. She squeals and retaliates, stabbing her cone in my direction, right into my chest. I jolt as the icy dessert smears across my pecs.

"That's cold!" I catch her wrist, twisting the cone back in her direction. Our amusement has reached new levels, and we're drawing attention. A man in the pool stares, his skin scorched red from the sun. He places his thick arms on the pool deck, a beer curled in one hand. His mirrored sunglasses do nothing to hide his leering.

When Rory throws a leg over my lap and straddles me for better leverage in our play fight, my annoyance flares. Her ass is directly in his view, and I don't like his eyes on her. At all.

I relent immediately. She smooshes the remnants of her ice cream all over me, and I sit there and take it, focused on hiding her from his revolting stare. My hands slide down Rory's sides, stopping on her hips, and I prop my knees to hide her ass. The motion unbalances Rory, and she plants her hands on my shoulders to steady herself. I shift to peek around her, checking on the creep. He's still watching, so I shoot him the nastiest glare I can muster, pouring all my disgust and protectiveness into the look. Finally, he breaks and wades toward the last place he should be headed— the bar.

When he's out of sight, I return my attention to Rory, who stares at the mess she's made. I wish it were a different kind of mess, one similar to the melted vanilla painting my skin.

I scold myself and try not to picture how pretty she'd look sitting on my lap like this and using me for her pleasure.

Too late. My cock makes its interest known once again, thickening between her thighs.

"Sorry," I grunt when Rory's eyes flick to mine. They're wide and innocent, blue like my fucking balls. I'll need to go tug one out in my hotel room if I'm going to stand a chance of spending the rest of the day with her.

"It's okay," she whispers, but doesn't move. I watch her internal battle as she decides her next move, holding my breath, afraid to shatter the moment. Slowly, Rory curls forward, and I'm all too aware of the way her pussy brushes my cock, even more so when she flattens her tongue between my pectorals and licks a stripe up my chest.

"Fuuuck," I choke. The air in my lungs abandons me as her warm mouth clashes against the ice cream.

No. Nope. This cannot be happening here, not right now. I want to have her for the first time alone, with no chance of anyone seeing and reporting us to hotel security.

My grip tightens on her hips. Rory must enjoy it because she gifts me a noise from the back of her throat. It's strained, like the way my cock is pressing into the fabric of my shorts. Her hips respond in jest, swiveling in a tight circle.

Before I can fist my fingers in her hair and pry her from my chest to tell her we can't do this here, that we need to find somewhere private *right the fuck now,* she draws away.

Her lips are red, and the urge to lean up and bite them, taste them, hits me. Her eyes swim with lust, pupils blown, and a wave of arousal crashes against me when her tongue pokes out to chase the taste.

"What did you say your room number was again?" She exhales.

It takes a second for the words to fully register, and when they do, it's game-fucking-on. Suddenly, I don't care which hotel-goers catch sight of the hard-on I'm sporting because I'm going to take Rory Wilson right now.

"I thought you'd never ask."

"Wow," Rory comments when I usher her inside my suite. I toss the ice cream-stained pool towel on the floor and take a cursory glance for my parents, who should be deep in the drink-mixing class they signed up for this afternoon. It's not uncommon for them to abandon their plans if important business springs up. All is quiet, and my shoulders relax. "If I'd known you were staying in the biggest room in the place, I would've taken you up on your bargain earlier."

The place *is* massive, with floor-to-ceiling windows showcasing the best view of the resort and ocean beyond. The furniture is classy and simple; creamy couches with warm wood accents create an airy and light space. It's the sort of expensive that shows instead of screams it.

I trail Rory to the glass, admiring her as she peers out at the expanse. She subconsciously twists her fingers together—the same ones I want to lace with mine and pin above her head while I press her into the window, my cock nestled against the peach of her ass.

"Rory?" She startles. "We don't have to do anything you don't want to. Say the word, and we can go back down to the pool."

"*No*," she answers fiercely. "I want this." Her brows scrunch for a moment, then she nods to herself in affirmation. I bite back a smile at her adorableness. "I want you to fuck me, Ace."

Good God, that's all it takes for me to close the distance between us. I guide her to the couch and plant her hands across the backrest, admiring how small they are beneath mine. Draping myself across her back, I growl huskily, "How about here, Rory-O? Do you want me to bend you over the couch? Take you in the kitchen? Do you want me on my knees for you in the shower?"

She grinds against me with each suggestion, already breathless. Fuck, I'm hard as a brick and sensitive, too. I haven't come in weeks, and if Rory keeps mewling and rubbing her perfect ass against me like that, I'm going to burst before we even begin.

"*Yes*."

I hum, body buzzing so hard I can't even think. I want her in every position she'll let me put her in, and I don't know where to begin with her, which is why she's going to decide how this goes. "You're going to have to be more specific, Rory-O."

"Whatever you want, Ace," she whines. She tries to jerk her hands from under mine, the leather screeching, but I don't allow it.

The creamy skin of her throat is mine for the taking, kissing and sucking ravenously like this is my first time tasting heaven. "No. I want to give you whatever *you* want." I'd give her anything she asks for right now. Oral, my fingers, a ride on my face. I'd give myself to her like I'm a fucking acolyte and she's my goddess.

Rory cranes over her shoulder to capture my mouth, and as soon as our lips touch, I'm useless to the world around us. All I know is Rory Wilson. I'm feral, spinning her and lifting her into my arms. She comes willingly, clasping her legs around my waist.

My forehead knocks into her baseball cap as I tilt my

head, and she's quick to catch it before it falls. I hate that fucking thing. Every time she tries to hide her pretty hair, I get an urge to rip the hat from her head and chuck it into the ocean. She doesn't need to cover anything of hers, and I'm going to make sure she knows it.

I stride through the suite to my room, lost to her tongue as she sneaks it into my mouth. Her nails scratch my scalp, and I give her ass a harsh squeeze of approval, eyes rolling into the back of my head. The sting reverberates down my spine, right to my excited cock.

Housekeeping must have come by because the large bed is made up. I don't experience an ounce of guilt for creasing the sheets as I lay Rory on the thick comforter.

She whines when I pull away, grasping for me, but I'm not going anywhere. No one could pry me away right now, not until I get an orgasm out of her.

"Have you figured out what you want yet, Rory-O?" I whisper, trailing kisses across the tops of her breasts where they peek out of her swimsuit. She tastes like sunscreen and vanilla, an intoxicating concoction.

"Everything," she pants, reaching between us to cup my groin. I grunt, bucking into her on instinct. "I want everything."

I nip at her skin playfully. "Greedy."

"I just know what I want."

"Then I'll give it to you," I promise, shoving the fabric of her swimsuit aside to suck bruises into the soft skin. I don't know how she's going to cover the marks later, but it doesn't matter; nothing matters except getting out of these clothes.

The front of her swimsuit is held together with a zipper. I snag the tab between my teeth and tug, taking my time to work my mouth across every inch I expose, nuzzling between the smooth valley of her breasts. I work my tongue over one of the rounds as I go. Rory arches for me, eager, and shoves my hands to the waistband of her shorts. She shivers at the breathy laugh I release at her impatience. Taking the hint, I quickly unbutton her, helping her slide out of the denim, leaving her in the unzipped swimsuit hanging off her shoulders and her ridiculous hat.

"Let's get you undressed, gorgeous," I exhale, and I swear, my cock bobs at the sight of the pink threatening to camouflage her freckles.

She comes willingly, sitting up with a shy smile, using the brim of her cap to avoid my gaze. I can't have that. I want her eyes on me all day, unless they're rolled into the back of her head in pleasure. Then, I'll settle for her screaming my name or dragging her nails down my back so hard she leaves welts.

"You have to promise not to laugh at my hair."

I frown. I've already caught a glimpse of the brunette strands when I stole her hat, and for the split second I saw before she plastered her hair back with a dip in the ocean, I thought the cut was pretty. She's entirely caught up on it, and if there's one thing I can do right now, it's reassure her I won't let something as small as an amused exhale slip.

"Why would I laugh at your hair?"

"Because it's ugly," she all but whines, crossing her arms. The motion causes the fabric of her swimsuit to bulge, and I swear I catch sight of one of her areolas. I wrench my gaze back to her face, or rather, the white baseball cap sitting snugly on her head.

I caress Rory's jaw and tilt her chin to meet my stare. My heart picks up when those icy blues land on mine. She's fucking beautiful, and having her attention at any point of the day is a gift. "There is nothing ugly about you, Rory. I promise."

Taking a deep breath, she squeezes her eyes shut, and on

the exhale reaches up to whisk her hat off before she can change her mind. She's bracing herself, I realize, as if I'm going to break my promise right away and tease her about the messy strands in a jumble from being tucked beneath the headpiece all morning.

Slowly, I brush my fingers through her soft hair, smoothing the pieces into place. They fall across her forehead, drawing me back to those crystal eyes peeking open to gauge my response.

"You're beautiful," I reassure her.

Heat rises to her face as she scoffs. Rory attempts to bat my hand away, but I catch her wrist and bring it to my mouth, planting a gentle kiss on the inside of her wrist.

"Hey!" she protests, giving a weak tug.

"You won't think of yourself as anything less than beautiful while I'm around, Rory. Or I won't touch you at all," I say sternly. If I have to make this a goddamn rule, I will. She's the most breathtaking women I've ever seen, and I won't have her feeling like anything less. "Promise?"

She swallows harshly. "Promise."

"Good." Now that we're back on track, we can do something about this sexual tension. My cock strains desperately in my pants, eager to meet Rory. "Now, let me taste your pretty pussy."

She moans in response and jumps into action, sliding the straps of her swimsuit down her shoulders. The tight fabric tries to cling to her body, but I yearn to touch, too, so I take over, peeling the cobalt spandex from her skin, exposing curves that make my mouth run dry.

I can't help myself. Before I can finish removing her swimsuit, I'm reaching down to touch. I tease one of her breasts, entranced. Massaging the soft tissue and strumming the pad of my thumb across the tightening bud, earning a pleasured gasp. When I peel the swimsuit over the curve of her ass, I leave her to kick it off while I dip to suck her nipple into my mouth. I roll the sensitive pebble between my teeth before soothing the hurt with my tongue, reveling in the way her fingers thread through my hair and her nails bite into my skull.

I trail my way down her glorious body, exploring, tasting, finding the places that make Rory squirm. The places that make her whine, beg, growl with impatience. Each noise I draw stiffens my cock more, and I need to get the fuck out of these swim trunks before I burst like a teenager who just met his hand for the first time.

I spread her thighs, tasting every inch. Rory whines desperately, legs melting open for me like her ice cream cone. I buck against the mattress and groan in response, pulling away to finally lay eyes on her pussy. It's wet and glittering, fluttering for me the longer I take my fill. I'm in a fucking trance until Rory cries my name impatiently.

"Ace!" I drag myself from her need and almost come on the spot. With her cheeks pink with frustration and blue eyes bright and begging, she looks well-fucked already. She wants my touch right this second, so I oblige.

My tongue peeks from my lips, and I hold her gaze as I trace the skin around her soaked pussy. Her chest heaves with each swipe, and this is torture for us both. I'm so close to finally tasting her, but the way she's squirming only urges me to tease longer.

A protest forms on her lips. Before she can complain, I bury my face between her legs and stroke my tongue over her hot core, moaning at the taste.

Rory arches off the bed like I've possessed her. My muscles jump with effort when her thighs threaten to clamp around my head as I lick a stripe up her pussy. God, she tastes fucking *divine*, like ambrosia, and I already can't get enough.

I feast. I eat Rory out until she's a writhing, whining mess, vibrating in my hold. I eat her until her thighs are firmly wrapped around my head, until my shoulders are raw with marks from her nails. I eat her until I'm drowning between her legs, and then some.

When the aftershocks subside and I find it in myself to detach from her, Rory's mouth is parted in a silent scream, her chest heaving.

"You did so good for me, Rory-O," I praise, and her body reacts all over again, arching for more. Perfect, because I'm far from finished with her.

I slip my shirt off and revel in Rory's eyes sliding down my body as they ping-pong between the tattoos littering my skin.

A wicked idea flickers to life as I kiss and nip my way back up her body. "That was just the beginning. Should we post a picture of you wrapped around my fingers? Or taking my cock? Surely that will make your ex jealous."

Rory's salacious moan sends those thoughts shooting right out of my head. She drags me into a deep kiss, hands sliding down my back before weaving between us to work at the knot of my swim shorts.

"Talk less, fuck more," she breathes.

So I do.

CHAPTER 12
RORY

"This looks so freaking stupid," I mutter, staring at my awful attempt of an advertisement. The flyer reads exactly like the cry for help it is with its bright, clashing colors and four different fonts. It's a wonderful showcase of just how bad I am at anything involving a computer, and now I can officially add "can't make a graphic" right next to "can't make a website" on my resume.

I'm on the verge of scrapping the entire mess and forcing Quinn to make one for me because this *was* her idea after all, and she would love to be in charge of finding someone to help me with my portfolio. The only thing stopping me from taking that risk is knowing she would use any means necessary to make it happen, including setting me up on dates in exchange for website knowledge, and I have enough boy problems in my life right now.

With a sigh, I lean back in my seat. The monstrous piece I've managed to Frankenstein together does not magically morph into a creation of beauty, no matter how long I glare at the screen. My plan was to print copies and hang them around the computer science buildings, but as I scan my ad for the third time, I overthink my usage of the word "help." It appears five times, twice in capital letters, and each instance of the plea is a different color. All of them are underlined, some more than once. It clearly screams "desperate," but that's exactly what I am at this point: desperate and discouraged.

I might be good at painting, but when it comes to digitally creative endeavors, it's clear I don't stand a chance. Not to say I had high hopes going into this project, but this is just sad.

The weather had been my saving grace, and now I've added it to the number of things working against me. Since the summer is beginning to cool down to something less sweltering in the mornings and evenings, I'd taken it upon myself to work at one of the tables scattered outside the art buildings. Apparently, the middle of the day hasn't caught on to the whole "fall is approaching" vibe, jumping to a more than toasty afternoon.

The shade I was once cloaked in has shifted, the sun's rays washing hot across my exposed shoulders. My hoodie lies abandoned on one of the empty chairs where I ripped it off in a rage. I'll have a nice sunburn to appreciate when I get home.

Sweat beads my hairline, causing my chin-length bangs to cling to my sticky skin in an irritating manner. They're not yet long enough to pull back into the ponytail the rest of my hair is captured in, and for the millionth time, I regret ever having cut them.

Stupid breakups always forcing rationality out the window.

The only positive about spending my few free hours before Beginning Watercolor worrying my ass off about my website is it's keeping my mind off the two boys who finagle their way into my mind more often than not.

I've filled every spare minute in my schedule in an attempt to drive them from my head. I've found inspiration on how to set up my paintings for the photoshoot I'm hosting this weekend. Quinn and I agreed on a much-needed Tipsy Canvas trip, and Slate is tagging along.

Hopefully, the photoshoot will be a relatively chill night, something Quinn and I can perfect over a bottle of wine and a large cheesy bread from the town's famous Cheesy's Pizzeria.

If I know myself and my best friend at all, the photoshoot will be pushed to Sunday in favor of popping open a second bottle of wine.

Running through my mental calendar for the weekend, the flutters in my stomach trip and tangle until they're a mess of knots.

Friday night is my date with Max.

The accompanying weariness is unsettling. I've never been so nervous to see Max, but after everything that happened between us—the wound of the breakup, the petty attempts at making him jealous over the summer—I'm more anxious than I was on our first date. He still holds the key to my heart, and that's terrifying because he can decide at any time to toss that key away.

A vibration on the table pulls me from my crisis. My eyes scream in relief when I force them away from the computer screen to pick up my phone.

It's Quinn, and I grin as I pull up our text thread. She always seems to know when I'm in a poor mood, and her message is a welcome diversion from the tension living in my shoulders.

QUINN

FMK: Ezra, Callum, & Johnny.

A puff of laughter escapes. She must be bored in Art History, but I can't bring myself to tease her about not paying attention in class because I need a good distraction. *Fuck, Marry, Kill* has been our favorite game to play since we received our first phones, using anyone from boys at school to famous athletes and movie stars, pitting them against each other. Sometimes we use strangers on the street, making up creative names for them. The silly scenarios never fail to make me smile.

This afternoon's gameplay consists of contestants from our favorite reality show, *Love Untouched.*

Fuck Ez, marry Cal, and definitely kill Johnathan.

I type, using Johnathan's full name because he's so evil he doesn't deserve the nickname Johnny.

It takes point two seconds for her reply to pop up, in total disagreement with me.

QUINN

I would definitely fuck Cal over Ez. That man is absolutely marriage material, but I bet Slate would agree with your rankings.

My jaw drops at the news, and my fingers fly over the keyboard. I've never typed a response so fast.

OMFG Slate is a Toucher too?!

The fans of *Love Untouched* have dubbed themselves with the nickname Touchers. It's not very creative, and it does sound incriminating, but the name has been coined since season one, and there's no changing it now.

I can practically feel Quinn's smugness wafting through the phone as I eagerly await her response.

QUINN

IKR?! He mentioned a direct quote from Layla and I swear I shrieked so loud dogs started barking.

My shoulders shake with laughter, picturing the moment. I wish I could've been there.

Ugh, that's hilarious. You invited him to watch the next episode with us, right?

QUINN

Obviously!

Sudden loud chatter draws my attention to one of the art buildings. The towering structure is large and intimidating, one of the oldest establishments on campus. The brick is in perfect condition, not at all how I would expect the multi-century old structure to appear, and the trim on the windows is peeling. There's already a maintenance man on a ladder scraping away the cream flakes, revealing a burnt crimson color beneath. The doors are propped open as students flood into the summer heat as a class releases for the day.

Examining the people descending the stairs, I try to come up with creative descriptions for my own FMK response when Ace steps outside. My lingering grin falls while my heart perks up at the sight of him.

Fuck. I'm definitely not prepared to see him, especially with how we left things at my sister's party.

I haven't seen him since. After scurrying from the bathroom like a coward, I prayed he'd forget what happened, like I planned on doing. The liquor I consumed did nothing to burn away the night's events, only what followed the fourth apple-something shot I downed with Slate.

Ace looks stupidly perfect with his disheveled blond hair, curling around the shell of his ears. His eyes are alight with laughter, and a smile stretches his totally kissable lips, dimples in full effect.

He maneuvers down the stairs with a swagger I'm sure guys only imagine having. A pair of straight black denim jeans dotted with paint splatters cover his legs, and a crisp, white t-shirt shows off the hodgepodge of tattoos speckled down his tan arms. He's utterly delicious and entirely fuckable.

Before our eyes can connect, I rip my attention from him completely, scolding my nether region that's decided to preen in his presence. Crossing my legs to stifle the tingling, I duck my head and jam my finger into the trackpad of my laptop to wake the screen.

I'd much rather aimlessly move text boxes around my shitty ad than face Ace right now.

Apparently, he doesn't share the sentiment, because when I dare peek to see which direction he's headed, our gazes catch, and he reroutes his path without hesitation. To make matters worse for my mind but better for my aching core, he's all too amused, mirth written all over his face and a shit-eating smirk curling his lips as he strides closer.

Heat creeps up my throat, finding a home in my cheeks.

"Please, please, *please* divine intervention save me from this moment," I mumble, offering him a tight-lipped smile while barely restraining myself from burying my head in my hands.

I'm not trying to call down a random strike of lightning to

hit him or anything equally horrific, but I need *something* to stop Ace from joining me. I'm not in the right headspace to muster the energy to discuss last weekend's bathroom escapade, which in *no way* compared to our Cabo bathroom endeavor.

"Hey, Rory."

Fuck. Fuck. Fuck.

The greeting isn't from Ace, but from Max.

This has to be some sort of sick joke. There is nothing *divine* about this intervention at all. Getting back together with Max has been a priority, but I'd be lying if I said Ace hasn't managed to sprout roots in my mind. We had a deal, and I don't know if I'm elated or upset he's continuously breaking our rules.

Max sets a bag in the middle of the table as he slides into the chair across from me. I eye it curiously, wondering about the contents inside, before taking in my ex. His sandy-brown hair is ruffled like he gave little time to tame it after practice this morning. His yellow-green eyes are focused eagerly on me, and the smile he wears sends my heart stumbling.

He's never visited me on this side of campus before. He doesn't usually amble past the football stadium that divides the newly refurbished business school from the historic arts and science buildings where I spend most of my days.

"Max, hi," I greet. Over his broad shoulder, Ace falters, brows knitting in confusion as he works out who joined me. Recognition flares the moment he realizes it's my ex, and his features harden. When we weren't fucking in Cabo, I remember breaking my own rules after a few too many drinks, complaining about Max. Ace had been a great listener and often the mastermind behind some of our more explicit revenge photos. He bore witness to Max's posts, too, so we knew what we were up against, which is exactly how he places my ex.

His stare flickers between us in silent question, tugging at my heartstrings. I nod while Max is distracted, unfolding the crumpled top of the bag and reaching inside.

Even from this far, the tick in Ace's jaw is visible. He doesn't seem satisfied with my answer, and with the way he's grinding his teeth, I'm worried he might waltz over here and drape himself in one of the empty chairs to *finally* meet the guy he's heard so much about.

My breath is stuck in my lungs as he mulls his decision over. When he spins on his heel and stalks down the path leading to our apartment building, I slump in my chair. He doesn't glance back once.

"Hey." Max's voice startles me. I return my attention just as he places a cardboard container in front of me. I recognize the bright blue sticker with the simple logo instantly, and a rush of nostalgia slams into me full force, smothering the sadness of Ace's retreat. Whatever is in the container, it's from the sandwich shop we met at. "I brought lunch."

I'd ventured into Stacks one afternoon while waiting for Quinn. I'd heard of the shop in passing from classmates and wanted to see what the hype was about. A retired professor and his wife originally opened the spot as a delicatessen, but quickly realized buying freshly cut meats was out of the budget for many students, and began selling sandwiches as well.

I wandered down the tight aisles in the small shop, not paying attention to my surroundings while I texted my roommate to see what she wanted when I ran straight into Max, my phone clattering to the ground like a fumbling fool.

"I'm so sorry—" My words had frozen in my mouth, my jaw detaching and falling to the floor alongside my cell when

he lifted his chin, his intrigued yellow-green eyes meeting mine.

The scent of bread was replaced with Max's smoky and woodsy cologne, with a hint of nutmeg, drawing me in. My mouth wasn't watering because of the freshly baked double chocolate chip cookies the owner's wife had pulled from the oven, but from the sight of him, clad in one of his practice jerseys, hair mussed and striking eyes looking me up and down with a charming glint.

I blink away the memory. "You didn't have to do that."

Max's grin is cheesy, cheeks pinkening with bashfulness. Normally, he exudes confidence, and the remaining uneasiness in my veins bleeds away at his nervousness. It's refreshing to see him out of his element like this, proving he really is trying. "I wanted to, Ro," Max answers easily, scooting the box closer. "Just say thank you."

My cheeks heat. I offer him a shy smile, shutting my laptop in favor of taking the container and unhooking the flaps to reveal the sandwich inside. Glimpsing the contents, my heart falls to my stomach, the flattery of his deed vanishing instantly.

Perhaps he mistakenly handed me his, but nope, Max is already pulling his sub out of its container and taking the biggest bite he possibly can. The bread overflows with meats and cheeses, and there's not an ounce of green—a telltale sign he's ordered his favorite, not mine.

"Thanks," I murmur, appetite replaced with disappointment. The smile I force to my lips is like pulling teeth.

Maybe it's silly to want Max to remember something as simple as a sandwich order, but we've been to Stacks on so many occasions, I've lost count. And I *always* order the same sandwich. Who can't recall something as simple as a BLTA?

Ace wouldn't have forgotten, my betraying mind offers. I tell it to fuck off.

"You're welcome, babe," Max says around a mouthful. He watches me eagerly; chest puffed with pride. It's sweet, I guess, that he's pleased he's done something kind for me.

Here he is, bringing me lunch, and I'm complaining when he didn't have to surprise me at all. I should be grateful he took time away from his busy schedule to trek across the university to track me down.

"So, what brings you to this side of campus?" I question, gently picking up the pastrami on rye. I'll eat it, though the sight of the deli's logo has me hankering for a BLTA. I'll pass off a couple bites—since Max is already halfway done with his meal—and go to Stacks for my own sandwich. Slate can have the rest of this one later. Quinn hates mustard.

At Max's response, the food turns to sludge in my mouth. "You haven't been answering my texts, and I've been wanting to see you, Rory."

"I've—" *Been avoiding you.* "Been busy." I wave my hand flippantly. "Classes and all. Plus, we're seeing each other this weekend."

The drink in his hand pauses halfway to his lips, his gaze narrowing in suspicion. I shift uncomfortably, like a bug under a microscope.

I haven't been ignoring Max's texts because I'm falling into bed with another guy, though Ace has been running rampant in my mind since the kiss we shared. Every memory I'd forced myself to forget wash up like a tidal wave, sucking me right back into the deep swell of passion.

My guilt grows. Max is trying his best to rebuild our rela-tionship, and I've been out kissing other guys.

Maybe I'm the problem.

"Yeah," Max agrees, sipping his drink. Unsweetened tea,

not soda, because of his regimen. "Football's been pretty hectic, too."

My shoulders slump when he accepts my excuse. "I heard you won the homecoming game. Congratulations."

"Thanks, babe," he winks, and I manage to force down a bite to distract myself from the revolt of my stomach at the nickname. Once, that would've had me ready to melt in his arms. Now, all I can think about is how many other girls he's called that.

Silence overcomes our table, but does nothing to soothe the strangeness budding in my chest. The one shouting that even though I'm sitting here, eating this awful sandwich, I'm doing something wrong. My stomach is in knots, and when I swallow, the pastrami threatens to make a reappearance.

"I'm excited for our date."

"Me too," I agree, though it sounds like a lie. Max doesn't notice, too busy readjusting the meat slipping from between the bread back into place. There's a dot of mayo above his lip. I stare at it too long. "Where are we going?"

Max tuts, a reprimand that straightens my spine like a scolded child. I place my sandwich back in its box, appetite melting away. "It's a surprise."

I don't like the sound of that either. "Sounds like fun."

Max grins, and I'm not sure I enjoy that look any more than the others.

CHAPTER 13
RORY

As quickly as I send the text, a response appears.

Out of pure desperation, I'd texted Quinn. It's Friday night, and I'm a mess of nerves in the passenger seat of Max's Mustang. Music plays softly from the radio, a DJ I recognize as his favorite, filling the car with an energetic and otherworldly beat.

The rhythmic drum does nothing to calm my restlessness. From the corner of my vision, Max appears at ease, content and not at all jittery. As he scans the intersection when we roll to a stop, I study the set of his strong jaw, and trail over the slight curve in his nose, the one I traced with my fingertips so many times. His hair is brushed to perfection, a gelled style stirring nostalgia in my gut. Being the one to mess up his perfect momma's-boy haircut was one of my favorite pastimes when we were together. I wanted everyone to know he was mine.

Streetlight pours into the windows, illuminating his

relaxed hands against the wheel. Completely opposite to the way I clutch my phone in my sweaty palms.

QUINN

Oh, fuck you.

I tuck my lip between my teeth, holding back laughter at her response. My shoulders unlatch from my ears, and I settle into my seat, welcoming the distraction.

More vibrations shake my phone, and I'm all too quick to read her responses.

QUINN

Fuck and marry Slate.

Kill and kill Knox and Ace.

You?

Darting a glance to my left, Max hasn't noticed how hot my cheeks have grown from the returned question. He's too entranced by the music, fingers tapping against the steering wheel with the beat. Shifting toward the window, storefronts pass as I mull over my options. Do I tell my best friend I would marry Ace in a heartbeat if given the choice?

Hypothetically marrying Ace leaves me between fucking or killing playboy Slate and broody Knox. I hardly know Knox aside from what I observed of him at my sister's party. That he's more than annoyed by my best friend. But there's something else there, something deeper, because his eyes hardly left her all night.

Kill Knox. Fuck Slate. Marry Ace.

QUINN

Knew it.

> Hey, I'm playing the game properly.
> Unlike you.

I can hear her eyes rolling from miles away.

QUINN

Fine. Kill Knox. Fuck Ace. Marry Slate.

Fire sparks to life in the pit of my stomach. She seriously won't give up her grudge enough to say she'd fuck Knox in a hypothetical game? She'd rather fuck Ace?

"We're almost there," Max's voice draws my attention. Hastily, I lock my screen, shoving down the jealousy crawling up my throat. I'm not jealous Quinn said she'd fuck Ace. She wouldn't really, because he was mine first, and this game is pointless.

So why does it feel not so pointless all of a sudden?

"I can't wait." I force a smile. *Focus, Rory, you're on a date. You shouldn't be thinking about Ace or the idea of him with someone else, either.*

It takes me half a song to calm myself enough to rejoin the night. The car rocks as Max maneuvers it into a parking lot, and when I lean forward to finally catch a glimpse of the location of our date, my heart falls out of my chest, the tires squashing it to bits.

The flickering neon sign taunts me, casting an eerie red glow through the windshield like a horror movie. Maybe this is one, because when I swivel to ask Max why we're *here* of all places, his illuminated smile appears ominous, the corners of his mouth pulled high, showing off pearly white teeth.

His excitement is spooky.

At least with the crimson light he can't see the mortification painting my cheeks the same shade of red.

Tin Can.

He fucking brought me to Tin Can.

Confusion and anger bubble inside me as I rack my brain for any plausible reason Max would take me to Hardwich's diviest dive bar. I don't consider the dilapidated building riddled with beer-bellied retirees and jocks grounds for a proper date. I wouldn't even consider it a place for a *shitty* date. My fingers fist in the skirt of my dress, disguising my disgust.

There has to be an explanation. If a guy brings a date here, he's either trying to get rid of them, or he's . . . actually, there isn't a second reason. *That's* how creepy Tin Can is.

This can't be right. I figured Max would take me to dinner. Or drinks. Or, hell, even a movie would be better than spending my night here.

"Tin Can?" I blurt. My sickened tone contorts the words, and I cringe, but refuse to shoot my . . . whatever he is to me, an apology.

Across the console, Max's brows knit, as if he genuinely doesn't understand why I wouldn't want to spend my night sitting around pool tables with bald patches in the green and $3.50 beers that are more foam than lager. "What? What's wrong with Tin Can? We used to come here all the time."

Damn me for being such a good actress when we were together.

Maybe I should audition for *Love Untouched* because I'd much rather be spending my days on a tropical vacation with a frozen, fruity drink in hand, laying out under the sun, and flirting with cute boys instead of here.

When I go to answer, not a single word escapes. There's nothing *to* come out because his confusion seizes my limbs. This is one of the worst surprises I've ever received. By fucking miles.

At my silence, Max slumps in his seat, a defeated edge to his words. "You used to love this place."

Guilt drowns me.

He's right, we used to hang out here all the time when we were dating, but he's wrong about the part where I loved it. I have never *loved* anything about Tin Can. It's abysmal for the word "love" to ever be used to describe the bar itself, or my feelings toward it.

The realization of how disheartened I am gnaws at me. I used to spend most of my weekend nights here of all places because spending time with Max was priority number one. We could have been doing anything else instead, but not even the temptation of me naked in his bed could lure him away from partying with friends, playing pool, and drinking cheap beer.

"I wasn't expecting our date to be at Tin Can," I admit quietly. Max traces a blunt fingernail across the horse emblem on the steering wheel, avoiding my gaze.

"We don't have to go in." His peers at the building uneasily. His nervousness would be adorable if my entire mood wasn't soddened by the location.

He's trying, I remind myself. Here I am, complaining about Tin Can, while for Max, the bar reminds him of the best parts of our relationship.

Fuck. I'm fucking this up.

Brushing away the lingering disgust gluing me to my seat, I plaster on a smile, hoping it conveys reassurance.

"No," I choke. "We should go in."

Max tilts his head to study me. His search is apprehensive, and I hold my smile while forcing my true feelings deep down inside, slamming the lid shut and locking them away.

After a few long beats, Max perks up, accepting my false

sincerity. His smile is genuine, and my body hums softly in response.

Even though my knees lock when I push the door open and attempt to stand, I get out of the car.

I'm hideously overdressed. The temperate weather is one of my last chances to wear a sundress before the chillier nights fully set in, and a denim jacket is slung over my shoulders. A gentle breeze caresses my bare legs, pulling at the hem of my dress, as if trying to steer me away from the bar. I smooth down the skirt and desperately try to rebuild what little confidence I left my apartment with as I make my way to meet him around the front of the car.

If I'd known I was coming here, I would've worn as many layers as possible. I will not be touching *anything* inside.

Max offers a hand, and after a beat, I thread my fingers between his and hold on for dear life.

"Philly and Cutter are here with their girls, too. You remember Hadley and Raven, right?"

I trip over his words, but Max doesn't notice. He's engrossed in his phone, shooting off a one-handed text, probably announcing to his teammates we've arrived.

This isn't even a one-on-one date; it's a fucking group date?

When I said I wanted our relationship to return to how it was before we split, I didn't mean *exactly* like before. I imagined deep chats as we found our way back to each other, working on rebuilding the cracked foundation we have. None of the scenarios I pictured involved an audience.

I don't respond, and Max doesn't ask about my silence as he leads me toward doom.

A combination of dust, stale beer, and over-spritzed cologne assaults my senses as soon as I step over the threshold, but nothing can cover the stench of sweat. Tears sting my sinuses as emotion swells, repulsion tightening my throat. The heat of the bar is affronting, but there's no way I'm taking off my jacket, not with all these men around, packed at the bar and stuffed like sardines at every table.

The atmosphere is loud. A couple of men shove each other good-naturedly as they joke around. A dart sails in front of our faces as Max leads me through the dimly lit tavern, and I gasp, whipping around to stare wide-eyed at the rugged man who tossed it. His brown eyes are dark, thick brow cocked as if somehow, it's my fault for walking in here. He lifts his beer to his lips and takes a deep swig while his greedy gaze trails me from top to bottom.

I shudder and clutch Max's hand tighter, quickening my steps. With my free hand, I grasp the back of his shirt as he slinks through the crowd, past foosball tables and TVs raging with sports games to the back of the bar, where his friends are gathered around a billiards table.

From the varying narrowed-eyed stares and deep frowns of the crowd waiting to play, they've been the reigning champions of the table for quite some time.

I desperately want to crawl into the bathroom, lock myself in a stall—even if they haven't been cleaned since the bar's grand opening—and call Quinn, beg her to take me home. She doesn't know I'm here, doesn't know I've been talking to Max at all. Once we broke up, he was dead to her and surely still is, because that girl does not forgive easily.

"Rory!" Phillip "Philly" Pendleton exclaims when he sees me. His big, chocolaty eyes are as bright as his smile. *At least someone is happy to see me,* I think as he pulls me into a bear hug. I all but sink into his arms, succumbing to his warmth despite the mugginess of the bar. I'm two seconds from bursting into a fit of tears because of how terrible this night has been so far, and it's only just begun. The nicest of Max's friends picks up on my poor mood because he leans down and whispers, "Are you alright?"

"Fine," I reassure him, offering a wobbly smile. This night will only be as good as I make it, so I need to put my big girl panties on and make the most of it. "Nice to see you again."

He beams, and I try to soak up some of his happiness. When he releases me, he wraps an arm around a girl's shoulders and pulls her into view. "You remember Raven, right?"

"Of course." I exaggerate my smile, which the onyx-haired girl doesn't return. Her equally dark eyes are sharp as she assesses me. She's never liked me, has always been cold and stiff when I'm around, and I try not to let her intolerable attitude toss me over the edge of the cliff I teeter on.

"Hey, girl," Hadley greets when Max ushers me over to join their table. My shoulders ease slightly. She's a sight for sore eyes, the only other girlfriend on the team I've actually missed. She hops off her barstool and squeezes me tightly. Maybe since she's here, the night won't be as bad. I'll have someone to catch up with, at least. Her hazel eyes are bright when we part, and her deep brunette hair is twisted into perfect twin braids draped long down her back. She's dating the team's quiet linebacker—who nods at me—Graham Cutter.

Hadley quickly became my confidante in the group of football girlfriends. At parties, events, and group hangouts, she and I got to know each other pretty well. We even sat together at the football games, too, cheering our asses off while Raven sat on her other side like a cloud of gloom.

Though I hoped tonight was going to be Max and me, if we have to spend the night at the unhappiest place on earth, I'm glad she's here.

Cutter offers me his seat, and I take it graciously. He rolls his shoulders and twists a cue in his hand, rounding the table for his turn.

Settling into the seat, I scan the small high-top table. There's a stack of empty cups starting to lean precariously toward the edge and an empty basket of what I assume was Tin Can's famous Trashy Nachos—if the remnants of grease and cheese on the paper are anything to go by.

My stomach growls, and I groan. I skipped dinner tonight because I assumed our date was happening at a restaurant, and now my poor organs will have to settle for gnawing on themselves or survive off whatever alcohol I manage to choke down. I won't be caught dead eating off the menu here, even if my life depended on it.

Tin Can's RRR score is a big, fat, zero.

A drink is set in front of me, drawing my attention from my complaining stomach. The soda is lacking bubbles and fizz, and I don't need to taste it to know it's flat. The ice clinks, and a drop splashes over the rim onto the rough hands I'd recognize anywhere.

"I got your favorite, rum and coke."

I didn't think it possible to be more disappointed than when Max brought me the wrong sandwich, but here he is again, confusing my drink of choice with someone else's. I'm not sure I've ever had a rum and coke in his presence before, and that alone smothers any hope I had to brighten my night.

"Thanks," is all I can manage. When I raise the glass to taste the concoction, Max clinks his cup against mine before abandoning me, striding for the rack of pool sticks to claim his own.

With his back turned, I slip from the chair and beeline for the bathroom. The bite of the chilled glass in my white-knuckled grip is the only thing keeping my quickly fraying emotions from bubbling over.

I shove past a horde of men who jump in their seats, cheering obnoxiously at the TV. I fold in on myself, hiking my shoulders up and ducking my head to avoid drawing attention. The last thing I need right now is a stranger trying to chat me up while my date's distracted with his friends. Someone throws their hands in the air with a curse, and I bob to avoid an elbow to the skull as I weasel my way inside the tiny bathroom. Immediately, I want to gag. The two tiny stalls are riddled with stickers and graphic graffiti, and I don't examine further as the door swings shut behind me. Fraying posters cling to the wall, the corners curling inward. The only good thing about the bathroom is its privacy—not another soul in sight.

I trapeze my way to the sink, narrowly avoiding a cracked tile and a crumpled strand of toilet paper. My drink teeters precariously when I place it on the corner of the sink, and I wouldn't be upset if it spills. With a heavy sigh, I stare at myself in the mirror, wondering how the fuck I ended up in this position.

A boy. Always a fucking boy.

It's a shame my bangs are finally cooperating, wasted on tonight. They've grown out considerably, nearly chin length, and *this* is what I envisioned when I had the brilliant idea of cutting them in the first place. There's a crease between my brows that I'm afraid is becoming permanent these days, between a frustrating love life and an equally frustrating portfolio. My eyes are red-rimmed and my mouth is down-turned in a scowl, because if I'm not angry, I'll cry.

"You can do this," I breathe. If I repeat it enough, maybe I'll start believing it.

My reflection doesn't seem so convinced.

Futilely, I search for a window to climb out of and come up empty. Damn.

Leaning my hip against the counter, my mind wanders to what my roommate's doing. If she's banging on the walls in retaliation to Knox, who refuses to lower his music to a decibel quieter than an airplane takeoff or if she's studying for Art History or watching re-runs of *Love Untouched* with a big bowl of popcorn on the couch.

Ugh, that sounds heavenly right now. My mouth waters. I'd give my left arm for a pizza or Thai.

Allowing myself a few minutes to wallow, I fix my hair. I wash my hands. I consider adding my own brand to the stall. I check my phone, but there are no texts waiting for my response. Social media proves just as dry, and I'm bored enough I even take a sip of the drink Max bought me and immediately wish I hadn't. It's heavy on the rum, and the soda is flatter than my features. For a brief moment, I consider downing the drink entirely in hopes the alcohol might ease the rigid edges of my shoulders.

Ultimately, I abandon the drink, and with one last somber glance in the mirror, I paste on a fake smile and make my way back to the group.

Slinking between tables and chairs, I dodge leers and stretched limbs, mumbling an apology as I accidentally cut through a group mid-toast. They only cheer louder.

When I clear the crowd, my limbs seize. A man juggling five full beer steins narrowly avoids slamming into me, grunting something unintelligible as he skirts by, but I'm completely frozen in shock at the sight before me. Ace, Slate, and Knox play pool at the table directly beside Max's. Worse, it's impossible to miss the glare Ace keeps throwing my date's way.

Fire bursts to life in the pit of my stomach at the sharp

gleam in Ace's blue eyes, like he'd never forget Max's face or what he's done to me.

His blond hair is tousled. It appears salt-kissed, like it had in Cabo, and my core tightens as the memory of running my fingers through the tresses arises.

I should hate the way he's staring at Max. With animosity in his eyes and tight, unforgiving features, he looks utterly delicious.

Someone brushes against my shoulder and I recoil, ducking away from the annoyed scoff the lanky bar back flings at me. His face screams with judgement, like I don't belong in this bar, and I hope the glare I pin him with conveys how much I don't *want* to be here.

With my heart in my throat, I step closer, unable to peel my attention from Ace. The navy shirt he wears accentuates the hue of his eyes, still the deepest blue I've ever seen. His muscles bulge where he stands with his arms crossed, pool stick gripped tightly like it's a staff and he's ready to attack.

The image of him fighting like a knight for my honor sends arousal shooting down my spine.

Our eyes meet, and time halts. The room vignettes around Ace, around the corner of his mouth that quirks into his signature smirk. My gaze narrows on those perfect pink lips, the game we're so good at playing quickly falling into place.

Flipping my hair over my shoulder, I stride to my table, ignoring the fiery gaze pinned on me. I slide into the seat I abandoned for the bathroom, across from Hadley, only to find her chair empty. She's giggling with Raven on the other side of the pool table. I wouldn't be welcomed into Raven and Hadley's conversation. Hadley's always been nice; it's Raven who would build up the unbreakable, solid wall with me on the outskirts. She's damn good at it, too. I've seen Philly after one of their arguments. The man was in shambles, and she went radio silent for four days.

I'm on my own, fidgeting under Ace's intense stare, waiting for me to acknowledge him. To keep from falling into his orbit, I stack empty cups and toss napkins in baskets.

A resounding crack snags my attention. Ace stands from where he broke the triangle, colorful balls rolling in every direction. A solid orange ball sinks in one of the far pockets. He shoves a strand of hair from his forehead, and it immediately slips back. My fingers twitch to curl the pesky lock around my finger.

Beside him, Slate holds a basket of mozzarella sticks, and it doesn't look like he's sharing with his roommates.

Knox follows the shot. He rounds the table, scanning his options before bending into place. The light hanging above the green casts a pallor to his skin that accentuates the dark circles beneath his somber gaze. He's entirely focused on his shot, blocking out the jibing of his roommates. Pulling his arm back, he drives the cue forward and the solid red ball rolls easily into the pocket.

I quickly grow antsy sitting alone. Max nor his friends notice my reappearance, but Ace does. Between turns, he watches me like a vulture circling a carcass. The muscles of his jaw tick and the daggers in his eyes show every vile word he's waiting to spit at Max.

If my dimwitted date doesn't even notice me, there's no way he's going to notice Ace or the rising tension in the bar.

Ace's stiff shoulders ease into confidence as his eyes light with a mischief that turns my stomach. He crooks a finger at me in invitation, and my pulse speeds.

I gnaw on my lip, glancing at Max. As much as I want to follow the wagging finger like an eager puppy, I'm in the middle of a date. I can't abandon him, can I?

It turns out I can, because Max is throwing his head back in laughter, clapping Cutter on the shoulder as he leads the way to the bar without so much as a glance in my direction.

Humiliation douses my body with heat, so I decide to take my leave.

"Hello boys," I greet, my first genuine smile of the night softening my stone-cold features. Ace sidles up to me, and the hairs on my arm rise at the contact. I stifle a shiver but am unable to mask the goosebumps prickling my flesh.

"Fancy seeing you here, Ro," Slate says around a bite of mozzarella. A speck of marinara clings to the corner of his mouth. "Doesn't seem like your kind of place."

I shrug. "It isn't."

Slate's thick brows knit in confusion. I nod to Knox, who surprisingly responds with a tilt of his chin as he scoots around the table, assessing his next shot.

"Hi, Rory-O," a deep voice rumbles beside me. Lifting my gaze, my breath hitches when my eye collide with Ace's.

He's too close. If Max returns to find me almost chest-to-chest with Ace, he'll be furious.

And he should be. The petty part of me wants him to feel the same way I've felt tonight. He brought me to a place I hate to hang out with people I'm not really friends with, and abandoned me the first chance he got.

Perhaps he's not who I once thought he was.

With that sour thought rolling through my mind, instead of stepping away from Ace like I should, I move into him, challenge igniting my blood.

A muscle in Ace's jaw flickers, and my lips curl upward.

He's right where I want him.

"Hi." I flutter my lashes, and he traces the movement greedily, then drops those pretty blues to my lips.

His hand slides around my waist and pulls me into him

for a hug I'm unprepared for, but fall easily into. The familiarity of his body against mine is a comfort I didn't realize I longed for. My stomach clenches at how much I've missed this. Missed him.

"That's the guy you've been trying to win back?" Ace mutters, breath hot in my ear. "He won't even look at you." His hand trails the length of my spine, and it's difficult to smother the shiver eagerly following his fingertips. "I could bend you over the table and fuck you right here, Rory-O, and he wouldn't even notice."

His words unearth a craving that hasn't been satiated in far too long. My core clenches at the image of Ace folding me over the deep mahogany table and pressing his thick, hard cock between my legs. God, I wouldn't even mind we're in Tin Can.

I'm wet. So unbearably wet, I'm on the cusp of giving in to Ace in record time.

"Do it," I bite, cheeks flushing at my boldness. Ace jolts in surprise. Why did I say that? I haven't finished a full drink, and here I am, blurting my fantasies like all of my filters have gone AWOL. There's no denying what I said, no magic erase button, and a side-eye to the table beside ours shows Max in the middle of telling a story to his buddies, a fresh beer in hand, gesturing animatedly as he speaks. Fire licks up my spine, so I square my shoulders and look Ace dead in the eyes. "Bend me over and teach me how to play pool."

Choking sounds somewhere behind us, and our intense stare breaks. Slate beats on his chest, free hand still clutching the red plastic basket of cheese sticks. His caramel eyes are wide and apologetic, while Knox snickers at his side.

"Sorry." Slate sounds like he swallowed gravel. "Got mozzarella stuck in my throat. That cheese pull was no joke."

At my amused snort, he waves a hand in our direction. "Please continue. Knox and I will get drinks."

He all but drags his roommate through the crowd.

As soon as they turn their backs, Ace hands me his cue. I hold it away from my body like it's going to poke me. Chuckling, Ace wraps his hands around my hips, and my heartbeat spikes. When he plasters himself against my back, I realize I should've been worried about something else poking me.

He guides me with two steps forward to the edge of the table and hinges forward, folding us so I'm eye-level with the green velvet surface. It's musty, stained, and reeks of stale beer, but it's impossible to focus on how disgusting it is while my brain short-circuits.

The familiar position reminds me of when Ace bent me over the counter in his hotel suite. Except, at that time, one of his hands was fisted in my hair with the other wrapped around my front, buried between my thighs.

My core tightens. It's been too long since someone touched me like that. I'm three seconds from offering to recreate that night, Max be damned. If my date is too occupied with his friends, I sure as hell can find someone to hold my attention, too.

Guilt at the thought causes me to glance in Max's direction. He and Cutter surround Philly's phone, propped on the bucket of beers they've brought back to the table, the three football players watching the screen intensely. They begin grumbling and glaring at the device, engrossed in a football game, our date forgotten.

"I'm still upset with you," I mutter to Ace over my shoulder. I use every ounce of energy not to melt as his breathy laughter rustles my hair.

"I know, Rory-O," he purrs. I pray he doesn't feel my body quiver in response, thighs trembling with the effort not to clamp shut. I'm hyperaware of where our bodies touch, pressed so tight he can feel every tremble, twitch, and shaky inhale I take.

He's enjoying this. That much is apparent from the hardness against the curve of my ass.

"Back to square one with you, am I?" He runs his hand up my planted arm on the table, stabling my cue. His teeth drag across the shell of my ear, and a metallic tang floods my mouth when I bite my lip so I don't tilt my chin and capture his mouth against mine. "That's alright. I got you once, Rory-O. I'll get you again."

A shiver lets loose. It sounds like a promise.

CHAPTER 14
ACE

Rory feels all too good in my arms again.

I've dreamed of this moment for months. Not exactly like this; if it were anything like I imagined, we'd be in the privacy of my room. She'd still be bent over, but there'd be no clothes between us.

There's a minute tremble to her hands I bet reflects the way her thighs quiver under this goddamn sinful dress, begging for my touch. Every noise she makes goes straight to my cock: the little hitch in her breath, her shaky exhale, the moan tucked in her throat.

I've lost all sense of everything around us. All I know is the curve of Rory's body, the round of her ass nestled against my front. The scent of her shampoo collides with her sweet perfume, fruity and warm. It reminds me of lazing on loungers, sipping cocktails under the sun. Her heart beats so hard I feel it in my chest, its rapid pace matching mine.

There are no roommates sharing knowing glances from across the bar, no patrons nudging each other's arms and nodding in our direction. There's no dad rock playing in the background, no stench of cigarettes and beer breath wafting through the bar.

There are no ex-boyfriends.

There's only Rory and me.

"Ace?" Rory's whisper shatters my daze.

I blink, our surroundings eke back into focus. Fuck. Tin Can. Teaching Rory how to play pool. I clear my throat. "Yeah?"

"That doesn't feel like the friendship we talked about."

What? My mind spins as I take stock of myself. My hands rest on hers, holding her in the perfect position to shoot. My chin is hooked over her shoulder, and I'm not currently ravaging the creamy skin of her throat, so I have no clue what's unfriendly about the position we're in.

Is it my chest pressed to her back? My feet between hers from when I kicked her legs further apart? Is it—

Rory wiggles her hips, and the motion zips through me like a lance, so visceral my knees almost buckle. Realization slams into me. She's referring to the raging fucking hard-on I'm sporting.

Yeah, that's definitely not very friendly.

I lock my legs to keep steady and let loose an exhale that brushes the hair thrown over her shoulder. She shivers, and her ass brushes my front again.

I stifle a groan. I want to do more than groan. I want to lift the skirt of this fucking dress and pull her panties to the side. Run my knuckles across her slit . . .

"Right, well . . ." I struggle to find words. I should back off, hide the bulge in my pants or walk my sorry ass home, but she's not pushing me away, either. There's no excuse to use as a cover. She knows exactly what's nestled against her ass. The truth is the only weapon in my arsenal. Maybe she'll take being turned on from the slightest touch as flattering instead of what it really is: mortifying. "I just can't seem to help myself when I'm around you, Rory-O. It's been a long summer alone."

I don't need to look at her to know she scowls at the nickname.

My cock throbs at the thought of her pout. I've been on the receiving end of it more times than I can count, and it never fails to light me on fire.

"I still don't like that nickname," she growls, fingers tightening on the cue in frustration. It's cute.

"I still don't care," I retort, brushing my lips against the shell of her ear. I can't help myself. What I wouldn't give to dig my teeth into her lobe, suck a little to draw that one noise out of her. The one that's a mix of annoyance and reluctance. She hates that she likes when I do that.

She wants to move just as badly; I can feel it in the tension of her body. She's as stiff as my cock, and I wonder if she's as aroused as I am from this public display, draped all over her like she's mine. Right in front of the guy she's been so desperate to get back.

The boy she's in love with, dumbass.

Before the thought foolishly slips out, Slate interrupts.

"Are you two going to shoot, or what?" He's at the other end of the table wearing a shit-eating grin. Knox is paying careful attention to the chalk he's rubbing on the end of his cue.

Oh, I'm about to shoot alright. Just not the ball.

Rory flinches at their sudden interruption, and I snap, both relieved and annoyed with Slate's superior cock-blocking technique. "Yeah, we are."

Concentrating on the girl in my arms, I refocus, wishing we had a few more moments alone. My body is a buzzing storm of emotions, mostly the sexual kind that urges me to lift Rory in my arms, drag her back to my apartment, and lock her in my room like a barbarian.

Fuck. I am too gone for her, and she's too in love with someone else.

The truth slides through my veins like ice, painfully dragging me into reality, where she's here with another guy and I'm just a pawn to get his attention.

You don't do feelings like this, my brain continues with the harsh truth. My weight shifts, withdrawing from her. *You don't do feelings*, period. *Get a fucking grip, Ace. She doesn't want you.*

Slowly, stiffly, I guide Rory's hand back and line up the shot. She reacts to my sudden change in mood, her body tightening, too. The lack of space between us is no longer agony, but awkward.

It's torture.

We rock forward, all in perfect motion. With a jerk of the cue, we shoot.

The ball rolls forward, slamming into the twelve ball with a *crack*. The force sends the blue ball careening toward the center pocket.

It sinks in.

"I did it," Rory breathes in disbelief. I'd laugh at how adorable she is, eyes wide and mouth gaping like a fish, if my head wasn't regaining consciousness over my dick. I back away as she shoots upright, spinning on her heel.

Her excitement is intoxicating. Her beaming smile sends all the air shooting from my lungs. My heart races, pounding like the hooves of a horse gunning for first in the Kentucky Derby.

I want to be the one who puts that smile on her face, always.

"*I did it!*" She repeats, louder this time. She throws

herself at me, wrapping her arms around my neck. Her body melds with mine, contorting to fill the empty slots I wasn't aware I was missing.

She feels perfect in my arms.

"You did it, Rory-O!" Unable to help myself, I brush through the soft tresses of her hair, cradling her head, holding her close. I could lean down and kiss the shit out of her right now like I desperately want to.

It's difficult to ignore Slate's smirk and Knox's amused stare.

I don't get to enjoy Rory's hug for long. A rough voice barks over my shoulder; the source from the next table over. "Hey, asshole! What do you think you're doing with my girlfriend?"

Honestly, I thought it would take longer for the prick to notice Rory's absence.

Rage washes my sappiness away. Now he wants to act like they're together? When he's been drinking and dicking around with his friends while she sat miserably at their table alone? I don't fucking think so.

Rory's nails dig at my arms in a frantic plea to release her. I loosen my grip, and she slides to the ground. Selfishly, I keep my hands on her hips, hoping my hold conveys how much I don't want her to run back to him to diffuse the situation. I don't want her anywhere near him. I don't want her to leave my side.

I turn, facing Rory's ex just in time for him to step chest-to-chest with me. I have an inch on him. My smirk only enrages him further, his squared features tightening. He's wider than I am, probably has twenty pounds on me, but I can be scrappy. I wouldn't back down from a fight, especially one over Rory.

I've emasculated him by stealing Rory right out from

under his nose. Insecurity swirls in those piss-colored eyes. His cheeks are crimson, and his knuckles are white from how tightly his fists are coiled.

If he wants a fight, he's got one.

A collective murmur surrounds us. We're drawing attention, braced for violence, and I'd say some of the bar-goers want in on that bet, too.

Rory slips into the hairsbreadth of space between her ex and me, and I don't like how quickly she's thrown herself in the line of fire.

"Ace, *don't*," she hisses. I break the stare with her ex to check on her, her concern raising alarms in my head. The shame on her face sets me on fucking fire. Is she upset we got caught? Or because we were all over each other in the first place? I pray it isn't the latter.

Ire eddies like smoke from my nose when she turns to *him*. There's no chance of reveling in the fact that I was the first one she spoke to because now she's addressing him. "Max, it was nothing. He was just showing me how to play pool."

I almost reel. *It was nothing. Nothing except my cock begging for your pussy, Rory-O.*

Max's glare is still pinned on me. He doesn't deign a glance at Rory as he growls, "So, you wanted his hands all over you like that?"

Rory's mouth drops in horror, and my muscles coil, more than ready to throw the first punch. "I—"

"If you paid attention to your girl, you could've had your hands all over her instead, douchebag," I interrupt with a harsh bite. Rory shouldn't have to defend herself; this isn't her battle to fight. It's mine.

My comment strikes a nerve, and not a happy one. Max's

chest doubles in width, readying himself for a brawl, and he sizes me up like the dumb fucking jock he is.

His friends inch closer, flanking his sides, like the sight of dumb, dumber, and dumbest is going to intimidate me. All I'm thinking about is knocking their heads into their leaders, and a surge of satisfaction rushes through me at the backup.

Anticipation burns through my veins like a raging wildfire. I haven't been in a fight since high school, and coincidentally, that one was also because of a girl.

I'm a rabid dog on a leash, snapping its jaws, ready to bite.

Slate and Knox step closer, making it known I'm not outnumbered. Max's focus stays pinned on me, but one of his friends assesses my roommates, calculating the threat. I'm confident the three of us can lay these sports fuckers out if it comes to a fistfight. They might be used to taking hits on the football field, but this is a bar; there are no rules here.

A too-nice-for-her-own-good petite brunette tries to tug Rory out of the fray, but my girl doesn't budge. She's always been stubborn. It's as fucking hot as it is worrying. I don't want her caught in the middle of this more than she already is.

From the corner of my eye, I notice drinks have been set down, conversations dulled, and attention is pinned entirely on us. No one dares break up the verbal match in hopes of it turning physical. Until first blood is shed, and maybe not even then. This will be the highlight of the week for these guys. I'm sure they can't wait for one of us to throw the first punch.

Slyly, a man slides a folded bill across the table to his friend, who adds it to the growing stack in hand. They're betting on us.

"If you're on a date with *me*," Max begins, turning to

address the woman he's speaking to, and my blood boils. I don't like his attention on Rory one bit. My fist itches to meet Max's jaw, but she's still standing between us like an unmovable force, and I'd never put her in danger, no matter how badly her ex deserves what I have in store for him. "Then you don't let another guy touch you. I'd think that was common sense, even for you."

My glare turns lethal on Max as his words ring in my head. *Even for you.*

What the fuck does that mean? A girl like Rory? A fucking beautiful girl he doesn't have the brain capacity to understand? The one who he's played and broken so terribly she somehow believes he's *the best she can get?*

Fuck that.

Fuck. That.

I'll show Rory how she deserves to be treated, right after I take care of this prick for her.

"He's my neighbor," Rory tries to defend, but the asshole isn't listening. I'm his focus once again, and my lip threatens to curl when I meet those eerie eyes. "It's nothing."

Ouch.

"Traded down for convenience, Rory?" His smirk is slimy. My nails threaten to break the skin of my palms, and the sting does nothing to ease my rage. "All you have to do is walk next door, and you'd have your mouth full—"

"You better watch your fucking mouth when you speak to her," I growl, voice deathly low. I'm a volcano on the cusp or eruption. Rory needs to move right the fuck now, but even with how hard her friend tries to remove her from the line of fire, she stays put.

"Or what?" Max sneers, and I fucking hate him. And I hate the way Rory still looks like his forgiveness means everything to her.

"Or I'll break your fucking jaw, asshole." I'm not bluffing. If he thought I was going to back down, he's sorely mistaken. I'd like to see his jaw unhinge and hit the ground before knocking him out cold.

Max must hear the promise in my words because a flash of unease hurtles across those ugly eyes. *That's right, bye-bye football.*

"Ace," Rory hisses, successfully gathering my attention. My shoulders drop an inch at her plea. Her fingers uncurl from the fabric of my shirt to splay wide across my chest in warning. Momentarily distracted by her touch, I wonder if she can feel how hard my heart beats for her.

She has that sad look in her eyes, the exact same one she wore when I met her. Like this is breaking her heart. Before she can speak, I know what she's going to say. "Just go. *Please.*"

"I'm not leaving without you," I murmur stubbornly. I'm not ditching her with alpha asshole and his pride of jocks. My feet are glued to the beer-laden floorboards, and only Rory has the power to move me.

"Don't do anything rash." Max's friend leans in to speak in his ear. I overhear easily with our proximity and because the chatter in the bar has softened to a whisper. "You'll get suspended from the team if the cops take you in."

The team. The fucking football team. The only thing that matters to these pig-headed fucks.

He doesn't love Rory; he loves the *idea* of her. Someone willing to endure whatever he puts them through because she's head over heels for him. She'd forgive him, no matter what he did. Already has, just by agreeing to this date.

He thinks she can't do any better.

Well, not my fucking Rory.

My jaw grinds as his sadistic eyes turn wicked. "Take

her," he waves a dismissive hand at Rory, and I swear the corner of his mouth twitches like this is amusing. Like he's not breaking the girl with the biggest heart. Before I can lunge, he turns away.

Rory's face crumples. Her shoulders deflate, and my stomach curdles when she calls out to him, following him and drawing away from me. Something in my chest splinters with every inch she puts between us. "We can finish our date, Max. I'm sorry!"

"No." Max rounds on Rory so fast I take a step forward to intervene. She shrinks under his brutal glare, and I'd bundle her up in my arms if it wouldn't make the situation worse. "This date is over. I'll text you when I'm ready to talk."

His words land heavy. Rory gapes, blinking furiously in an attempt to hide the glossy tears quickly gathering in her lashes. The urge to kick his ass is still strong, but attending to Rory takes precedence.

Her face is pinched in pain. She glances around, red blossoming on her cheeks when she realizes the attention we've drawn. Mortification twists her features, and fuck, her devastation cracks my ribs.

This is my fault. I'm the one who disrespected her date, even if Max was ignoring her. I had no right gluing my body to hers like the desperate idiot I am. I know how much getting back together with Max—however scummy he is—means to her, and I've fucked everything up.

"Come on, Rory." Gently, I hook my fingers around her elbow as Max and his friends disappear through the disgruntled crowd. Dissatisfied glares linger from the lack of fists and bloodshed. They can all fuck off. "I'll walk you home."

Rory allows me to guide her away from the wreckage, and I'm thankful for the win, however small it is.

Slate and Knox are equally as eager to leave this hovel,

but I can't have them trailing us back to the apartment building when I have some major apologizing to do.

I give them a look that says, *please stay here while I grovel.* Knox picks up on my silent request, and a frown deepens his features.

"Oh no," he hisses when I pass. "I didn't want to come here in the first place. And now we can't even leave?" His green eyes flicker over Rory and I don't miss the scrutiny there, like he's as annoyed with her as he is with her roommate.

I'm still four seconds away from blowing a gasket, and if he keeps looking at her like that, I'll snap.

I tuck Rory closer to my side, where she deflates. Shit. I intended to leave with her tonight, just not like this.

"I don't care what you do, but don't follow us."

Knox rolls his eyes, which tells me they'll stay behind long enough to give Rory and me a block's head start, and not a foot more.

"We're right behind you, Acey-boy," Slate says to irritate me. He succeeds.

At least it amuses Rory, who giggles wetly at my expense. If it means uplifting her after this awful night, I'll be the butt of every joke for the rest of time.

Leading Rory through the throng of regulars, I earn stabbing stares for disturbing the night, but I brush them off. The only person I care about right now is the girl I've managed to continuously push away since we've reconnected.

As we shove out the door, the brisk night washes over us. My lungs expand with a much-needed deep breath, and the chill quells the fight response clinging to my muscles. The silence between us is thick in the first few blocks we stray from Tin Can. Trees glowing with fairy lights illuminate our way home. They shine mockingly at me, casting a much happier aura than I deserve.

I stare into the windows of the storefronts we pass, all closed for the night. The pastel blue of a dental group with a giant set of straight, white teeth in the window. A ship-lapped décor shop. A boutique with mannequins contoured into impossible positions. My reflection is the same in each window: dejected. With my lip tucked carefully between my teeth, I grasp for what to say. I beg my brain to string together a sentence, but I'm not sure anything can heal the damage I caused tonight.

I've never been good at communicating my emotions, and I can't say I've spent the years since my last failed relationship asking or caring about another woman's feelings. My life has been strictly hookups and one-night stands since then. Never anything serious.

Rory's beginning to feel like the chink in my chain of armor. What's worse is I can't give her what she wants—*deserves*—because I'm not capable of such.

Every other step, I chance a peek at Rory, and every time, my chest tightens at the sadness she fails to hide by staring at the sidewalk.

I royally fucked up tonight.

It's her sniffle that jolts me into action. "I'm sorry." I cringe. It doesn't sound apologetic, and I suppose it's because I'm selfishly not sorry at all. I don't have it in me to lie, because I need Rory to realize how horribly Max treated her tonight. How she deserves so much more.

You're supposed to be trying, Ace, my conscience supplies unhelpfully.

Right.

Those usually bright blue eyes find mine, and my lungs collapse at the sight of unshed tears, redness puffing her lids.

Guilt wraps around my throat like a snake, choking me. I have no one but myself to blame.

"S'fine," Rory says feebly, and I fucking hate it. I hate that I had anything to do with upsetting her. "It was kind of a shitty date, anyway."

"Yeah," I offer lamely and silently kick myself.

She's quiet for a long time before she says, "Where would you have taken me instead?" Her gaze is firmly attached to the sidewalk. The stupid concrete doesn't know how lucky it is. The urge to reach out and lift her chin is strong, but I refrain. The last thing she probably wants is me touching her. Even if I'm sure she might like it.

I'd take you literally anywhere else, Rory-O, I think bitterly. *Even somewhere as lame as my apartment would have been better than that shitshow.*

"I don't know," I say instead. "I don't date."

It's as much of a reminder for me as it is for her.

"Right," she agrees, nodding to herself. I swear there's a thread of disappointment in her tone, and I could kick myself all over again.

The chattering of bugs fills the silence. Tension clouds around us, thick like smoke. It's stifling and makes me want to claw the skin from my arms. I've never been so thankful yet discontent to see Third Street Apartments. The brick building looms up the street, and we're only one block from this terrible night ending.

Rory has given up on speaking. If she's pretending I'm no longer beside her, I don't blame her. I've been an ass, coming onto her only to tell her sleeping together is all I can offer. She wants a relationship—one with Max—and I may have ruined her chances at what she's been working toward since we met.

Fuck. I'm so stupid. Selfish and stupid.

The silence eats at me, and I can't take it. I need to hear her voice, need to drown out the thoughts of how she should really be going home with *him* right now instead of me. "Please don't do this."

She startles, brows scrunching in confusion. "Do what?"

"Shut me out."

Her arms come up to hug herself. There's a gentle breeze, but otherwise it's a balmy night.

"I'm not shutting you out, Ace. I'm just . . ." She pauses as she searches for a response, then releases a frustrated sigh. "I'm upset my date went up in flames."

"All because of you" goes unsaid, but lingers in the air.

I'm not sure how to respond. An apology isn't enough, and I can't promise I can help fix the situation. All I know is to destroy. To be alone.

At my lack of response, Rory continues. "It's my fault anyway, for—"

"It's *not* your fault." I frown, finding my words.

"Yeah?" She laughs humorlessly, kicking an invisible rock. "What do you know about it, Ace?"

"I know you deserve better than him," I answer gruffly. Truthfully. We near the apartment, and I suddenly wish there were miles separating us and the front door. Once we go inside and that door is between us again, she's going to ghost me. I can feel it. I might even deserve it. "You can't seriously want to be back with that guy."

Rory shrugs defensively. I want to shake her by the shoulders, make sure she understands she deserves so much more than what that airhead football player can offer.

So much more than *I* can give her.

"You don't get it, Ace."

"Then *help* me get it, Rory," I beg, tugging open the front door. My heart picks up pace until it's jackhammering, the sound so loud it drowns out the conversation another student is having on the phone in the small lobby of our building.

We both ignore the girl, and I follow Rory into the god-awful elevator I hate. It's slow as shit and is never on the right floor, except *tonight* of all nights.

She jams her finger into the fourth-floor button and crosses her arms tightly over her chest. The motion pushes her breasts together, and I can't help but follow the silky skin on display. The top of her dress is cut low, and I realize anyone at the bar could've been staring down her top when I had her bent over the table. My anger flickers back to life at the thought, and it's difficult not to press the ground floor button so I can go back to Tin Can and kick everyone's ass.

"You don't know what it's like to—" The elevator stops on our floor with a jolt that rocks us both. A shiver crawls up my spine, and thankfully, the doors grind open. The jarring motion steals enough of Rory's attention that she doesn't finish her explanation, instead stalking quickly for her door, a mere twenty feet away. "Never mind."

"Never mind what?"

"I don't have to defend my relationship to *you* of all people," she hisses, whipping around on her heel to face me. The fire in her eyes goes straight to my groin. Fuck. With how the night has gone so far, I'm going to have blue balls come midnight.

Her words sting, but she's absolutely right. The nature of her relationship with Max is unknown to me, other than what I picked up over the summer: he wanted a break and to pick back up when school started again. She'd always known where she was going to end up, which is why she set those rules for us in the first place. The ones I barely followed because I didn't think I'd ever see her again.

Perhaps I let myself fall too far into the deep end with her.

The way I acted tonight, like she was mine, of all things, only proves her point.

"No," I agree quietly, accepting defeat. Waving a flag of surrender won't help. Rory's already buried me in the sand. "You don't."

I walk her to her door. It's more me following than walking beside her, and the urge to drag my feet is fucking *strong*.

"Goodnight, Ace." Rory jams her key into the lock and opens the door just enough to slip inside. She doesn't offer me a last glance, doesn't give me the chance to return the farewell. For once, I appreciate the gesture because I hate myself too much to form words.

The door shuts tightly behind her, and I wish she would've slammed the damned thing instead of closing it so quietly I barely hear the click.

It's a full-circle moment, staring at the door like this, my chest heavy.

I fucked up tonight. I fucked up her night.

Maybe Rory blocked me for a good reason, is all I can think as I trail next door and shut myself inside.

CHAPTER 15
RORY

From behind my camera, I snort at the text that appears at the top of my screen.

"What is it now?" Quinn's complaint is muffled by the canvas she's crouched behind, propping my artwork up as I attempt to capture the perfect photo.

When she crawled into my bed at the ass crack of dawn with a grumble of how loud Knox was and an offer to assist me with my portfolio this afternoon if I let her nap—even though she agreed to this days ago, there was no way I could kick her out. I desperately need the help.

"It's Slate with his daily Fuck, Marry, Kill," I answer distractedly, pulling up the last few photos to scrutinize my work. The background is all wrong and the lighting in our apartment is too yellow. With the afternoon sun shining through our windows, Quinn's curled silhouette shows through the canvas.

What I thought was going to be the easiest part of

building my portfolio has proven to be another iron-spiked hurdle in Roryy's Expedition to applying to the Royal Academy of Arts. Yes, still two Y's because I haven't figured out how to change my name yet.

Frustration lances down my spine like a whip. Nothing has gone according to plan since I had the bright idea of applying for summer classes well outside the state lines of Washington. Don't get me wrong, I adore the city I grew up in and love the fact that I live only blocks away from my bestest friend of over fifteen years, but I've always felt the urge to be elsewhere, trying new things, experiencing everything life has to offer.

Art kept me company when my sisters locked me out of their rooms to giggle over boys or indulge in the newest episode of *Love Untouched*. Out of every medium I tried, painting quickly became my favorite. I'd create portraits of friends and stuffed animals until the pages of my paint pads were filled front-to-back. Mom always thought I'd grow out of that stage in my life, but with no one besides my best friend to turn to, the buckets of brushes and stacks of canvases became the one thing that would never disappoint me.

The further I get from my disapproving mother, the happier I might be.

"You can come out now," I sigh. Selecting the photos from today's shoot, I hit delete with a jam of my thumb into the screen. There isn't a single image worth uploading, and I contemplate chucking my phone out the window to blow off the simmering failure sticking to my skin.

I don't need a phone. I live with my best friend, and the only other person I message besides a few friends hasn't texted me since Saturday night's fiasco where I let Ace bend me over the billiards table like I was Easy Barbie.

"*Thank God*," Quinn huffs. She stretches, limbs poking out from behind the canvas, and I puff out a laugh at how ridiculous my painting looks with legs sticking out of one of its ears. Standing, I help rest the art against the wall behind her while she twists her torso in a deep stretch. The *pop* of her spine makes me wince. I'll hate every bit of telling her we haven't gotten the shot, but right now, we can both use a break.

Her hazel eyes are bright with amusement as she swipes through her phone. She aimlessly tucks a loose strand of blonde hair behind her ear, fallen from the clip that haphazardly holds it back. The oversized hoodie and fuzzy slippers she wears are making me sweat. Then again, all she had to do was sit behind my canvases while I loped around the apartment like a fool, finding lamps for better lighting and angling the camera a thousand different ways for the perfect shot.

"Do you have any idea who these guys are?" Quinn asks, face twisted in confusion.

I pull open the group chat and reread his message. Slate is the only one of the three boys next door we're currently on good terms with. It was difficult to stay upset with him, especially with his carefree attitude and charming personality. He wouldn't have stood for us holding a grudge against him anyway, because he quickly managed to weasel himself right into our good graces on the first day of drawing class.

The cherry on top of this friendship is that Slate is also a fan of *Love Untouched*.

He's scoring perfect hundreds while his roommates sit in the low twenties . . . or tens right now.

I wonder how Ace would react to that tidbit of information. I shove the thought away quickly.

"No idea," I frown, scooting closer to Quinn, whose

fingers fly over her keyboard as she types the name Kash Bailey into Google.

My jaw drops when his pictures begin to load. Fireworks crackle and zip throughout my body at his tanned skin and glistening muscles. I swear, hearts pop out of my eyes just like in the cartoons. If I weren't already perspiring from the effort of shooting perfect pictures, I sure am now.

This guy looks ridiculous. As in ridiculously fucking hot. So hot I almost tear Quinn's phone from her hands for a better view.

Warm brown eyes resemble melted chocolate. A slightly crooked nose. Full, kissable lips. Chestnut hair styled in a classy mullet, a cut I never thought I'd deem sexy.

And his *thighs*. Mother of pearl, his *thighs*. It's like they're carved from marble. I can make out every single muscle on them. Who knew rugby players were so hot, and why am I only finding out right now?

Somehow, I manage to pry myself from the literal god on Quinn's screen. Swiping a hand across my mouth in case I've started drooling, I search the other name Slate sent, Bruin Williams. My jaw doesn't just drop this time; it plummets to the core of the earth when the dark-haired man appears in the same tight-fitted jersey as Kash.

He has perfectly bronzed skin earned from hours spent practicing in the sun. Clicking on a photo, I ogle the sweat rolling down the hard lines of his chest. His dark hair is soaked, clinging to his forehead the way I'd cling to him if I ever came across him in real life. I've never been the kind of girl to shy away from a sweaty, attractive man, and today is not the day I start.

The apartment is silent except for the sound of our careful shallow breathing. When I stumble across a photo of Bruin's thick thighs, packed with layers and layers of muscle, I nearly excuse myself from the room.

Maybe I *am* Easy Barbie.

"Holy shit," Quinn breathes when we trade phones. All I can offer is a disbelieving noise of agreement.

Seriously, they're both *specimens*. The finest pedigree of athleticism. Forget football. Those players might be muscular, but they're covered in protective padding. Rugby . . . it's like football on steroids. No pads, no timeouts, just eighty minutes of raw strength and brute force. It's animalistic. It's vicious.

It's the most attractive thing I've ever seen.

And while Slate could easily be a rugby player with his similar stature, these men have years of the sport under their belts, which makes them even more appealing.

I don't know how long we're lost in the wormhole of the Terrapin's rugby team, but Quinn and I both startle when Slate's impatient follow-up appears in the chat.

A pang of guilt gnaws at me as I type my answer. I hover over the send button, chewing my lip. I could change my answers, put Slate somewhere in the running, but I can't lie.

Sorry, Slate, these men are just too handsome.

I peek at Quinn. Her cheeks are rosy with a blush, and I bet she regrets her sweatshirt right now. She appears just as ready as I am to crawl back into bed for a few hours of alone time.

"Are you thinking what I'm thinking?" I ask almost dreadfully.

Quinn gives me a forlorn look that says, "it needs to be done," so, together, we press send.

As expected, Slate's offended texts chime in one after the other.

SLATE

There's no way you'd BOTH KILL ME!!

I'm wounded, WOUNDED I TELL YOU!

I'm out for Tipsy Canvas. Can't be doing art
with people who don't appreciate my
beauty. And tell Beatrice she's going to have
to find another model because I quit.

Laughter bubbles from my chest at his dramatics. Surely, he should have known what kind of mess he was getting himself into when he sent his own name with those demigods.

I respond quickly before Slate bombards us with another slew of affronted messages.

I'd love a turn appreciating their beauty.

Quinn snorts, eyes gleaming with delight as she joins in on the fun.

QUINN

Of course we looked them up! We don't go
into FMK BLINDLY, Slate. And have you
SEEN their thighs?

She's not kidding. I zoomed in on Bruin's thighs until they filled my entire screen. There might be screenshots saved to prove how nice they are. Each defined, bulging muscle was mine for the taking. If Slate quits, they'd be great figure models . . . they'd be great for other things, too.

I should thank Slate for helping lighten my defeated mood.

SLATE

I'd let you appreciate mine if you didn't KILL
ME OFF. Plus, you know what I'm working
with ;) My thighs are just as good.

QUINN

That's why we decided to kill you off, S,
because we know what you're working with.

A single bang on the wall beside our dining table turns our giggles into full-blown hysterics. Tears brim the corners of my eyes, and there's a stitch in my side I only manage to get rid of when I sprawl out on the floor.

Quinn collapses next to me with a blissful sigh, stretching her arms high above her head. I don't blame her; she's been coiled up behind my paintings for almost an hour. I owe her one.

My phone lights up with another message.

SLATE

Hey! It was COLD in there. I'll come over
and show you both right now.

"Oh, my God," I mutter, trying to swallow back my amusement. The thing is, Slate *will* come over here and show us. The boy has no shame whatsoever.

My stomach aches and my cheeks tingle happily with glee as I respond.

Don't do it! We don't want to see it again.

SLATE

I don't think I've ever been so offended in
my entire life. I'm a good man with good
muscles and a nice cock, dammit!

He then proceeds to bombard the group chat with a list of

reasons we should consider him as a fuck or marry, instead of a kill.

SLATE

I'm local.

I've been known to rock ladies' worlds ;)

With my cock, fingers, and tongue.

I'm very creative.

And flexible.

I chuckle and lock my phone, casting it aside. It could be hours until he's done.

I will *finish this portfolio, and it will be the best-looking portfolio the Royal Academy of Arts has ever seen,* I manifest, sending the affirmation into the ether.

When I'm positive my request is received, catalogued, and begun, I loll my head to the side and crack open my lids to meet Quinn's. She's staring at the painting I relieved her of with a slight frown, her brows knitted together in deep thought.

"Hey Ro?"

"Yeah?"

She swallows, and concern piques at her sudden shift in mood. Since I returned from Cabo, she's been different. Avoiding talking about anything art related, and her feud with Knox has only made Quinn's off attitude worse. Something's up with my roommate, but she's headstrong and has trouble admitting when things get rough. Right now, she's as serious as I've ever seen her, and I'm more than willing to set my own art struggles aside to lend an ear to my best friend.

"Do you ever think your artwork just isn't goo—"

Knocking on the door interrupts. Her muscles lock and

her features harden as she shoves away the truth she was about to spill. Sadness and frustration drape over me like a blanket.

Before I can press further, she climbs to her feet and heads for the door, where Slate begins shouting for us to let him in.

I stare as she retreats, hoping my best friend will find the courage to open up soon.

I'm lost inside a painting.

Music blasts from my headphones, but the lyrics don't compute with how entrapped I am in the brushstrokes of color I layer over the canvas.

They say the eyes are the windows to the soul, but in this case, they're a reflection of mine. My warring thoughts are laid bare in the bright, sandy browns and rich reds. Hues of blue have overtaken the figure's irises like a tsunami crashing against shore in a harrowing storm, determined to rip me off my feet.

I pour myself into the piece. Brash, conceited yellows, flecked with strokes of envious greens. Emerald peeks through like rays of sunlight between branches of trees. Each press of my brush to the canvas is fueled by my embarrassment of the date I fucked up so terribly I still haven't heard from Max days later.

And the blues . . . the waves of something lost creeping back to shore. Sea foam bubbling to the surface as soon as Ace laid his hands over mine and pressed himself against me.

With a sigh, I sit back on my stool, pluck my headphones from my ears, and scrutinize my work.

What stares back is a confliction of emotions. My stomach churns as those sinking thoughts come wading back in, anxiety twisting wildly.

I had time before Creative Writing to kill, so I set up an easel in the art building and pulled out my oil paints, falling into their familiarity hoping to ease the stress that's clung to my shoulders all week.

Last weekend's shitshow, paired with my failed attempt at taking photos for my portfolio, has dragged the past few days on and on and *on*. I haven't mustered the courage to confide in Quinn about what happened on the date. She doesn't know Max and I never *really* stopped talking, let alone that I spent my Saturday night at Tin Can with him on a date to reignite our relationship.

I didn't believe in Murphy's Law until that night, when everything that could go wrong, did.

I'm hiding a monumental secret from my best friend. She briefly heard about my summer excursion, but that boy being Ace isn't something I've advertised. With the vendetta she has against Knox—and Ace—I doubt mentioning I've slept with our neighbor will improve her sentiments toward them.

Swapping the brush for a paint knife, I shovel white onto a clear spot on my palette. A dab of burnt sienna follows, mixing them as my mind wanders to one of its favorite subjects: Ace. He overstepped the boundaries I set once again, and it's no surprise I folded for him like a fool. I've been touch starved for months, and my date occupied himself with other people, ignoring me. It was easy to fall back into routine with the boy next door.

I wish I'd been able to resist, but alone in the middle of

Tin Can, I'd gotten caught up in Ace's magnetic presence all over again.

Maybe things would be different if we hadn't made our agreement over the summer. If I hadn't blocked his number. If he didn't have his heart locked in a dungeon, featuring everything from a moat to armed archers ready to shoot at the slightest hint of genuine affection.

Maybe I'm waiting for him to give up on me.

Maybe the chase is half the fun.

A low creak cuts through my thoughts, and my hand stills. I glance over my shoulder, and my heart skips at who stands in the doorway.

Speak of the devil, and he shall appear.

Except in this case, the devil looks a lot like one of the gods, and his name is Ace Broden.

His presence alone sends my pulse skyrocketing. He's handsome, clad in a blue flannel matching the exact hue of his eyes. It'll be too hot come afternoon, but in the white shirt underneath, he'll look just as good. Maybe he'll roll the sleeves up to his elbows to show off his impressive, tatted forearms and really give me something to daydream about.

It takes effort to turn away. The knife clinks softly against the palette as I mix aimlessly. My mind bursts with ideas, his appearance inspiring me.

"Hey," Ace says like he's approaching a rabid animal. I would laugh if I had the energy.

"Hey."

A stool screeches against the floor as he drags it near, taking a seat beside me. He's a consuming presence that draws my gaze like a magnet.

He slowly analyzes my progress. I wonder if he can see the confusion in my strokes, the frustration and anxiety brewing inside me.

"Who's this?" He asks, and I snort. That's fine; we don't have to talk about what happened or the crackling attraction between us.

"No idea," I shrug. The painting doesn't have any of my signatures yet, like the glowing ring of color around his irises or the pointed ears or sharp canines, but he will soon. He's a character I haven't quite figured out yet, a combination of two personas as flawed and puzzled as me.

Silence settles between us, filled only by Ace's bouncing leg. His fingers twist nervously.

I'm not sure what to say either.

I've spent days dissecting every second of what went down at Tin Can and the conversation that followed. I played into seeing Ace at the bar, and I got caught up, falling back into our old routine of trying to make Max jealous. Ace had only been responding to my cues.

"Rory," Ace starts. As soon as our eyes latch, my body reacts, heart kicking into gear and pulse fluttering so hard my head swirls. Ace doesn't have to touch me to send electricity zipping through my veins. His existence alone does that.

He resembles a kicked puppy with his hair sticking in every direction. His brows are bent in worry, and he chews his lip as if I'm about to ask him to leave me alone for good.

If I were smarter, maybe I would.

"Ace," I prompt, swallowing tightly. Our stares have lingered for too long, and all it does is fill me with the memories of his touch, how wide his grin is when he laughed, and how rosy his cheeks turned when he collapsed beside me after a particularly exhausting round of sex.

Reel it in, Ro. Reel it the fuck in.

"I wanted to apologize for what happened last weekend." There's something in the way he says it, so genuine I almost forgive him immediately. "I was way out of line not only with my actions, but how I spoke to you on the walk home. I didn't mean to hurt you, and I'm sorry I did."

My heart swells with the sentiment. I place my brush down and turn to face him fully.

"Thank you, Ace. I appreciate the apology, and I'm sorry too. I should have put a stop to what we were doing earlier." I duck my chin in shame. "I wanted to make Max jealous, and I regret using you to do so."

His finger hooks under my chin, startling me. The touch is scalding in the best way, and the tingles shooting from the contact intensify as Ace tips my face to meet his. When our eyes latch, my breath leaves me at the vibrant blue.

"In case you didn't notice, Rory-O. I like making that fucker jealous. He doesn't deserve you." I should protest, should come to Max's defense, but Ace doesn't give me the chance. "I accept your apology, even though I don't need one."

I search his face, and nod when I find nothing but the truth.

Like the snap of fingers, the tension in the room begins to fade. Ace removes his grip on me with a parting brush of his thumb across my cheek, and I almost fall off my chair and into his lap. The sensation lingers, but it's easier to catch my breath now that one of my problems is solved. My shoulders ease when the conversation shifts to something lighter. Gossip in classes, assignments, plans for the rest of the day.

"I should be packing up soon," I admit, checking the time on the clock hanging above the door. Creative Writing starts in half an hour, and it's halfway across campus. "I have class."

"Can I see you tonight?" He asks eagerly. "We can catch a movie or something?"

We may have apologized, and while the idea of watching a movie alone with Ace is tempting, it never really ends with watching the movie. It ends with clothes strewn about, red marks on skin, and a satiated sex drive. All the things I can't recreate with him right now.

"I can't. Quinn, Slate, and I are going to Tipsy Canvas."

A muscle in Ace's jaw ticks, and I smother a smile, beginning to pack my supplies. His jealousy is amusing. Slate and I don't have any complications that will jeopardize our relationship, like seeing each other naked.

Well, we have *half* that problem, but Slate will *not* be seeing *me* naked. I can promise that.

"Tipsy Canvas?"

"Yep," I confirm, stretching the cling wrap from its container to fit the length of my palette, preserving the paint.

"That seems unfair, you know. With how talented you are," Ace comments as I collect my dirty paintbrushes and head for the sink. Twisting on the water, I dip a brush into the steady stream. "Is it even going to be fun for you?"

I can't help but grin. "Of course it'll be fun. It's about the company, Ace, not the painting. Plus, depending on how much I drink, it'll even the playing field."

He rolls his eyes and crosses his arms, leaning against the wall. I try not to notice how his flannel stretches around his biceps. Splotches of water splatter my forearms, and I jump, not realizing I've unconsciously moved closer to the spraying faucet. "You know, for some reason, I don't think you'll be able to outdrink Slate."

"Want to come and find out?" I challenge, smothering my brush in soap. A green so bright it's almost yellow streaks across the bar, bubbles forming as I scrub the bristles clean.

Ace smirks like I've fallen into his trap, and dammit, I

did. There's no rescinding the offer, because he accepts all too easily.

"Absolutely."

CHAPTER 16
RORY

ce might not realize it, but he's two seconds away from bursting into flames under the severity of Quinn's glare.

Selfishly, I'm happy to no longer be on the receiving end of that razor-sharp look I've been victim to since inviting Ace to join us at Tipsy Canvas tonight. While I struggled to pick out the perfect top, Quinn went to gather the rest of our painting party next door, grumbling incoherently under her breath. If I had to guess what she was huffing about, I'd bet all the money in my bank account—all sixty-seven dollars and fifty-three cents of it—it had something to do with Ace. When I met our group in the hall, I was surprised to find Knox there, hands stuffed deep in the pockets of his jeans, looking like he'd rather be anywhere else. I also didn't miss how he and Quinn kept as far away from each other as possible, with Quinn leading the group to the elevator, and Knox bringing up the rear.

How he managed to score an invite, I don't know. The chances that Quinn invited him aren't high, but I do find myself watching the pair closely, sitting beside each other across the table from me.

"When do you think she'll stop staring?" Ace asks from the corner of his mouth. He leans closer, but his canvas does nothing to conceal him from the death curse scrawled on my roommate's face.

I snort softly, dipping my paintbrush into the beige on my palette and dotting it meticulously along the bottom of my canvas to create the illusion of sand. The instructor slips between painters after demonstrating the technique, and although I chose not to follow her direction to splatter the paint on with a toothbrush, Slate is enjoying the step, his joyous pride echoing through the room. "When you apologize."

"She doesn't seem like she's open to hearing an apology right now," Ace whispers back, ducking behind his painting when her hazel eyes flicker this way. I take the brunt of the daggers, but my roommate's face softens when she lands on me. Her brows raise in a "how the hell did I end up in this situation" look, and I stifle a laugh. I lift my wineglass to her with a sheepish shrug. Reluctantly, Quinn follows suit, then drains the contents of her second—or third?—glass of wine.

Whilst deep in her cup, Quinn fails to notice Knox's lingering gaze, but I sure do. The corner of his mouth twitches as he watches her chug, and I zone in on the interaction, entranced as he trails her lips against her glass to her throat, bobbing with each sip.

As I reach out to swat at Ace for his attention, Slate interrupts. Surely, I can't have been the only one to see the interaction, but Knox returns to his canvas as if I didn't just witness something as groundbreaking as a smile from him. Quinn frowns as Slate reaches over her for her palette, zeroed in on his masterpiece. I'm all alone on Secret Feelings Island.

"When do you think I should do it?" Ace asks, checking across the table. Quinn's chair almost teeters out from under her when Slate forces his body between her and her canvas, and my heart jumps like I was just defibrillated when she slips.

Knox is the one to save her, catching her arm as she flails. Slate disappears from her space with her palette in hand, and I wonder if he also witnessed Knox's stare. I remind myself to ask him later, entrapped with the scene before me. It's like an episode of *Love Untouched*, and I'm secretly voting for them to win.

When Quinn is righted in her chair, her cheeks are bright red, and it's not a color she can pass off as merely drinking too much wine. I bite my lip in excitement.

"Earth to Rory-O." Ace waves a hand in front of my face. I blink, scowling his way for distracting me. I quickly return my focus to my roommate, but she's out of her chair, palette and empty glass in hand, making a beeline for the paints and bar.

My chest stings for Quinn. Since the night of the photo-shoot where she almost opened up about whatever has been eating at her this semester, she hasn't been acting like herself, and I want to get to the bottom of it. She can tell me anything, and if there's something more than the hatred I believe there is between her and Knox, as her best friend, I'm not going to judge.

Sickness swirls in my stomach. She's not privy to my life lately, either. It's about time we both come clean with each other.

Only half paying attention, I reply, "What?"

"I asked when you think a good time to apologize to Quinn will be," Ace says, face scrunched. He juts his chin at our friends. "What are you staring at?"

Quinn's at the bar. Knox is conversing softly with Slate. Much to my chagrin, he didn't turn to watch Quinn trail from her seat. Did he want to? Was I reading too much into the situation? I have been watching a lot of *Love Untouched* reruns lately.

"Nothing," I shake my head, turning toward Ace. The sand he painted is realistic as fuck, so much so I swear if I laid his canvas on the ground and stepped on it, I'd be able to feel the grains between my toes. "Now," I continue. Quinn's alone at the paint table, mindlessly grabbing a bottle of blue to refill her palette. "Now is the perfect time to apologize."

"Really?" Ace quirks an eyebrow, shooting a nervous peek across the table. His shoulders relax a notch when he notices Quinn by herself.

"Really," I agree, all but shooing him from his chair. "You do want to be friends again, don't you?"

Ace makes a face, and I'm sure it's because he would've found a way to get me to talk to him whether he apologizes to Quinn or not. There's something about Ace I can't seem to resist, but luckily—reluctantly on his part—he strides for my best friend.

This time, Knox watches his roommate approach Quinn, features carefully neutral.

Oh yeah, it might not have clicked for him yet, but I know a possessive stare when I see one.

Ace startles Quinn so badly paint squirts from the bottle with the loudest squelch. Of course, there just so happens to be a lapse in conversation, creating an even more embarrassing scene. Slate snorts with laughter, and I can't help but muffle my giggle in my drink.

"Oh, my!" A voice exclaims. I choke, hammering on my chest as the teacher of the class expresses her apology, hands out like she's considering patting my back. I hold up a hand to warn her away. "I'm so sorry! I didn't mean to startle you! I was going to compliment how stunning your painting is turning out!"

"Thank you," I croak. When my throat is clear, I ease the sting with another swig of wine. "My friends and I are really enjoying the class."

She beams, my near death already forgotten. "I'm glad to hear it."

Slate calls the teacher over with a question. I situate myself in my seat, exchanging my wine glass for my paintbrush while I determine what color to use next. Scrubbing my brush clean in a jar of water, Ace peeks over his shoulder with wide eyes as if signaling for help. I offer him a nod of encouragement, and he rewards me with a playful smirk. A flutter rouses in my stomach at the slightest curl of his lip, and I scold myself.

I'm too far to hear, but I'd pay any amount of money to be a fly on the wall for this conversation, especially when Quinn bites her lip to smother a smile. She raises an accusing brow, and I'm locked in on the scene, knowing my roommate is going to make Ace work for her acceptance of his apology.

If this really were *Love Untouched*, I'd be equally entertained. I'd be eating up the different camera angles, the commentary from the narrator, and, *oh,* their confessionals would be top-notch. Ace would make a comment about how unapproachable Quinn is, and she'd be grinning like a madwoman, satisfied he's sweating over this confrontation.

Not that I would want them to be a thing if this really were a season of my favorite show. I'd have to vote against them when the time came because Ace is off limits.

I'm so enthralled, I don't notice Slate making his way over, which is funny since he's well over six feet tall and built like a linebacker. He's at the table before I can send a silent prayer, hoping Ace and Quinn have made amends.

Slate reaches between them, and Quinn hasn't detected his presence either, because she startles, stumbling, only to run into Knox's chest, who prowled closer in Slate's shadow. Their eyes lock, and I swear I'm scorched all the way over in my seat from the intensity.

I finish off my glass to chase away the heat. With the interruption, the mood shifts. Slate makes a comment that has Ace rolling his eyes and Quinn laughing. I can't help but grin. Once Knox and Quinn get over their feud and Ace and I reinstate our rules, there's a chance we can become great friends with our neighbors. We're a good bunch.

The teacher begins to demonstrate the next step, and I stand, abandoning my station in favor of gravitating toward my friends. My body is warm with wine and my limbs light and airy, my smile contagious.

I snag Quinn's hand, and she grins broadly as I drag her away from the paint table over to the bar. She squeezes in reassurance, and I know everything is going to be just fine.

CHAPTER 17
ACE

Apologizing to Quinn Conroy almost killed me.

She didn't make it easy either. I had to explain—in lengthy detail—exactly what I'd done wrong while she listened with her arms crossed over her chest, unimpressed. The grueling process was worth it for Rory's beaming smile afterward.

And apologizing does have its perks.

Like right now, as I walk beside Rory heading to our apartments to begin the weekend.

So far, this trip is faring far better than the one we shared the night I found her at Tin Can with her douchebag ex.

Rory is blind to how awfully he treats her. Not that I can compare views on relationships with my track record. I haven't dated in years and haven't found someone worth breaking that rule for until she appeared in my life without warning. The fear of a new relationship ending like my previous one is partly what keeps me away. If I hadn't built concrete walls around my heart and vowed never to date again, I'd be begging to make her officially mine.

My fortress isn't holding up so well in Rory's presence.

She's managed to find a fissure and work her magic, slowly chipping the crack into a full-blown cavity. Whatever this is between us, it's so much better than what I had with she-who-shall-not-be-named. Our relationship is built on bigger feelings, bigger losses, and better fucking. Rory and I are teetering on a threadbare wire between fully shattering whatever twisted friendship we've built and finally giving in to everything that could be.

My eyes dart in her direction. Her fists are circled around the straps of her backpack, and the urge to uncurl her grip and thread my fingers through hers is immense. She's sans baseball cap today, and I'm fucking grateful because I never liked when she hid her face. I told her a million times the bangs weren't bad, but she refuses to acknowledge any conversation about the haircut.

I've saved my own ass many times by sticking to that rule when all I wanted was to prove to her how much I liked the haircut. Now that her pretty brown hair has grown out, I must give her props: this length would be much easier to gather around my fist.

"Ace?" Rory's voice cuts through my sinful thoughts.

"What?" We've stopped in front of our apartment building, Rory propping open the door to the lobby. Was I lost in my head that long? Have I been ignoring the real Rory for my deluded imaginative one? Fuck, I'm such an idiot. "Sorry," I offer sheepishly. "I was just thinking about something."

She searches my features, and my heart clenches at her concern. She cares about me, and I wish it were more than just in a friendly way. "Was it about your meeting? How did it go?"

I take a careful breath as the irritation returns. My afternoon was spent in my academic advisor's office, conversing about advice on querying an art manager. So far, I've sent out a few feelers but haven't received any particularly good news, so I stopped by for assistance on constructing a better email. I received help, but not without a lecture on how I should be accepting my mom's offer instead. Not many people are as lucky as I am to have not only one but both parents in the art business.

My parents don't know I'm exploring other options. It'd break Mom's heart if she found out I'm thinking of working with someone else, and I don't have the guts to hurt her like that.

"Yeah," I agree, and the lie tastes sour. I take the door from her, and she ducks inside the building. "It went better than I thought, but I feel guilty."

It's not that I don't want Mom to be my manager . . . okay, that's exactly what it is. Reaching out to other talent managers feels like I'm betraying her for exploring my options as an artist. And in a way, I guess I am. I should be grateful for my parents' help and excited for the opportunity to work with the people who have literally given me everything in life. The painting lessons, the travel and culture—it's a life most people only dream of.

What does that say about me? I'm in the perfect position an artist can be—one parent with connections to the most prestigious galleries in the country, and the other is one of the best art managers money can buy, and I don't use them to my advantage?

"What are you feeling guilty about?" She stops at her mailbox, shoving the key into the lock. A single slip of paper sits inside; one Rory scans quickly and tosses into the garbage at the counter behind us. I'm too distracted to check my own. I may have managed to save myself from admitting I was daydreaming about her, but I wasn't expecting to bare my soul.

Shrugging lamely, I busy myself with punching the button to the elevator three times because I can never be sure if the temperamental machine will answer my call. The doors don't immediately grind open, and my nerves coil. There's nothing to deflect from the conversation at hand, but maybe talking about what's going on will help me figure out how to go about the situation.

With a deep sigh, I confess, "I've been struggling to find an art manager, and my advisor more or less told me I'm a fool for not accepting my mom's help."

Rory's features scrunch in confusion, and it hits me she doesn't know anything about my life due to rule number six: no personal questions.

"What does your mom do?"

I smother the smile threatening to break out as Rory unknowingly breaks one of the rules she tried so desperately to keep in place.

I indulge her because I'm no rule-follower, either.

"She's an art manager." Rory's lips part in shock. It's as cute as it is nerve-racking, and paired with the disbelief written across her face, I'm afraid she'll side with my advisor.

The elevator slams to a stop at the lobby. The doors scrape open, reminding me of a haunted mansion, eerily beckoning us inside. Alarm bells ring in my head, and I glance around for slime oozing from the ceiling or smoke wafting through the shaft as I tentatively step on.

"Dad owns a few galleries, so they're always traveling. And Mom finds the talent to house."

"So, your parents are like the super-couple of the art world?" Her voice is pitched with a mixture of surprise and awe. I shift uneasily, wishing I could take the information back.

"I guess you could say that." I brace in anticipation of her telling me I'm a fool, like my advisor said, but it doesn't come.

She's quiet, and when I slide my gaze to her, that damned lip is tucked between her teeth. Worry eddies from my mind as I zero in on the motion. I want to lean in and place my mouth on hers to distract her as much as she's distracting me.

The elevator beeps as we pass the second floor, and I force my attention away. I'm careful to keep still so she doesn't notice the sudden rush of blood collecting between my legs.

"I think that's very brave of you, Ace." She surprises me by saying.

"You do?" I blurt, stunned. Did I hear her right? *Brave*? Not taking the help my parents can give me is *brave*?

Damn. Maybe this girl *is* the one.

The elevator creaks to a halt, and the doors roll open with a sound that causes shivers to spindle down my spine. I trail Rory like a puppy, eager for her explanation. The linoleum shifts to gaudy airport carpet under my shoes, and the ugly cream walls guide us to our apartments. "Yeah. I mean, I can't imagine having that kind of support from your parents," she starts, and I frown. Her parents don't support her art career? She's talented as fuck; anyone with working eyesight can see that. I remind myself to circle back to that later as she continues. "But to have it and want to develop a career of your own? That takes guts, Ace."

My chest swells. If I were a simpering man, I'd preen. Fuck it, I do preen. To have support from someone as amazing as Rory has me flying high.

Why can't I kiss the daylights out of her for what her pretty words are doing to me?

The self-sabotage kicks me in the ass. *Because she's not yours, and she never will be.*

"So, you don't think I'm an idiot for not wanting my parents' help?" A sliver of vulnerability slips into my tone, something I swore I'd never be around another girl again. Rory's caught me off guard, and there goes another *crack* in my fortress.

She grants me a sly smile that sends my pulse skittering. "Well, I didn't say that."

"Very funny," I reply drily.

We reach her door, and she turns to face me fully, blue eyes sparkling with humor. "In all seriousness, yes, you're incredibly brave for chasing your dreams on your own terms." Her smile dulls, and it takes less than a microsecond for me to decide I'll do anything to make that grin reappear. "I'm trying to do the same, but it doesn't seem to be working out too well at the moment."

"What do you mean?" She unlocks her door and gestures me inside. I'm too thrown by her admission to realize this is the first time I've been inside her place. We're really taking our friendship to a whole new level tonight.

Rory shoots me an apologetic look that tells me she's sorry for the shift in conversation. I don't care; I care only about fixing this for her. I wave for her to continue, kicking my shoes off and letting my backpack fall to the floor beside them. Following her into the bright white kitchen, I prop a hip against the counter as she rifles through a drawer, plucking out a takeout menu.

"Dinner?" She asks as a lame attempt to distract me. Food is not a deterrent, and the only way I'd forget this conversation is if she dropped those skintight jeans. They accentuate the curve of her ass in a way I haven't noticed until now. They must be new. *Shit, Ace, back on track, buddy,* I mentally scold, discreetly adjusting myself as she pretends to scour through the menu.

Prying the paper from her grasp, I toss it on the counter. We're toe-to-toe, and it's difficult to ignore my body's reaction to the way her breath hitches at our proximity. My focus skews, attuned to every little thing that has to do with Rory Wilson. The scent of her perfume—strawberries and coconut. The way the strands of her hair tease the apples of her cheeks. Her blue eyes revealing a hint of apprehension the longer I stare.

"It's okay, Ro," I say softly, not wanting to scare her off. "You can tell me anything."

She hesitates, eyes growing red. Tears build on her bottom lashes, and a spike of anger stabs me in the gut. She doesn't allow herself to confide in many people, or perhaps they don't take the time to ask. I want to find everyone who has ever made Rory feel like shit and put them in their place. I'd start with that fucking ex-boyfriend of hers.

A tear slides down her face, and I'm there before she can wipe it away. Resting my hand gently on her cheek, she tilts her head almost unconsciously into my palm, and my body hums. I catch the droplet, brushing it away.

I'd offer her the whole damn world if she asked for it.

Her words catch in her throat when she tries to respond, and she gives me a broken smile instead. Whatever she's going to say is important to her. I smooth the groove between her brows, waiting patiently. Her hands absentmindedly find my waist, and I swear my knees wobble when she hooks her fingers through my belt loops.

"I've been trying to build a portfolio so I can apply to a class at the Royal Academy of Arts next summer, but I'm helpless when it comes to anything digital," she chuckles wetly and another tear escapes. I capture that one, too, and vow to catch all her tears, even if she doesn't want me to. She sucks in a breath. "My website is a mess, and don't get me started on how poorly the pictures are going."

Unable to help myself, I tug her closer. She clings to me just as tightly, and my body lights up. I bite back a triumphant grin at having her in my arms again. I've missed how she molds perfectly to me, like we're two colors blending to create one perfect shade.

"Rory-O, I actually might know someone who can help with both of those things."

"You do?" Her question is muffled by my shirt. I huff with laughter, and when she pulls back, her lips are pressed together in a pout, like the fact I find her amusing is annoying. I smooth the crease between her brows again, then indulge myself by tracing a finger down the bridge of her nose and across those tantalizing lips. Rory shivers beneath my touch, lashes fluttering and mouth parting with a shallow breath. My cock rouses in response.

"Yep." It's the only word left in my vocabulary. She's fried my brain.

"Who? You?"

I mock offense. I could be a phenomenal photographer for all she knows.

"I can probably help with the website, but I have a friend who loves photography, and I bet I can rope her into assisting you. She owes me a favor." She doesn't, but Rory doesn't need to know that. The blossoming hope in her eyes is thanks enough.

"Really?"

I grin. "Really, really."

To my horror, her tears are back in full force. I frown, cradling her face. "What's wrong? You're supposed to be happy, Rory-O, not upset."

"I'm sorry." She bites her lip to stop the trembling. Her fingers brush across my waist, and electricity coils through my body. Shit. Is it hot in here? The collar of my shirt is suddenly tight. "I'm just shocked. I didn't mean to make this about me, and I certainly wasn't expecting you of all people to have the solution, but of course you do."

"Of course I do," I echo cockily. My chest puffs with pride, which causes Rory to release a genuine laugh, swatting me playfully. "Please let me help you."

She hesitates for a long moment, and I hold my breath.

Her hands slide up my chest, and the slow pace is excruciating. I come alive, every nerve ending firing beneath her touch. All this time, she's been trying to put a buffer between us. Just friends. Because we can't be trusted alone together. We've always been destined for more.

Hooking her arms around my neck, her fingers twist into the hair at my nape. The insatiable part of me wants her to grab a handful and pull. I'd fall to my knees if she did so. My heart thunders in my chest as I battle the urge to slam my lips against hers, allowing her the lead.

I don't have to fight the craving for long because she breathes out a soft "yes" and hauls herself into my arms.

I stumble as she crashes into me. Regaining my footing quickly, her ass is in my hands, and I'm readjusting us so our hips sit flush against each other. Our desperate moans meet as our lips do, devouring each other.

Maneuvering across her apartment proves difficult, because I'm more interested in the way her hips press into mine, and because I've never been here before. My foot catches against the leg of a stool, and I grunt, but the pain drifts away as Rory's fingers trail down my torso. Somehow, I manage to make it to the couch, both of us tumbling onto the navy cushions, but our jostling limbs don't deter us from ravaging each other.

Rory's hands rake down my shoulders, clawing at my shirt as I buck against her. It's been too long since I've had her like this, and I've never been so desperate. All I know is *Rory Rory Rory*—

She tastes just as sweet as I remember. She feels just as good, too. Her perfect breasts in my palms, her piqued nipples rough against the pads of my fingers, inked onto the tip of my tongue. *God*, and the way her pussy hugged my cock . . . I need to be as close to Rory as she'll let me, skin to skin, hopefully with my cock buried so deep there's no doubt she wasn't made for me.

An impatient whine pierces my depraved imagination, spurring me into action. I press up onto my knees, tearing at the fabric of my shirt, eager to rid myself of the constricting garment. Rory's fingers latch onto my skin, clawing marks as she explores and tries to tug me closer simultaneously. Chest heaving, I peer down at her work, reveling in the throbbing raised marks already forming, standing starkly against the black ink dotting my torso.

My cock throbs at the plea in Rory's big round eyes. She grabs the waistband of my pants, and I almost topple forward when she pulls, catching myself against the arm of the couch. I placate her with a swift roll of my hips and a few soft kisses. "I know, Rory-O. I'm coming right back to you. Take your clothes off for me."

"Need your cock," she gasps into my mouth.

"Anything," I pant, just as wrecked. "Anything you want. It's yours."

She kisses the words from my lips before shoving me away. The fabric of her shirt is already bunched in her hands, and my mouth waters with each inch of skin she exposes. I've wanted this moment since I first found out she was my neighbor. Hell, I've been waiting for this moment a lot longer than that, since the morning she walked away from me on the beach.

Our clothes disappear quickly, and we're unable to take our eyes off each other as we drink our fill. The air in the room is thick with anticipation, and my body is buzzing as if a thousand bees are trapped in my chest. As much as I wish I were the one peeling each piece of fabric from her skin, Rory isn't waiting around. She's made it perfectly clear what she needs right now—just sex—and I can give her that.

I'm good at that.

When the last piece of clothing between us is shed, time slows to a standstill. Rory's hair is disheveled from where I've had my hands in it, mussed perfectly around her face. Her cheeks are a pretty, ruined red, and we haven't even begun yet. I catalogue the shade to mimic with my paints later. Her icy eyes blaze with heat, lashes fluttering as she shivers when I trail down the column of her throat to her breasts. Her blush-pink nipples are hard, ready for me to tease.

My eyes rove down.

And down.

And down, right to my second favorite spot on Rory's body.

"*Ace.*" Rory cries my name like an invitation, one I'm more than happy to accept.

We collide, and this time, there's no stumbling. We're a clash of skin and heat, mouths and hands, wet and wild. Her heart pounds hard against my chest, matching the thrashing of mine. Her nipples drag against me, and my skin breaks out in goosebumps. I mouth across her neck, sucking at the delicate skin until she's whimpering for more.

She cranes her neck and, at first, I assume she's giving me more room to roam, but her hands find my biceps, and she's pushing at me.

Confused, I pull back, but she doesn't let me go far.

"What? What's wrong?"

Rory swallows thickly, and I try very hard not to let my mind wander to her swallowing something else. My cock aches with excitement. If I don't get a hand on it soon, it might fall off. "Do you remember rule number three?" She asks, and my stomach plummets.

This is the game she wants to play? Keeping me at arm's length in hopes she won't become as attached to me as I am to her?

Annoyance threatens to straighten my spine, but I shove the irritation away. Fine. If she wants to do this, I can play her little game.

"No marks where anyone can see them," I recite, because how the fuck could I forget *anything* that happened during the best vacation of my life?

"Good." She nods to herself. "Keep that in mind."

I don't have to ask because I know why she's making sure I remember this rule. No marks where anyone can see them because she's still going to work things out with her ex.

I'll just have to fuck him out of her existence.

Before my dick can deflate at the wrench in this situation, Rory wraps a hand around my base, and she jerks me from root to tip in a motion that obliterates any coherent thought in my head that doesn't revolve around sex. The sofa rasps as I sink my nails into the cloth with the stroke of her thumb over my tip, collecting a bead of precum.

"Condom?" She reminds me, breaking my trance. My fingers are stiff as I forcefully unwind them from the spongy cushion to wrap around hers. I mean to stop her motions because I can't think, barely even know what she just asked, but my body has another idea, only adding more pressure as she starts to fist my cock. I'm glued to the scene until the fire smoldering in the pit of my body ignites into a rolling burn. Rory repeats herself, and my breath is ragged as I snatch my jeans from the floor.

As cliché as it is, I have a condom in my wallet.

Impatiently, I tear the packet open, then stop Rory with a hiss. If she keeps touching me like this, I'll come. It's been far too long since I've been with a girl, so if Rory's hoping this will last more than a few passionate minutes, she's going to be disappointed.

I'll make it up to her all night long.

Rory watches me roll the condom over my length with rapt attention. Her eyes are hazy with lust, and she's staring at me like I'm the damn moon in the sky, and I battle the urge to admit she's the sun that makes my days brighter than they've ever been.

Circling my fingers around her ankles, I yank. With a squawk, her arms give out, body flattening against the cushions. I smirk, guiding her legs forward, exposing her. It's a glorious pussy, one I'd like right up against my mouth, but now isn't the time to put my wicked tongue to use. She wants my cock, and I'm more than happy to oblige her demands.

A plea forms on the tip of her tongue. As much as I'd love to hear her wanton cries, I'm just as eager. I tug myself once more and guide the head of my cock to her entrance, teasing myself slowly through her arousal.

"*Ace*," she breathes, lashes fluttering. My stomach burns with anticipation. Goddamn, I love when she says my name like that.

"Yes, Rory-O?" I prod for an answer, knowing she won't respond. Not while her eyes are rolled back in her head as I press the breath from her lungs with each inch of my cock I feed her.

Her nails sting where they dig into my flesh. I offer murmured encouragement while continuing to push my way inside her. It's difficult to focus with her pussy hugging my cock tightly, and the warmth has my mind swimming. Fuck, she's perfect. Rory's legs wind around my waist, gripping me tight, and our chests move as one. She bats those long lashes at me, and the fucked-out look alone is enough to bring me to the edge. Her sultry tone is almost my undoing.

"I want you to fuck me."

I don't need to be told twice.

A roll of my hips elicits groans of pleasure from us both, and I fall into a quick rhythm because I can't seem to control myself when it comes to anything having to do with this girl. I'm selfish. I'm drowning. I'm completely drunk off her, and if this is all I get before she's back in her ex's arms, I'm going to indulge.

"Oh God, *Ace*!" Rory's moans are music to my ears, and I lose myself in my favorite song. The fabric of the couch scrapes my knees at the pace I fuck into her, and I'm going to have rug burn to show for it later, but the annoyance isn't enough to stop me. Neither is the size of the sofa. It's not made for more than one person. We're a mess of limbs and touches and kisses, overlapping in the best of ways.

I plant my forearms, framing Rory's face. Her pretty lips are parted in a silent moan, and I dive down to taste it. Bliss blooms throughout my body, and I want to bask in this high, to paint it to life and keep it forever.

We're so lost in each other the sound of a lock flicking open goes unheard. The high-pitched scream of terror doesn't go unheard. It shrouds the lewd sounds we emit, and the slamming of my heart in my chest isn't from ecstasy anymore, but from panic.

"*Holyfuckingshit*," Quinn's screeching pierces the apartment. My limbs freeze, buried to the hilt in Rory's tight, wet heat. Whipping my head to the door, I catch a glimpse of her roommate's wide and tortured eyes before she promptly slams the door shut.

Silence descends upon the room with the exception of our heavy panting.

Returning my attention to the girl beneath me, she stares back, eyes wide in shock. Her lips are swollen from my kisses, her hair a mess, and I can easily go a few more rounds with her. The lock slides back into place, drawing me back to the situation at hand, and we break into a fit of laughter.

I've never had anything like this. The ease, the playfulness. Sex for me is always transactional, because it has to be. We fuck, she leaves, nothing more. No relationships, and certainly no feelings.

This is so much better than all of that combined. With Rory, there's a carnal urge I need satiated. Our sex has always been amazing, and although it was a rule not to get to know each other, I feel like I've known her forever. She's loyal to a fault. She finds beauty in everything. She's gorgeous, flirty, and funny. Being around her is easy, and I never want to leave her side.

Her face is alight with amusement. Her pussy contracts with her giggles, pulling a deep groan from me. She's so tight I can't see straight. My hips buck on instinct, unable to help myself, and Rory dissolves into a puddle of pleasure beneath me.

"Oh my God," she gasps, and it's a mix of horror and desire. She shoves at me but hooks her legs around my hips.

"My roommate just walked in on us fucking. We have to stop!"

I think the fuck not. I ignore the protest, using my vantage point to kiss her. She melts immediately, jaw slackening, so I dive my tongue inside. When I thrust my hips, eager to resume our escapade, she's back to the mewling mess I can't get enough of.

"Sweetheart, I wouldn't stop if the walls were coming down around us. I'm sure as fuck not stopping for her."

CHAPTER 18
ACE

CABO

A smile threatens to split my face in two. Rory hasn't taken her eyes off me since the moment she sat down, and even though I know why she's staring, I still feel like a million bucks. The Hawaiian shirt I'm sporting is awful, but it's the reason for her focus, and any day with Rory's eyes on me is better than most.

Dad bought matching shirts for dinner tonight, and I couldn't say no when he held up the gaudy teal button-downs with large pink tropical flowers and colorful parrots. His face screamed with pride while my mind screamed at me to run.

How Rory and my family's tables ended up beside each other at the hotel restaurant is a mystery. Or perhaps it's a sign from the universe that we keep meeting like this. The resort is huge, but somehow, running into each other has been too easy.

Her icy blue perusal sends electricity dancing through my veins as she drinks me in for the fourth time. My heart rate spikes when she bites her lip to hide her amusement.

She looks incredible in her floral dress. It hits mid-thigh, showing off her long legs, crossed under the wrought-iron table.

I wonder if she feels it too. The call to be nearer. The spark when we touch. How the sex we've been having blows every other moment I've spent with a girl out of the fucking water.

There's something about Rory that's addicting, that keeps me searching for her every time I enter a room, that keeps me wanting more. I haven't experienced a longing like this in forever, and even then, this is way more intense. I don't want to give this up in a few days' time, not when I can picture something real with her.

"How are you liking school so far, son?" Dad asks from over the top of his menu. He doesn't need to look at it at all. The man has never ordered a different meal from any restaurant he goes to: steak and salad.

I tear my eyes off Rory, but not before gifting her a sly smirk. "'S good. I miss Knox and Slate."

Mom makes a sympathetic noise. "Oh, sweetie, you'll see them soon." She pats my hand in reassurance. "How is Knox? You should have invited him!"

"I did." Mom's all but adopted him and encourages him to join any trip she can since she found out he doesn't have a good relationship with his family, but he almost always declines in favor of spending the summers at our off-campus apartment. "He doesn't like sand."

"Poor thing," she coos, sipping her drink. It's the same bright color as her lipstick. "Don't let him think he's getting out of Thanksgiving. I need my sous chef in the kitchen with me."

I hum in agreement. I'm on the same page. I'd rather have him around than leave him on campus all alone, but he's stubborn. Mom hasn't worn him down quite yet, but it's only a matter of time. She accomplishes everything she puts her mind to.

A clang and a soft curse draw my attention. A fork lies on the ground in the space between my chair and Rory's. The culprit wears a sheepish look, cheeks red and mouth turned into a timid smile.

She ducks down for the utensil, and I take this as my chance, bending to meet her halfway.

"You know, I'm beginning to think you're following me," I whisper, reaching for the fork so our fingers brush. Her touch zips up my arm, and the feeling lingers when Rory snatches her hand away. I wonder if she felt it too, and if that's why she glares.

I offer a polite smile she sees right through. I understand her jitters, but she doesn't have anything to worry about. No one knows a thing about our secret rendezvous, and I'm not going to be the one to out us in front of either of our families, but that doesn't mean I can't have a little fun.

"Don't flatter yourself," she hisses, and I like her bite. My cock stirs. Her gaze flits over my shoulder to my parents, who are busy discussing the wine list, not paying a lick of attention to us. At her table, her sisters giggle together, attention locked on one of their phones. Her parents haven't noticed us either.

"They don't know a thing, do they?" I tease, gripping the fork. Of course they don't know, it's rule number whatever-the-fuck. I just want to see Rory squirm. "They don't know how wet I make you, how loud you are for me . . ." I trial off at the pretty blush reddening her cheeks. Fuck, she's perfect even with the scathing glare she pins me with. I twist the utensil in my grip, offering it handle-out for Rory to take. Her gaze flickers from the fork to me then back again, and I offer a polite smile, when all I want to do is grab her by the hips, flip her dress up, pull her panties to the side, and sit her on my lap. I need her like I need fucking air, and I want her right this second. "Meet me in the bathroom," I whisper when she finally snatches the fork from my grasp.

She shakes her head softly, but I'm not kidding. I'm going to bend her over the counter or get her into a stall and fuck the daylights out of her. She might be fuming on the outside, but I'd bet good money she's clenching her thighs under the table. *Fuck.* If I keep thinking like this, *I'm* the one who isn't going to be able to get up.

Without a response, she returns to her dinner, flicking her hair over her shoulder. The action only makes me harder, and I clench my jaw, straining to hear the conversation at their table—an offhand comment about how polite I am for helping her. My muscles loosen at the compliment, and I try to smother my grin as I focus my attention on my parents. Dad's asking what I was so busy with at lunch yesterday that I couldn't spend a few hours with them before their virtual meeting with their gallery in New York.

Rory. It was Rory I couldn't tear myself from.

"I was getting my tan on," I shrug easily. "You don't get this kind of coloring from sitting indoors." It sounds more like a jab than I intended, and I wince. Business for my parents doesn't take time off, and I'm grateful to have someone to occupy my time with while they work.

"How about I book us some time at the golf course this week?" He asks. I hesitate for a split second, not long enough for him to notice. I planned on going to the beach to try and catch Rory there again, maybe even give her a good morning orgasm, but the guilt spiderwebbing in my chest at his eager smile has me agreeing. We're only here for a few more days, and I should make the most of my time with my parents before we're back home and they're elbow-deep in work again.

The waitress arrives to take our orders, and as suspected, Dad orders a steak and salad. In the corner of my vision, Rory sips her drink, tracing a spot on the table while her family converses animatedly around her. My chest constricts, and when it's my turn to order, I mumble the same thing as Dad, attention completely focused on the girl at the next table over with somber features. When the waitress collects the menus and disappears, I'm already half-way out of my seat. Rory finds me like a beacon as I abandon my napkin at the table and raise a suggestive brow her way before heading toward the restrooms.

Not even thirty seconds later, she meets me in the hall.

Rory takes my breath away—she always does—but now that I really get a good look at her in this short, floral dress, she's absolutely fucking *stunning*. My heart skips a beat even with the annoyance written on her face as she approaches, but when I open my arms, her features soften and she sinks easily into my embrace.

"You look good enough to eat," I compliment. I can't resist bending to catch a taste of the sun-kissed skin of her shoulder. The familiar smell of her perfume permeates my senses, and I inhale greedily.

Her fingers curl into the fabric of my shirt as I drag my lips up her throat. Rory releases a soft noise when I find the spot that makes her melt, flicking my tongue to taste before I suck gently, making sure not to leave the mark I so badly wish to put there.

"*Stop,*" she whines. Her plea is a growl of frustration, like she's battling her inner self and doesn't want me to stop at all. My chest rumbles with laughter, and she shoves me half-heartedly, blue eyes round as saucers. The desperation in them has my cock straining against my pants. "We are *not* having sex right now."

"Give me one good reason we shouldn't." I trail my touch over her hips to the exposed skin of her thighs, reveling in the way she shudders.

There are a million good reasons we shouldn't fuck in the restaurant bathroom when our families are sitting right outside, but I'm most definitely thinking with my southern head rather than my northern one right now.

"How about the fact that my sisters could walk in at any moment! Or my mom! Or *your* mom!" She jabs a finger into one of the parrots on my shirt, then blinks as if she's just now noticing what I'm wearing. I'd laugh at her confusion if I wasn't actively trying to talk her into receiving a glorious orgasm in the un-glorious bathroom. "That's *four* times as likely that someone we know is going to catch us."

I'm not hearing a no.

"I didn't know you were a math major," I tease, and she zeroes in on me, gaudy shirt forgotten as her gaze narrows. My cock throbs, and I tug her closer in an attempt to both shield my erection and tempt her.

"Shut up, Ace." Rory huffs, bracing her hands on my chest like she's going to push me away. She doesn't, and I take that as a win. "We don't have time for this right now!"

"You're right." I lean in so we're eye-level. I want to hike the skirt of this sinful fucking dress up over her ass and plunge my cock into her. She wants the same, or else she wouldn't have followed me. "We don't have time to bicker, but I'll be fucking damned if I don't get to taste you."

Rory responds so prettily, eyelashes fluttering and lips parting with a mewl of agreement. Her hips roll into mine unconsciously, and we share a groan. I press my forehead to hers, needing to be closer. I've never been so fucking desperate to have someone before, which should scare me, but I'm too caught up in Rory Wilson to notice.

"*Fine*," she all but pants, giving in to her body's demands. I grin victoriously, and she swats me again. "Where are we going?"

"I would sneak into the women's bathroom with you, but it would look better on my end if we get caught and you're in the men's room."

Rory's eyes grow wide. "We're going to get caught?"

A strand of hair has fallen across her cheek, and I brush it away, admiring the innocent shock on her face. Poor Rory's never been fucked in public before; that much is obvious from the redness of her cheeks and the way her heart pounds against my chest. Her gaze flickers nervously, tucking a soft pink lip between her teeth, and I think she likes the thought of potentially getting caught because she rolls to the tips of her toes to brush her hips against mine while her hand snakes between our bodies to rub my thickening erection.

Fuck, the things this girl does to me.

"Just in case, Rory-O," I whisper gruffly, patience gone. Time is running thin, and if we're going to fuck, we need to do it *now,* before either our families become suspicious of our absence.

I drag her into the men's room and thank my lucky stars this is a five-star resort because the bathroom is both nice and clean. The walls are emerald and covered with a floral wallpaper that almost perfectly matches my shirt. I'd cringe, but Rory's mouth is a *very* good distraction.

She tastes like vanilla and sunshine, if sunshine had a taste. I lose myself in her so easily it'd be concerning if I paid it more attention. My body is buzzing, and when she whimpers desperately, nails scratching my scalp in a silent request for more, my cock jumps. I delve my tongue into her mouth, and she meets me just as eagerly.

It's difficult to tear myself away from the dream come true in my arms, even more so when she pouts at the loss, lips red and ready for more. Her eyes are wide and innocent and need lances down my spine. The urge to bend her over the counter and fuck into her so deeply she feels it for days is fervent. I want her in the worst way, with my come leaking from that pretty pussy of hers while she's forced to sit through the rest of her family dinner, where all she can think about is me, feel the imprint of me between her legs.

"One second, beautiful," I reassure with a gentle brush of my thumb across her swollen lip. Rory's tongue darts out to chase the taste, and it's almost impossible to tear myself away to check if we're alone. When I'm sure the coast is clear, I flip the lock on the door. I don't care if someone tries to come in, but there's no way they're getting a front-row show to what I'm about to do to her. "Pull that dress up and take those panties off for me, Rory-O."

She shivers and follows my instructions without complaint. *Fuck*, her obedience is hot, and so is that pretty, pink pussy that appears when she hastily flips her dress up and tugs down her lacy red underwear.

I make quick work of my belt, tossing it on the counter with a clang before impatiently reaching for the button of my pants. Rory watches intently, as ready for this as I am.

Shoving my pants and briefs down my hips, I firmly grip the base of my cock, trying to stave off the orgasm already building from her presence alone.

Goddamn, she's fucking gorgeous.

With a sultry smile, Rory flicks her panties at me. I catch them easily, gripping them firmly in my fist. The silk is soft, and I hope she realizes I won't be returning these any time soon. I stuff them in my pocket for safekeeping. Rory lifts a brow, and I want to fall to my knees right fucking now. "Well, are you just going to stand there or are you—"

She doesn't get the chance to finish because in a single stride, I'm on her. Our mouths fuse desperately, and I swallow the rest of her sentence like the hopeless man I am. Her hair is soft as I weave my fingers between the strands, tightening my grip to guide her into an angle that allows the kiss to deepen. My other hand has a palmful of her ass, squeezing firmly before I give her a firm slap, humming in satisfaction when I'm gifted a moan in response.

A delicious sting trails down my back as Rory claws at me, and I hope she tears right through the gaudy fabric of my shirt. We stumble as I push toward her, the lewd noises of our kisses bouncing off the tiles. I sweep her onto the counter, and she gasps as her thighs touch the cold marble. Her legs find my hips to draw me closer. The head of my cock meets her wetness, and I choke at the warmth, hips unconsciously jerking into her.

"Okay, Rory-O," I appease, reluctantly prying myself away. My hands find her ankles, which I unhook from my waist. An irritated groan slips as I help her down but shifts into a surprised noise as I spin her to face the mirror. With our eyes locked, I gently guide her so she's bent over the counter, on full display for me. I admire the handprint on her ass, working my way to her glistening pussy as I fumble for the condom I've started carrying in my wallet for moments like this.

If we had more time, I'd spend hours exploring her body with my tongue. She's sweeter than any dessert, and she always sounds so good when she's grinding on my face.

She's laser-focused on my dick, and I'm lost to her as I stroke myself. Stepping forward, I slide my tip through her wetness. In return, Rory's lashes flutter in bliss. She's hot and soaked and more than ready for me.

Nipping the shell of her ear draws a needy whine from her that tightens my balls. When those piercing blue eyes slide to mine in the mirror, I ask, voice more ruined than I'd like to admit, "You're going to watch everything I do to you, right, Rory-O?"

Heat floods her gaze, and she bites her lip to smother a groan. My muscles strain as I hold myself back from notching my cock in her pussy and fucking in with abandon. I'm not moving until she answers, no matter how torturous every second that passes is for both of us.

"Yes," she hisses, trying to shove her hips back, fighting for friction.

"Good girl." I smack a sloppy kiss to her cheek that shifts her features from soft and gooey to demanding. Her mouth parts with what I anticipate is a snarky retort, but I'm already lining myself up and plunging into her with a throaty groan. "*Holy shit*," I heave. Rory keens, squirming for more. "So good for me. Right, Rory-O?"

Pulling out to the tip, I admire where we're joined. Rory's hugging my cock perfectly, snug around my girth, and her body sucks me in greedily when I drive forward. *Fuck*, I'm not going to last long, which works in our favor since we're on limited time, anyway.

Her head rolls back with a loud moan of my name that has my hips jerking faster. Her fingers scrabble against the marble countertop for something to cling to, while mine dig into the meat of her hips.

Desperate to have her in every way, I lean in to kiss her. I fuck into her, arousal setting my veins on fire. She makes me fucking crazed, like I'm an addict and she's my drug of choice.

I hush her moans with my mouth the best I can, but my girl is *loud*. Her noises eke between our kisses, echoing through the room. Snagging her plump lip between my teeth, I give a rough tug before soothing the spot with a sweep of my tongue. "You have to keep quiet, Rory-O, and we have to be quick."

"Almost there," she whines in response, circling her hips. Ripping her hand from the counter, her nails find home in the muscle of my ass, urging me faster.

I weasel my hand around her front, fighting the bunched fabric of her dress. My blood surges when I find her braless, nipples so hard they can cut the granite beneath her chest. I pluck the tight bud, body singing with her rasp of encouragement. I'm feral, a man unhinged as I continue thrusting while sliding my free hand between her legs in search of her pussy. She's so wet, and her knees buckle when I circle her clit, reveling in the sight of her wrecked reflection.

The intensity of her icy blue eyes hurtles me toward my orgasm. Keeping a firm hold of her stare, I suck my fingers into my mouth, tasting her. Rory's breath hitches at the lewd moan I release when her sweetness explodes on my tongue. Her pussy tightens, and I almost come on the spot.

"You taste so good, Rory-O." My voice drips with approval.

"Better than dessert?" Her question is seductive, peering up at me beneath long lashes.

I buck into her, grunting as my core draws tight. There is nothing innocent about Rory, not when she's wrapped around my cock like this, about to milk me dry.

"Better than any dessert in existence," I purr, returning my hand to circle her swollen clit. Her back bows with the motion, and her nails bite into the skin of my thigh so hard I'd be surprised if she doesn't draw blood.

I fuck into her with fervor, ravaging her in the middle of the restaurant bathroom.

"*Ace*," Rory cries out, shuddering as she comes. Her pussy is a hot brand I'll never forget, even after this vacation ends.

"*Rory*," I grunt back, on the cusp of oblivion as I continue to work her through her orgasm. Her pussy squeezes me like a vice, and I'm a goner.

Fucking fuck. My vision darkens as I spill into her, still playing with her clit because I like the way she keens and writhes around me. Her legs tremble as she tries to keep herself upright, and her quivering muscles only heighten my release.

My breathing hasn't evened out by the time I pry myself off her. Drawing away is a feat when all I want is scoop her in my arms, and take her to my hotel room where I can clean her up and fuck her all over again, but we have dinners to return to.

Rory peers at me over her shoulder as I tug the condom off. She wears a soft and sated smile that makes my heart do things it shouldn't after only knowing someone for a week. She's gorgeous like this—though she always is—fucked-out, picturesque blue eyes sated and her body limp.

Snagging a few paper towels from the dispenser, I help her clean up, then press a gentle kiss to her lips. It's a promise of another round later, one where I'll take my time with her, let her take whatever she wants from me. I brush her mussed hair back into place and cradle her face, stroking my thumbs across her cheeks. "Meet me tonight." It's not a question. If anything, it's a tender prayer.

"I'll see what I can do." She rolls onto the tips of her toes for a last fleeting kiss. She's gone far too quickly, dropping away, and holding her hand out for the panties I figured she forgot about.

"You'll get them back later, Rory-O, when you meet me," I muse, turning to check myself in the mirror. My hair is intact, but I run my fingers through it anyway, trying to dispel the desperation in my request. *This little fling isn't going to last more than the summer, Ace, and you shouldn't want it to. Cut it the fuck out.*

Rory's jaw drops. "You want me to go back out there like this?" She gestures to her rumpled dress. I bite my lip because her face screams "thoroughly fucked," and I hope none of her family members have caught on to her disappearance. That interrogation would not be fun.

I shrug, stuffing my hands in my pockets, where I fist the lacey underwear. My cock twitches, readying for round two. "If you didn't want me to hold onto them, you shouldn't have given them to me, Rory-O."

Her hip juts, and she crosses her arms over her chest, scoffing. It's paired with a roll of her eyes all in the same motion, and my grin grows. She's too cute for her own good.

"I'm not walking out there with no panties, Ace," she huffs. I wait for her to stomp her foot like the little brat she can be. "It's breezy out!"

My laughter echoes off the tiles. She's adorable, but she's not getting these panties back. Not a fucking chance.

"Maybe the wind will cool you down," I suggest, striding for the door. Rory's hot on my heels, and when I spin to get my last remark in before we return to our tables, she stumbles into me. I smirk into those blazing eyes. "Because you look well and truly fucked right now, and everyone's going to know."

CHAPTER 19
RORY

"I can't believe Ace is the guy you met over the summer," Quinn repeats a week later while I set up for the photographer to arrive.

She's been in a state of shock since The Couch Incident™. And with our families surprising us with an early arrival for parents' weekend, this is the first chance she's had to fully interrogate me.

I confided in my best friend about things with Ace, but never mentioned his name or the fact that he turned out to be our neighbor when we moved into Third Street Apartments.

Quinn's timing for this conversation is shit. I've been an anxious wreck all day, scrambling to prepare my work for Ace's photographer friend. Against the wall is a stack of canvases I keep mindlessly reorganizing in a different order every time I pass by.

I'm more than nervous. Not only because these photos *need* to be perfect before I fall further behind on preparing my portfolio website, but because Ace is tagging along tonight, and I haven't seen him since Quinn walked in on us defiling the couch.

My emotions are also on the fritz because of what Mom had to say when she and Dad were in town to torture me all weekend. The disapproving "are you sure this is what you want to do for the rest of your life?" when I showed them my studio area in the arts building was a knife straight to the chest. Somehow, I managed to grit out a simple "yes" while blinking back white-hot tears, and survived the rest of the weekend by diverting any further conversation to Peep.

Mom's words taunt me as I shove a canvas to the end of the line after just switching it to the front.

Concern was clear in her tone when I showed off my latest piece. It's nowhere near complete, and Mom doesn't understand the process I go through to create my art, how layers upon layers of paint need to be built to construct something beautiful, but her words stung.

I understand she's worried, but I'm *good* at painting. It's my passion, and there is nothing else I'd rather be doing.

I'll prove it to her when I get into this class.

If I can get my website up and running.

"Yeah," I respond, shoving the doubt from my mind. I wish Mom's opinion didn't mean so much, and no matter how hard I try to keep her negativity from affecting me, I'd be lying if I said her words didn't haunt me.

The nervous energy in the room doesn't seem to affect Quinn, who can't get past the fact that I fooled around with Ace. She found out in an awful way, but there is no Ace and me. There was a moment of weakness, a really, *really* hot moment of weakness, and I broke the most important rule I put into place: what happens in Cabo, stays in Cabo. I made it more than clear to Ace that we can be friends, but sex is off the table. At least while I figure things out with Max.

Max. The thought of him alone twists my stomach into

knots. If he knew what I did after how hard he tried to mend our relationship, he'd be both furious and devastated.

With the way Tin Can ended, I may have royally fucked everything up.

When I brought up my concern to Ace once the post-orgasm haze cleared, he'd taken it better than expected. He strongly reiterated that he doesn't do relationships and that the sex that transpired between us was just that: sex. No-strings-attached sex. Instead of relief, hurt nettled my chest, and the coldness in his eyes told me if I did involve emotions in whatever transpired between us, it would be a major waste.

"I can't believe I . . ." Quinn trails off, shuddering violently on her stool at the counter.

As horrible as it must have been seeing Ace on top of me on the couch, a weight has been lifted off my shoulders now that Quinn knows more of the truth. Most of our nights have been filled with extensive details of Ace and me, and I even scrounged up the courage to admit somewhere deep down, there's still a place in my heart for Max.

Quinn was more affronted by that revelation than the entire couch escapade.

Her cheeks are still pink with mortification, as if the thought of the scandal alone is enough to make her blush. Under different circumstances, I would laugh, but with the war she's declared on the boys next door, she must feel betrayed. As her unspoken second in command, I crossed a line by fraternizing with the enemy in a moment of weakness, forcing her into spending the night with Knox at the apart-ment next door after she walked in on Ace and me. Knox is the last person in the world—her words, not mine—she wants to be around.

And yet . . . he somehow convinced her to accept his offer of a ride home that night.

Their bickering didn't penetrate the thin walls, so I'm curious how her evening really ended. I'm too afraid to ask because while a distraction from my own problems would be nice, I've also heard too much complaining about the "tattooed fucker" to last an eternity.

"Talked about his dick?" I supply, body warming at the mere mention of Ace's cock.

"*Complimented* his dick!" A snicker bursts out of me. "*Oh God*," Quinn's hazel eyes widen comically. "I asked you if I could borrow it since you blocked him after your vacation. *Ew*!"

I double over in laughter, stress dissolving for the moment. Leave it to my best friend to help ease the anxious butterflies running rampant in my stomach.

"Yeah, well, I think it's safe to say that's never going to happen," I respond, wiping a tear from the corner of my eye. The image of Quinn and Ace is so ridiculous, especially because her and Knox are so obviously into each other it's incredible neither of them have figured it out yet. Poor Quinn can fight her emotions all she wants, but she's only prolonging the inevitable. Slate and I have bets going for when the realization is going to kick in, and I'm going to be twenty dollars richer within the next few weeks. "Plus, it's not like I haven't thought about Knox the same way," I add, carefully gauging her reaction.

As suspected, my words sober her up. Her nose scrunches in disgust. "Ugh, *no*. He's the worst." A blatant lie because her gaze falls to her lap for a fleeting moment before her mask is back up. I'm sympathetic, but she's holding onto this grudge all on her own, and frankly, I'm surprised she hasn't broken yet. Is arguing their way of flirting with each other? Isn't Quinn exhausted from putting up a constant fight? She's stubborn, but this is next level.

Maybe Knox should take a page out of Ace's book and irritate her incessantly until she finally throws herself at him and lets him bend her over the couch.

I eye the banished sofa in the corner of the living room where I moved it to give the photographer space to work, since Ace mentioned she was bringing her supplies. Quinn declared she's never sitting on it ever again, even when I offered to flip the cushions over.

"So, what does this mean for you and Max?" Quinn asks, switching the focus of the conversation. She swivels on her stool to track my frantic pacing through the apartment. Guilt surges through me, and I wince.

"Ugh." Do we really have to talk about this right now? "I miss what we had together, but . . ."

Quinn finishes my sentence. "But you have feelings for Ace."

I shrug, head buried in my canvases. Hopefully my lack of response conveys how much I don't want to talk about this.

As if a higher power hears my prayer, my phone buzzes, and my stomach twists at the message displayed on my home screen.

MAX

Can we talk?

Irritation flares. Of course, he'd message me while I'm in the middle of something important. It's like he has a nose for these things. He should have reached out sooner about what happened at Tin Can nearly three weeks ago, and all I get is a "can we talk?" No apology, no "hey, how are you" or an "I've been thinking about you"?

"Yes. No. I don't know," I answer distractedly, staring at his message. I flip my phone screen down, trying to banish

Max from my mind with a few controlled breaths. "We can't be anything more than friends."

"Because he's kind of annoying?" Quinn grouses, smiling sheepishly at the side-eye I shoot her. It's no secret she's not Ace's number one fan, but she said she would try, and I'm holding her to that promise, come hell or high water.

"Because I told him we couldn't have sex again," I mumble.

Her brows bend in concern, and perhaps she's rooting for Ace and me the same way I'm rooting for her and Knox. "What? Why not? You don't want to?"

"*Of course,* I want to," I moan, conflicted. With a sigh of defeat, I abandon my ever-changing order of canvases. I consider myself lucky I'm getting pictures of my paintings at all. At this point, I can't be picky. There is still a lot of work to do if I want to apply to the program, like figuring out how to upload the images to my website, and then the struggle of resizing and placing them where I want.

I'll have the chance to fret over the order of my artwork again soon.

I am *so* screwed.

"I don't see the problem." Quinn pops up from her seat just as I slump onto the stool beside her. She rounds the island to the refrigerator and snags a can of soda. Cracking it open, she slides it across the counter like I'm an exhausted cowboy with the weight of the world on my shoulders.

The sugar tastes like heaven on my tongue.

"Ace doesn't do relationships."

Quinn rolls her eyes. "Ro, that's what they all say."

"What do you mean?" I ask skeptically, tracing a divot in the aluminum. Quinn hasn't been in a relationship since junior year of high school, and I use the term relationship loosely because they never made it past second base, so what is she talking about?

"Because it's more socially appropriate for men to say they don't do relationships when they've been hurt than it is for them to express how they really feel," she answers matter-of-factly. I pause with my drink halfway to my mouth, mulling over her explanation.

The memory of Ace admitting he'd had a relationship that deeply scarred him manifests. I'd always assumed with his cocky manner and insistence on the fact we were only hooking up that he'd gone through something traumatic, but everything is beginning to make sense.

My hand falls to the counter in realization. The aluminum clinking against the marble counter mirrors the pang in my chest.

Quinn offers a sympathetic smile. Is this why she won't take a chance on Knox?

Before I can ask, my phone buzzes again. I almost refuse to check, in case it's Max again, but there's a chance it's the photographer, so reluctantly, I flip it over.

My heart jumps into my throat at the contact. Upon accepting Ace's help, I'd been all but forced to unblock his number to set up a date and time to meet. So far, our message exchanges have been sparing, and all business. None of the cheeky, flirtatious banter I expected.

I shove my disappointment away and click into the text chain.

ACE

Be there in ten.

Blunt and to the point, exactly how I expected things to be between Ace and me when I told him we couldn't sleep together again. It's easier to keep myself in check when there's nothing to read into.

I didn't think normalcy would be so painful.

Scrambling from my seat as a fresh wave of nerves crashes over me, I don't bother responding to either message.

"Oh my gosh, they're going to be here in ten minutes and the place is a mess!" The apartment, in fact, isn't a mess. I made sure of that this morning when I cleaned every inch. The stool scrapes loudly on the floor as I shove it under the counter, searching for something else to occupy myself with. Ah-ha! The vase that hasn't held a single flower arrangement since we moved in is off center. I reach for it.

"Wait, they? Ace is coming too?" Quinn eyes me like I'm crazy as I scoot the vase to the side, then shift it back. Maybe I am crazy. Maybe I should have bought some flowers. I'm a terrible host.

"Apparently. And I need you to play buffer for me," I all but beg.

"It didn't look like you needed a buffer with the way he was mauling you on the couch," she grumbles, and my jaw hits the floor so hard it reverberates through my bones.

"*Quinn Stephanie Conroy!*"

Scolding does nothing to wipe the satisfied smirk from her face. A glance at the couch manages to do the job, her face morphing into a grimace.

Quinn slips around the counter, cutting off my pacing by planting her hands on my shoulders. She offers me the same stern look men usually shy away from. I've seen it all my life, so the hard set to her features has no effect on my haywire nerves. Okay, *almost* no effect. "It'll be fine, Rory. You focus on your paintings, and I'll be a supportive roommate and throw myself into the line of fire with Ace if he tries anything."

I would appreciate if she were nicer to Ace, but my brain is fried and I don't have the energy to stop whatever tactics she might use tonight.

I just hope neither of them ruins this photoshoot for me.

"Thank you." I wrap my arms tightly around her. Quinn doesn't hesitate to return the much-needed embrace.

"Should I order some food or something?" I ask when we detangle, flicking through the contents of our cabinets in my head. "I don't think we have any water bottles!"

Quinn stares at me like I've grown a second head. "What? They can't drink from normal glasses now?"

"I don't know!"

"Here." Quinn flings open one of the white cabinets beside the fridge. She grabs a long-necked bottle of—"We have rum. No one will complain about the lack of water if we serve rum and Coke instead."

Rum and Coke? She wants to serve rum and Coke? Is *she* crazy?

The protest on the tip of my tongue is interrupted by knocking. My pulse skyrockets, jitters attacking my limbs once more. "Fuck it. Pour me one," I call, heading for the door. I'm going to need the liquid courage if I'm going to survive Ace's presence. "But make it light. I have to keep my head for this photoshoot."

"Rory!" A familiar voice freezes me on my trek to the Chrysler Art Building early the following week. "Babe, wait up."

Shit.

How long has he been prowling around here searching for me? I was bound to run into Max at some point, but I figured I'd be safe tucked away on my side of campus. He didn't care to learn my course schedule when we were in an actual relationship, so how did he find me? Is his luck that good, or is mine that bad?

"Hey Max," I greet, plastering on a fake smile. He trails me into the grass, and I'm hesitant to accept the hug he opens his arms for. If he notices my apprehension, he doesn't show it.

As badly as I don't want to admit it, as soon as his muscular arms wrap around me and pull me into his chest, I melt.

"You've been avoiding me," he teases, and plants a chapped kiss on my hairline.

He's as handsome as ever. Sandy hair longer since I saw

him last. It curls gently around the band of his VU football snapback. His captivating eyes are narrowed in playful accusation, but suddenly, his words don't seem like much of a joke, and his arms begin to feel like a steel trap clamped around my shoulders.

Clearing my throat, I carefully remove myself from his embrace, putting distance between us. "Not on purpose." It's not a complete lie; I just haven't had the energy to respond to his message. The one that left a sour taste in my mouth. "I've been busy with class and stuff."

"Stuff like Tipsy Canvas?" He questions, referring to the picture I posted online when I went painting and drinking with my friends a few days after our failed date. Digging the toe of my shoe into the grass, I rack my mind, trying to remember exactly what I uploaded, wondering what Max could possibly be so irritated about. Was Ace's hand or Slate's leg accidentally in the photo? Is he annoyed I was having fun with friends of my own instead of him and his?

"Amongst other things," I answer, angling my body toward the art building. I don't find the harsh set to his jaw or the accusation in his eyes very appealing. If anything, it turns me off further. Has he always been so controlling? "Look, Max, I have class right now, but I'll text you later."

Hurt creases his eyebrows and guilt falls heavily on my chest. He came all this way to talk to me when I refused to answer his message. I should at least give him the benefit of the doubt and hear him out.

Max steps in line with me, blocking my path.

"I want a redo," he says earnestly.

Surprise straightens my spine. My head snaps up so quickly pain flares in my neck. He appears genuine, fidgeting with the straps of his backpack.

Those soft eyes have always made me weak. I force my gaze elsewhere.

"A redo?" I echo, unsure.

"Of our date," he explains. "I shouldn't have taken you to Tin Can or invited my friends, and I understand that now. I want a chance to do better. Just Max and Rory, like old times."

Like old times.

I chew my lip, mulling over his admission. Yes, Tin Can is an awful date spot, but I can't blame him for thinking it would make for a great night. We used to spend a lot of weekends there when we were together, and his buddies from the football team and their girlfriends joined more often than not. Tin Can was the place to unwind after a hard practice or daunting game. That hasn't changed.

"Come on, Rory," Max pleads. He grabs my forearm and gives what is supposed to be a reassuring squeeze. I startle at the contact, and he pulls away as if I've burned him, his eyes fixed on me, wounded. "I said I was sorry. You can't hide from me forever."

Frustration stirs like a rake over smoldering coals. He, in fact, did *not* apologize for anything about that awful date.

I can admit I didn't put in the effort to make the most of the night, especially when I allowed Ace to put his hands all over me. The scene would have humiliated anyone in Max's position. If our roles were reversed, seeing him with another girl like that while all my friends were around, I'd have been livid, too.

Carefully, I study my first love. Here he stands, attempting to repair what should never have broke in the first place. My heart twists painfully as my warring emotions rage for round two. Shame and regret. Anger and annoyance.

Heartbreak and love. None of this would be happening if he had never suggested we split in the first place.

"I'm not hiding, Max. I've just been busy," I repeat.

"Too busy to respond to my texts?" He raises a brow, and I'm offended by his doubt. He's probably still used to when he was the center of my universe, when I would jump at the chance to respond to a simple message from him. For fuck's sake, I was in so deep I bailed on my friends more times than I can count. The space we had apart was good for me, and it's taken me longer than I'd like to admit to come to this conclusion. Alone time forced me to rethink the way I treated my family and friends. The break opened my eyes to what I really want and need in a relationship, and I don't ever want to be the person I was when I was with him again.

I'm better than I was before, but is Max?

If he can prove he can support my newfound views on relationships, there might be something worth fighting for, after all.

"Okay," I relent. One more chance. The relief that overcomes Max's features stirs my confidence. "I'll go on a date with you, but no Tin Can."

"No Tin Can." He nods firmly. "You won't regret this, baby. I'll make sure of it."

I hope so.

"I have to get to class before I'm late, so text me when you're available and—"

"Can I have a hug?" With the puppy eyes he flashes me, it's difficult to resist. I lean into his arms, and he wraps me up easily, holding tight as if he's never going to let go. Pleasant memories resurface, and I shut my eyes, focusing on the sound of his thundering heart.

He was nervous to talk to me.

Something inside me flutters at the sentiment.

It isn't the butterflies I get when Ace is around; they're tamer than that. When Ace infiltrates my mind, my heart jackhammers and excitement caffeinates my body. I'm drawn to him like a magnet, and his presence is like basking in a ray of sunshine.

Max's muscles bulge as he gives me a final squeeze, snapping me back into the moment. Remorse bleeds like ice in my veins for my wandering mind.

Ace doesn't do love, and I want to be in love enough to give Max another chance.

Third time's the charm, right?

CHAPTER 21
RORY
CABO

This deal with Ace might be the best idea I've ever had. Not that I'd ever admit it to him.

I get to have sex with one of the hottest men I've ever met. I get an orgasm whenever—and *wherever*—we find the time. *And* I get to show Ace off to Max, who's been living in my messages rent-free, just like I hoped. The photos I posted of Ace's hand on my thigh, the selfie with his arm wrapped around my front with his patchwork tattoos on full display, and on the beach with my salted hair and sun-kissed skin in his hoodie are some of our best works.

And they say revenge isn't sweet. It's so much more than sweet; it's hot and sweaty, skin sticking to skin. It's rough and sexy, teeth against my throat, lips against my jaw. It's hands caressing my body, knees nudging mine apart, and a cock that makes me forget my name.

Things with Ace are fun. We don't ask questions about each other's lives, we post our pictures and get each other off, and we *never* spend the night together. That would be difficult anyway, with our families around. Sneaking around under their noses hasn't always been easy, but we've become creative with our excuses, one of which I happen to be planning right now: devising how I'm going to get out of the bonfire Peep has been berating me about all day.

"Come *on*," my sister whines as she drags me across the lobby by my arm. *Damn, when did she get so strong?* Tonight is Bonfires on the Beach, which is exactly what it sounds like: a multitude of bonfires on the resort's private beach. I'm sure it's great—I heard there will be music and drinks and dancing, right up my alley. The friends my sister met at the pool were raving about the party, but there's something else that's stopping me from jumping at the occasion.

Or rather, someone else.

Aisling is as thrilled as I am, her unimpressed gaze floating around the lobby. Somehow, Peep convinced her to join this evening's excursion. She mentioned something about sisters having to stick together, which is funny because this mentality wasn't a thing every time I've snuck out with lame excuses to see Ace. Not that I'm complaining, it's made my life easier.

I'm surprised my oldest sister isn't in bed already, reading the novel she has tucked under her arm.

Mom and Dad are at a salsa dancing class that's offered in the hotel's event space. When they asked if we wanted to join, I'd used the excuse of the bonfire to get out of dancing, unaware Peep was listening, hence her towing me through the lobby like an excited puppy tugging on a leash.

It's a real shame I'm stuck attending because, conveniently, Ace's parents are also occupied with the salsa class.

My phone buzzes in quick succession, and I use it as an excuse to rip my arm from Peep's grasp with an annoyed, "*I'm coming.*" Hastily, I fish the device from the pocket of my dress. Since Ace's near-feral reaction to the floral one I'd worn at dinner a few nights ago, I've put a lot more thought into my outfits. Anything with a flouncy skirt means easy accessibility and quicker dress time. Plus, the dresses never fail to make Ace horny. I'm really starting to enjoy the way his eyes glow like the bioluminescent waters at night when he catches me in one.

My steps falter to a stop at the names lighting up my screen.

It's like two worlds colliding, seeing Ace's and Max's names stacked on top of each other. My head whirls with comparison: sunburnt kisses and roaming hands versus a longing that hits me so hard it steals the breath from my lungs.

"Ugh, I'm not going to wait for you forever, Ro." Peep's complaint draws me from my inner turmoil.

"I'll meet you there then." I wave her off distractedly. She huffs dramatically and latches onto Aisling instead. They stride from the lobby onto the pool deck, while I collapse on the nearest plush couch.

I stare at the notifications. Ace's is a text, and Max has reached out over social media. He's most likely replying to the photo I posted when Ace and I met up at the beach this morning for another sunrise painting session. The image was of our finished watercolors side-by-side. With the way Ace's hand was angled, it appeared the scorpion inked across his hand was trying to catch the early morning wave I painted.

Curiosity gets the best of me. My heart thuds as I click on Max's notification, pulling up the app. He hasn't sent a direct response to my story, but the message is a tell he's seen it all the same.

MAX

Hey. When r u back in town? We should link up n talk.

Giddiness explodes throughout my body so hard I almost begin kicking my feet like a lovesick fool. This is the message I've been waiting for, and it's finally here.

Hook, line, and fucking sinker.

I won't be back until August when classes start up again, and I chew my lip timidly. Is he willing to wait that long for me?

My phone vibrates again, startling me. I didn't realize how hard I've been clutching the device, my knuckles white. I shake my hand out, and Ace's name appears with a second text.

Stuffing my worry aside, I open the thread.

> ACE
>
> I'll meet you there. We should be able to sneak away, or would you rather I finger-fuck you in the ocean?

I shiver at the idea, scanning over the newest message:

> ACE
>
> I found your sisters but not you. Are you waiting for me to come find you, Rory-O?

My knees turn watery, and I'm thankful I'm sitting.

> Got caught up, be right out.

I respond before returning to Max's DM, re-reading it.

Two weeks ago, my world flipped upside down because of this boy. The thought of spending the summer apart from Max was abhorrent, and I couldn't wrap my head around how he so easily broke things off when days prior, he claimed he loved me more than anything. I miss him, but I must admit, each day that passed was spent examining our relationship. He broke up with me so he wouldn't feel guilty if something happened between him and someone else during summer break.

Ace has been the perfect distraction. He happily agreed to my plot for revenge, and I can't help but wonder if he's in any way living vicariously through me. If someone had presented him with an opportunity to get back at his ex when they split, would he have taken it?

He won't always be here to fill the void. In a few days, our agreement ends, and I'll be on my own again. Sure, I'll be in Seattle with my best friend, but a best friend isn't the same as a boyfriend. Not that Ace is boyfriend material. He's made his stance on relationships more than clear, and his views are perfect because I'm not looking for anything more with him. I want Max, end of story.

Without responding, I tuck my phone into my pocket and head to the bonfire. My sandals slap loudly against the pool deck, but the bass from the music at the edge of the resort drowns out the sound.

When I reach the end of the landing, I kick my shoes off and squish the cool sand between my toes. Bonfires of all sizes litter the beachfront, embers drifting high into the sky to meet the stars. There's a handful of patrons celebrating already, huddled together around the flames, dancing in the shallow waters, and enjoying the balmy night.

Clearly, this event is a big hit for the hotel. I pass a long line for drinks at a tiki-themed pop-up bar. I have no clue where my sisters wandered off to, though if I had any guess, I'd say Aisling is sat in the front of whichever bonfire has the least amount of people with her head tucked in her book. Peep could be anywhere. I'll have to keep an eye out for her if Ace and I plan on staying.

I squeak as strong arms wind around my waist and lift me

off my feet. My sandals fall from my grasp as I grip tightly to the limbs keeping me clutched to a solid, warm body. I'd recognize the tattoos littering his skin anywhere.

My heart jumps into my throat and sticks when the man at my back leans in to whisper, "Did you wear this dress just for me?"

I quiver as his lips caress the shell of my ear. Ace sets me on my feet but doesn't let me go far. I don't want him to with his excitement pressing into the small of my back. Leaning against him, my body lights up as his touch skates up my front to rest a hand around the base of my throat. He doesn't squeeze; his grip is a warm weight that conjures numerous dirty ideas of how this can end.

Heat pulses through my core, and my breathing fractures. My body tingles in all the right places, and to know he's just as affected has me glowing.

"You're just begging for me to bend you over and fuck you in front of all these people, aren't you, Rory-O?"

A noise of pleasure trickles up my throat. I catch it just in time, but my body betrays me, reacting to Ace's growled suggestion. My nipples pebble and my bones turn to mush. My hips press into him, and he hums, pleased with the response. Ace is the only thing holding me upright.

I tilt my head back against his broad chest to peer up at him. His features are bathed in the amber light from the bonfires surrounding us. His gaze is just as hot, blue eyes blazing with arousal. Ace looks good enough to eat, good enough to agree to whatever plans he has in store.

"Yes," I breathe. I reach up, fingers finding his hair. I thread the salty strands between my digits and use the leverage to pull him closer. Ace's breath catches when I brush my mouth against his in a sensual tease, not quite kissing, then releases in a shaky burst when I slowly roll my hips. "All of this is just for you, Ace."

Until our agreement ends.

My stomach swirls until Ace's lips meet mine and everything around us disappears.

Kissing Ace is like standing on the edge of a cliff. He is reassurance and confidence and pleasure in their finest forms, and the tornado of butterflies in my stomach reaches an entirely new level when he twists his tongue around mine. My knees shake, but his hold is firm, like he won't ever let me plunge off the side.

His touch elicits sparks wherever his skin brushes mine. He palms one of my breasts and swallows my eager plea for more, knowing exactly what I want. He continues his path until he's slipping beneath the hem of my dress, hovering right above my aching core.

Twisting in his arms because I can no longer help myself, I plaster myself to his front. My fingers find the tie to his board shorts, fumbling with the strings.

"I think your sisters are coming," he whispers. The words seize my muscles. My heart plummets to the pit of my stomach, and my hands fall from Ace's shorts like he's on fire. With my frantic shove, Ace stumbles away from me. I smooth down the skirt of my dress and hold my breath in anticipation of my sisters' reactions.

My head stays ducked in expectation. Shouts from a fire further up the beach and the pop of logs at our bonfire fill the night with no sign of Aisling's teacher tone or Peep's dramatic gasp.

Peeking up, I find neither sister in sight, but Ace's shoulders are shaking with laughter like I'm the butt of the greatest joke in history.

"You *ass*!" I exclaim. Swatting at him does nothing to

silence his hysterics. Little does he know, his joke has ruined the entire mood, and he won't be getting anything from me tonight.

Okay, maybe if he's really good, I'll let him go down on me, but as of right now, I plan on making his night hell.

I swear, there are tears in Ace's eyes when he ambles closer and very sneakily tries to slide his way under my dress again. I dodge his attempts, crossing my arms over my chest and pinning him with the most unimpressed stare I can muster, ignoring my amusement as he attempts to apologize. *Attempts*, because he's still chuckling over his lame joke.

"I'm sorry, Ro," Ace says, dimples disappearing as he forces his mouth in submission. They don't stay hidden for long. His ocean eyes sparkle with delight, and paired with the endearing boyish smile, I'll accept his apology in two seconds flat. Which is why I turn and stalk toward a different fire.

Ace catches up in two long strides, and dammit, his husky voice does unspeakable things to me. "Are you really sure you want to walk away from me right now, pretty girl?"

A shiver crawls up my spine and—*oh*, I like that tone entirely too much.

Where has *that* nickname been these past few days?

I manage to keep from folding in hopes he continues speaking to me like that. Reaching the biggest campfire, I plop down onto the sand, taking a cursory search for my sisters. Peep laughs with a group of people by one of the tiki bars. She has two leis around her neck, and I wonder if the boy who stands so close their arms brush gave her his.

Aisling is nowhere to be seen. She probably snuck off to the hotel room to finish her book, and I hope that's the case, especially when Ace sits behind me, cradling me between his legs.

"What are you doing?" I ask when he tries to pull me into his body. As much as I'd enjoy relaxing against him, this position is too precarious if my sisters appear. I shift, feet digging in the sand as I prepare to scoot beside him.

"Oh, stop it," he scoffs, wrapping an arm across my front to keep me in place. He plucks the cap from my head like he does every time he's around. I hate when he does that, but damn does he look good in a backwards baseball hat. I duck my head, flattening my disheveled bangs. "There's no one around." Ace catches my hand, halting my tedious movements. "And you look beautiful. Even better without the hat."

"Respectfully, I disagree," I huff. My bangs haven't changed in the week and a half I've been here. It's going to be a hellish summer until they're long enough to style, and until that time comes, I'm wearing the hat.

Ace leans out of my reach and takes my grabby hands as a playful invitation.

"You forget I like when you squirm," he jeers, trying to capture my limbs. I'm confused until I realize I'm all over him, almost sitting right in his lap. "I just wish you were sitting on my cock instead, Rory-O."

My throat dries. I'd very much like that too, but we can't. We're in public, and my sisters could catch us at any moment.

If they weren't around, I might consider it.

I relent, slipping off to sit beside him. It takes a few readjustments to settle due to the arousal dampening my panties. He can have the damn hat; there are more in my suitcase.

We fall into an easy silence. The weather is perfect tonight with a slight chill from the ocean cooling the warmth of my cheeks. Howls of laughter permeate the air, along with crackling logs and crashing waves, serving as the perfect background to the music drifting our way. The sky is full of the moon and dotted with stars, and if I remember correctly, one of the dippers.

Despite our cheerful surroundings, I itch to fill the silence. Ace and I have spent a lot of time together, and I've vehemently put "no personal questions" in the terms of our agreement, but as I admire Ace from my peripheral, relaxed with an easy smile gracing his features, the urge to learn *anything* about him before this vacation ends consumes me.

I want something to remember him by.

I memorize everything I can about Ace because the first thing I'm going to do when I get home is break out my oils and paint the man beside me. The curve of his lips, the straight lines of his jaw and nose. His eyes, the color of choppy waves. My gaze traces the curl of his blond hair around the shell of his ear, where I spot a tattoo I haven't noticed before.

Curiosity gets the best of me. "Is that a diamond behind your ear?"

The corner of Ace's mouth tips into a smirk, catching me breaking my own rules.

"Yeah. I have all the suits tattooed on me."

"Really?"

Ace readjusts, leaning back on a forearm. His head falls back on his shoulders, and he closes his eyes like he's basking in the sun.

I can't complain because the move allows me to admire the length of his body.

"Yep," he says, popping the "p."

"Where are the others?" My gaze skirts down his body like I might be able to catch a glimpse of the ink through his clothes.

Maybe he'll let me undress him so I can find them myself.

Ace's eyes pop open, dragging me in like a riptide. The blue burns with arousal, as if he knows exactly where my mind has wandered off to. My cheeks heat, and I blame it on the campfire. "Rory-O, you've seen them before. Or do you need a reminder? I'd be happy to refresh your memory."

My toes curl in the sand.

Yes, please.

Now that he mentions it, I *do* remember them. I've studied all the ink on his skin, each stroke of black burned into my mind.

Ace lifts his shirt, exposing tight abs. I'm glad I broke my rule for this because now I can ogle his body without shame. "The spade is here," he taps the small shape tattooed over his heart. At my confused face, Ace explains. "It represents wisdom."

He holds up his hand, showing off his ring finger, where the heart symbol lies. "Heart, for obvious reasons. Diamond behind my ear for brilliance," he grins dopily, and a bubbling laugh escapes my chest. "Do you want to reacquaint yourself with the club, Rory-O?" Ace winks, flicking his eyes toward his shorts. Heat surges in my veins. I'm more than familiar with the clover inked beneath the cutting line of his hip.

I've been eager to see it all day.

"Come on, Acey-boy," I decide. Climbing to my feet, I reach down to help him up, his grin widening. "Let's go see if this lucky charm really works."

Ace winks. "It already has."

I try not to think too deeply about that.

CHAPTER 22
ACE

ear Mr. Broden. My mood plummets. I know what the rest of the message is going to say before I continue. I've been receiving the same responses for the past few weeks.

Every email has been a variation of the same fucking thing. *I appreciate the time and effort—you have a unique style and perspective, but I'm currently focusing on artists whose work more closely aligns—I enjoyed reviewing your pieces, however, I believe there are areas for further improvement, yadda, yadda, fucking yadda.*

Because I'm a glutton for punishment, I read on, frustration building with each word. *Thank you for your interest and for sharing your portfolio with me. It was a pleasure to see your approach to your work. At this time, I am not taking on new clients—*

"And that's enough of that." With a heavy sigh, I slam my laptop shut and rub my eyes. Rejection letters never get easier to read, and they're piling up in my inbox.

It's like I'm applying for college all over again, except this is my entire future on the line, and not just a place I'd spend four years studying, partying, and fucking. Except, I don't remember receiving this many nos when deciding where to attend college.

Maybe my advisor was right. Maybe I *should* get my head out of my ass and accept the help my parents have offered me my entire life.

It wouldn't be a hardship to work with them. I love my parents to bits, but there's a nagging in the back of my mind demanding I do something for myself. I'm proud to have the last name Broden, but I don't want to be viewed as the boy that gets everything handed to him on a silver platter.

Mom hassled me day and night from the moment they arrived for parents' weekend. She even went as far as to shout how happy she is from the window of their rental car when they rolled away from my apartment at the end of the trip. They'd forced me to visit Brodie, their newest gallery two hours from Vulcan University. While we walked through the half-renovated space, I endured an hour of Mom pointing out the best placements for my paintings while Dad name-dropped my favorite piece with a proud smile. Meanwhile, all that prattled in my mind was how much of a coward I am for not telling them I'm searching for my own representation.

I am so fucking screwed.

The one thing keeping me from melting into a helpless mess is Rory. Her words ping-pong in my head, calling me brave. My chest warms at the memory, her blue eyes wide and vulnerable, filled with unshed tears as she shared her own struggles.

I never believed a grinch's heart could grow three sizes, but when Rory broke rule number four—no learning about each other's lives—to express her grievances, I swear my heart swelled so much it almost tore through my shirt.

Did she notice the effect her words had when she ripped

my top off following our heart-to-heart? Or did she feel it when she pressed her naked chest against mine?

Everything pales in comparison to Rory. When she left Cabo, I longed for something that compared in the slightest to what we shared.

Unsurprisingly, I found nothing close.

She'd been impossible to replace, no matter how hard I tried. Her phantom touches haunted me. Falling into bed with other women to erase the feeling of her body against mine did nothing to paint over the memories of her laughing, glaring, and orgasming from my mind.

I have *rules* to uphold. She's still seeping into the fissures I thought I sealed shut. Having an infatuation with a beautiful girl who rocked my world isn't catching feelings. I hardly know anything about her besides the noises she makes when she comes, for fuck's sake. None of that could make me fall for someone. It's just lust, and now that Rory's back within reach, my body is excited to be with her again.

The crack she's struck into my soul splits the longer I'm away from her. It's been days since I've seen her, and we live next door to each other, so she must be avoiding me again. She's damn good at it, too.

Or maybe she's been spending all her spare time with her ex.

Fuck, I need to stop overthinking.

I lock away all thoughts of potential art managers, galleries, and girls as I push away from my desk. I need to find something to take my mind off the stressors in my life before they eat me alive, like playing video games or helping Slate with his car or hitting the gym.

Sketchbooks and homework are strewn across my mattress. There's an unfinished painting sitting on my easel, and normally, I'd grab my brushes and paint to distract myself, but I fear if I sit down, blue eyes, brown hair, and freckled cheeks will appear beneath the half-colored tree.

"Why didn't anyone tell me that finding a manager was so difficult?" I complain as I enter the living room, where Slate sits watching TV with rapt attention. I'm beginning to think my parents were lying all these years when they said I was talented. Maybe they paid off the competitions I entered growing up.

I collapse on the couch beside Slate. The black leather squeaks in protest under my weight. A whiff of sour cream and onion chips in my roommate's grasp hits my nose when he shoves his hand in the bag. There are two beers, frosty with condensation dotting the aluminum cans on the coffee table and my mouth waters.

"Dunno, dude," my roommate responds distractedly. He doesn't so much as glance in my direction, attention glued to the rugby game playing loudly on the TV. I wonder if Quinn is aiming her unbridled anger at the right roommate, because the cheering emitting from the TV rivals that of Vulcan's stadium during home games.

And just like that, Rory floods my mind again. Well, not so much her but that douchebag of an ex she has that just so happens to be on the football team.

I've never felt *less* school spirit than I do this year. The only thing that keeps me from spiraling into a full-blown psychosis is that I was the one kissing her the night of the homecoming game, not him.

Take that, sucker.

"You're not worried about finding one?" I ask. As much as I crave chips, I don't attempt reaching for the bag because: the heavens only know where Slate's hands have been—seriously, he once offered me a handful of M&M's and I was rewarded with clay covered chocolate because he hadn't washed his hands after his focus hours. He's not big on sharing and sour cream and onion is only good when it's the real stuff.

The game breaks to a commercial before Slate graces me with his attention. "Nah." He shrugs, leaning forward to swipe one of the beers. He swallows down the drink with a sigh of enjoyment that causes me to eye the distance to the fridge. "Figured I'd ask your mom if she'd take me on. She loves me. And daddy B has all the connects."

I roll my eyes at his blasé attitude. He's always joking around, and I wonder if Slate will ever take anything seriously. We're almost seniors.

A pang of remorse needles me. The list of people wanting to work with my parents is miles long. Am I blowing this out of proportion? Should I hunker down and sign with Mom? I love her dearly. Art has always been the thing that's brought my parents and me together, but it's also been the very thing to keep us apart.

My parents have traveled for work for as long as I can remember. Sure, they were home for birthdays and holidays, and there were times when I was allowed to join their excursions, but sometimes vacations felt more like work than time to spend together. Sometimes, I'd stay with my aunt and uncle, my grandparents, or wander around whatever hotel or resort we stayed at while they met with artists and attended showrooms. If we weren't touring a potential gallery site for Dad, it was Mom on her phone, emailing clients. The trip was never truly Mom, Dad, and me.

Apprehension leaks into my question. I've successfully gained Slate's attention. His hand paused halfway to his mouth, concern threaded in his thick brows. I fight the urge to duck from his gaze. "What if it doesn't work out?"

"If art doesn't work out?"

I nod once. Slate's features soften.

I worry my lip when the game flicks back on and doesn't immediately steal his attention. He's reminiscing about the career he's already lost. Slate was destined to play rugby until an accident on the field left him with a ruined knee and crushed dreams.

"Then I guess I'll go home and work at my dad's shop." He answers like it's so simple, giving up on art if things don't go well and turning to something else. I guess that's who Slate is—a go-with-the-flow guy who has more than one talent to fall back on. Rugby doesn't work out? On to ceramics. Doesn't make it in art? He'll work on cars at his dad's shop back in Hawaii.

Life isn't like that for me. Painting is all I've ever known, and I'm terrified I might lose it if I can't prove myself to managers out there. There is no plan B.

Apparently, Slate has a backup to his backup's backup, because he adds, "And if *that* doesn't work out, I always have nude modeling." He smirks and kicks his feet up onto the coffee table. "Easiest money I ever made."

Damn Slate for making me laugh in the midst of my crisis.

"I'm pretty sure ladies won't be paying to see you nude when you're seventy," I gripe, shoving off the couch. Now that the conversation has turned to a lighter topic, I'm grabbing a beer, hurdling over Slate's legs as I aim for the kitchen.

"Pretty sure they will, Acey," Slate calls from the couch. "By then, science and technology will be so evolved, I'll be my young, dashing self forever."

I sigh into the fridge. Make that multiple beers.

Snagging a can off the shelf, I pop the tab and swallow a sip of the crisp drink before scouring the cabinets for a snack. Apparently, we need to go grocery shopping because all I find is a bag of rock-solid marshmallows I'm not sure microwaving will soften, and an empty box of cereal that was half-full yesterday.

"You're paying for dinner," I grunt when I return to my seat, sans food. I glare at the bag of chips Slate sheepishly offers in apology. "No way, dude. You're the only one with the car capacity for groceries, and you ate the last of the cereal. It's your turn to ante up."

Before he can reply, the front door opens and shuts with a slam. Knox stalks into the apartment like a rain cloud, dressed in all black, face stormy with fury. He doesn't acknowledge us as he crosses in front of the blaring TV to his bedroom, shutting the door tightly behind him.

"What the hell is that all about?"

Slate sighs dramatically. "Tell me about it. I swear, living with the two of you is totally killing our cool factor. It's like I'm the only one ever having fun around here while you two sit on your asses and mope all day. If this is what it's like falling for a girl—" I open my mouth to protest, but Slate isn't having any part of it. He trudges on. "Then I don't want any part of it."

"I'm not falling for anyone," I object a little too quickly. Slate arches a disbelieving eyebrow, and I sink further into the cushions.

"*Right*," he scoffs, raising the volume of his TV when Knox's music begins blasting on the other side of his door. "And I'm not sexy as fuck."

I'm particularly fond of the cyberpunk skyscraper I'm peering into the window of.

Dots of color speckle the building I've painted, rooms holding different moments of my life.

A corridor in a New York City high-rise where I'm eight years old and it's Christmas. Snow falls heavily outside as my cousin and I race down the hall toward the sound of holiday music. It's one of the two Christmases we didn't spend at my family home in Colorado, and it's different and new, but even at the ripe age of eight, something's off.

My teenage bedroom on floor five. Nights I spent staring at my ceiling, fruitlessly trying to work out why the girl I loved cheated on me.

On another level, there's a view of the ocean, reminding me of a summer spent in Cabo with a girl that makes my heart soar. She's hiding her hair with a hat again, and her face is in her hands when I lift it from her head. The room is warm and pastel, the colors of her blushing cheeks mixing with the setting sun. I'd like to spend the rest of my days there.

On the rooftop is an arch of neon light. Plants crawl over the edges of the building, and I'm there, too, staring into the vast night. The darkness is a taunting void. The sky is starless, nothing to wish upon for help to sort through the clouds of confusion that close in. The fate of my future cloys my throat. Confusion swims in my mind, but I manage to push the creeping thoughts away and continue adding strokes of paint to the scene.

My trance is broken by the vibration of my phone.

The world around me rushes in. It's late, or maybe it's so late it's early, with the way the sun peers through my blinds. The stiffness in my back draws a groan from me. Shit, it's been a while since I've been so consumed by a painting I didn't sleep. Pulling all-nighters was the norm for me in high school, especially after she-who-shall-not-be-named did what-shall-not-be-spoken.

Since I started at VU, I more often trade paintbrushes for booze and girls. I rub my eyes, gritty from lack of sleep. My bones protest as I reach for my phone, abandoned at the foot of the bed.

I grunt unhappily at the message.

PAULA

I need you to cover for me for an hour this morning. Running late.

Shit. The time in the corner of the screen has me jumping from my chair. I hiss as my knees pop at the quick adjustment after sitting so long. I'm going to be as late as Paula for my shift at Art Haven if I don't get my ass moving.

Making quick work of my clothes, I exchange my shirt for a fresh tee and sweatpants for jeans. I roll on deodorant as I toe off last night's socks, kicking them at the basket beside my door before gunning for the bathroom.

I do my business, drag a hand through my hair and scrub my teeth before stumbling to the dryer where I pluck out the first two socks I see. One is a crew sock and the other ends at my ankle, but I'm running too late to care.

In an impressive feat, I'm up and out the door in five minutes flat. There's no time to pat myself on the back at my speediness because as soon as I turn from locking the door to make my way down the hall, I trip right into Quinn.

She appears as sleep-deprived as I feel. Her blonde hair is bound messily in a clip, showing off the exhaustion in her hazel eyes. The very ones that spark with fire when she realizes who stands in front of her.

She and Knox would make the perfect pair with their stubborn attitudes and matching frowns.

Quinn and I might be on friendlier terms, but I can tell her walls are still very much up. We haven't encroached on best-friend territory, even though I answered any and all questions she tried to distract me with while Kaye—my photographer friend—and Rory took pictures of her artwork for her website.

I vow right now to have a conversation with Knox about giving up this feud, for all our sakes. If there's one way to make sure I have *any* chance with Rory, having Quinn in my corner will help.

"Hey, is Rory around?" I ask, trying to peer over her shoulder into their apartment. I get an eyeful of a vase with fresh pink flowers on the counter before the door snaps shut.

Quinn is less than impressed with my greeting.

"Good morning to you too, Ace," she says flatly. The lock clicks over, and I wince, remembering how Rory did the same not so long ago.

I try again, ramping up the morning cheer she seems to be seeking. "Good morning, Quinnie." I use the nickname Slate donned for her because I'm not in a cheery mood this morning either, and to be honest, irritating her still fills the petty part of me with joy. I layer my bubblegum enthusiasm with a cheesy grin. "Didn't my day just brighten up in the presence of your smile?"

The corner of her mouth twitches, but her eyes stay locked in a glare. Either way, I take it as a big fat win.

"Come on," I goad. "Let it out. I know you want to smile."

Quinn manages to swallow her amusement. Damn. She's good. I trail her to the elevator, where she presses the call button. Taking this shoddy contraption will guarantee my lateness, but if it means the possibility of finding out if Rory is free, Art Haven can open a few minutes late.

"No. She had an early morning and has an afternoon study session, and then she's finishing up a painting at the studio. I'll let her know you asked for her when she comes home to get ready for her date." We both still at the slip. The elevator doors screech open, but Quinn's feet are glued to the floor, staring at me with wide eyes, like she can't believe she just let out that tidbit of information that has officially ruined my entire morning.

"A date?" I echo, my voice sounding far away, like I've left it in my apartment. My heart gives a painful thud in my chest.

I would never forget having a date with Rory, which means I *don't* have a date with Rory and she's going to be basking in the company of her ex tonight. The boy she pined so hard for the entire summer. The boy she's *in love* with.

My unhappiness must show because Quinn can hardly hold my gaze. If my body wasn't actively trying to revolt over the news, I'd crack a joke. I've never seen her look so guilty.

Of course, Rory's going out with him. It's not like we didn't agree that our fling on her couch was anything other than casual sex. We're not together, so why is there a crushing weight pressing down on my shoulders from knowing she's going out with someone who isn't me tonight?

"Yeah. I'm sorry, Ace," Quinn apologizes. She sticks a hand out to stop the elevator doors from rolling shut, and I have to admit, she has some balls because no one would willingly put any of their limbs anywhere near those doors.

I force a shrug and try to tamp down the way my heart seems to be crawling up my throat. "No need to be sorry. She can do what she wants." I take a step toward the stairs because I have a sudden urge to move. Quinn calls my name as I shoulder my way through the stairwell door. I pause, voice echoing as I call back. "I'm late for work, so I'll see you later. Need anything from Art Haven?"

Her features are soft and sympathetic, and I'd be freaked out over how *human* she seems in this moment, but my mind has fallen into a tailspin. She doesn't need to feel bad about how disappointed I am that Rory will officially be back with her boyfriend any day now. I'm Ace Broden, and I don't do relationships. Rory does. That's how things have always been between us. How they always will be.

"No. Thanks, though," Quinn answers. Something flashes across her features, but I'm in the stairwell before she can question it. I wonder if she's come to the same conclusion about Rory and me that I have about her and Knox.

I don't stick around to find out.

CHAPTER 23
RORY

"Wow," I breathe, awed by our surroundings. "Max, this is . . . beautiful."

I'm thoroughly impressed. Max kept his word when he said he would put more effort into this relationship because this date is completely opposite of Tin Can. We're at one of the fanciest restaurants in Hardwich, the kind with white tablecloths and no prices on the menu and so many pieces of cutlery I feel inadequate. The lighting is hardly lighting at all. The only glow comes from a votive set beside a vase with a single rose in the center of the table. It's so dark I can hardly see Max's beaming smile across from me.

Right off the bat, the restaurant's RRR score is off the charts.

I swallow the pebble of guilt in the back of my throat with the sparkling water the waitress pours me.

Max doesn't have a good track record with choosing locations for dates, and in the beginning of our relationship, that didn't matter. Spending time with him in any capacity was all I cared about, no matter where we were.

The breakup has allowed me to rethink what I want in a relationship. What I deserve.

"I'm glad you like it," he grins triumphantly. I can't help but return the sentiment, basking in his eager energy. He's handsome in his button-down and dark slacks. I'm so used to seeing him in sweats or repping college gear around campus I've forgotten how well he cleans up. The linen fabric of his shirt accentuates his broad shoulders and muscular arms.

His hair is brushed and his eyes sparkle as he gazes across the table at me. I place the crimson napkin in my lap to busy myself. I shift in my seat under the intensity of his stare.

A thread of unease tugs at the pit of my stomach, keeping me from being fully present. And not in the *oh my god*, butterflies in the tummy kind of way. The knots are more of a *holy shit what am I doing* kind of feeling.

I haven't been able to stop overthinking how the night will play out all day. Every time my mind wandered through outcomes, I imagined what a date with Ace would be like instead. Would he pick me up with a bouquet of flowers? Offer me an arm while walking me to the elevator? Would he open the car door and pull out my chair? Both of which Max has failed to do.

I don't *need* a man to do any of those things for me. It's more so the fact that those courtesies wouldn't take a second thought from Ace that makes him even sexier.

"Ro?" The call of my name snaps me from my thoughts. Max's brows are creased in question, and perhaps the darkness of the restaurant is a good thing, obscuring the color of my cheeks from being caught thinking about another man.

"Sorry." I take a careful sip of water to wet my throat. It bubbles as it goes down, and I bask in the coolness washing over me. I forcibly relax the muscles of my thighs that always coil whenever my mind drifts to Ace. "What were you saying?"

"I asked if you knew what you wanted to eat?"

I frown. Did he miss the part where I haven't picked up the menu?

When Max fails at discreetly checking his phone, his sudden rush makes sense.

"Why? Am I keeping you from something?" I can't help but blurt. Arguing is the last thing I want tonight, but this is the second date we've had where he's been more interested in something other than me. Annoyance bubbles like the sparkling water in my glass. It's becoming apparent I will always be number two in Max's life, which begs the question: why is he trying so hard to get back with me in the first place?

As annoying as he might be, I'm not as upset as I would have been when we were together. Back then, the action would've been completely overlooked. Maybe we both changed over the summer. Maybe we don't fit together like I once thought.

Maybe I'm too stuck on someone else.

A deep sigh grinds in my ears as Max stuffs his phone in his pocket. "Please, Ro, let's not start with this. We're at a nice restaurant. Can we try and have a pleasant dinner?"

It's difficult to keep my features neutral. I had every intention of having a pleasant dinner, but now I'm suspicious. What is conflicting with our date tonight? Why bother making plans in the first place?

Despite the tidal wave of hysterical laughter threatening to crawl up my throat, I don't want this night to end in gunfire. I peer into the yellow-green eyes I once wished my future children would have, searching for an ounce of fault, and come up empty. Max stares right back, almost daring me to continue. To salvage what sliver of peace we still have, I force the fight from my shoulders and drop my gaze to the menu.

Suddenly, I'm no longer hungry.

"I'm sorry." It pains me to say. The desire to slip into the bathroom or sneak out the back door is heavy but abandoning him after we've worked so hard to find our way back to each other this semester keeps me in my seat.

"I'm sorry, too." Max reaches across the table for my hand. The cuff of his shirt slides up, revealing a woven bracelet around his wrist. It's mighty similar to the one he gifted me at the beginning of the semester—the ugly one I've never worn, not that he's seemed to notice—and I can't help but speculate whether he used the same line on whoever gifted this to him as he said to me. That when he comes back into town after the school year, they can pick up where they left off?

As I place my hand in his, a red flag waves wildly in my mind, screaming at me to get away from the danger. This is all wrong. Max's hands, rough from training and years spent playing football. His grip isn't reassuring, but dominating, nothing like the way Ace's hands feel on me, gentle and teasing. He's a comfort, while Max has the opposite effect.

What the hell am I doing here?

"It's just . . ." Max starts, and my stomach rolls. "You make me crazy, Ro."

He's awfully good at making insults sound like compliments, but his words hit me like a truck. The time apart has opened my eyes to the way he speaks. The things I once found endearing, I now receive differently. It's always *my* fault. *"You make me crazy," "that never happened," "you're overreacting."*

I've been blaming myself for our failed relationship all this time, and now I'm finished making excuses for him.

I could stand up, toss my water in his face, and stalk out the door with what little pride I have left, but I stay put. I don't want to cause a scene, lest Max grow more upset. So, as I've done many times before, I sit in my seat and take whatever warped words he has to offer.

"I don't mean to make you crazy, Max," I reply demurely, exactly how he likes. My skin is crawling where our hands connect, and all I want is to break the contact, take my phone out of my purse, and ask Ace if he'll come pick me up.

He'd drop everything in a heartbeat to meet me because he's a good man. If he knew how uncomfortable I am, he'd be here as quickly as possible. My heart thumps at the thought alone.

And all I've done this semester is reinforce our rules, reminding him how we were nothing more than a hookup when I wish we could've been so much more.

The worst part is, Ace is so adamant that he doesn't do love. He's not looking for a long-term relationship. He doesn't trust anyone after what happened to him, but that was years ago, and I haven't made a good case for myself with flaunting Max all this time. I regret parading around in front of Ace even more than trying to reconstruct my relationship with my ex.

I don't care anymore. I want any part of Ace's heart he's willing to give me, even if it's only in the form of incredible sex.

"Let's start over, okay?" Max says, squeezing my hand. Maybe he thinks it's reassuring. Maybe it's a warning. I try not to recoil. "I want this night to be perfect."

"Yeah." I force a smile. "Me too."

I use the excuse of picking up my menu to tear my hand

away. I barely pay attention to the words; all I see is *steak* and *lobster* and something with such a fancy name it really is a crime to call it anything other than a Caesar salad.

None of the dishes sound appealing. They aren't soggy sandwiches and chips on the beach. They're not sticky fingers from melted ice cream or chocolate-stained kisses. They're not fruity drinks and red and blue tongues clashing together to make purple.

He's not the boy I want sitting across from me.

If Max were a quieter man, I might be able to pretend I'm alone, but as the date continues, I find my eyes lingering on my fork, the need to jam it into my eardrum strong. No one should legally be allowed to talk this much about themselves.

Max orders for me, and I'd care if I weren't sick to my stomach. It's no surprise he chooses something I wouldn't have ordered. I pretend to listen to Max spout off stats about how the team is faring this year, but I don't absorb the words. I've spent enough time pretending to enjoy the sport.

I hem and haw in all the appropriate places, laugh along to his stories like I haven't heard them a million times, and wish my sparkling water was something stronger to sip on every time he checks his phone.

When the waitress places the check on the table, I almost jump up in glee. Equally as hasty to get back to whatever was on his phone, Max slaps down his card before the billfold even touches the table.

We leave the restaurant hand-in-hand. As grating as this evening is, the food *was* delicious. Definitely a ninety-seven out of ten on the RRR scale. The company of my ex-boyfriend—who might be better off as an ex after all—sits at a three out of ten. A *generous* three out of ten.

"That was nice, wasn't it?" Max asks, guiding me down

the street. I clock the direction change from the path to my apartment as soon as we turn down Main Street.

"Yeah," I agree absently. I'm more focused on where he's taking me. His place? Tin Can again? Since he seemed so eager to be on his phone, I hoped the night would simply end after dinner. "Where are we going?"

"Cutter's hosting a watch party tonight," he says excitedly. He shoots me the very grin I once never argued against. It no longer has its moral melting abilities. "Supposed to be the biggest matchup of the season. I thought we could join."

If my standards weren't already dragging on the sidewalk behind us, they are now. So, that's what he's been not so slyly checking beneath the table. The score of an NFL game.

A wave of exhaustion hits me. I'm not in the mood to hang out with his friends, and I sure as shit don't want to watch football. I've endured enough talk of the sport throughout dinner alone, with the constant info dump of stats and standings flying right over my head. If I never see a brown leather ball in the shape of an egg again, it'll be too soon.

"I don't know." I offer my contemplation to see how he responds. Max frowns, and unease churns the delicious dinner in my stomach. He must think my response is weird since I'd normally placate him and go along with his plans, despite wanting to be alone with him. I'm still seeking alone time now, only without Max. "I'm kind of tired, but you should go, spend some time with your friends."

Max releases a heavy sigh that causes the hair at the nape of my neck to stand. He drops my hand and turns to face me fully, running a hand through his hair in exasperation, like *I'm* the problem here.

"What have I done wrong now, Ro?" He asks, shaking his head in disbelief.

He seems just as upset as when he caught Ace teaching me how to play pool at Tin Can. I've never been wary of Max before, probably because I never realized the nature of our relationship, but right now, with his looming frame, I'm successfully intimidated.

"What do you mean?" I cross my arms over my chest to fight the sudden chill sweeping past my bare legs. It's well and truly autumn now, and the sweater I pulled on over my dress isn't enough to combat his frosty eyes. "I'm tired, Max. I want to go home and—"

"I don't get it." He abruptly cuts me off, drumming his fingers against his legs. "I've waited, Ro. I did all the things I was supposed to do—"

Anger momentarily blinds me, drowning out the rest of his declaration. The things he was *supposed to do*? Like there's a fucking checklist to win me back?

"Oh, like taking me to Tin Can?" I snap, irritation boiling over. I spin on my heel, only to swing back around with another retort. "How romantic, Max. My panties are soaked just thinking about it!"

Every date—or what Max proclaimed a date—we've ever been on suddenly flashes through my mind. The parties at his friends' houses he'd consider a group outing, the lunches we shared between his practices and classes, when I'd trek all the way to the other side of campus to see him for a few minutes. He'd take the bag filled with food, kiss me on the cheek, and claim he had to hurry to class. Old Rory was filled with warmth at the fact that she got to see him at all, even if it was only in ten-second spurts.

Earlier this semester, he finally brought *me* lunch for the first time. I actually thought it was sweet only to uncover a sandwich that wasn't even close to my favorite. He *never* paid attention to the things I enjoyed, what I needed from our relationship. Everything always revolved around *him*, and apparently, it still does.

Well, I'm officially fucking done with that bullshit.

I don't wait for a response, pivoting and trudging down the street. I'm fuming. How dare he think I could ever fall back into his bed so easily after what he did? I'm a fool for wanting this, for wasting my entire summer thinking about the moment he'd ask me to be his again.

Max calls my name. Growls it, almost. His shoes thud loudly against the sidewalk as he bounds after me, but I ignore him. He no longer deserves my attention. Not anymore.

"Rory." I jump when he catches my wrist to stop me. I whirl around and rip my arm away, eyes blazing.

Surprised, Max holds his hands up in surrender. Something akin to fear creeps into his gaze.

"Easy now," he says, like I'm a rabid dog ready to attack. I feel like one, and his explanation only pushes me closer to completely snapping. "You make me insane, Ro, and my mind's a fucking mess when I'm around you. I'm *trying*, and I'm pent up because I haven't gotten any since—" The words die in his throat, but I've already dug my canines in and latched onto his words.

"Since when?" I quirk a brow in mock interest. There's no stab of hurt accompanying the notion of him sleeping with someone else, no spike of insecurity. Of course he spent the summer burying himself in other girls. I'm not completely naïve. It just makes me all the happier that I spent mine with Ace buried inside me.

And that's the difference between Max and me. Women are objects to him, to chase and parade around and use. He had his fun with however many women opened their legs for him. I found Ace and stuck to him like glue because even without our agreement we were both broken and seeking comfort. We needed to find each other in order to begin healing our fractured hearts.

Only I think I took pieces of Ace's heart to fix my own, and I know I gave him some of mine.

It's almost funny, how I'm standing in front of my unhappy ex while thinking about how much I'd rather be with Ace.

Awkward as shit, but still comical.

"Since we broke up?" Max answers, tone wavering. The lie is as clear as the night sky we're arguing under.

Honestly, I don't know how to respond other than to walk away, block his number, and scrub him from my life.

So, that's exactly what I do. I turn and begin a freeing walk home.

"*Ro?*" Max calls. I squeeze my eyes shut against his grating voice. "Hold on!" The slight desperation in his shout almost makes me smile. Almost.

Unless I start running, there won't be any getting rid of Max until he has the last word. Another red flag I completely ignored. "So, I had some sex over the summer," he tries to defend, but I no longer need his excuses, nor do I want a play-by-play of what he chose to do with those girls while I sat heartbroken on the beach. Well, mostly heartbroken. "But they weren't you, Rory. They were *never* you."

His face softens in the way that used to get me to forgive him. Now, I recognize it's another ploy, more tricks and pretty words, making everything seem like it's my fault when it isn't. *He's* the one treating me like I'm Play-Doh, manipulating me into whatever mold he wants me to fit. Quiet. Demure. Arm-candy. Don't have too much fun or be too loud. Don't embarrass him. *He's* the fucking embarrassing one, not me.

"Well, it sure seems like you didn't have any problem falling into bed with someone else afterward, instead of, I don't know, trying to contact me?" I reply angrily.

Max runs a hand through his hair, pulling at the strands. His face is a distraught crimson, and his eyes are stoked flames. He's panicking because I'm not so easily putting my head down this time.

I almost preen, proud of finally sticking up for myself.

"You were with *him* all summer," he spits back. "What would you have wanted me to say?"

"I *wanted* you to say you missed me. I *wanted* you to feel the same way I did seeing you with all those girls. I *never wanted* to break up in the first place, Max!" I laugh hysterically, and I really do feel as crazy as he thinks I am. "Now? Now, I think splitting up was the best thing you ever did for me."

His teeth grind so loudly, I hear it over the chatter of a group passing by. One of the girls eyes me, and I soften enough to reassure her I'm okay with a single glance. Her gaze flickers to Max whose arms are crossed over his chest as he towers over me, but she continues on.

"You can't mean that."

I turn back to my ex. "I do." I really do.

"So, what? This is it, then?" Max deflates. To give him credit where I shouldn't, he *does* sound genuinely hurt by the outcome of tonight. He has only himself to blame, though. He's the one who began digging this canyon between us. The little rope bridge I spent months trying to sling across is officially irreparable. "You strung me along all semester, just to break up with me?"

A wave of fury slams into me so hard I momentarily forget how to breathe.

Max uses my silence to his advantage, stepping into my

path. Apparently, we're about to go in for round three of this verbal spar.

Steeling myself, I tip my chin and set my jaw. My fingers curl into fists. Then, I meet Max's gaze with a furious glare of my own.

"I didn't string you along." Once I get home and can properly replay this moment, I'll pride myself on how calm I sound. Of course, it's a front for the tsunami of anger building inside me. Max better move before I explode. "Three months ago, I thought we could work this out, but like you said, there's someone else."

His face darkens. "*Him.*"

"Him." I agree and fully mean it. I've been wary of the outcome of rekindling my relationship with Max for a while; I just didn't want to face the scary thought of being alone. I've been throwing myself into a doomed relationship because the person I do want to be with doesn't do relationships.

No relationship is worth *this*.

With that admission, I walk away from Max Denton for good.

This time, he doesn't follow. I'm more than thankful, because when I make it down the street and around the corner, my adrenaline comes crashing down.

"Holy shit," I mutter, taking a second to catch my breath against the wall of a building. I can't believe I just did that.

My hands tremble. My chest aches in a good way. I don't ache for what I've lost, because I'm finally free. I stood up for myself, and I'm damn proud. No more sticking my head in the sand to please others, no more downplaying what I deserve.

Max has shown me I deserve real love.

Ace has shown me what real love is, even if neither of us can admit it.

A surge of happiness threatens to lift me into the sky. I can't wait to tell Ace that Max and I are officially over. That we don't have to follow the rules I was so scared to break with him in the first place.

Well, maybe not *all* of them. I quite like rules number seventeen and eighty-seven.

And selfishly, rule number six.

I blush just thinking about our rules and the ways Ace worked around them. My body reacts to the image of his charming smile, his glittering eyes and wicked grin. I shove away from the wall with newfound energy. I want to sprint upstairs and pound on Ace's door until he answers. I want to throw myself into his arms and kiss the daylights out of him. I want to hold him tight and admit everything I've been too scared to face. That maybe he can find it in himself to be in one more relationship because I'd never do anything to hurt him. If Ace gave me his heart, I'd protect it. Nurture it. Love it. Love *him*.

As I reach my block, the door to Third Street Apartments swings open. From this far, the pair that exits doesn't notice my presence. I'm unsure how they could anyway, with how hard they laugh. Time slows, and my excitement bleeds out onto the sidewalk beneath my feet.

Ace. My heart jackknifes at the sound of his happiness, at how freely he offers it. My body lurches toward him on instinct, like we're two magnets in orbit of each other, ready to snap together at any second.

It's the person he's with that has me precariously close to withering into a heap on the sidewalk. Right alongside my heart.

The girl beside him is gorgeous. Under the buttery streetlamps, her long, blonde hair is curled to perfection. She's swallowed in a Vulcan University sweatshirt, one I can only assume is Ace's, her sky-high legs on full display.

Jealousy entwines with the heartache. I'm not sure who she is, but they look good together. Happy. Ace pulls open the door of the rusty red Bronco parked on the curb and offers her a hand to help her climb inside.

She must be another conquest, more than eager to spend the night with him. I wonder if they're going to her place or perhaps the store because he ran out of condoms. Whatever the nature of their nightly excursion is, this serves as a reminder that Ace doesn't do relationships, and I'm a fool for thinking we had a chance at one.

CHAPTER 24
RORY

"Pass me a chocolate," Slate groans, waving flippantly at the bag of candy on the coffee table he's too lazy to sit up and reach for. Unlike Quinn, who vehemently refuses to sit on the sofa post-Couch Indecent™, Slate is sprawled out across the small, navy piece of furniture like it's his own personal bed, beefy limbs strewn over the sides.

"Can't. Move." Quinn answers remorsefully from where she lies on the patterned rug. I can't say my position is any better, because I'm shoved into one cubic foot of space in the corner of the couch trying to avoid Slate's legs. He's spread out like a spider. I can't imagine it's comfortable.

I'm sure if he actually had any of those fancy spider powers, he'd utilize them for little things like that. Reaching for candy on the table. Snagging a beer from the fridge. Helping remove the clothes off whatever girl he brings home that night.

My living room is a full-on pity party. Candy wrappers scattered across the table, where mismatched candles burn as a vigil of sorts. There's a box of tissues that have thankfully, gone unused thus far, and there's a pint of ice cream in the freezer waiting for us to bury our sorrows in as soon as one of us can muster the energy to get up from where we collapsed after learning the devastating news.

"I can't believe they broke off their engagement," Slate sighs again. I think he keeps repeating himself because the gossip hasn't sunk in yet. We're still fully in shock.

"If they can't make it, how the fuck are any of us supposed to?" I complain. My heart thumps a rueful beat in my chest. Our favorite couple from *Love Untouched*, Layla and Jace, who we watched fall in love as soon as their eyes locked on television, have broken off their engagement and entire relationship two months prior to their wedding.

I'd like to believe we're moping because we all have our own problems with love. Quinn and Knox, who every day grow closer to cracking those thick walls they have up. Slate and the way he's been acting lately. He's very good at masking whatever's bothering him, but there's a fissure in his finely crafted pottery.

And me, obviously, with my love life that could have its own show called *Love, Yeah Fucking Right*.

Quinn and I have had the date marked on our calendars since the celebrity couple announced their wedding would be televised. We had a big night planned to celebrate: cocktails and food orders from our favorite restaurants in town. We were going to have popcorn and chocolate, and it was going to be the most perfect watch party for the most perfect couple.

And now we have nothing.

The news has only worsened my week. I've been avoiding Ace like the plague since I saw him with the blonde. Not that he's sought me out, either. They must be having a grand time together.

And great sex, too.

The thought leaves a sour taste in my mouth, and I grimace. I need another chocolate, too.

"You're telling me," Slate grumbles, crossing his arms. His brows are bent, and he's either thinking very hard or practicing levitation on the candy. Selfishly, I hope it's the latter.

"What does that mean?" Quinn heaves herself into a sitting position to scrutinize our neighbor. She seems to have caught on to what I've noticed in regards to Slate. I was going to let his solemn mood go, but my roommate has no such qualms about interrogating our friend.

"Fuck it. I need the ice cream," Slate announces, climbing from the couch. Quinn and I release twin noises of complaint at the poor attempt at distraction.

"No fair!" Quinn whines, snagging a candy to toss at him. Slate catches it with ease, gifting her a wink as he bounds over to our fridge with a saunter that says he owns the place. Swinging the freezer open, he grabs the pint of chocolate brownie ice cream and pops the lid, shouldering the door shut. Silverware clangs as he digs in the drawer for spoons before he returns, slumping back into his spot on the couch. "We're all in this together. We deserve to know!"

Slate rolls his eyes, hacking a spoon into the creamy goodness. The scoop he pulls out is the size of half the carton, and my jaw slackens. Affronted at the missing chunk of ice cream, I lunge for the dessert. I want my share before the chance is gone.

He pouts when I snatch the pint and escape to the carpet with Quinn. We stare eagerly, like children ready for a bedtime story, begging Slate to explain the slip in his normally good-natured mood. If he insists on intruding on girls' nights, rule number one is he has to be emotionally open to gossip.

There I go again with my rules. I cringe, aching as I wonder what retort Ace would have if I were to put that rule into effect.

I'm being a hypocrite. I've been wallowing in bed for days, overthinking my love life. Quinn hasn't questioned why I've been so quiet lately, waiting for me to come to her when I'm good and ready to talk. She found me after my date with Max, our first pint of ice cream in hand, and quietly climbed beneath the plum-colored sheets with me where we watched reruns of some ghost hunting show I accidentally clicked on but was too lazy to change.

"Fine," Slate huffs. "But you can't tell your boyfriends."

"*He's not my boyfriend!*" Quinn and I exclaim simultaneously. Slate arches a brow, fixing each of us with a pointed look. I shrug sheepishly, and Quinn glares, stabbing her spoon in the ice cream.

It's a stalemate. We stare at him and he stares at us. I will not be the one to break first, and I sure as hell know my stubborn roommate won't either. He must read this on our faces because his shoulders droop in defeat. I bite back a winning cheer, and Quinn smothers her smile, offering him the emotional support ice cream.

"It's just . . ." Slate sighs. He avoids our imploring gazes by digging through the carton like he's discovered a new planet inside. Maybe we shouldn't push.

I'm about to say as much when he admits, "I think I like this girl . . ."

Quinn and I release earsplitting squeals of joy that earn us a *very* unimpressed face from Slate. He *never* thinks twice about girls, so this is earth-shattering news.

"Well?" I question, waving impatiently for him to continue. "Go on!"

"I can't believe I'm telling you this," he mutters, handing the carton over before running a distressed hand through his shoulder-length hair. "I haven't even told Knox and Ace yet, for fuck's sake . . ." My heart jumps at the mention of Ace. Before the thoughts can fully form, I push them away and busy myself by shoving a spoonful of ice cream in my mouth. I almost moan at the chunk of gooey brownie I bite into and return my attention to Slate. "I can't stop thinking about her."

Silence fills the apartment as we wait for further explanation.

He stares as if this is some sort of crazy revelation, like he expects us to combust in surprise.

After a few long seconds, where I drag my tongue across my teeth to suck the sugar from them, Quinn prompts, "That's it?"

Slate sighs in exasperation, throwing his hands out wide. "What do you mean, *'that's it?'*" He pitches his tone in a terrible impersonation of my best friend. Quinn scrunches her nose in distaste while I burst into laughter. "This is huge! I haven't given a third thought to a girl in like . . . all of my twenty-one years!" He slumps into the cushions, gesturing for the dessert. We're going to have to make another trip to the store, but for something with more alcohol content this time.

"There's been second thoughts of girls before?" I ask. My question cracks Slate's dramatic flair for as long as it takes for him to smirk and retort with a wise-ass reply.

"Well, some girls are more confident the second time around." He winks. Quinn and I groan in unison. Slate can be too much of a playboy sometimes.

My phone pings with a news alert. I pluck it from where it

lies face down on the coffee table and scan the notification, mouth parting in shock at the headline.

"This breakup is messier than we thought," I say, drawing Quinn and Slate's attention from the interrogation of his mystery girl. He can thank me later with something in the form of cold and alcoholic. They both listen intently as I read. "Apparently, Layla and Jace were seen deep in argument after the reunion of *Love Untouched*. The headline also says something about an elopement, lawyers involved, missing property, *and* alleged cheating rumors." My mind spins with the new information. I eagerly scroll through the story, skimming the words.

"Oh my God! Does it say who's accused of cheating?" Quinn asks, leaning close to peer over my shoulder.

My stomach plummets at the highlighted pull-quote.

"Layla," I murmur in disbelief. "Jace says Layla's been cheating on him for *months*."

I immediately want to call bullshit. We don't know the reality show star personally, but she seems like the sweetest, most badass girl ever. I don't believe for a second she would cheat. She's more of the determined and self-assured type. Layla would have broken up with Jace straight up, not cheated.

There must be more to the story. This has to be clickbait to draw attention to the already hurting couple.

And their hurting fans.

"Shit," Slate says, staring at the coffee table. "I guess life's too short not to be with who you want."

His mumbled epiphany shocks me more than what I just read. My mind shifts from Layla and Jace to Ace and me and how we've been playing this game of cat and mouse all semester. I've been avoiding him, trying to remind myself of why we wouldn't work out. He doesn't do love, and I do. It's simple, and yet it isn't. I swear, the way he looks at me, all tender and soft, doesn't scream hook-ups only. In fact, from what I recall of our Cabo excursions, he never kicked me out of his bed or asked me to leave. That has to mean something, right?

Then again, there was the blonde I caught him with. Was he using her to get his mind off me? If he doesn't do relationships, is she the new flavor of the week? Dread pools in my stomach. Neither option is favorable.

I should tell Ace that Max and I are done for good. I should explain how I'm finally facing the emotions that have only grown for him since summer vacation. How I want to try this with him, if he wants the same. And if he doesn't, we need to stop whatever this is between us because losing Ace would kill me.

It's time I tell Ace how I really feel.

CHAPTER 25
RORY

"I was beginning to think you weren't coming," Ace says when he opens the door. He looks like pure sex in his simple black t-shirt and dark-wash jeans. He smells like sex, too. Not actual sex, but his heady cologne makes my knees weak and core throb. It must be another Pavlovian technique he's perfected because I'm ready to strip and throw myself at him.

His knowing smirk tells me he wouldn't be mad at the outcome, either.

I didn't think my heart could beat any faster, yet here we are. I've been shamefully dodging Ace because I still haven't figured out how I'm going to confess I want more than casual hookups with him.

I want dates, lingering looks, and soft touches. I want to hold his hand as we walk across campus and to kiss him over coffee. I want Ace Broden like I've never wanted anything before.

The only problem is I don't know if he reciprocates. If he's emotionally available enough to return the sentiment.

I've kept busy with coursework and trying to tackle my portfolio website so I can finally attach it to my application. I'm so close to pressing submit I can almost taste it. I even managed to remove the extra Y from my name, so I don't have to go through the grueling process of changing it to Roryy on all my paintings, which I seriously considered. It's unique and would definitely help me stand out against competitors.

I have to forcibly remind myself of the company we're in so I don't grab Ace's hand and lead him down the hall straight to my room. Quinn and Slate both bear witness to the way Ace's ocean eyes leisurely trail me from head to toe, like we have all the time in the world and there isn't a party raging two feet behind him. I hate that I enjoy the publicity of this moment, how he only has eyes for me.

His appreciative stare makes me feel *wanted,* makes me think there's a part of his heart he can give to me.

Slate shoves past Ace with Quinn's hand tucked firmly in his own, more than eager to join the festivities. My roommate appears less than thrilled to attend, but its either join or mope while the music blares through our walls, so she reluctantly follows.

"Sorry, it took some time to decide on whether or not I wanted to show up," I tease. Ace doesn't need to know I jumped off the couch like a giddy teenager at the mere mention of seeing him.

He doesn't believe me in the slightest, but he humors me anyway. "Well, I'm honored you were able to find the time in your busy schedule to join me."

My heart picks up in pace.

Not join the *party.* Join *him.*

"Truly. It was quite tedious rearranging my to-do list." I brush my hair over my shoulder with dramatic flair, giddy my bangs are no longer an issue. They almost reach my chin now, and I can finally pull the strands into a ponytail.

It's the small victories.

Ace answers with a pleased hum. We break out in grins, and he gestures me into the party with a wave.

Ducking inside, I'm instantly swallowed by the crowd. Raucous cheers and laughter tear through the apartment along with a wall-shaking bass I'm shocked Quinn and I didn't notice sooner. We were far too engrossed in the horror movie we chose for our marathon tonight.

Crowd is the wrong term to use to describe the number of partygoers crammed into Ace's apartment. There are people from the windows to the walls, pressed together and flopping around as they grind to the music.

Ace's hand finds the small of my back, and everything else dims. He's warm, and each stroke of his thumb against the fabric of my shirt sends jolts of electricity up my spine. I want him to slip his hand beneath the hem so I can feel his touch on my skin.

I peer at him, but his attention is focused on the crowd as he guides me through the room. People part for him like he's a hot knife gliding through butter. A guy nearly stumbles into me, but Ace plants a palm on his shoulder and shoves him away, all while his other stays firmly—protectively—on me. Arousal coils low in my belly at his warning glare.

I greedily drink in the expanse of Ace's apartment. The lights are shut off, but two mini disco balls on each side of the living room toss orbs of colorful light across the walls. Unlike my apartment, the cabinets in his kitchen are painted black with silver finishes, and the countertop laden with cups and bottles and a smoking ashtray is a dark stone to match.

Ace sure is popular, though I shouldn't be surprised. Guys clap him on the shoulder with passing greetings, compliments on the party, and dibs on being his partner in the next round of beer pong. We maneuver around the counter, straight for the liquor, and more than one fiery glare prickles my neck. When I catch eyes with a pretty brunette with perfect, bouncy curls, a nasty scowl contorts her entire face.

I level her with a scathing glower of my own, jealousy surging through my veins like I've just downed a shot of hundred proof.

He's mine, I evoke into my stare. She rolls her eyes and returns to whispering with her friends.

I try not to preen too noticeably.

"You're quite the social butterfly," I comment when Ace shoulders between two boys who hand out shots of amber liquid to anyone within reach. Their matching bleached hair stands out in the darkness of the apartment. I gasp, stumbling into Ace when one shoves a glass into my hand and the other flicks a lighter over the top, the drink bursting into flames.

Excited cheers mask my squeak of surprise.

"What the fuck?" I'm careful not to let any of the liquor slosh over the sides of the glass, but it's difficult. If someone so much as brushes against me, it'll slip from my grasp.

Ace is quick to come to my rescue. He closes the space between us, steadying me. His body pressed against my back threatens to buckle my knees. It's enough of a distraction from the great ball of fire I hold as far away from my body as I can manage. The bleach-blond boys balk under Ace's glare and attempt to slink into the crowd, a difficult feat because everyone is raring for a flaming shot now.

"It's okay, Ro," Ace reassures calmly. My breath hitches when his fingertips press into my waist while he reaches over my shoulder to confiscate the flaming drink.

I lean into him while he holds the glass before us. My heart keeps its erratic beat when he hooks his chin over my shoulder, and I grasp onto his pant legs, watching intently. I don't get to revel in his closeness because he proceeds to scare the shit out of me by placing a palm over the entirety of the cup, snuffing out its flame.

My nails dig into the meat of his thighs. Over my shoulder, Ace's breath catches. If I could tear my gaze from the scene before me, I'd be able to taste the cinnamon whiskey he's been drinking as it wafts from his parted lips.

Ace would enjoy that too, because when he shifts behind me, the bulge in his pants rubs deliciously against the curve of my ass.

I bite my lip to stifle the noise of pleasure creeping up my throat.

I want him. *Badly*.

With the flame completely out, Ace uncovers the glass. His hand comes to a rest at my jaw, and my nipples tighten as he tilts my head back until I'm resting against his chest, staring up at him.

His eyes burn the same hue as the flames he put out. He devours me like I'll disappear at any moment, and the only way that will happen is because I'm two seconds away from melting into a puddle under his heady gaze.

Ace dusts a finger across my lower lip, and it pops open for him like magic. I'd be embarrassed if his cock wasn't hard at my back. Electricity shoots directly to my core, and whatever is happening is much too intimate to be standing smack dab in the center of the kitchen.

"Good girl," Ace praises softly. Slowly, he delivers the glass to my mouth and tips the liquid in.

I choke in surprise but swallow the liquor, all the while keeping our gazes locked. With the way his eyes flare with lust, Ace likes it too. I hope he acts on his arousal soon, because at some point tonight I plan on admitting what's been on my mind all week. Maybe after we reacquaint ourselves with each other's bodies, get an orgasm or two in, because if this is the last time I'm able to be with him before putting my heart on the line, I'm going to make the most of Ace's tan, naked body in bed.

I arch against him, partly to tease, partly to get the point across that I'd much rather be in his room than eye-fucking each other in his kitchen.

"Hey! Get a room!" A pitchy voice shatters the moment. Ace's grip tightens a fraction around my neck, and holy shit, I almost sink to my knees right here.

That is, until I rip my attention from the gorgeous man at my back, following the call. My heart plummets when I realize who the owner is. Every pleasured charge that just fired through my body is extinguished when I recognize the girl Ace escorted from the apartment last weekend in front of me.

Her wicked smirk is painted ruby-red. Her lashes are full and dark, making her blue eyes pop. Her hair is silky and long, and from this close I notice brunette streaks throughout the blonde. Her roots are dark, too, and I wonder if a hair-stylist and makeup artist follow her around 24/7 because she looks professionally maintained.

Insecurity tightens my throat. She's everything I wish I was: confident, flawless, and most importantly, Ace's.

I try to shift away from Ace as she prowls closer, but he wraps a solid arm around my waist, firmly keeping me in place. I peer around in search of my best friend, and pray she will interrupt. There are too many people crowding the kitchen to see her. I'm on my own.

"You're one to talk, Mandy," Ace scoffs in amusement. His thumb shifts beneath the hem of my shirt, and my brain all but short-circuits at the jolt of electricity blooming beneath his touch. Heat lances through my body, skin tightening over my bones. I relax into him on instinct, allowing the rumble of his chest to soothe my taut muscles.

The girl's—Mandy—laugh is a song. Melodic and sultry, like a siren, matching the rest of her perfectly. Bitterness unfolds in my stomach as she swats Ace playfully, and I'm unable to check my glare. At least I don't bare my teeth at her like I want to. Small wins.

Mandy misses my scathing scowl, which is a shame, really. She's too busy pulling three Solo cups off a stack on the counter, mixing drinks like she does it for a living. She flips a bottle with a flare that stops a burly boy in his tracks. Mandy winks, and he grins like she just lifted up her shirt and showed him her goods.

The boy leans closer, inviting her to converse. My shoulders drop their fight when she accepts and eyes him when he turns to pour them each a shot. Mandy shoves two cups in our direction and brushes us off with a quick "see you later."

I take a sip of the drink and blink in surprise. I can hardly taste the alcohol, which I've learned from many days spent drinking in Cabo, always spells disaster. It's now or never. Mandy's presence has fueled me. When Ace turns his attention my way, I ask, "Can we talk somewhere?"

Ace frowns, studying me. I wonder what he's thinking behind those blue eyes, what read I'm giving off. After a moment, he nods, leading me through the apartment.

He shoves open a door and drags me inside. The light flickers on and I squint against the shift in brightness. When my vision adjusts, I'm thankful not to be assaulted by the sight of a couple getting handsy on his bed.

The thick comforter does look mighty fluffy, though.

An easel by the window catches my attention. My jealousy and jitters ebb as I move closer to inspect the unfinished painting. The beginnings of a forest with the last remnants of the day cast deep shadows across the dirt path. A figure hides between the trees, and I strain to make out the creature.

"This is . . ." I breathe in a trance. It's so realistic, I can practically feel the mysterious forest looming all around me. "Incredible." I face Ace, who's watching me nervously, like he's scared I'm about to declare the painting terrible when it's anything but. "Tell me about it."

A faint dusting of a blush spreads across Ace's cheeks, and I melt even more for this boy.

He gestures to the stack of books on the floor beside the easel I didn't notice before. The spine of the novel on top is cracked with love.

Ace swallows, gaze flickering between the artwork and me. "I paint landscapes of the worlds I read about in books."

The tips of his ears are bright red. He has nothing to be embarrassed about. That's one of the most endearing things I've ever heard.

"I love that," I compliment. Ace searches my face like he's going to find a sliver of a lie. He won't. I one-hundred percent mean it. This is beyond adorable. He's so creative. "You captured the trees perfectly. I feel like I'm really there."

He beams. "I know, right?" Drawn by my compliments, he strides closer and tugs me into his chest. I wind my arms around his waist and revel in his comfort. I shut my eyes and inhale his familiar floral yet musky scent.

Ace presses his forehead against mine, his fingers scraping into the hair at my nape. My heart kicks up a notch with excitement. This is exactly where I should be, safe and sound in Ace's hold where nothing and no one can interrupt. I refused to believe it for so long.

Worry sits in the form of a rock in my gut, and I draw away to see his face.

"What's wrong?" He asks, immediately knowing something's up.

I'm not sure I can do this. I don't want to sound jealous when we're not even together. When I don't know if he wants a relationship like I do. He wants to sleep with me. That much is obvious from the thickening length in his pants. I'm flattered he's aroused from me admiring his work, but the thought of him reacting the same to *any* girl who compliments his art curdles my stomach.

"It's okay, Rory-O. It's just me," Ace murmurs, stroking my cheek tenderly. While I contemplate what to say, I burrow closer, soaking up every bit of him. "You can tell me anything."

This is more serious of a moment than I imagined. The party rumbles outside the door, but in his room, its just the roaring of the blood in my veins and the loud brash beat of my heart. My thoughts are so dizzying I can hardly make sense of them.

"Are you sleeping with her?" I blurt.

My brain catches up to my slip quickly, and I'm completely mortified, eyes widening comically. I've never been so jealous of someone before, not even during my relationship with Max. The thought alone of Ace entertaining someone else makes me sick, makes me want to rage. I should be the only one he touches and kisses. He's mine.

Ace's brows knit in confusion. "Am I sleeping with who?"

"That girl," I gesture to the door, suddenly feeling very foolish. "The one in the kitchen."

His puzzled features melt when he registers exactly who I'm talking about. It's how I know I've gravely misunderstood the situation.

And then Ace bursts into a hearty fit of laughter. The kind that humiliates me more than I already am.

I try to shove away from him, but Ace is quicker. He catches my wrists and draws me closer, easily overpowering my attempt to run back down the hall to my apartment. The flex of his muscles almost distracts me, but my mortification is too fresh.

He pins my arms behind my back, and no matter how much I squirm, I'm unable to free myself. Unless I knee him in his pretty dick. I wouldn't enjoy that one bit, although I'm sure it would make the smug grin slide right off his face. I hate that smirk. I hate the conceited gleam in his blue eyes. I hate that I'm so turned on by him.

"That's my cousin," Ace explains simply.

I blink.

"Your cousin," I echo. My mind races a thousand miles a minute, trying to compute his response because it isn't clicking. Mandy is his cousin. His family.

I compare them in my head. Now that I'm taking the time to actually think about it, they have similarly shaped noses. Their eyes are the same shade of cool blue, and they share the same wicked grin.

Shit. I *am* a total fool.

Ace swipes an imaginary tear from the corner of his eye, and my embarrassment fades. My features flatten into an unimpressed mask, but I can't ignore the rush of relief with the news.

"Yeah. I wanted to introduce you to her properly, but I haven't seen you in so long that introductions kind of slipped my mind." His eyes flare with heat, and my body responds so easily, blood boiling. "She was here visiting for the week since her university is on autumn break. She leaves tomorrow."

"Ace!" I exclaim. "You should be spending time with her if it's her last night here!" He releases my hands when I tug, and I plant them on his chest to nudge him hastily toward the door. He lets me, still grinning like I'm the best thing that's ever happened to him. Butterflies flap rampantly in my stomach.

He lets me manhandle him all the way to the door. When I reach for the knob, Ace spins and leans against the wood, crossing his arms in a move that stirs interest between my legs.

"Don't worry about it," he reassures. "I spent the week with her. Besides, I'm pretty sure she already found someone to occupy her time, so interrupting will only ruin both of our nights." Ace draws me nearer until there's no space between us. He leans down to nuzzle the skin of my neck, and almost all of tonight's events fly out of my mind. "You were jealous?"

My features scrunch. Unable to help myself, I wind my fingers in his hair. It's impossible to focus on crafting a response with his teeth scraping my skin. I tug lightly and he groans, flicking his tongue to lick a stripe as he pulls away. Goosebumps explode on my arms.

I swallow harshly and manage to rally a glare. "No, I wasn't."

"You were irate," he teases, eyes glowing with mirth.

"Wrong."

"Furious."

"Never."

"Territorial."

"Not even a little bit."

Ace's smirk is killer. Paired with the hardness in his pants poking me in the stomach, it's safe to say he enjoys my claim on him.

He must notice how I crave him so inherently because his self-righteous smile transforms into a hungry look that tightens my nipples. A charged silence passes between us, his pupils dilating with lust.

There are so many better things we can be doing than bickering. Things that involve less clothing.

We move at the same time. My fingers find the fabric of his shirt, and his hands smooth over the curve of my ass where he grabs a handful. I moan wildly, finally receiving what I've been waiting for.

"*Fuck*," Ace growls when I circle my hips against his. My clit throbs, and I'm desperate for more.

I'm not sure who leans in first. His mouth is on mine, and nothing else matters. Not when he's splitting the seams of my lips with his tongue or when his hands slip beneath the hem of my shirt to cup my breasts.

The air in the room is thick with lust. Our frantic movements are everything I've been missing since the last time I tasted him. Since the summer when I had this every single day. Had *him* every single day.

It didn't take long for Ace to become my vice.

He brushes a thumb across my nipple roughly. I whine into his mouth when he rolls the sensitive nub between his fingers, then tugs just how I like.

His hands are gone too soon, slipping down my torso, burning my body up. Before I can protest the loss, Ace draws my shirt up my body until I take over, ridding myself of the fabric. Thankfully, Ace does the same, stripping and tossing his clothes every which way, not caring where they land. I drink in his long, toned chest like the suddenly parched woman I am.

"What's this?" I question when I notice a new stretch of ink on his shoulder.

"What does it look like?" Ace asks, voice taking on a soft note. Glancing up at him, I catch a nervousness that only confuses me more.

"It's a billiard ball," I whisper, tracing the number scrawled in the center. My heartbeat is loud in my ears. "With the number eighty-seven on it."

He's giving me the look that makes my heart swoop. Like he's admiring his favorite painting, memorizing every inch of me, savoring the moment.

I feel warm.

I feel loved.

Ace smiles fondly. I hardly realize he's corralling me toward the bed until he grasps me by my waist and twists us around, dragging me onto the mattress with him. He takes the brunt of the fall, landing on his back. A breathless laugh slips from my lips as I straddle him, but I can't stop staring at the tattoo. "Do you remember what rule number eighty-seven is, Rory-O?"

Of course I do. I could never forget anything involving Ace Broden.

"Rule number eighty-seven says you can kiss me whenever you want," I recite, awed. He got a tattoo for me.

He got a tattoo for me.

That *has* to mean something, right? He wouldn't do this for just anyone, would he?

He would, I try to rationalize. This is the same guy with playing card suits tattooed on his body for fuck's sake. Who knows what else he'd get a tattoo of if given the chance.

"Exactly." His charming grin causes my body to tighten. He stretches up to kiss me, and I melt. There isn't time for teasing, not when we've been craving each other for this long.

As soon as Ace's fingers curl into the waistband of my jeans, a knock on the door interrupts us.

Ace groans into my neck like a wounded man. I swear, my thighs ease open further in response to the noise. "Do you think they'll go away if we don't answer?"

I hope so, because I can't stand not having you for another second.

Before I can voice the thought, the knocking resumes. It's not a polite sound, either, asking if anyone occupies the room. The knock is brash and loud, a demand to be let in. Whoever it is on the other side, they know we're in here, and they won't leave until they're seen.

The rhythm takes on a frantic pattern the longer it continues. Ace and I exchange silent conversation. He's annoyed, but I'm beginning to worry. His features soften when he picks up on my apprehension, and I slide off his lap, allowing him to slip from the bed. Grumbling under his breath, he strides for the door, adjusting himself in his pants as he goes.

I admire the way his jeans hang low on his hips. I tuck my lip carefully between my teeth and busy myself with searching for my shirt. Scanning the room, I locate the fabric draped over the corner of his easel, and I like the way it looks there. I smile and lift his comforter over myself to hide my bare chest.

Ace's eyes darken when he sees me tucked beneath his sheets. My cheeks burn in response. He looks like he wants to devour me. And I'd let him, if it weren't for the incessant knocking.

"Answer it," I hiss, waving at the door. The faster he answers, the faster we can get back to undressing each other.

Ace smirks and opens the door a crack.

"Knox?" Confusion floods his voice. "What's up? I'm a little . . . busy at the moment."

I hide my grin under the blankets.

I'm not expecting Knox to shoulder his way into the room. At the sudden intrusion, I squeak and pull the sheets tighter.

Knox dives into a meticulous pace across Ace's room like a caged animal. He runs a hand through his dark hair in distress, brows bent tight. I've never seen so much emotion from him, and my spine straightens with alarm.

"*Knox*," Ace warns when he strides a little too close to the bed. "Are you okay? What's going on?"

Ignoring Ace, Knox whirls to face me. "Did you know your roommate is passed out in my bed?"

"What?" I gasp. Immediately, I want to race across the apartment and check on Quinn, no matter how scantily clad I am. If she's hurt, I will bring wrath upon this party without hesitation. That's my best friend. "Is she okay?"

Ace appears at my side with a shirt in hand, scowling at his roommate as he helps me into it, making sure to block Knox's view. The soft material drapes over my body. It smells like him—lavender and spice. I manage to control myself from nuzzling into the fabric and focus on the important matter at hand.

Knox resumes the path he's wearing into the floor. "Think so. She's sleeping."

Ace and I exchange a confused glance. Quinn arrived with me, and last I saw she was trailing Slate into the kitchen for drinks. Did she have too much and stumble into Knox's room by accident?

I pull my phone from my pocket. There aren't any messages from Quinn, but the blinking numbers stun me. Shit. How have I lost track of so much time?

Ace rests a reassuring hand on my knee, and the loss of hours suddenly makes sense.

"And you weren't the one who put her there?" Ace prompts. I shoot him a warning glare because while it's clear we both agree that whatever is going on with Quinn and Knox will eventually reach a boiling point, it's obvious Knox has no idea what Ace means.

He frowns, coming to an abrupt halt. "Why would you think I put her there?"

Ace and I fall silent. The party outside rages on, but in here, it's like a different world. The air is tight with concern and confusion. Trepidation and denial.

Knox is worried about Quinn. He clearly cares for her more than he knows. Perhaps he just needs a little help realizing it.

"Knox." I keep my voice soft, calm like I'm approaching a frightened animal. "You like Quinn, don't you?"

Ace's grip on my leg tightens. Knox's mouth parts, probably to reject my statement. All he manages to get out is an, "I—" then he's spinning on his heel and booking it for the door, ignoring our calls.

The door shuts tightly behind him, plunging the room into silence once more. I didn't expect that to happen.

"Well," Ace sighs from the door, having followed Knox to lock it. He leans against the wall, drinking in the sight of me and heat reignites between my legs. "That was something. Can't believe he didn't figure it out until now."

Yeah, I think, pushing back the blankets in invitation, *if you thought that was a show, wait until you hear what I have to confess.*

CHAPTER 26
ACE

"Then, you click this," I explain, circling the cursor over the save button while glancing at Rory to make sure she's following. Her wide eyes are pinned to the screen with rapt attention. I smother a smile. "And it saves the progress we made."

Her nose wrinkles cutely, and I'm a second away from leaning down and planting my lips on hers when she replies, unimpressed, "That's it?"

I blink. Was she expecting something more? "Uh, yeah?"

She sighs, throwing her hands up in defeat. I dodge to avoid a wayward hand whacking me in the face and immediately move back into her side as soon as she relaxes against the foot of the couch. "Well, I could have done that!"

I can't help it. The way she glares at the computer is adorable. I sling an arm over her shoulder and plant a kiss on her cheek. When she angles her head for more, my heart skips. I grant her wish without a second thought. Rory melts into me, the kiss distracting her from her portfolio.

Trying to keep myself from falling for Rory was the

dumbest thing I've ever done. She is the light of my day, and just the thought of her brings a smile to my face. When we're together, everything seems right in the world. I've never been so comfortable with someone before, and knowing I could admit my deepest, darkest secrets to Rory and she wouldn't judge me is surreal. That alone should terrify me, yet it doesn't. If anything, it only makes me want her that much *more*.

I'm way the fuck past falling. I have tattoos dedicated to her, for fuck's sake. If that doesn't scream "down bad," I don't know what does. I need to man the fuck up and talk to her, but each time I've tried broaching the subject, the words stick in my throat. After years spent single, dating seems daunting, but the thought of a relationship with Rory eases my anxiety.

The only problem is her asshole ex. It pains me to see Rory so upset over someone who is leagues below her. I need to figure out how to prove that I'm the better man for her.

Thinking back to the party my roommates and I held over the weekend, the beginning of the night had gone perfectly. I only wish I would've gotten the chance to ask why Rory was so jealous of my cousin. If she reacted like that, she must feel similarly about me as I do her, right? Otherwise, she wouldn't have gotten so fired up about the idea of me with someone else.

As unwelcome as Knox's interruption was, I'm glad the impromptu intervention helped him realize his feelings for Quinn.

He stormed out of the room with determination. I was envious of him in that moment, how once it hit him, he was more than ready to do something about it. Nervous as fuck, but committed nonetheless.

"Well, why didn't you?" I chuckle.

"This thing hates me," she grumbles in response, dark brows narrowed as she scrolls down the page, assessing the full experience.

Not to toot my own horn, but the website is perfect. I implemented every change Rory meticulously noted in a bullet-point list in the back of her notebook. The only thing we missed was adding a Creative Director title to her resume with the way she instructed me on how she wanted everything. I was more than happy to follow her charge, especially with the excited noises and pretty smiles she rewarded me with.

Rory slowly maneuvers through each page. The photos of her paintings are professional as fuck, which reminds me I owe Kaye a huge favor for helping out. I paid her, but this is some truly professional work, and she'd definitely have a successful career in photography if she pursues it.

A vibration pulls me from the computer. Sliding my phone from my pocket, I fully expect a message from Slate about dinner or from Knox with an idea for a new tattoo, but it's not a text at all. It's an email from an art manager I recently sent my portfolio to.

My pulse hammers. I gave up expecting a yes after the last two declines I received. I barely notice I'm squeezing Rory tighter until she turns toward me. "What's wrong?"

"I got an email from a manager," I answer, still struck.

Rory immediately gives me her focus, placing a comforting hand on my leg. My heart is probably soaring in my chest, but I'm numb with nerves. With bated breath, I click the email and skim the message.

Good morning, Mr. Broden. I hope my email finds you well—I'd be thrilled to extend an offer—

Holy shit.

I found a manager.

An array of emotions slams into me like a wave: disbelief, guilt, pride, regret, remorse. I'm thrilled I finally found someone willing to give me a chance after sending out so many fucking emails, yet the excitement gutters in the pit of my stomach.

This isn't right.

"Ace? How are you doing?" Rory asks, giving me a gentle squeeze. I'm unable to tear my attention from my phone, or the sick swirling in my stomach. "Are we happy about this?"

"No," I whisper as reality settles like cement in my gut. My voice sounds far away. "No, I'm not."

"That's okay," Rory reassures, rubbing a soothing pattern across my back. This time, I'm the one leaning into her. My mind spins, and I latch onto her free hand to ground myself, intertwining our fingers tightly.

I've spent so much time this semester—and the past few years—adamant about searching for my own manager so as not to be portrayed as the kid who got where he was because of his parents' connections. The process ended with me distancing myself from Mom and Dad, from my dreams, all because I had this notion in my head that I needed to earn something on my own.

It's taken me until this very moment to realize I *do* deserve these things. Working with my parents would be an honor, and here I am, trying to find someone else to help pave my way in the art world? *They're* the ones who have helped me get this far, and signing with someone else would be the biggest slap in the face. There's a reason they're renowned in the art community globally, and it's not because they don't know what they're doing.

A sliver of pride grows when I reread the email. For

finding a manager who wants to work together and believes in my artistic talents outside of my parents. If I had to endure the rigorous process of applying to agents only to realize that the people already in my life are the key to my happiness and success, I commend myself.

My answer has always been my parents.

I drink in the girl at my side. Her pretty blue eyes shine with concern as she allows me time to process. My body warms at the sentiment, and I show her the delight of my decision with a grin. Rory beams, and, fuck, she's so beautiful my heart aches.

I drag our linked fingers to my mouth, brushing my lips across her knuckles. She shivers, and I revel in her reaction to something as simple as a kiss. If we didn't have important matters to attend to right now, I'd defile her on this tiny blue couch all over again.

My confession rears its way up my throat, and I almost admit I've fallen for her right here in the middle of her living room, with Knox's muffled music pulsing through the wall and an awful reality show playing reruns on TV.

I refrain because it isn't the moment, and I can do much better than this.

"You finish up that application." I beam from ear to ear, confident in my decision. Excitement radiates off Rory, and I decide right here to make all my life-changing choices with this girl at my side, and hopefully one day, we'll make these important decisions together. Giddily, I smack a kiss on her forehead and gather my things. She stares at me, cheeks flushed as if she had the same idea about the couch. I force myself to step closer to the door before I forget the very reason I'm leaving at all. "And I'll catch up with you later. I have a call to make."

After a long-awaited conversation with my parents, where I confess I'd been searching for my own representation and made the ultimate decision not to go through with signing, I had to blow off some steam. Tears were shed, not only from Mom. Dad's eyes were red-rimmed, and I'm man enough to admit there wasn't a dry eye on my side of the video call, either. They were so understanding I felt foolish for keeping my worries from them in the first place.

"Dude, you really need to get your head out of your ass," Slate grunts from his spot on the bench, pressing more than I weigh over his head. If his arms give out, I won't be able to save him, and I secretly think he knows this, which is why he refrains from finishing his jibe until he re-racks the bar and sits up. "It's probably starting to stink up there."

Knox snorts from where he's working on his biceps. I shoot him a nasty glare, surprised he's even at the university gym. Perhaps I should be honored he's taking some time off from annoying the shit out of Quinn or brooding in his room to be here with us.

"What the hell are you talking about?" I grumble, removing some of the plates for my turn.

"With Rory-O." Slate rolls his eyes as if the explanation is obvious, but I'm fucking lost. Annoyance sparks at the use of the nickname I coined for her. I'm the only one allowed to call her that, not anyone else. "You know, because you obviously want to be with her."

I frown. Is it that obvious? Of course, it's obvious to me that I want more with Rory, but I didn't realize anyone else picked up on my infatuation with her.

"Dude, fuck off. I'm not listening to any advice *either* of you have to say because *you*—" I point at Slate, "Haven't been in a serious relationship *ever*, and *you*—" I swing around to aim my accusing finger at Knox. "Just figured out you've been into Quinn since she moved in."

They don't react how I expect. I want one of them to bite back, to take a shot at me like they always do. Instead, Knox takes Slate's advice and throws the allegation right back. "And how long have you been in love with Rory?"

I recoil, muscles drawing tight. *Love* and *Ace* do not belong in the same fucking sentence. My heart rate doubles like I just finished sprinting a marathon at full speed and haven't been standing here spotting Slate for his three sets.

Rory's been the first to consistently occupy my thoughts, day and night. And it's not only images of us fucking, either. Oftentimes, I daydream of her smile, the tenor of her laugh, or how she might react to a situation I'm in if she were around. As hard as I've worked to avoid fueling the spark we shared from the moment our eyes caught across the pool, I ended up falling for her, anyway.

It was terrifying coming to the realization that I *am* deserving of love. For so long, I've been envious of my parents' relationship. I had that with someone once, only for her to hurt me beyond repair, or so I thought.

Rory made me realize it's okay to try again. When we met, we were mirrors of each other. Heartbroken. Confused. Hopeless. But there was also that fire, determined to teach us a lesson. She gave her trust to me on so many occasions, and I gave her mine without noticing. She reignited the love I'd been so adamant to extinguish.

My lungs seize, then crumple in the bottom of my chest at the reason she handed me her trust to begin with: because she wanted to make her ex-boyfriend so jealous he'd realize what he lost.

He doesn't treat her like she deserves. I bore witness to that at Tin Can, watched how he ignored her in favor of his friends. How he brushed her off as if she were some sort of football fan. How he spoke to her like he fucking owned her.

Rory is like the finest of paintings. She needs someone who appreciates her. I want to admire her like she's the most beautiful painting in the room, in the world. To care for her until I'm no longer able—

Holy shit, I'm in love with Rory Wilson.

And, because I, Ace Broden, can't seem to fall for a girl who actually wants me, am totally and completely screwed, because Rory has made it perfectly clear she wants another man.

And exactly like my last relationship, he isn't me.

My stomach revolts. *This* . . . this is why I don't fucking do love.

If there's anyone I can open up to about my warring thoughts, it's my best friends. And while the university's gym is not the ideal place for this conversation, our corner is currently empty, and I can't hold it in any longer.

"Since the first time I laid eyes on her. Over the summer."

Slate's jaw drops in shock. "Summer? You two met over the summer?"

My shoulders slacken with the relief of finally admitting what happened between Rory and me. "Yeah. We met in Cabo. She was on vacation too, and things sort of . . . clicked."

"Why the hell didn't you say anything?" Knox asks, setting down his dumbbells. I raise a brow. Knox is the master of not sharing. He shrugs almost sheepishly, and I hope he can find it in himself to trust us with whatever is going on in his life, too. Slate and I are worried about him.

"We made an agreement not to tell anyone." I explain everything that happened between Rory and me from the beginning. My roommates listen intently. I keep the finer details of our relationship, like our sexcapades and how she's pining after her ex, to myself, and I make it to the part of our story where we met for the first time back on campus when a sultry voice interrupts us.

"Excuse me," the girl says, drawing our attention. She stands a few feet away, twirling a strand of caramel hair where it's loose from her ponytail. She bats her eyelashes, and in the past I would've taken a longer glance, but she's not Rory. "Are you using those?"

She points to the weights we're clearly not using on the rack behind us.

Slate openly ogles her. Knox has been glaring since the second she broke up our conversation, but she either doesn't notice the scathing look or doesn't care. I busy myself by untying and retying my shoe.

"No, help yourself," Slate answers.

"Thanks." She winks, passing by. She juts her ass out for his viewing pleasure as she reaches for the weights. Slate takes full advantage of her offering, while I silently urge her to move faster.

"Go get her, big dog," I clap Slate on the shoulder when she returns to her friend on a yoga mat beside the stair steppers. They peer over their shoulders at us, quickly turning away when they catch us staring right back. Their giggles carry across the gym. "Don't let us stop you from getting any."

"Never have before," Slate replies easily before lying

back on the bench. I frown, realizing I completely missed my set. My roommate grins wickedly. "Put the weights back on, Acey. I'm going to get one last pump in before I go over there."

I shake my head but follow his request. At least Slate isn't having any trouble with his love life.

Lucky bastard.

"So, what other advice do you need?" He asks with a grunt, pressing the weight to his chest. I linger nearby in case he burns out, but who am I kidding? I'm not going to be of any help. It'd take both Knox and me to lift the bar if he fails. "Anything to do with that girl I heard you with last night?"

"What? I wasn't with a girl last night," I lie. I was *definitely* with a girl last night, and that girl was Rory, but we spent the night at her place because Quinn was busy with something I failed to listen to, immediately distracted when Rory said we had the place to ourselves.

"You weren't? Then who did I hear moaning like a fucking champion?" Slate questions.

The puzzle clicks for us at the same time. If it wasn't me and it wasn't Slate, then it was—

We slowly turn to our other roommate, whose head is ducked and cheeks the slightest shade of pink. "*Knox*?"

"*No.*" I breathe in disbelief. Knox doesn't answer, doesn't even glance in our direction. "Who?"

"Quinn?" Slate asks.

"Not a chance," I refute. There's no way he's moved this quickly. They've already slept together in the time since he barged into my room to interrupt my night with Rory? Knox was in distress, and now he's sitting here trying to smother a self-fucking-satisfied smile twitching the corners of his mouth. "Knox, is it true?"

He peeks at me, jade eyes brimming with happiness. After all this time, after everything he's been through, Knox is finally at peace, and seeing him like this has me yearning for the same.

"Yeah, it is."

CHAPTER 27
RORY

Divine intervention has finally sought its revenge.

Between adding the finishing touches to my application, studying for upcoming exams, and working on my oil portraits, I haven't seen much of Ace, no matter how hard I've tried to run into him.

Okay, that's a lie. I've seen *a lot* of Ace—mostly in the nude, with those big hands trailing the sensitive skin of my body before parting my thighs and diving between them and eating like a man tasting his first bite of food after being lost at sea. Those blue eyes boring into mine with a tidal wave of passion so consuming I couldn't form the words so desperately trying to slip from my soul. I was unable to do anything but wind my fingers into his blond locks and drag his lips to mine.

It's safe to say my mouth has been occupied by better things than confessing my feelings for my neighbor.

But tonight is the night.

The music blasting through the speakers of Iggy's is exactly my taste: a beat to nod my head to and lyrics that have my hips swaying from side to side as I wait. I'm jammed between two stools, elbows planted on the edge of the wooden bar, waving down the first bartender I make eye contact with.

She wipes her hands on a towel and flips it over her shoulder, leaning in for my order. I get a full view down her low-cut tank top and avert my gaze, only to catch the man on the seat beside me staring right down the canyon of her breasts. I grimace and spout off drink orders as quickly as I can. She nods and doesn't deign me nor my neighbor a second glance as she begins crafting the cocktails. Simultaneously, she pours shots of liquor into glasses while reaching under the counter for the beer the woman on my other side has been waiting for, and I'm impressed by the display of multitasking.

"See, I told you I could get drinks faster," I tease when Ace finally gives up his spot farther down the bar in favor of carrying cups. He's delicious in the t-shirt beginning to cling to his chest with the mugginess of the bar. His tattoos are on display, and I get an eyeful of the scorpion on the back of his hand when I hand over a beer.

Downtown Hardwich has been packed to the brim lately with students avoiding studying for tests, just like us. Iggy's is the best bar in town for the ultimate night of not remembering, and everyone seems to be on the same page about one last banging night out before finals begin next week.

Ace rolls his eyes, guiding the way to where our friends have staked a claim in the throng of people. The three of them stand awkwardly—drinkless and shoulder-to-shoulder like they're glued together—and maybe it's because of the unnatural frown plastered on Slate's face tonight.

An hour ago, while the five of us ate at Rhonda's, a diner a few blocks down the road, Slate's evening plummeted at the appearance of the red-headed server who worked our section.

The tension between them was so thick I could've used my spoon to scoop it from the air. The waitress had been all glares, and Slate had been the one thing I'd never seen him before: silent.

He refused to explain why poor Isla had run off so quickly after taking our orders, and I'm beginning to think she might be the girl he confided in Quinn and me about.

Ace's jab about how Slate forgot her name had been a harsh blow for the boy who normally allows jokes to roll off his shoulders like he's made of rubber. The entire table fell into a delicate state for a few long beats at Slate's uncharacteristic brooding. His sharp glare settled on Knox, accusing him of not giving a proper warning she was on shift.

Arms folded over his chest, Slate scowls at the packed bar. Normally, he'd have charmed his way into a table by now, as the serial flirt of our group. His harsh features don't seem to be scaring anyone off as a few girls peer at him over the rims of their glasses, making a show of slurping their drinks through their straws, trying to snare his attention.

He downs the drink I hand him in one go before grumbling something about buying another round. Ace and I share a concerned glance. He sighs and zigzags through the tightening crowd after his roommate. They need to hash it out and make up more than I need to confess my feelings to Ace in the middle of a bar where we can barely hear each other over the music, anyway.

"Let's dance," I suggest to Quinn, doling out a drink to her, then Knox. Their hands are clasped firmly together, and my chest swells with happiness. Finally, after almost an entire semester of petty grudges, she and Knox have finally called a truce. They've done a lot more than that, from what I've heard from my best friend and through the thin walls of our apartment. Not that I'm one to talk. At least now when we all hang out, the scathing glares and uncalled for comments are no longer filled with malice.

The sight of them together makes me yearn. I want to hold Ace's hand like that, grin at him like he's the center of my universe, to have him all to myself. My stomach sours at the possibility of him shutting down as soon as I mention the taboo topic of a relationship.

Brushing the nerves that begin to crop up at the thought, I lead the way deeper into the belly of the crowd. It's difficult to wedge through the horde of people on the dance floor, but with a little elbowing, gentle shoving, and not so apologetic smiles, we find a gap large enough to form a small circle.

The air is muggy, warm with bodies rubbing against me from all sides. All the shouting, chatting, and heavy panting don't help. I slug down my drink faster than normal, the ice-cold drink soothing my rising body temperature. The hair at the nape of my neck clings to my skin as I dance with Quinn, and a stray clump of bang sticks to my cheek. I scrape it from my face with a grimace as the memory of hot summer days and an itchy forehead resurfaces.

Summer always reminds me of Ace. I peer around in search of him, but there are too many people around to get a clear view of the bar. Hopefully, when he and Slate rejoin us, they'll be back to their teasing and cheerful ways.

I'm lost in the thick of a song, dancing against Quinn when the eerie sensation of someone's eyes on me prickles my skin.

Taking a cursory scan, I hope to find Ace's attention latched on me, but the shivers raking down my spine aren't from lust, but of an impending storm ready to crack open the skies.

Then I see him.

"Hey." I try to catch Quinn's attention, clutching her arm

in alarm. I'm half-distracted by the man scouring the dance floor like he's searching for an open player to make a touchdown pass. Those yellow-green eyes lock on mine before I can duck, and my stomach churns at the determined gleam. My pitch rises when Max begins bulldozing our way. "I'll be right back."

"What?" Quinn frowns. "Where are you going?"

"I'll be right back," I insist, all but shoving her into her new boyfriend's arms. She can't see Max. Hell, *I* don't want to see Max, which is why I'm preparing to tell him to leave me the fuck alone before any of my friends notice he's here. "I promise."

My half-empty drink sloshes over the rim and up my arm as I brush between a couple who have seen nothing but the insides of their eyelids all night, and a loner who leers at me when I accidentally bump into him.

Why wouldn't we run into each other again? I was dumb to believe I'd never see him again. We live in the same town and attend the same university. It was always wishful thinking that Max Denton would disappear from my life.

"Rory!" He calls. I'm met with a wall of broad shoulders as he slips in front of me, effectively halting me in my tracks. Muffling my apprehension, I straighten my spine and tilt my chin, staring up at him.

This is far from what I expected to happen following what I hoped was our final conversation. He shouldn't be seeking me out at all. *Max and Rory, together forever*, is *forever* over.

Max's sandy hair is a disheveled mess, his eyes ringed with sleepless circles. He's so unlike the overly confident Max I used to love, and the sight would be jarring if I cared.

He steps closer, and I edge back. Keeping space between us proves difficult when I bump into someone behind me and they respond with a sharp elbow in my direction, warning me away.

Max's brows pull taut, and he attempts infiltrating my space again. I recoil, a bead of sweat spilling down my spine. My foot lands in a puddle of unidentifiable liquid and almost comes out from under me. Luckily, I manage to steady myself by using a couple grinding against each other like it's going out of style. One of the girls peeks over her shoulder. I offer an apologetic smile that goes ignored because her partner cranes her neck around her girlfriend's torso and packs every warning she needs to in her cutting glare. *Yeesh.*

Eagerly, I remove myself from their bubble, shifting out of the massive crowd. "What are you doing here?" I curse myself for prompting conversation. There could be a million reasons why Max is here: celebrating with the team, a night out with friends, and I'm not at all prepared for his honest response.

"I miss you."

I'm pretty sure my jaw is sitting at the bottom of my cup.

Under his intense gaze, I shift from foot to foot. Suddenly, I regret entertaining this ambush.

The urge to glance around for my friends is strong. There's a rock in my throat, and even if I could speak, I have no words. I'm too stunned to respond, and Max takes my silence as an opportunity to continue.

"No, listen, Ro. I know I fucked up, but I should never have broken things off between us to begin with." Once upon a time, this confession would have meant the world to me. The earnest glimmer in his eyes is almost concerning. I've never seen him in such distress. Well, there was that scare his favorite team wouldn't make the playoffs, but I've never seen this sentiment aimed at *me*. Could this be another ploy to turn things around on me? Does he really want me back as badly as he says? "I didn't know how good we had it before the shitshow of a summer happened." He rolls his lip between his teeth, fingers burying in his hair. "You were messing around with some guy to get back at me, and I was hanging out with girls, playing into your little game—"

Fury seizes my body, and I finally find my words.

"*Hold on.*" I raise a hand, putting a stop to his declaration. Surprisingly, Max's jaw snaps shut, his attention fully mine. That response alone is almost odd enough to distract me from the anger boiling my blood. "That's not how it went at all! *You* wanted the break, *you* wanted to see other people, *you* wanted this." Anger fuels me, poking his chest with every offense I shoot off. People are beginning to notice our spat. I catch whispers about how the quarterback of the Vulcan University football team is all but being castrated in the middle of Iggy's dance floor on a Friday night. I can't find it in myself to give a fuck.

"*You* are the one who started with the pictures." Manic laughter bubbles up my throat, but my frustration and betrayal and all-around *hurt* supersede my hysterics. "And sleeping with those girls, too," I tack on, and hate how pained I still sound.

"And *you're* the one who started sleeping with *him*, Rory," Max fires back, and I imagine how pissed he would be to know I'm currently still sleeping with *him*. Before I can turn the thought into fuel for this useless argument, Max's demeanor morphs like a fourth-down switch-up. His face softens, his shoulders drop, and I'm dizzy from the 180. "The time apart has been eating me alive, Ro." And well, he might not be lying about that. He does appear worse for wear. "I haven't been playing to my full potential. I can't stop thinking about you, about us, and—and I love you."

The noisy bar softens to a dull rumble as Max's words

ring in my head. *He's in love with me? What the actual fuck is going on?*

This admission is what I expected to hear the night we split. What I yearned for when I flaunted myself on social media to get his attention. All he needed to do was pick up the phone, tell me breaking up was a mistake, and he loved me.

They're still words I want to hear, just no longer from him.

A million questions roll around my head like an over-stuffed bag of marbles finally exploding. How can he possibly be admitting this right now of all times?

Realization rocks me back on my heels with its strike. Max hadn't been so desperate at the time of our first breakup because he always knew he was going to get me back.

I made my disparity known. I would've done anything for a second chance at our relationship, even agreeing to going our separate ways over the summer. *That's* why he spent the split between other girl's legs—because I was there waiting.

The only thing Max didn't account for was Ace's inter-ference.

And thank goodness for Ace Broden, because if not for him, I would never have realized how low Max set the bar. How poorly he treated me and how much more I deserve. All this coming from a man who doesn't *do* love says something, and it isn't difficult to imagine what Ace would be like if he *did* do love.

"You love me?" I scoff, but Max doesn't seem to hear over the roar of the music. He closes the space between us, and before I can raise my hands to warn him away, he's cupping my cheeks and planting his lips firmly on mine.

My drink slips from my grasp, and I grow rigid. There's an urgency on his lips, and his mouth is pressed so tightly to mine it stings. My consciousness slams into me as his posture regains that confident poise while mine crumbles in disgust. My heart pinches in my chest so fast tears sting my eyes. I don't want this. I don't want his body pressed to mine, pinning me to him like I have no choice in the matter.

Squirming, I manage to wedge my hands between us and push him off. If I hadn't lost my drink from the shock, I'd toss it right in his face.

"What the fuck are you doing?" Adrenaline pounds loudly in my ears, like my very own bass system.

Caught off guard by my response, Max stumbles into a group behind him. One of the guys catches him with a scowl that transforms into awe when he recognizes the star football player in his grasp. Over Max's shoulder, time stands still as I lock eyes with Ace.

"What do you mean? I love you, Rory," Max presses. I barely hear him over the sound of my world imploding.

The pain on Ace's face has my heart disintegrating in my chest. He stares at me as if I've personally taken a blade and plunged it right between his ribs. Which is funny, because I feel like I'm bleeding out, too.

The circle of partiers shoves Max back into me with hoots and hollers of excitement. His wide frame rips my contact with Ace. I raise my hands to stop Max from moving any closer, rolling to the tips of my toes to seek out the boy I'm mad for. My mind races, figuring out how I'm going to get away from Max and go to Ace, who I finally spot stalking for the exit.

"Fuck!" I lunge around my ex, ignoring his calls as I chase Ace with my heart in my throat. This looks bad. I've been flirting with him all night, and the moment he steps away, he returns to Max and me locking lips. Of course, he's betrayed. What Ace doesn't know is I was an unwilling participant. He must think I'm still pining for Max, when in reality, I haven't spoken to him since officially breaking things off. "Ace, wait!"

I force my way through the crowd, not caring if I bump someone too hard or spill their drink or interrupt their dancing. All I care about is not losing Ace this time. My name is called somewhere behind me, but my attention is tunneled on the boy I love, making his way out the door—

The line of eager partygoers waiting to get into the packed bar surely enjoys the sight as I burst out the door, frantically calling Ace's name like the best thing that's ever happened to me is walking straight out of my life. And he might just be.

We probably resemble a rom-com where one of the love interests chases the other in an anguished attempt to right their wrong. My eyes are rimmed with tears, nose prickling with emotion, heart pounding against my ribcage as I tighten the distance between us.

Ace's hands are tucked deeply in his pockets; his head is dipped toward the sidewalk. There's a defeated slant to his shoulders; the heels of his shoes scuff the pavement as he goes.

"Ace, *please*," I beg, latching onto his wrist when I catch up. He stops, but won't meet my eyes, no matter how hard I try to catch his gaze. It's difficult to swallow the emotion clogging my throat. At least he's allowing me to say my piece, but his avoidance cuts deeper. Brushing the sting aside, I take a calming breath when calm is the last thing I'm experiencing right now. My mind is a mess, a flurry of emotions as I stare at the boy who I almost gave up. I won't let him walk out of my life. "It's not what you think. Max, he and I—"

"You don't need to explain, Rory," Ace interrupts softly.

The fact that he doesn't want to hear my explanation isn't the first thought that crosses my mind. He *never* says my full name unless it's something serious. It's always Rory-O, which has grown on me so exponentially that hearing my full name rolling from his lips feels so *wrong*. "This is how it was always going to go." He shakes his head and smiles defeatedly, finally lifting those sad, ocean eyes. His brokenness makes me crumple; pain splintering my soul. My lungs seize, and a hot tear escapes, rolling down my cheek. "I should've blocked your number after the summer ended, just like we agreed."

I shake my head frantically, emotion keeping words from escaping. My fingers dig deeper into his forearm when he tries to pull away. This isn't happening right now. This isn't the end. I won't let it be. We've been through too much to give up now.

"I'm not with Max," I explain vehemently, voice breaking when he shakes his head like he can't bear to hear this again. Well, he's going to, because I'm not giving up on us. I press on. "I broke it off with him weeks ago. What you saw in there," I point back to the club. "*He* kissed *me*. I didn't—" My breath hitches with distress as the memory of what happened only moments ago rekindles. "I didn't want that."

Ace's entire body tightens. His shoulders go rigid, fingers curling into fists, and this time, when he meets my gaze, his features are stony and his eyes are filled with flames of blue fire.

"You didn't want that?" He searches my face with urgency. I nod in confirmation, and the hand he was just using to pry me off him twists around in mine, lacing our fingers together and offering me a reassuring squeeze. He looks like an avenging angel with his gold hair and menacing face. All he's missing is wings and a halo.

I don't know what this means for our relationship, if we're okay, but for now, I'm not letting go.

Ace has a one-track mind, on a warpath not even the bouncer tries to stop. He allows us back inside with a warning stare that says if we continue to make a scene, he's going to kick us out. I duck under his glare, trailing after Ace, who strides across the sticky floor with purpose.

His eyes pin on Max before I can warn him not to do anything stupid. I'm apprehensive about what happened outside, and all I really want is to talk to Ace somewhere private, but he won't be deterred, heading straight for my ex, who nurses a dark-colored drink with a stormy set to his brow.

Max's gaze sweeps right over Ace, not knowing he's the target of the fuming boy at my side. He doesn't know who Ace is, how much of a part he's had to play in us not getting back together. Instead, Max's eyes latch onto me. Surprise flickers across his face, and he straightens from where he leans against the edge of the bar.

"There you are," he greets with a cunning smile, abandoning his drink, like he knew I'd be back. My face twists in disgust and only reinforces my decision to cut ties.

I come to a stop beside Ace, curling my fingers into the back of his shirt as a warning not to do anything crazy, like punch my ex right in his smart fucking mouth for kissing me without consent. He slips an arm around my shoulders in reassurance. He's going to behave for now.

Max finally seems to notice the boy at my side. His gaze trails across the arm draped over me, to his face, where recognition flickers. I've witnessed this many times, like two alpha predators sizing each other up. In a few seconds, one of them will puff their chest or release a warning growl. Max probably has twenty pounds of muscle on Ace, but my boy isn't backing down.

"What's going on, Rory?" Max asks. He doesn't look at me as he speaks, eyes locked firmly on Ace. He jerks his chin. "Who the fuck is this?"

Ace's arm tightens around me as if to say, *watch this*. I brace for the storm, sliding further into his side in a silent show of support. I want Max to get the picture and Ace to get me as far away from him as possible.

"I'm the other guy," Ace answers, all too smugly, and a surge of satisfaction zips through my body. He's already pulling me through the crowd. It's only when Max is no longer in my line of vision that I can take a full breath, relaxing into Ace's side.

It's also now that the effects of what the hell just happened fully settle.

The discomfort of Max's touch drags me under its current. My throat tightens, and it takes all my effort to choke back an uncomfortable noise. Tears brim my eyes without permission, and my nose tingles as I falter. Ace notices my sudden freak out and draws me aside, safely guiding me to an empty spot by the wall while he blocks the crowd, standing in front of me. His hands are a solid comfort on my hips, blue eyes concerned. "Rory? Tell me what's wrong, baby. Are you okay?"

I curl my fingers into the fabric of his shirt and cling to him like a lifeline. My head is swimming. "He just appeared out of nowhere and confessed his love for me. And then—" My throat constricts as I recall how Max gripped my face and planted his mouth on mine like I was going to let him do whatever he wanted. Frozen in shock and helpless in the moment until I gathered the confidence to push him away.

Ace soothes me, brushing away a tear. "I know. I saw," he

says, and I'm sure he's cursing himself for misreading the situation. It's not his fault. He wouldn't have known. "You're shaking, Rory-O."

I all but sigh at the sound of my nickname rolling off his tongue.

"Sorry," I apologize out of habit. Ace frowns deeply, but before he can respond, I clasp his hand and tow him toward where we left our friends. "Will you take me home?"

His touch is grounding, settling the coil in my stomach. There's too much going on in this setting to filter through my rampant thoughts: the pounding music, the bodies brushing along mine, the thought Max might still be in this bar quickens my pace.

When Quinn spots me, concern flickers through her hazel eyes before rage consumes her features, reading me like a book. The sight of her so ready to go to war for me makes my tears thicken, but I manage to hold them back, offering a broken smile as she pushes away from Knox to meet me.

"Ro, what the fuck is going on? Are you okay?" Her gaze flashes to Ace before she peers over my shoulder, trying to pinpoint the cause of my sadness.

I wrap my other arm around her, keeping her from interrogating every patron in the bar until she finds who hurt my feelings. Quinn's like that, stubborn as hell and ready to kick some major ass without asking questions first.

"I'm okay, just ran into a little trouble," I reply, suddenly exhausted. I need this night to end.

I don't have to explain because Quinn knows exactly who I'm talking about, features tightening.

"Where is he?" Her voice takes on a threatening edge. Her eyes are narrowed, and if I didn't have my arm around her, she might slink into the crowd like a hound dog and track Max down. The image brings a small smile to my face.

"Already taken care of, Quinnie," Ace answers smugly. The comment is paired with a reassuring squeeze that has me focusing on his hand in mine. We're going to talk, and soon.

My roommate peers over her shoulder to where she left Knox, as if only now realizing she abandoned him to fight for my honor. Knox stares at Slate, who has rejoined the group, appearing just as grumpy as he did at the diner, glaring into his drink.

I wonder how many he's had.

"We're going home," I announce loudly enough for the group to hear. Slate doesn't acknowledge me, but I know he heard because Knox nods in agreement and steps close enough for his body to flank Quinn's. I'm so happy for them.

My roommate and I share a questioning glance. She shrugs and I shake my head, neither of us having an idea why Slate's acting so unlike himself. Tonight has been much too long for interrogations. I need a scalding hot shower to wash the skin-crawling feeling of Max off me, and I want to collapse in bed and sleep for twelve hours.

"You coming, man?" Ace asks Slate, clapping him on the shoulder. Slate swings his cutting glare from his drink to his roommate, and I'd hate to be on the other side of that look right now.

"No, I don't think I will," Slate answers flatly, shrugging Ace off. His attention catches on something across the bar, but I'm too short to see where his gaze strays. The crowd parts for him as he stalks away, leaving the rest of us more confused than before.

"What's his problem?" I ask, rubbing my aching eyes. Ace strokes the nape of my neck with his thumb, and I lean into him, reveling in his warmth.

Knox answers, watching Slate disappear into the mass. "Not a fucking clue."

CHAPTER 28
ACE
CABO

The sky is picturesque tonight, but it has nothing on the girl tucked into my side.

Rory's head rests against my shoulder, tracing lazy circles across the logo on my sweatshirt. She's lost in her thoughts, her vacant blue eyes cast over the vast waters, and I wonder if she's memorizing this moment like I am, as our time is running out. The breeze of the ocean caresses us, the night chill tickling my leg hair and raising goosebumps on my exposed skin. Neither of us could resist sneaking away from our families one last time.

Conversation has been sparse. A few words shared here and there; bittersweet kisses and unspoken confessions linger in the air. This has been one of the best summers of my life. When I came to Cabo, the last thing I thought I'd find was a girl who drives me wild the way Rory does. She's everything a man could want and more: beautiful, charming, loyal, kind. She's successfully infiltrated my mind, tattooed herself on my brain. It feels like I've known her much longer than a few weeks. It feels like I've known her for a lifetime.

She leaves tomorrow, and I wish I had the fucking balls to tell her not to go.

Not that she'd listen. Rory's a stubborn little thing, and we made an agreement I need to stick to, because I can't hurt her more than she's already been hurt by that douchebag ex of hers. She got what she wanted from our playing around anyway, if the constant buzzing of her phone and her hidden smiles prove anything. Her quick glances in my direction paired with the nervous biting of her lip gave her away.

We had fun this summer. That's all this was, I try to convince myself. Some innate part of me wants her to stay because I'm here for another week, and I don't know how I'm going to occupy myself once she's gone. Our agreement was perfect. Not many girls would take the whole casual fucking thing well, but Rory has. And I've performed better than ever knowing she didn't expect anything like labels or deep, serious talks. No, this has been *all* of the fun and none of the difficult stuff.

I can't even be mad. Rory was perfectly fine wallowing her weeks of vacation away in a book and the photos I bet she never deleted from her previous relationship. I had been so caught by her beauty on day one I couldn't stay away, couldn't help but blurt that I'd help her.

Knox would have rolled his eyes, and Slate would've egged me on had they been here, but I haven't told my best friends about any of this. Not a soul knows what happened between Rory and me this summer, and it's going to stay that way because I owe it to our promise, even when we're both back at our respective homes.

I can't believe I'll never see her again.

Rory's head lolls tiredly, drawing me from my thoughts. The moonlight washes over her face, pale from days spent hiding beneath a baseball hat. I don't understand why she hates her bangs so much; she's gorgeous, and the brunette strands frame those stark eyes I've found myself drowning in on more than one occasion.

Said eyes are shut. She's relaxed, a comforting weight pressed against my side. I'll wake her soon so she can sneak back to her room before her family notices her absence. A strand of hair falls across her cheek with the soft breeze, and I catch it between my fingers before it can disturb her. I tuck the strand behind her ear, mesmerized. She's beautiful, and if I weren't emotionally unavailable or we didn't come from opposite sides of the country, I'd try to steal her away from her undeserving ex.

Even if there were a possibility things could work out, we're too different. She wants another man, and I don't do commitment. I won't throw my heart on the line again.

Tomorrow she'll be gone. My stomach churns at the thought of never seeing Rory again. We agreed nothing could happen between us after tonight, but maybe there's a chance we can still be friends? The idea of going no-contact sits heavily in my chest.

We didn't get to spend our last day together. Her parents rented a boat to take out with their daughters, while mine insisted I hang out with them. I did little more than move to the next cabana over while they prattled about plans for an upcoming gallery opening somewhere near my school.

The bottom of the horseshoe-shaped pool never looked so inviting.

We lay in the sand until the moon is well into its descent. My arm is way past numb, and if losing the limb means a few more hours with Rory, I'll saw it off myself. The sand is cold, but her warmth seeps through my sweatshirt and into my soul. I can't wrap my head around how such a short amount of time with someone has created this kind of connection, like

I've always had a spot just for her in my heart. I hardly know anything about her, and yet she's utterly captivated me.

When the moon is a few hours from touching the horizon, I wake her with gentle kisses until she rouses enough to capture my mouth against hers. My heart gives a painful thump, and I quickly shove it aside, losing myself in her. If it's the last kiss I get before she leaves, I make it count.

Rory releases a soft noise I'm going to miss. My cock twitches, but I'm too sad to do anything about it. Her fingers tighten in my sweatshirt, and my chest squeezes with the motion.

She responds so prettily, like she always does, mouth moving slowly and softly against mine, as though she's savoring this moment like I am. I cup Rory's cheek and her lips part beneath the gentle trace of my tongue, tangling with mine as we grow more desperate.

I pour every ounce of unspoken emotion into the kiss I can, praying if anything, she'll change her mind and won't cut contact with me as soon as she steps off the resort property.

When my hope is in the ether and our kiss draws to an end, I escort Rory back to her room.

"Hey, you." A voice startles me from where I have my ass planted in the sand in the exact same spot she'd been sitting the second time we met.

"Rory?" My surprise is clear. I thought she'd be gone already. It's early, the sun having only made her grand appearance an hour ago. I hadn't gone back to my room after we parted ways with a final, sad brush of my lips against hers outside her hotel room. I'd found myself wide awake, and wandered my way back down to the beach, where I've been wallowing ever since. "What are you doing here?"

She sits beside me, hugging her knees to her chest. I drink her in like it's my first time seeing her, heart stumbling like it's the first time, too. She has that damn hat on, sunglasses perched on the brim. She's wearing a sweatshirt I've seen her in occasionally, white with the word CABO printed across the front, and my eyes narrow on her shorts resembling a pair of boxers I own, the red gingham ones she made fun of a few days ago.

I stifle a smile at the memory. We'd been hastily undressing each other in one of the pool changing room stalls, and she'd almost doubled over in laughter at the sight. Rory teased me relentlessly about how they resembled a picnic blanket and made her hungry, so I pressed her up against the wall with her hair wrapped around my fist and fed her my cock.

She peers out over the water, a sad twinkle in her eyes. My chest stings the longer I stare, building myself up for the inevitable.

I thought saying goodbye to her last night was difficult. I'm not prepared to go through this all over again.

"Wanted to catch the sunrise one last time," she admits with a smile that makes me want to tug her into my arms. I'm not sure how she'd react, if she'd pull away because it would hurt her as much it would me, or if she'd lean into me, lay her head on my shoulder one last time and tell me she doesn't want to leave. "It's so beautiful here."

"Yeah," I agree, committing every freckle, every eyelash, to memory. "It really is."

The world waking up fills the mournful silence between

us. The soft waves lapping the shore, birds cawing at each other, and my heart cracking behind my ribs.

A montage flashes before me. Rory and me in the ocean, when she made up those ridiculous rules, the both of us splashing around, not knowing what we were getting into. The fleeting smiles she gifted me, cheeky stares from across the hotel whenever we'd catch eyes. She ran into her sister once, distracted by my good looks. I snorted a laugh when she cringed away as her sister whirled around with a glare, then had to stifle my amusement when Dad asked what I found so funny.

Another memory features Rory peering down at me between her legs as I swirled my tongue around her clit. I blink, and it's her up against every wall, bent over every piece of furniture, splayed out across every surface we could find to have sex. It's Rory all the other times, too. Laying out in the sun, trying her hardest not to ogle me from across the pool. Her face buried in her book, reading so intently she didn't even notice me at all. Taking pictures to send to her friends, playing her favorite songs and dancing with me under the stars. The skirt of her dress flowing as she spun around and around in circles until she couldn't walk straight and fell into my arms in a fit of giggles that made my stomach swirl just the same.

Fuck, I'm such an idiot.

I like her. The sensation is so foreign it's taken me this long to notice, but now that I have, it's so fucking obvious.

I like Rory far too much to let this summer go, to not *try*.

My pulse spikes. Sweat slicks my palms, and I rub them down my shorts, clearing my throat to encourage the words I desperately want to say. The admission catches on the tip of my tongue when Rory shifts her gaze in my direction.

She looks eerily similar to the day we met; her cerulean

eyes sad, shoulders slumped. *Broken.* The shadows under her eyes tell me she hasn't gotten much sleep since I dropped her off at her room, and I frown at the soft smile she's clearly putting on in defense.

I take a steadying breath that does none of the steadying.

Here goes fucking everything.

"Rory-O, look. Before you go, I need to tell you—"

"Ace," she protests weakly, shaking her head. My mouth snaps shut at the sadness in her voice. I swallow thickly as she tears her gaze away, like she can't bear to look at me while she delivers this crushing blow. My stomach sinks to the sand. "You promised me we wouldn't—"

"I didn't forget." I cut her off because I can't hear her say it. This can't end like this. There's something special about Rory, about the connection we share. She's sweet and funny and gorgeous and so fucking far out of my league. She stars in all my dreams and I've never had such an itch to get my hands on paint because for the first time in my life, the landscape I want to create is one of her body—the planes of her face, the valley of her collarbones and the hills of her breasts. I want to paint the sky in her eyes, the cotton candy clouds of her cheeks, and the chocolate swirls of her hair.

Fuck. How did I drown in her so deeply without even realizing?

We can still be friends, I try to remind myself. We don't have to block each other's numbers and forget this happened. *I* won't ever forget this summer, and I hope she won't either. I don't know much about Rory outside of the physical, but I'd like to think I understand the part of her soul she laid bare for me all the times we came together.

The ocean is loud in the terse silence hanging between us. I've put my foot in my fucking mouth and maybe it's better not to say anything at all, because her feelings on the matter are clear: she's going to block my number as soon as she leaves, and she's still going to get back with her ex.

My heart rocks painfully in my chest when Rory gently takes my hand.

My heart cracks when I clutch her tightly, pouring every unspoken word into the motion. Her eyes well with tears, and I *know* she knows my confession. Maybe she returns the sentiment a fraction of the way I do. I hope she knows I've never been happier, hornier, and more content with my life than when she's around. She brightens every room she walks into, and makes me the best man I can be.

My heart shatters when Rory pulls away, stands, whispers an "I'm sorry" so softly the waves almost eat it up, and walks away from me.

CHAPTER 29
ACE

"Ace . . . ." Rory trails in disbelief, pausing in the threshold to drink in the view. My heart takes off in my chest as nerves officially take over. "What's all this?"

I've anticipated this moment all week. When exactly my body stopped recoiling at the idea of a relationship, I have no idea, but every time I think about Rory as officially mine, I'm filled with a warmth I haven't experienced since I was sixteen. *Before* the incident. *Before* I found my girlfriend fooling around with my best friend at the time.

Rory consumes me, day and night. There isn't a minute that passes when I'm not thinking about her in some way, shape, or form. Even when we're in the same room, I'm wondering when I can get her alone. And when we are alone, all my mind seems to scream is how perfectly we fit together, both figuratively and literally.

I forgot what being in love was like. It's better than I remember; all the teasing touches and soft kisses that make me soar. I'd do anything to put that breathtaking smile on her face. She doesn't deserve to be treated like she comes second to anything or anyone, and I'll prove I can be better than her ex ever was.

After what I witnessed at the bar, Rory's reaction to her ex and the admission that she no longer wants anything to do with the fucker, it was hard to hide my satisfaction at the outcome.

Rose petals line a path to my bed, the crimson color popping against my gray duvet. I meticulously crafted the walkway with this moment in mind, and even washed my sheets. Candles are scattered all around, glowing as brightly as the flattered awe in Rory's blue eyes.

"This seems suspiciously romantic," Rory teases, and I don't miss the emotion in her tone. It sounds like no one's done this for her before, and equal parts of me preen that I'm the first and rage because she deserves so much more, and I'm going to give it all to her.

My hand finds hers, giving her a loving squeeze. "Nah, these roses are left over from last night's conquest," I play along. Rory tries and fails to smother a smile. She was the one I was in here with last night.

"The bed is perfectly made. I take it didn't go so well?" She fires back, and goddamn, her smile fills my heart.

I hum in amusement, falling into her icy blue eyes. She stares back like I'm everything she's ever dreamed. I would know, because I return the sentiment. I have no witty retort to make her laugh. The only words I manage to get out are the ones I've been mentally preparing to say for far too long.

"I'm sorry."

Rory's smile fades, and I damn near lose my breath. Her brows bend in confusion. "What are you sorry for?"

I brush a strand of hair behind her ear and caress her jaw, stroking a thumb across her lip. Her mouth parts in response, and I have to hold back a groan as my cock rouses in my pants. And she jokes that I've Pavlod'd *her*. It's definitely the other way around.

"I'm sorry it took me so long to realize I've fallen so fucking hard for you, Rory-O." My voice is hoarse, filled with more emotion than I knew I had left in regards to love. Finding Rory has made me face my past head-on. "I haven't made things easy for you this semester,"—*understatement of the year, Ace*—"but I realized I fell in love with you the moment you walked away from me on that beach."

With the admission, a weight lifts off my shoulders. Nothing and no one can stop me from pursuing what I want. I'm proud of starting again, and for it to be with Rory.

Her fingers squeeze mine, but she doesn't respond otherwise. I scan her, trying to gauge what she's thinking. Her gaze darts between my eyes, searching for something. I've dropped a bombshell on her, and she's trying to see if I'm serious. I've been adamant about no relationships since we met, and here I am, not only changing my mind, but confessing my love to the girl who stole my heart in Cabo.

Well, she won't find anything but the truth behind my words.

The longer she's quiet, the harder my heart beats, to the point where it's painful. Anxiety begins to bloom in my veins like ice, stiffening my muscles one by one. My breath sticks in my chest, and when I'm about to blurt out something stupid and self-depreciating, Rory responds.

"You took the words right out of my mouth," she breathes, and it's my turn to be stunned. She feels the same? *She feels the same*. Her grin is megawatt. "I love you too, Acey-boy."

Relief crashes over me like a wave. My lungs expand, and I greedily gulp down air. My heart bursts with happiness, and I can't help myself; I tug Rory into my arms, crushing her against me as I slam my mouth against hers. Rory laughs at my desperation, and I drink the sound down eagerly. Her fingers lock in the fabric of my shirt as she responds, holding me just as close.

"I'm sorry I took so long," I whisper against her lips. I can't get enough of the taste of her, so I kiss her again.

She gives me a soft squeeze in response. "I forgive you. And I'm sorry too." Rory tilts her chin so I can see her beautiful face. A stray tear slides down her cheek, and I swipe it away. She's staring at me so earnestly I ache. "I fell in love with you so long ago, Ace."

And if hearing that doesn't make me want to kiss her again, I'd be a fucking fool.

Rory melts for me so beautifully. Her movements are urgent, pressing into me like we're not close enough, even standing chest to chest. Her fingers twist through my hair, and I moan when her nails scrape my scalp. The sensation tingles down my spine, straight to my aching cock.

When we part, there's still a worried knit to her brows. I smooth the crease away. "What is it?"

"I'm scared," she admits, gnawing her lip.

The feeling is mutual. Since I've met her, my walls have been up. I've been a broken record, making it adamant I didn't do love. Of course she's terrified of stepping into these choppy waters with me. Before Rory, I wasn't sure I was capable of loving again.

"Why?" I ask around the lump in my throat.

"We barely know each other," she admits, and my heart seizes.

That isn't the entire truth. Her eyes dart away with her words—her tell—but I can work with this. I can ease her anxieties; prove to her I can be the man she's been dreaming of. The one there to support her, listen to her, and be there for her in all the ways her ex never was.

I can be so much more than that prick.

So, I say, "What do you want to know?"

She blinks. "What?"

"What do you want to know?" I repeat, enunciating each word. I squeeze her hips, urging her response.

She scrutinizes me. She's wondering where I'm going with this, so I let her read the primal need stirring my blood for her. Her eyes spark with intrigue, and she can barely smother a shiver. I love playing with Rory, love the way she made me chase her, but right now, I'm not playing.

When she fails to answer, I continue.

"Do you want to know my favorite color?" I ask, drinking her in with my hungry gaze. The hue of her eyes, a color I could recognize in my sleep. The red her face turns when she's thinking something naughty. The speckles of freckles doting her skin. She's so beautiful, and heat pools low in my stomach. "It's the shade of pink your cheeks glow when you blush." I track a thumb across said cheek, and as if smearing paint across her skin, the exact shade appears.

I take a step into her, groaning when my hips brush her front. Rory backs away, eyes wide. She swallows hard, arousal flooding her pupils, and satisfaction threads through my blood. Her lids flutter as I give chase.

"Do you want to know my favorite song?" I taunt, prowling closer. A wicked smirk pulls at my mouth when she mirrors my movements, retreating. My eyes flicker to her chest, where her nipples stand starkly against the fabric of her shirt, and holy shit, do I want to devour her whole.

Rory can only nod, and a part of me loves that I've rendered her speechless, but the other part loves when she makes those pretty sounds for me, which is why I answer, "The noises you make for me when you come."

We traipse across the room in a game of cat and mouse until she runs into the wall. Her palms splay wide as she braces herself, and I close the distance easily, pressing the hard length of my cock against her. I revel in the way her eyes flash and that beautiful blush dips down the column of her throat.

When she moves for the waistband of my pants, I snag her wrists and pin them above her head, threading our fingers together.

I'll give her what she wants after we finish our conversation.

"My favorite place?" I whisper, dipping low so my lips brush the shell of her ear. Her breath catches, and my body thrums with anticipation. There's a desperate, yet futile tug as she tries to free her hands, but she's not going anywhere yet. Not until I allow it. Her lashes flutter shut as she tilts her head, giving me more room to work my mouth across her soft skin. "Between these thighs, Rory. Right where I know you like me."

I roll my hips into hers in a gentle tease, and this time there's no hiding the noise she's so desperately trying to hide. A cross between a moan and a whimper escapes, signaling for more. Rory lifts her feet and wraps her legs around my waist, locking me against her. My breath leaves me in a harsh pant, fanning across her face.

"And your favorite taste?" She asks when she finally finds her words. Her lustful eyes are dark with challenge.

A chuckle escapes me. Freeing a hand, I situate the other to keep her wrists glued to the wall. Rory jerks, but the attempt garners no results. All in good time.

My grin is wicked as I drag my hand down the curve of

her body. I make sure my movements are as slow and torturous as possible, loving the fire in her eyes. Pausing over the curve of her breast, I tweak a pert nipple, eliciting an aroused hiss I can't help but lean in and taste.

She melts into the kiss, and I use the distraction to my advantage, hand falling to the apex of her thighs. I give a rough swipe, pressing the seam of her jeans into her clit.

Rory gasps. She chases me when I pull away, but I don't go far. No one could pry me off her right now. I do so only to answer her question.

"*You.*"

She arches and captures my mouth. The sudden shift of her weight forces me back a step. Dropping Rory's hands, I hook mine around the curve of her ass and haul her against me. Her fingers thread through my hair and pull. The tug reverberates all the way down to my groin, and I groan as her touch drives down my chest to fist in the fabric of my shirt, hastily tearing at the hem.

"Easy now, Rory-O," I breathe, amused. I'll give her exactly what she wants. I can't believe the girl I love is in my arms. She's finally mine, and she loves me back.

"*Need you now,*" Rory gasps like she can't get enough. I don't have the time to respond before her mouth is against mine and we're stumbling toward the bed.

Fuck. I need her too. I need her like I'm stranded in the ocean and she's my lifeboat.

I lay her on the duvet and crawl after her. Her eyes are hot, demanding. I'll give her anything she wants, as long as she says she's mine.

On my knees before her, Rory watches greedily as I tug my shirt off, tossing it away. I shiver under her pretty blue eyes, drinking in every inch of skin.

I bite back a smile when she latches onto my newest ink.

I want to preen like a show dog as she studies me. Rory leans closer, successfully distracted by the tattoo I got just for her. My heart gives a slightly anxious beat as I wonder how she'll react. Usually, she wears her feelings on her sleeve, but she must be practicing because right now, I can't seem to read her at all.

She traces a finger over the tattoo, and my abs tighten in response. Her touch spreads like a wildfire, blossoming to my cheeks and down my chest and to the tip of my cock straining painfully against my jeans.

When her gaze flickers back to mine, hand still caressing my tattoo, she laughs brightly, and her amusement unlocks my taut muscles.

"Is that an Oreo?"

I can't help but beam. I thought the billiards ball was my favorite tattoo, but this idea hit me out of the blue. I didn't hesitate; I asked Knox to ink me up the same night.

"No," I tease. I hook my fingers into the waistband of her jeans and pull her closer. The gleam in her eyes is intoxicating, and I'm drowning in it. "It's my Rory-O."

The shape *is* everyone's favorite cookie, but where the middle usually says Oreo, I had Knox write Rory-O, as a tribute to my girl.

"Ace, this is . . ." Rory trails off, tracing the shape. Her face is a mixture of awe and disbelief, like I'm crazy for this, when in all reality, I'm just crazy for *her*. "I can't believe you did this."

"I wanted a piece of you with me always," I admit, leaning in to brush my lips against hers in a sweet kiss. I settle my weight onto her, laying her flat against the bed. Rory moans when I begin working my way down her body, shoving her shirt up and latching my mouth against the soft, silky skin of her stomach. She's quick to rid herself of the fabric, and I feast on every inch she exposes. I tug at the straps of her bra and follow with my tongue. "You're mine, Rory-O, and I'm never letting you go again."

"Is that a promise?" She keens as I pop the button on her jeans. My cock twitches at the sight of the little pink bow at the waistband of her panties. I growl headily and surge forward, trapping it between my teeth. I pull and release, the elastic snapping against her skin. Her back arches off the bed.

Impatiently, she tries to shove out of her remaining clothes. It's difficult to bite back my amusement at her eagerness. "Rory-O, it's more than a promise." I crawl up her body. She stares at me with those big, round eyes I adore so much. "It's goddamn rule number one."

I kiss Rory just as enthusiastically as she kisses me, fireworks bursting behind my eyelids. Fuck, what this girl does to me.

Together, we rid her of her pants and panties, and then I'm parting her smooth thighs and settling between them, admiring her glistening pussy. God, she's fucking perfect. And all mine.

I paint pictures against her with my tongue, swirling, stroking. I'm fucking masterful with it, if the nails scrabbling against my shoulders and the lewd moans spilling from her lips tell me anything.

"*Oh my God.*" Rory's voice is a desperate plea. I don't hold back, flicking my tongue against her clit in a fervent pattern. I need this as much as she does, enjoy it just the same, too.

She's sweet, and I love how she goes crazy for me. Her fingers slide into my hair, holding me where she wants as she grinds desperately on my tongue. I get so fucking hard when she takes what she wants from me. My cock throbs, and I squeeze my eyes shut, focusing on Rory so I don't come in my pants like a fucking teenager.

Her body jerks as she chases her pleasure. I don't pull away until her moans become wanton and her thighs threaten to clamp around my skull. She's close, but I don't want her to come yet. I want to draw this out, revel in those whines and gasps, the way she's begging me for more. Rory lifts her head from the pillow, and I almost come on the spot at the dazed look on her face. Her lips are swollen from her failed attempts at hiding her noises from me, but her softness doesn't last long. Her blue eyes sharpen when I don't let her come, and my grin grows.

I lick my lips and watch her track the motion. She bucks her hips, demanding I lower my head and get back to tongue-fucking the shit out of her. My Rory-O wants an O? I can make that happen.

"You want to come, Rory-O?" I challenge.

"That's right, Acey-boy," she purrs. "Now get back to work."

And work I do. Teasing my tongue through her slit, the air falls from her lungs. The muscles of her thighs strain beneath my hands. I lick around her clit in tight circles that have her crying out, but I'm not done yet. Slipping lower, I stick my tongue right into her wet pussy.

"*Ace*!" Rory cries, and I fucking love the way my name sounds on her lips.

I add a finger into the mix, sliding inside her tight heat. Fuck, I can't wait for this to be my cock. Her jaw slackens when I brush over the bundle of nerves that drives her wild. Moving my mouth back to her clit, I trace and suck, stroking my tongue against the nub so quickly she can't hold back any longer, coming with a war cry of my name I would get tattooed if I could.

Her body shakes as I continue to ease my finger in and out of her, drawing out her orgasm. Rory has deflated into the mattress by the time I pull away, eyes shut in bliss, the occasional tremor rocking her. Her hands smooth up and down my back weakly as I slowly climb up her body.

"I think I just found my new favorite song," I tease, pecking her on the mouth. My body burns with the need to be inside her right this second, especially when I grind my cock between her legs, feeling her heat against my jeans. Rory moans breathlessly, eyes flying open as she clutches onto me, nails biting deliciously into my shoulders as her second wind appears.

Her hands claw down my skin, leaving red streaks in their wake. I hum a noise of appreciation and help her undo the button of my jeans.

"*Off*," she murmurs against my lips. "Please, Ace. I need you."

I almost come right on the spot. She's relentless, frantic and wanting, and it's so fucking hot there's no way I'm going to last more than a few minutes inside of her.

"*Fuck*," I breathe, sliding out of my clothes. My cock springs up, and Rory zeroes in on me. Reaching out, she wraps a firm hand around my shaft like she can't wait the seconds it will take to find the condom I'm searching for.

I hiss with pleasure as she tugs. Biting her lip like that, she's the poster girl for innocence, and all I want to do is untuck her lip and shove my cock past it.

"Just a second, Rory-O. I'm coming." I almost beg, trying my damndest not to burst in her hand like this is my first time. Where the fuck is the condom?

Ignoring me, she flicks her wrist. Black vignettes my vision. I have to grab her arm to stop her before I fucking burst.

"I sure hope not." She teases, blue eyes glittering. "Need you in me before you come, Acey-boy."

CHAPTER 30
RORY

Ace's smile might be my favorite thing in the world. The way it curves higher on one side, creating the tiniest, cutest divot in his cheek. The way it's directed at me. That smile is all mine, and I can hardly believe it. It takes my breath away.

Just like the press of his hard cock inside me does.

The sheets bunch between my fingers as I grip them, clawing for something to ground me because his hot, thick length never fails to make me ascend.

Ace hums with pleasure. "Always so good for me, Rory-O," he praises, and my spine arches in response. Realizing my eyes have fallen shut, I manage to pry them open, peering up at Ace. Arousal floods between my legs at the sight, his deep blue eyes focused hungrily where our bodies meet.

When we made our little agreement over the summer, I only intended to dip my toes into the water with him, enjoy what we had for what it was: just sex. I wasn't prepared to fall in headfirst, and I've been drowning in him since.

His hips slam into mine, and I exhale at the delicious tightness. Ace admires me while allowing me time to adjust.

His eyes dancing across my skin alone has me straddling the fine line of orgasming. Beneath his gaze, I feel *sexy,* like I'm his favorite artwork.

"I can't believe you got my name tattooed on you." I try to distract myself because he's not moving. He's going to torture me like always, which is both the best and most annoying thing ever, but I love being on the edge with him. I reach out to trace the newest addition on his skin, heart pounding in disbelief. Ace is truly a wild card.

When I'm done drawing, my fingers drift across his collarbone and beyond, winding in the hair at the nape of his neck to pull him closer.

"Now, we just have to get my name on you," he teases, biting back a groan at the way his cock slips deeper with the change of angle. Slowly, Ace begins pumping his hips. His pace quickens as if his name inked across my skin turns him on even more. I must admit, the mental image of how he might react if he ever found his name on my body is arousing as fuck. I circle my legs around his waist and moan deeply at the thought.

"*Fuck.* Yeah, you'd like that, wouldn't you, Rory-O?" Ace growls, pressing his hips to pin me to the bed, fucking with abandon. I writhe desperately, dizzy with euphoria, on the verge of release.

He sucks a harsh kiss to the underside of my jaw, making his way messily across my throat. He hooks an arm beneath my knee and lifts so he can fuck deeper. My body responds with pleasure, hips seeking his. His eyes are dark, hungry, and oh-so sexy. "Want to have my name on you? Right where everyone can see, pretty girl?"

Calloused fingers trail up my sides to play with my breasts. Ace circles a nipple, thumb stroking the tight nub roughly as he continues to tease. "Or would you want it somewhere else? A secret just for you and me?"

I can't help it. His words are erotic, and when his hand snakes between my legs to play with my clit, the combination drives me over the edge. I come *hard*, stars blackening my vision.

Ace hisses as I clench around him, nails digging into the perpetually sun-kissed skin of his back.

With a groan, his tempo quickens, prolonging the rush of euphoria I'm experiencing. Ace dives to suck my nipple into his mouth, dragging his hot tongue across the hard nub. Desperation and pleasure blind me. I pull at his hair, his skin, anywhere I can reach.

"*Ace!*" His name breaks free from my chest. It's the only word I can manage to say. I've forgotten everything except the boy who milks pleasure from me like no one else.

He knows exactly what I need. Always has. His fingers slow, and the pressure keeps me from completely relaxing into the bed. I'm a shuddering mess, and Ace makes it known he enjoys my eager responses.

When I finally manage to crack my eyes open, Ace is staring at me with so much emotion I don't know where to begin deciphering the look. My mind is a melted pool of desire, and I'm pretty sure I've lost control over my limbs.

"There she is," Ace grunts, hitching his hips into mine again. The hot slide of his cock plucks a debauched whine from me. "I'm going to come for you, Rory."

And *fuck*, if that isn't the hottest thing I've ever heard. I want to go for round two before this one's even finished.

I lock my arms around his neck and say, "Come for me, Ace."

He does, and his face is so fucking pretty when he releases. His mouth red and lips bitten raw, parted as harsh pants and grunts escape him. His eyes are hidden behind fluttering lashes, like he's fighting his body to keep them open and on me.

Ace collapses beside me and immediately pulls me into his body as if the mere inches between us were too far already. I don't mind, because I love being close to him. He rests his forehead against mine, chest heaving as he tries to catch his breath, tickling my cheeks with every exhale.

His heartbeat is a steady thrum in my ear. The silence between us is blissful as we revel in our post-sex haze, like we could spend days doing exactly this and wouldn't be missing out.

"And what does this one mean?" I ask, perched on Ace's lap the next morning, pointing to the various tattoos littering his skin. Neither of us felt inclined to crawl out of his bed yet, but with the way Ace's stomach growls, we may have to face the rest of the world soon.

I giggle at the noise. Ace rolls his eyes but wears a fond smile that twists into a mischievous grin when his hands move from resting on my waist to tickling my sides. I squeal, batting at him as I gasp through laughter.

When he relents, Ace catches one of my wrists and tugs me into him. His cock is hard against my leg, and I'd love nothing more than to ride him like I've been thinking about all morning, but he distracts me with peppered kisses to my cheeks.

"I got bit by a spider once," he explains, and I lift a brow, unimpressed. He mimics me, and I stick my tongue out in retaliation before peering at the tattoo in question. It's a menacing spider, blacked out with delicate webbing stretching between its long limbs. I shudder at the thought of it skittering across my skin, and my grip tightens on instinct. "I thought I was going to turn into Spiderman," Ace continues, stroking a long line down my back. I relax into him, fingering the thin webs. "It was a big moment for me."

"What, was this like two years ago?" I joke. I can feel him grin where his lips are near my hairline.

"*No*." He pinches my side playfully, and I squirm. Ace's breath hitches when my leg brushes against his cock, and I instantly still, body lighting up. His heartbeat kicks in pace, but he trudges on. "It happened when I was six, but I never forgot that moment. Still working on the whole web-shooting thing, though." He frowns, flexing his fingers. He extends an arm toward his easel, like the first thing he'd pick up if he had magical web-shooting abilities is a paintbrush.

I fail to smother a smile, picturing Ace as a child, crying about a spider that was probably way more afraid of him than he was of it. I imagine his small fingers trying to shoot webs at the cookie jar before dinner.

"How about this one?" I run my fingers over a Doberman painted across his ribs. It has three heads, and two of the canines snap at each other while the third growls, lips pulled back in a snarl, drool hanging from its sharp teeth. "Did a dog bite you? Should I expect your super sense of smell to kick in any day now?"

"Okay, Little Miss Jokester," he scolds, rolling us easily, so he's pinning me to the bed. I part my legs, and he settles between them, my breath hitching when his length rests against my entrance. I'm not too sure we're going to make it out of his room for breakfast. Not that I'm complaining. "That's enough making fun of your boyfriend for today."

My chest swells at his official title. Ace Broden is my boyfriend. My fucking boyfriend.

"But it's only eleven," I pout, reaching to grab my phone from the bedside table to check the time. There are a few texts from Quinn and one from my sister, asking to meet up for dinner. I quickly type an agreement. "I still have a few more jokes left in me."

I swipe out of my texts and click into my email while Ace jostles me playfully, dipping low to nip at the sensitive skin between my collarbone and shoulders. "How about I give you something to laugh about?"

As fun as the intention in his voice sounds, my body pulls taut at the email sitting at the top of my inbox.

"What is it?" Ace stills, concern lacing his tone. "What's wrong?"

"I—" I swallow harshly, eyes glued to the screen. "I got an email from the Academy of Royal Arts."

He presses a gentle kiss to my shoulder before shuffling off me, giving me space. My chest seizes with affection.

"Do you want to open it?" Ace murmurs, helping me sit up. The cotton sheets are soft against my legs as he pulls them over us. He leans against his headboard, and if I weren't so nervous, the sight of his muscular torso would be more than distracting.

His features are soft and understanding. I've worked all semester to curate the perfect showcase of my work, and I'm proud of myself. I want this more than I've wanted anything in my life.

If I don't get in, I don't know what I'll do. My mom creeps into my head. How weary she is of me making art my career, even if I'm following my dreams. I shouldn't be put down or mocked because what I want isn't similar to the paths my sisters chose.

Painting is my passion, and I made a promise to myself I'd follow through on art no matter what anyone says. If I love it, I'm chasing it, just like I did with Ace.

So, with bated breath, I open the email.

Dear Ms. Wilson,

Congratulations! It is with great pleasure I inform you of your acceptance to Oil Painting: The Expressive Portrait at the Academy of Royal Arts in London, England . . .

"I got in," I exhale in shock. Hysteria bubbles up my throat as I face Ace. Tears of joy blur my vision, and I latch onto him, planting a hard kiss against his lips. "Oh my God, I got in!"

"I knew you could do it," Ace says, sharing my enthusiasm. His proud kisses only elate me further. I didn't think it was possible to be happier than I was last night, but here I am with the man I've completely fallen for, sharing one of the most important moments of my art career with me. "Congratulations, Rory-O. You deserve it. You deserve the world."

CHAPTER 31
RORY

"Mom says you've been screening her calls," Peep interrogates, setting a plate of spaghetti in front of me. The whiff of garlic bread in the basket that follows has my stomach growling like a beast. Combined with the wine warming my belly, this sister's night started out great. We caught up on the latest drama on *Love Untouched*, chatted about classes and plans for winter break in a few weeks while I cooked the meat and Peep prepared the sauce.

The red wine in my stomach sours at the mention of Mom. It's true, I've been dodging her calls like my ass is on fire, only because I don't know how to tell her—or any of my family members—I'll be spending my summer in London, honing my painting skills.

While one of my greatest achievements, I'm apprehensive about her reaction. She's not the biggest fan of me pursuing painting as a full-time career, and she's made her opinion more than known. Holidays are the worst, where she talks my sisters up to the rest of the family and brushes over my accomplishments like I'll never be able to make a living doing what I love.

She wants more for me, and I get that, but I have everything I've ever wanted.

I hum as if Peep's comment is news to me, twirling pasta on my fork and biting back the urge to shove the utensil in my mouth to avoid answering. "That's because I am."

Peep's brows furrow in confusion, like not answering the phone when our mom calls is a mortal sin.

News flash Peep, it isn't even close.

"Why?"

This time, I do shove the fork into my mouth, giving myself time to devise an answer that doesn't draw attention to my strained relationship with Mom. Flavor bursts on my tongue, and I'm momentarily distracted by the RRR scale of this dinner. It's a solid eight point five out of ten.

I wash the food back with a sip of wine. I want to talk about avoiding my mom just as much as I want to answer her calls. With a shrug, I decide that being truthful is the way to get them both off my back. "I don't feel like talking to her."

Peep shoots me a look from the corner of her eye. Dutifully, I ignore my sister and busy myself by ripping off a chunk of garlic bread and using it as a vessel to scoop sauce.

"Why?"

I roll my eyes, annoyance bubbling in my gut. "What are you, two years old? Quit asking 'why'."

"Fine," she huffs, pulling her phone from her pocket. The hair on the back of my neck rises with my defenses. If she calls Mom right now, I'm going to be pissed. I'm using almost all my willpower to stay seated at the table and not skip out on the rest of the meal because of the interrogation I had no idea I was walking into. If this spaghetti weren't so damn good, I'd be out the door already. "I'm calling Aisling."

Shit. Talking to Aisling is almost as bad as talking to Mom. She's like a mini-Leah Wilson. Even has the same features, minus the nose she inherited from Dad.

It's my turn to ask "why." So they can gang up on me like they always do? Story of my life.

Peep fixes me with a deadpan stare. I duck my head like a scolded child and stuff another bite of food into my mouth while she dials.

Aisling answers on the fourth ring.

"Hey! What's up?" She greets. Peep props the phone against the bottle of wine to get us both in frame, and when Aisling sees me, she smirks. "Uh oh, Ro looks like someone shit in her spaghetti. What's going on?"

I mutter into my glass, "Peep's forcing me to talk about Mom."

"*No,*" Peep refutes with a glare. "Ro's acting like a child and refuses to tell me anything going on in her life."

I wince. She's not entirely wrong. I'm normally left out of conversations with my sisters, so they have no idea the whirlwind this semester has been. They've never been choice number one of people I confide in, and to see the hurt in Peep's gaze has my stomach clenching with regret.

"*Oh.*" Aisling grins, settling on her bed. She's wearing a pink robe, and her hair is wrapped in a fluffy towel. I'm momentarily distracted from my defeat by the bright pink depuffing mask under each of her eyes. I wonder what *she's* keeping from us. I can't be the only Wilson sister with secrets. "Tell us more."

"There's nothing to tell." I try to stand strong, I really do, but the pointed stares my sisters give me are my weakness. The two of them are thicker than thieves, and I know what happens between us won't reach Mom's ears until I'm ready.

"That's statistically impossible," Aisling says, propping

her phone up, too. The placement gives me a better view of her cloud-like duvet as she reaches over and snags a nail file from the bedside table. "When I was your age, I was—"

Peep's phone vibrates with a message. My jaw falls onto my plate of spaghetti at the contact name, but the picture attached to the message is quickly swiped away by a frantic Peep before I can make out what it's of. I'm pretty sure I saw a winking face emoji in the accompanying text.

She snatches her phone from the table and clutches it to her chest. Aisling's squawk of confusion rings through the phone, wondering why it's gone dark on her end. I can't answer because my focus is completely zeroed in on Peep, whose cheeks are redder than the tomato sauce.

"Peep." I try to speak calmly. I want to burst into the wildest cheer routine either of my sisters has ever seen, back-flips and all. The urge to pull out my phone and text Quinn right this second is so strong I tighten my grip on my fork to keep from fishing it out of my pocket. "Why is Sam Conroy sending you a winky emoji?"

Sam Conroy, Quinn's older brother. She and I—and secretly both of our entire families—have been waiting for something to happen between the pair for *ages*. They've always been close, flirting the line between family friends and more, and when Sam made a sudden appearance at the beginning of the semester to attend Peep's homecoming party, Quinn and I caught them kissing in the hall. I have never been happier for my sister, but she hasn't divulged any information since.

"I don't know," she squeaks, tapping away at the phone. I assume she's switching her device to Do Not Disturb so that any more promiscuous messages Sam tries to send won't appear on screen. Upon my unimpressed face, she shoots right back, "We're not talking about me right now, we're talking about you!"

"I'll tell you if you tell me," I barter. She ponders my proposition for a moment, and when her shoulders drop in defeat, I grin into my pasta.

She pours herself another hefty glass of wine, then refills mine before propping her phone back against the quickly emptying bottle.

"*Fine*," she sighs dramatically, failing to hide a cheesy smile in the rim of her glass. "Sam and I are officially together."

Aisling and I screech so loud I'm surprised our wine glasses don't shatter with the frequency. Peep ducks her head, but there's no hiding her blush. *Finally*. We've been waiting for this moment forever. I'm so excited, like it's the last week on *Love Untouched* when there's only two couples left and the one I've been rooting for all season finally wins.

I cannot wait to tell Quinn.

"Ohmygod! This is the best news ever!" I can't help myself, launching from my chair to wrap my arms around Peep. She returns the hug, and we sit there for a long minute until Aisling stops cheering and starts complaining about how she's not here to celebrate.

"Okay, okay," Peep waves off the questions we begin rattling at her. "Questions can be saved for winter break," she insists. "Where we can all be together and drink bottles of wine to our heart's content. Now it's your turn, Ro."

My excitement deflates. I pick up my fork and push the food around my plate.

"Yeah," Aisling tacks on, carrying her phone into the bathroom where she begins peeling the masks off her face. She's glowing, and I remind myself to ask for the link later.

"What's been going on with you? You've been a wreck since the beginning of summer."

"Wow, *thanks*," I grouse. Normally, I'd appreciate Aisling's bluntness. She's always been a tell-it-like-she-sees-it kind of girl, but her words sting. "How thoughtful of you to point out what a wreck I looked like, *five months later*."

Life has flipped since Cabo. Everything is finally falling into place. I've been accepted into the painting class of my dreams, I've gotten rid of the boy who had only been dragging me down longer than I care to admit, and I'm official with Ace. If anything, I should be glowing.

Minus the fact that Quinn and I need to start apartment hunting for next year since Knox's father decided to kick out every renter he has in order to renovate the building and double the cost of living at Third Street Apartments, I'm doing dandy.

"You know what we mean," Peep waves me off.

"I just don't feel like hearing how it's not too late to change my major."

My admission stuns my sisters into silence. They stare, and even though Aisling is the size of my fist right now, her eyes are like lasers.

"What are you talking about?" She questions, sounding shocked enough that I raise my gaze from the table.

My brows knit in confusion. "Mom?" I explain. "She doesn't like that I'm majoring in painting. She hates that I would rather spend my time creatively than doing anything else."

Peep's face is contorted like I've grown a second head. "Ro, she doesn't hate your major." She shakes her head in disbelief. I glance at Aisling, who has stopped washing her face, her attention on me. She leans as close to the phone as she can get, and if we weren't having a serious as fuck discussion right now, I might joke that I can see her nose hairs. "She's worried about you."

"*Yeah*," I defend, though the swirling in my stomach signifies I might be wrong. "Because she doesn't think I can make a career out of painting."

"Because she doesn't want you to forget about her," Aisling argues sternly, and now I'm the one shocked into silence.

I frown. What? Because she doesn't want me to forget about her? How could I possibly forget about Mom when she's always trying to butt into my life and interrogating me about my future for years?

"What are you talking about?"

Peep's face softens with concern. "You're incredible at painting. Really, you have a talent anyone can see, since you were young. Not even Mom can deny it, and she never has. I mean, has she ever said anything bad about a single one of your paintings?"

I rack my brain, searching for a moment in time where Mom has made a negative comment about any of my paintings, but come up empty. Every instance I've shown her my work has been her standing in silence, her hand over her mouth. Maybe she hasn't outright said anything bad, but I swear I could read it in her posture and face quite clearly.

I swallow harshly. Unless . . . I've been misconstruing her silence for disgust and disappointment when it's really pride?

"Well . . . no." I slump in my chair and stare at my pasta, appetite gone.

"Because she thinks they're amazing, just like the rest of us," Aisling explains, wiping the soapy water collecting at her chin with a towel. "She's worried about an art career for you because it might take you away from us."

"How could art ever take me away from you?" I mumble, neck growing hot at the news I have tucked in my pocket.

"Painting will take you all over the world," Peep explains. She places a gentle hand over mine. Tears well in her eyes, and when she squeezes, my heart mirrors the action. "She's going to miss holidays and summers with you. Aisling and I, we're close enough for Mom and Dad to drive and visit, but if you're off gallivanting around the world . . . she's worried she won't see you as much. You'll be too busy to call and text and visit once in a while." She smiles weakly, and I feel like a truly horrible daughter. "It's never been about changing your major; it's about the possibility of rarely seeing you."

I don't know what to say, what to think. All this time I've been drawing my own conclusions about Mom's feelings about me being an artist, and I've been so fucking wrong. How did I not connect the dots sooner? Why couldn't I just ask?

"Why wouldn't she tell me?" I question, throat tight. I take a desperate gulp of wine, and the liquid sticks on the way down.

Peep wipes the corner of her eye with her napkin. "What? When you were actively avoiding her calls?"

Shit. She's right. I need to remedy this ASAP.

My sister catches my wince and rolls her eyes. The heaviness of the room lessens when she teases, "You can be such a brat sometimes, Ro."

I gasp dramatically. "You take that back!"

Peep raises a brow in challenge, swirling her drink in her glass. She resembles Mom so much it's uncanny. "Or what?"

My responding grin should strike fear in her, but since I'm the youngest, neither of my older sisters have ever feared me. "Or I'll tell Sammy you're a Toucher."

Her hand freezes in its motion, and her eyes widen comically. On the line, Aisling snorts and begins applying concealer. "You *wouldn't*."

"Oh," I laugh evilly. "I *so* would."

Peep and I bicker until Aisling's scolding breaks us apart. I slump in my chair in defeat. A weight has been lifted off my shoulders, but an equally heavy one has taken its place. Calling Mom will help, but there's something else I must confess to be completely free of secrets.

"There's something I have to tell you," I say, and the nerves return. I finger the stem of my wineglass and try not to duck away from my sisters' heavy gazes. "Okay, two things." I shrug. I wish I could pull my phone out and text Ace for a confidence boost, but I'm pretty sure his response would involve a cheeky remark or a shirtless picture, and I can't get worked up like *that* in front of my sisters.

It does have me wondering what kind of picture Sam sent Peep.

"What is it?" Aisling asks wearily. She leans so far into the phone all I can see are her eyes, face stretched as she applies mascara. She must have propped us against her mirror.

I grin sheepishly. A twang of guilt hits me. I've been going to school with Peep for two years, and I've never talked this much about myself before. "You know, Ace?" I ask. "The blond boy I brought to your homecoming party?"

"Yeah . . ."

I twist my fingers in my lap. I shouldn't be nervous to tell my sisters we're dating, but they can be judgmental at the best of times. They hated Max, so sue me if I'm a little anxious.

Aisling cuts me off before I can continue. "Is that the boy from Cabo?" She asks, and hey, there's my jaw on the table again. "*Please* tell me you're together. He was cute."

"What the fuck?" I squawk. "How do you know that?"

"Ro," Peep chides. "You two weren't as sneaky as you thought you were." She shudders in her seat as if recalling something she witnessed. A hot flush of embarrassment rises up my throat.

Ohmygod, this is mortifying. I didn't think we were flaunting our secret around the resort by any means. We made sure neither of our families were near when we fooled around. How many times were we caught? I shudder. What the hell did they see?

"I recognized him as soon as he showed up on my doorstep," Peep waves me off, sipping her drink. I'm still in shock at the revelation and how neither of my sisters decided to bring this up sooner. She answers my unspoken question of *how the hell do you know anything about Ace and me?* "When your attitude did a 180, Aisling and I did a little snooping."

"The restaurant bathroom?" Aisling chimes in, and I want to melt into the floor. "Not very original, Ro."

"*Okay*," I bark back, the desperate urge to defend myself rising. "It's not like we had time to go to either of our rooms! And not very original? Where the hell are *you* having sex?"

Aisling grins like the cat that got the cream, and I'm on the edge of my seat. When she admits one of her high school boyfriends fondled her at the top of a Ferris wheel at a local carnival, I can't help but gasp. The real kicker is she claims to have had sex in the showers at her gym, but I don't see how that's much different from my bathroom escapade with Ace. Peep confesses she hasn't had sex in any nefarious places, but with her newfound relationship, maybe that will change over winter break.

We laugh, and it's nice to gossip with my sisters like this. Our age difference doesn't seem so monumental anymore.

I'm no longer on the outs. Right now, we're three peas in a pod, all on the same page.

"Yeah, we're dating," I confirm, and I can't help the smile accompanying the admission. I feel like I'm fucking glowing, and I must be, if the matching mega-watt smiles my sisters wear prove anything.

The next half hour is spent gushing over our love lives. Aisling is getting ready for a date, so she asks what the other thing I wanted to tell them was before she has to hang up and get dressed.

Guilt sluices over me again, my happiness dwindling. After what they said about Mom and my endeavors in art, I'm not sure how they're going to react when I tell them my plans for next summer.

I decide that ripping the band-aid off quickly is the way to go, so I say it while silently preparing myself for the worst. "I got accepted into a class at the Academy of Royal Arts in London this summer."

Silence follows for a second, then two. I jump in my seat when my sisters erupt in high-pitched cheers.

"That's amazing, Ro! Congratulations!"

"No way! London is such a dream! I'm so proud of you!"

I peek my eyes open, drinking in their beaming faces. "You're not upset?"

Aisling's face scrunches. "Of course not! This is such an accomplishment, how can we not be happy?"

Peep adds, "Plus, this means a Euro trip is on next summer for the Wilson family," she winks. "After your class ends, of course."

Their unabashed praise means so much to me. I wasn't prepared for positive reactions, and I feel foolish for thinking they wouldn't support me.

"Really?" I ask tentatively. "You don't think Mom will be upset?"

"I think Mom will be the proudest of us all," Aisling answers seriously. Then she blows us both kisses and says, "I have to go, but I love you both and I am so proud of you, Rory. Keep me updated on how things go with Mom, and I'll tell you all about this date. Who knows, maybe he could be the one!" She waggles her eyebrows in exaggeration and then hangs up.

My pasta is cold when I take another bite, but that won't stop me from finishing my plate, especially when I have so much more to ask Peep.

"So, about you and Sam…"

My sister fails miserably at hiding her smile, and I'm giddy. "Let's open another bottle, and I'll tell you all about it."

CHAPTER 32
RORY

"Hey, I hate to do this, but my mom's calling. Can we finish this later?" I ask Ace, who has been sitting somewhat-obediently on my desk chair by the window. The sunlight this morning streamed into my bedroom in such a beautiful way I had to capture the slats of light across his face for my next portrait. So far, the painting has gone well, minus the two much-longer-than-necessary breaks.

Ace sighs dramatically, stretching his long, strong arms over his head. I almost reject Mom's call, dragging my gaze across the bulge of biceps and his flexing abdominals. He stands and waltzes over, hooking his chin over my shoulder and winding those arms around my waist, admiring my progress. I drew a rough sketch and laid down the base colors for his features and hair. I was able to begin some detailing on his eyes with my favorite shades of blue, all mixed into one.

"You'll have to let me paint you one of these days," Ace says thoughtfully. He pecks me on the cheek, then on the lips when I turn for more. My chest blooms with adoration, and I fall into his little trap all too easily, the hot teasing demand of his mouth distracting me.

My phone stops buzzing where it's propped on my easel. I swat Ace on the arm, and he gives me an innocent grin in return. I want to kiss him all over again.

"I thought you didn't paint portraits." I reply, standing to stretch my back, arching until I hear a soft pop. Ace's gaze flares with heat as they dip down my body, and I all but shove him out of my room before we end up naked on my bed for the third time today. We're definitely revisiting this later.

"I meant finger painting," he teases, and I'd never admit how my body lights at the idea. "My fingers, your body . . . I can make something great, don't you think, Rory-O?"

I groan. He's killing me. "Hold on to that thought, Acey-boy." I pinch his butt as he leads the way to the front door. He jumps and retaliates with a firm slap on my ass that forces a surprised half giggle, half squeal from me.

"How much later?" Ace groans. "Because we're supposed to be hanging out with everyone tonight, and I don't want Slate interrupting—"

I roll onto the tips of my toes and cut his complaint off with a kiss. Ace's arms fold around me, tugging me closer. He's half-hard against my hip, and damn, he's insatiable. I'm one to talk because I can't seem to get enough of my boyfriend, either.

"Trust me, Slate won't be interrupting anything I do to you later."

His throat bobs, and my stomach mimics the motion. He brushes his thumb across the sliver of skin between the hem of my shirt and the waistband of my sleep shorts, and I shiver in his hold. "What are you going to do to me?"

I grin wickedly, reaching around him to open the door. "You'll have to wait and see, Acey-boy."

"*Fuck*," he curses under his breath. His cock is fully hard in his pants, and normally I wouldn't kick a man out while he's this vulnerable, but he's only traveling next door, and I really have to call Mom back. "I want to enact a new rule."

A flutter stirs in my stomach, adoring how we're slowly replacing the rules we came up with over the summer. "Let's hear it, then."

"Rule number fifty-one." Ace gestures to the strain in his pants. "You can't leave unless you finish what you've started."

"I'll bring it to the board," I play along, though my core clenches at the thought of getting on my knees and sucking him off right here in the doorway of my apartment. Something tells me if Quinn walked in on us, she'd appreciate the moment a lot less than The Couch Incident™.

Ace's fingers find a home in the hair at the nape of my neck, startling me back to the present. He tilts my head and kisses me hard.

Before I give in to the arousal that floods my veins, Ace pulls away, eyes glittering with mischief. "Let me know what they say," he murmurs with a wink, and leaves me with one last, gentler kiss.

I watch him strut down the hall. He looks good enough to eat in those gray sweatpants, and his worn, white shirt only draws attention to the tattoos scattered down his arms. His blond hair sticks up in all directions, aftermath from our sexcapades.

I want to chase after him.

The hungry look Ace shoots me over his shoulder as he opens the door to his apartment tells me he knows it, too.

Reluctantly, I tread back to my room. Plucking my phone from where it's propped on my easel and double-checking I didn't accidentally get paint on myself—truly a feat because the messy medium almost always manages to get *somewhere* on my clothes—I fling myself onto my bed.

Propping a pillow beneath my head, I dial Mom back. A coil of nervousness manifests in the pit of my stomach, and I inhale deeply. I won't allow my fear of telling Mom I got into the class of my dreams deter me today. The conversation with my sisters has eased my anxiety some, but if what Aisling and Peep said about Mom is true, I've been a terrible daughter, avoiding her because I'd misread her intentions. This conversation has been a long time coming.

"Hi Rory," she greets happily, and my heart clenches.

"Hey Mom," I reply, rolling onto my back to stare at the ceiling. "Sorry I missed your call. I was painting."

"How is that going?" She asks. There's nothing in her tone that gives me the impression she doesn't want to talk about art, but she doesn't sound very interested either. Instead of latching onto the pang of hurt that normally accompanies her disinterest, I wonder what she could be feeling. Perhaps she's standoffish because I usually respond poorly when we broach this touchy subject.

"It's going well so far," I answer, peering at said painting. Indeed, I'm pleased with what I have, and while Ace might not be here in the flesh, even his presence in the form of a painting eases the tension in my shoulders. "I think this one is going to be one of my best works yet."

My head falls to the fluffy pillow again, and I begin nervously picking at the fabric of my comforter, rolling the cover between my fingers to try and expel the nervous energy coursing through my veins. I realize I'm preemptively bracing myself for her reaction, something I never noticed before, but am fully aware of now. I force the breath out of my chest while I wait for a response.

A pot clangs over the line, and I imagine she's in the

kitchen, cooking. I wonder if she's making my favorite dinner she always remembers to serve when I come home for breaks, or if she's trying something she saw on the cooking channel and is going to force Dad to taste-test later.

"I'm happy to hear that, Rory."

"Are you?" I blurt, voice betraying me. If she's too busy to talk, she can say so, but she doesn't know the gravity this conversation holds for me. Perhaps I should ask for her full attention.

"Of course, I am," Mom defends vehemently. "Why do you ask?"

I swallow the thickness in my throat. I've pursued art despite assuming this wasn't what she wanted for me, but if what my sisters said is true and Mom has always supported me, hearing it from her will make my craft mean so much more.

My voice sounds small when I respond. "Are you upset that I'm majoring in art?"

The line goes silent, and the rock in my stomach doubles in size.

Mom's quiet for so long I tap my screen to make sure the call hasn't disconnected.

When I'm about to respond with an excuse to get off the phone so I can call my sisters and ream them for lying, Mom says, "I could never be upset with my daughters' passions. You love painting, and you're incredibly talented at it. I'm so proud of you." My nose prickles with emotion. "What brought this up, Rory?"

I release a slightly relieved sigh, but my worries have latched onto me like cactus thorns. "I feel like you never wanted this for me," I admit. "It seems like every time we talk, you compare me to Aisling or Peep, and I know what they do is steadier than painting, but art is truly what I love.

There might be times when it's difficult, but I wouldn't change a thing."

It's freeing to get this off my chest. The effect is almost immediate, and I can finally breathe again. This semester has been a whirlwind of emotions, and I've been slowly unlocking my self-made shackles and living my life how I want to.

A hysterical laugh bubbles through the phone. A chair scrapes, and Mom heaves a heavy sigh as she collapses onto it. "Rory," she sounds broken, and I ache. It's difficult to hear the woman who is always so hard-headed sound defeated. The thickness of her voice has tears prickling my eyes. "You can be anything you want to be. A mathematician, an actress, hell, an underwater basket weaver for all I care," she says wetly. I laugh with her, not sounding any less emotional. "You're chasing your passions, and I'd never want anything less for you."

I gnaw my lip. "Even if it means moving away from you?"

"Even then," she confirms strongly, and I can hear her melancholy smile. "One day, you're going to be off doing your own thing. You won't come home to me during summers or breaks. You'll have your own place and family and *life*." I wipe a stray tear sliding down my cheek. I might not know what my future holds, but I will never forget who raised me. The best mom in the entire world. "I will miss you as much as I miss all my babies already."

"I miss you too," I say around a lump in my throat. It hits me when I say the words; just how much avoiding her phone calls has hurt me. I miss Mom more than anything.

There's a lull as we absorb the conversation. I hope the invisible barrier between us has been knocked down, because it feels like it's well on its way to crumbling. There's another thing I have to come clean about first.

"Hey, Mom?" I ask tentatively. My nerves have dissipated some, but there's still a ball of anxiety when I broach the subject that might burst whatever solace we just built. "I want you to know I applied for a summer class at the Academy of Royal Arts in London, and I got in."

"You got in?" She gasps in awe.

I bite back a smile as pride sweeps through me. I did that. "I got in."

"Oh, honey, I am so proud of you! That's an incredible accomplishment!" Her joy rivals mine. It seems all too real now that the most important people know. I'm going to be spending my summer in London, doing what I love most. I couldn't be happier with myself because yeah, I fucking did it!

I voice the one concern niggling at the back of my mind. "You're not upset I'll be spending most of my summer in London instead of at home?"

"Of course, I'll miss you more than you know, but you're chasing your passions, like you've always done, and I won't ever stop you from following your dreams, Rory." At her genuine happiness, a smile breaks out on my face. "Besides, it will give me somewhere new to travel. Can you imagine me and your father waltzing around London, telling all the Brits my daughter attends the Academy of Royal Arts?"

I laugh, and the pressure in my chest dissolves. "Well, let's not get ahead of ourselves."

"Too late," she laughs. "Already there. Zak!" Mom calls loudly, and I wince at the shout in my ear. She should pull the phone away from her face when she's yelling, but her utter excitement has me buzzing. I can stand up and jump on my bed with the amount of elation flooding my veins. "Rory has something to tell you!"

EPILOGUE

ACE

I've told myself for the past four years I don't do love.

Because love is messy. Because someone always ends up hurt. Because it left me feeling buried alive under piles and piles of hurt.

Boy, am I glad I was wrong.

Love with the right person makes everything I ever worried about seem insignificant.

I tighten my grip on Rory. She rests in the curve of my body like a cat lounging in the sun. The steady sound of her breathing as she dozes almost sounds like a purr. A strand of hair falls across her cheek. I tuck it away, rolling the brunette strands between my fingers. There's no fighting the smile accompanying the memory of the bangs she had when we first met. She despised them, but I never thought they were all that bad, and I adore the way her cheeks still pinken whenever they're brought up.

I count the freckles dusting the bridge of her nose. I admire the curl of her dark lashes, the arch of her brow, memorizing every feature. She's a masterpiece. I tuck this moment in my brain, immortalizing her nine o'clock in the morning beauty on a chilly December morning.

Rory is my person, my muse, my *love*, and I can't believe I finally get to call her *mine*.

She stirs against me, nuzzling into the warmth of my body, inhaling a deep breath as her lashes flutter open. My breath catches when she offers me a soft, sleepy smile. There could never have been any other outcome than this right here.

What we have is the real deal. After all we've been through this semester, from the pining to the chasing, to the sad attempts of stifling our feelings. It was never in the picture for us to just be friends. We were always destined for more, from the very first moment I laid eyes on her.

What Rory and I had over the summer . . . it wasn't a dip your toes in the ocean kind of love. There was nothing slow or gentle about how we met. We were both broken seashells on the beach, and she was a wave that knocked me off my feet, grabbed my ankles, and dragged me in.

And I don't ever want to come up for air.

"Good morning," I grin. I can't help myself, leaning in to press a chaste kiss to her forehead, then to her mouth when she stretches up for more.

"Morning," Rory sighs happily, returning her head to my chest. My heart races. She has that effect on me, and I hold her tighter in response. This morning in my bedroom is calm and quiet and I'm not ready to part from her yet. "I could hear you thinking in my sleep. What's on your mind?"

"You," I admit softly. "Always you."

Rory's cheeks pinken, and the sight makes me soar. "Can you believe how far we've come?" She asks, tracing the spade over my heart. Goosebumps arise with the motion, and my cock twitches beneath the blankets.

She plucked the words straight from my head. Soon, we'll

depart for winter break. Rory is going back to Washington with Quinn, and I'm headed down to Colorado with Knox, while Slate spends his time off in Hawaii with his family. As much as I'm going to miss Rory, I am looking forward to visiting my parents and talking more about my future with Mom as my manager.

"It's crazy," I agree. "Seven months ago, you were just a girl in Cabo trying to hide your adorable bangs from me."

Rory groans and smooshes her face into my pec. A playful pinch in the side accompanies her shyness.

"And you were just a boy stealing my sister's lounger."

I poke her until melodic laughter trickles out of her. My favorite sound.

"I saw a pretty girl, and I took a chance," I defend, stopping my attack in favor of caressing Rory's cheek. She peers up at me with a soft smile and sparkling eyes, and I'm a goner all fucking over again. "Looks like it worked out pretty well."

"And to think I blocked your number at the end of summer."

"I didn't," I respond, smoothing the wrinkles between her brows when her features tighten in confusion.

"You didn't? Even though we promised we would?" Her eyes glisten with emotion, and I squeeze her affectionately.

"I didn't, Rory-O. That was the one promise I couldn't keep."

ACKNOWLEDGMENTS

My second book is officially done and I don't think finishing a book will ever feel real. Painted Promises took longer than expected, but after learning what I did through the process of Midnight Muse, the time was well worth it.

To Paigey—Slate's number one fan—thanks for always being such an incredible support system, letting me interrupt your work because I'm so excited to share a blurb or editing chapters on planes…I couldn't do it without you. I love you to the moon and back.

To my parents who have always been my support system, thank you. Allowing me to chase my dreams and helping in any way you can is monumental. I love you so much and looking forward to visiting soon.

To Alyssa, Hannah, Jill, Abe, Trista, and all my best friends, thank you for being by my side through thick and thin, through terrible dates and unfortunate situationships (that may or may not have blossomed ideas for some of the content in this book) where all we can do is laugh, nothing comes close to the good times we share. Here's to many more years of friendship.

To Christian, my editor, thank you so much for all the help. Thank you for giving as much love to this book as I did. Your comments gave me life, your suggestions helped ease my worries, and you are an incredible person. I cannot wait to work with you again soon!

To you, the readers. If you've been with me from my

fanfic days…can you believe this?! Thank you so much for the continued support throughout my writing journey. If you know me from Midnight Muse, thank you so much for reading and I hope you loved Rory and Ace's story just as much.

To Books and Moods for the incredible cover! You smashed it out of the park and I can't wait to work with you on the next one.

And to Slate…you're next buddy!

ABOUT THE AUTHOR

Lanie Tech is a graphic designer by day and author by night. Her writing stems from many years spent as a fanfiction author and she's sorry if it shows. She is currently in her contemporary romance era but hopes someday to dip into the romantasy world with her novels. *Midnight Muse* is her first novel.

She currently lives in SoCal with her younger sister and enjoys strawberries, traveling, creating delusions during walks or work, and loves anything and everything creative.

Connect with her at lanietechauthor.com

Instagram: @lanietech
TikTok: @lanietechauthor